Beyond the Blue

Definitely 5 stars from me. Great love story. Great and different. Different because instead of a long slow burn with a quick ending... while you wonder what happened next. In this story, the romance is in the first 20% of the story and the remainder is how they are together as lovers. How do they deal with the age gap and how do they each resolve their past loss and grief? How do the family members accept the relationship? It is a very thoughtful, interesting, and warm story. I loved the sex scenes. They were very hot without describing every minute detail. I enjoyed all the characters, and felt they were all very natural and the dialogue insightful. I understand this is O'Shea's first published story. Amazing...hopefully there will be many more.
                                                    -Cheryl S., *NetGalley*

An excellent age-gap romance that was actually one of the better romances I have read in 2022. I often talk about the amazing track record that Bella has in finding debut authors and with O'Shea, they have proved it again. If her debut is this good, it makes me so excited to read her future releases.
                                                    -Lex Kent's Reviews, *goodreads*

What a beautiful, heartwarming, heart-wrenching debut romance from TJ O'Shea. If I had not known this was a debut novel I would have assumed that it was penned by a more experienced writer. I would rate this stellar debut 4.25 stars with high recommendations to other readers. I can't wait for future books by this author.
                                                    -Michele R., *NetGalley*

Oh my goodness! What a sweet amazing read this book was!
This is a character-focused book and I really liked how the book was able to delve deep into the makeup of these two. As each part of their relationship evolved, I found I couldn't put this book down. Each mini situation/moment was filled with a mix of witty banter, dry sarcasm (Mei), affection, emotional confessions and totally made this a page turner. This is a "late coming out" story as well, and I liked how it wasn't made to be a big deal. There was no angsty crazy and the processing was managed like the mature adults they were. So refreshing!

Lastly kudos to O'Shea for representation. I love it when authors introduce characters of color, ethnicity, body types and gender. It makes the story so much more real and I really appreciate the effort that goes into that. As a debut book this is absolutely fantastic and will probably end up in my re-read pile. 4.75 stars.

-D. Booker, *NetGalley*

TJ O'Shea has done a masterful job in creating this story. Mei and Morgan were three dimensional, relatable women. The supporting cast of characters really helped to enhance the overall plot. The dialogue was witty and engaging. And the chemistry between our mains was spicy! I loved everything about this book from Morgan's need to help others to Mei's dry humor to Ruiz's snarky wit. How can this be TJ O'Shea's first book?

-J.Beebs, *NetGalley*

To Be With You

Other Bella Books by TJ O'Shea

Beyond the Blue

About the Author

TJ O'Shea is a New Jerseyian by birth and a New Yorker by proxy. When not working in the video game industry and writing sapphic romances, she enjoys playing video games (this time for fun), shouting answers at Jeopardy! reruns, amateurishly baking, spending time with her wife and daughter, and singing to their cat.

To Be With You

TJ O'SHEA

BELLA
B O O K S
2022

Bella Books, Inc.
P.O. Box 10543
Tallahassee, FL 32302

Printed in the United States of America on acid-free paper.

First Edition - 2022

Editor: Heather Flournoy
Cover Designer: Kayla Mancuso

ISBN: 978-1-64247-419-0

PUBLISHER'S NOTE

Acknowledgments

A thank you to Bella Books for their continued support and fostering this wonderful community of authors. To my friend Kylee, for her great beta read and edit, as well as her patient sound-boarding when I spam her with different ideas. To my editor, Heather, for her amazing editing and continued support in my journey to understanding hyphens. And finally, a forever thank-you to my wife, Valerie, who is the best partner a girl could ask for, and is always good to sing the response to a call-and-response song.

Dedication

To my daughter, Ellie. Being your mom is the greatest privilege and joy of my life.

You can't read any of Mommy's books until you're 25.

2005—CURRENT DAY

Ambivalence. The word stuck in Tori's mind like bubble gum in hair, the rhythm of its vowels and consonants moving at the speed of her tires over bumpy asphalt. Each letter of the word could be found sprinkled over Garden Hills as ubiquitous as pollen, touching every square mile of the town. Not a big town, but not a small one. Not a rich town, but not a poor one. Wooded and mountainous on one side, flat and listless on the other. A railroad track that announced itself with X-shaped warning signs and red lamps, but no trains had shrieked against the rails in over seventy years. A town stuck in the past like a Wild West facsimile, yet had changed enough to disorient Tori as she rode down the single county road serving as the only entrance and exit to Garden Hills. It looked as if it had waited for her return—buildings and fixtures standing in the same place—but also like it had moved on without her.

Their car took them through the downtown—a generous term for one intersection of shops, family-owned restaurants, and standard utilities. Climbing up the hills which gave the town its name, Tori gazed upon it from the perfect view each block possessed due to the intentional way rich prospectors blew into the sides of the mountains and dropped luxury homes. From here, the town and much of the unimpressive county lay at their feet, the industrial park just outside the town limits and the busy interstate highway winding around the homes in the valley like a noose.

Several blocks from her own home, the car's dashboard lights blinked, and all at once the car stopped. Tori understood deeply—she, too, would rather die on the side of the road than go back home. Her fiancé, Ben, got out of the driver's seat, ostensibly to check under the hood. Reaching over, she pulled the lever to unlatch the hood, knowing full well Ben had no idea what to do. After a minute or two, he closed the hood and looked at her through the windshield, laughing.

"Babe, I don't know what I'm looking at."

Tori chuckled and exited the car to join him near the front bumper. "Really? Your 'looking concerned at the engine' face is pretty convincing."

"Yeah? Do I give off big 'frustrated dad on the side of the road during a family road trip' vibes?"

"Definitely." Rows of McMansions blocked the view uphill, but Tori knew they were close. "I guess we could call my parents?"

"Please don't," he replied quickly. "The last thing I need is to show up at your parents' house with my car on the end of a tow truck. Can you imagine the look your mother would give me? I would turn to stone and the gardener would drag me onto the lawn with the rest of the sculptures." He sighed. "I'll get it towed to a shop."

Tori's heart skipped a beat. "Right. Okay. Probably one close by, I'd think." She knew.

Tapping on his cell phone, Ben walked in the street to chase better cell service. Tori rested on the side of the car and stared out into Garden Hills. Behind downtown, over the railroad track, smaller homes stood in neat rows like sets of teeth. Hemmed in by trees, Tori traced the blocks in between with her memory. Eyes closed, she vividly recalled cruising those streets with her head back, the summer heat blowing in through the open window and cooling her glistening skin. One hand out the window, the other clasped in the strong grip of someone else. Feeling unlimited and invincible in the way only teenagers can. Now twenty-two, light-years away from the teenager who soaked up summer nights, Tori stood at the edge of her old town, deathly afraid of it. Her memories lurked around every corner, waiting to rob her of the armor she'd built to keep hidden the sad, heartbroken girl who left Garden Hills and never looked back.

Ben sat next to her on the side of his expensive sedan, folding his hands in his khaki lap. In the context of Garden Hills, Ben fit perfectly, just as she thought he would. His placid demeanor, model good looks, Lacoste wardrobe; everything about him screamed "I am comfortable in a mostly white, small suburb."

"Pretty town." Ahead of them summer gasped out its dying breaths, the green foliage resisting the encroaching yellow touching the tips of the leaves. A mild breeze jiggled the branches, marbling the sunlight across the grass. Idyllic and banal, just as she remembered.

"It is." Garden Hills never lacked for beauty. What it lacked for Tori ran deeper than the flora and fauna.

"I'm looking forward to seeing it. The town that built Tori Lockwood," he said, imitating great fanfare. "Plus, it's not every day you get to attend a Sweet Sixteen as a twenty-six-year-old man. Gonna try out my sick dance moves at the party."

"It's laser tag, Ben. There isn't any dancing."

"Not with that attitude there isn't." He put his arm around her shoulders. "I hope we get to see some of the town."

"You did. That's the town. Two elementary schools—one nearby and one across town. The middle school and high school share one building, right there." She pointed to a plus-sign-shaped building to their left. "The industrial park over there? That's where Lockwood Industries is. It's a boring office building surrounded by other boring office buildings. There's the duck pond and the park, which are fine, I guess. And, on the other mountain over there, a make-out spot for horny teens. Our downtown is one block."

Ben nodded along like he understood, but for a man raised in a luxury suburb of Boston, Garden Hills likely looked like a sandbox in comparison. "Nothing like Boston, huh? The bars here probably won't even play a Sox game." Sensing tension, she looked up at him to find his face pensive. "I'm sure coming back for you is tough. I know your relationship with your parents is…strained."

"That's putting it mildly." Tori fidgeted with the hem of her sweater. She kept Ben's knowledge of her relationship with her parents fairly limited. Better to ease into the dysfunction than baptize him in it. "I'm only here for Ward. I left him here alone with them for five years. I owe him. I mean, we're lucky Ward is still a boy and not metastasized into whatever deep sea creature Mother would like to groom him into."

Ben grimaced. "Now I can't stop imagining your mother as Ursula from *The Little Mermaid*."

"Yeah right, she wishes she had the gravitas of Ursula."

He chuckled, pressing a kiss against her temple. "Well, I can't be entirely negative about your parents, because they made you."

"You're just saying that because they love you." Of course they did, because Ben represented everything her parents valued. A third son of an old-money family from Massachusetts, the only kid to follow into the family law firm. Their roots dug so deep, he had an ancestor on the Mayflower. Pedigree, money, whiteness—a dream for Cassandra and Victor Lockwood, Sr. "It's just going to be exhausting. The reunion is whatever, and Ward's party is fine, but this stupid award dinner is basically going to be my debutante ball. Where Dad introduces me to the old men who will be my subordinates because it wouldn't be Lockwood Industries without massive nepotism."

"Maybe it's nepotism, but you're smart, you've got a degree, and there's no reason why you can't step into a CEO role."

"Not wanting to isn't enough reason, I guess," she mumbled, drowned out by the crunching of gravel behind them. Ben strolled toward the oncoming pickup truck as Tori ducked into the passenger seat to grab her purse and phone. Rummaging around the passenger side floorboard, she heard the tow truck driver's voice call to them.

"Hey, you the one who called? Ben?" A pair of boots thunked against the asphalt. "I'm Leah. What seems to be the problem?"

No, no, no. Tori's breath caught and she froze, bent over in the passenger seat. Air rushed around her, a hurricane of anxiety where she sat in the eye, anything but calm. It couldn't be her voice because every other sentence out of her mouth was about getting out of Garden Hills. Those couldn't be her boots because she said she'd never set foot in this town again. But her voice, its low rasp and familiar intonation, Tori could pluck it out of thousands of voices. A voice she heard whisper, banter, moan, and sing. A voice that told her the sweetest words she'd ever heard, and then never spoke to her again.

Ben scratched his short brown hair and sighed. "Oh, man, I don't even know. I'm garbage with cars. The lights inside went nuts and then the thing died."

"Okay. Let me take a look." As Leah came into full view around Ben, Tori dropped her purse and phone. Rooted in place, hands outstretched, she stared at Leah in open shock. A thousand memories swarmed her like bees, but she kept immobile, lest one of them sting. Tori struggled to find a coherent emotion among the many battling for dominance. Dejection, bittersweet nostalgia, and oddly, relief, as if she could finally expel the breath she'd stored in her lungs for five years.

Their eyes met and Leah paused in her step, boots kicking loose gravel down the road. Her eyes, always so wonderfully expressive, conveyed surprise and perhaps even excitement for the briefest of moments. They then quickly moved to Ben, then to Tori, and dismay ghosted across her face before she banished her emotions. The chilling effect unexpectedly devastated Tori, and she clutched her stomach in the place Leah's eyes hollowed out.

"Pop the hood for me?"

"You got it." Ben did as told and Leah lifted the hood to inspect the machine. Unlike Ben, Leah could divine a car's problem like tea leaves. Tori watched her do it many times, instinctually finding issues even Leah's experienced father couldn't spot. After long, agonizing minutes of inspection and testing and ignoring Tori's presence, Leah took a few steps back and placed her hands on her hips.

"I think it's your alternator, but I won't know for sure until I get it to my shop. I can tow you there, or I can tow it somewhere else if you want." Leah's gaze flitted up the road, in the direction toward Tori's childhood home. "If you're not too far from where you're going."

Ben glanced at Tori, who only now picked up her phone and purse off the ground, hands trembling. "We have to get it fixed, I'd think. Is that cool, babe?"

"It'll have to be," Tori replied in a strangled voice. "Otherwise, we're walking."

Leah smirked. "It is a long walk back to town. Good thing it isn't raining."

Dumbstruck, Tori stood off to the side of the road with Ben as Leah hooked the car up to the tow truck. Her father's auto shop didn't used to do any towing, but Leah appeared to know her way around it. What else had changed? Did she still only drive with her left hand, firmly placed at twelve o'clock? Did she still keep her guard up, letting only the lucky ones in? Did someone reside in her heart now?

Once she secured the car to the truck, Leah jerked her thumb toward it. "I'll give you a ride."

"Oh, nice. Thanks!" Ben climbed into the cab of the truck in the middle of the bench seat, and Tori sandwiched herself between him and the door. The interior of the car smelled fresh, like leather cleaner and pine. Terribly neat, which came as no surprise, as Leah had always kept her car immaculate. A small cross dangled from the rearview mirror, a pack of gum thrown into the cubby below the radio, and a black CD binder lived on the floor near Tori's feet. Currently, a CD played soft rock at a decent volume, though none of them tried to speak over it. Well, except for Ben. "So, is this your shop we're going to?"

"No, it's my dad's."

"Neat, a family business. Have you always worked for him?"

Curse Ben and his insatiable curiosity about other people. Normally, Tori found it kind of charming, but right now she wanted to throttle him. "Pretty much. Other than when I was away at college."

"Oh yeah? Where did you go?"

"MIT."

"No kidding! Practically neighbors! Tori and I went to Harvard." Ben slapped himself on the forehead. "Where are my manners? Yikes. This is my fiancée, Tori."

Tori watched carefully as Leah withdrew her sunglasses from her pocket and placed them over her eyes. Even with her shield up, Tori caught the furrow of angst drawn between her eyebrows. Leah nodded but didn't respond, her fingers clenched the steering wheel until her knuckles nearly turned white.

Drumming his palms on his thighs to the music, Ben spotted Leah's thick CD binder on the floor and eagerly nabbed it. "Wow, this is a lot of CDs. Most people do MP3s now, right? Old school, though. I like it."

"You can't touch that," Tori said automatically. Ben's curious gaze tilted to her and she picked out Leah's snickering over the music and the ambient road noise. "I mean—it's her car and her music. I'm sure she doesn't want us pawing through her stuff."

Ben placed the binder on the floor with the exaggerated precision of Indiana Jones switching out an artifact. "My bad."

"It's fine," Leah replied coolly. "I prefer discs. I don't like music I can't touch."

Ben smiled. "I can dig that."

The conversation died down as they turned down the block toward the shop. VASQUEZ AUTO SHOP used to blare in big metal letters atop the garage door, visible from blocks away. In its place, the marquee read: VASQUEZ FAMILY AUTO.

Leah pulled in backward and the three of them climbed out of the cab, their football echoing off the cement walls. Ben and Tori stood to the side as Leah methodically removed the car from the tow. "I'll park the truck and be right back."

Stepping away, Tori ran her hand along a bright red toolbox, inhaling the scent of oil and rubber. Her olfactory senses sent her hurtling through time, back to when this shop functioned as a third home for her. Perhaps if it looked the same, she'd have drifted into the past even further, but modern upgrades like computers and new machinery grounded her in the present, as well as the lack of music. Years ago, anyone within five feet of the shop could hear Hector's traditional Mexican music playing from an unseen old stereo. The eerie quiet unnerved her.

But not as much as Leah unnerved her. Tori silently took her in as she strutted across the floor of the shop upon her return. The blue machinist jumpsuit hugged her more closely than it had as a teenager, emphasizing a broader, more athletic physique. She'd tied her big, wild curls up into a ponytail, a red bandana hung loosely around her neck, and the same worn, clunky boots on her feet. Still achingly gorgeous, making Tori's insides clench with no effort at all.

Leah, however, didn't appear affected by her. This infuriating indifference made Tori want to grab her by the lapels and shake her, demanding an answer for the feelings she engendered without permission. Tori jammed her hands in her pockets instead.

"I'll need at least an hour. I'll give you a call and read you the estimate, and you can tell me how you want to proceed."

"Yeah, don't worry about the estimate. If you can fix it, I don't care what it costs. Consider it a blank check to make sure I don't roll up to my future in-laws on a bicycle with their daughter in the front basket."

Leah pushed her sunglasses to the top of her head and nodded in agreement. Gazing into Leah's eyes, Tori lost sight of everything else in the room. For a single, dizzying, insane moment, she considered throwing her arms around Leah and hugging her tight. But you can't embrace an open flame, and that's what Leah was. Crackling, burning, magnetizing, luring her in. The instinct to draw closer to her became almost too powerful to ignore.

Disturbed by the frightening sharpness of her urge, Tori slid closer to Ben. Leah looked between them, where Ben had casually taken her hand in his. "Fine by me. I have your number. I'll call when I'm done."

Her gruff dismissal couldn't put off cheery Ben. "Sounds good. Any recommendations for a quick bite while we wait?"

"The diner is close, and the food's good. The industrial park is a bit of a walk from here, but they've got food trucks. Better food, longer walk. And there's always the Starbucks, I guess."

Ben frowned. "I look like I drink yuppie coffee, don't I?"

"Little bit."

"Is it the khaki pants?"

She nodded toward the car. "The Beamer doesn't help."

"Gosh, that's true. Nuts. Well, thanks for the help, Leah."

After giving a quick wave Leah did not return, Ben led them back out into the street. Just one block off the main road, they walked together around the corner toward the diner. The streets smelled strongly of fresh asphalt, and Tori noticed the unblemished yellow lines bisecting the road. A facelift, she figured, as they passed quaint streetlamps and sophisticated garbage cans. Maybe the money in the hills had finally trickled downtown.

"I'm famished. This diner any good?"

Tori nodded absentmindedly, watching her feet as they walked down the block. "The food is good, but it's just a diner."

Of course, it wasn't just a diner, it was *their* diner, but that didn't matter. One of many places they'd painted their love, splashing it in bright neons across Tori's memory, only to be washed away by time and intentional scrubbing.

She and Ben grabbed a booth and a young waitress immediately popped up to take their order. Tori caught her admiring Ben, an almost comically common occurrence. Good-looking and polite, Ben charmed just about anyone he met. Still, no matter how beautiful the woman—or man—who gave him attention, or how shamelessly they flirted with him, the attention only ever embarrassed him. Besides, Tori simply didn't have the energy to be jealous.

"Did you come here back in the day?" Ben asked, leaning on the Formica table.

"Not a lot. I do know the food is exponentially better than the décor."

"These kinds of places always have the best food, right? And this is a lot cleaner than some of the spots we've been to in Boston, for sure." He gave an appreciative look at the place as a whole, its dust-covered knickknacks and wallpaper yellowed from the days before it became unfashionable to smoke indoors. His eyes dropped to the bench, where he shifted in his seat to look at something. "Huh."

"What?"

"Somebody carved in the seat." He tilted his head as the color drained from Tori's face. Unbeknownst to Ben, she inhaled shallow breaths, gripping her seat like her life depended on it. If she let go, she would surely slingshot into the past. "Let's see. What is that, 'honk'? Why would someone take the time to carve 'honk'? I guess maybe a clown enthusiast. Or a car enthusiast. Oh, or a clown car enthusiast."

"Ben."

"What else do we have here? An LV over a VL. Weird. Looks like roman numerals. Who carves roman numerals into a seat?"

"I—I don't know. Probably the same person who carves the word 'honk.'"

She knew. She knew exactly who. The "who" took shape like a desert mirage, shimmering to life in the seat across from her. In Ben's place sat the younger versions of herself and Leah, cozied into each other and lost to the rest of the world. Wrapped in her warm embrace, her nose tucked into the crook of Leah's neck, breathing in the salty musk of her skin. Tracing the divots in between her knuckles, outlining the tiny cuts on her hands. The same hands that wielded the knife and carved their initials into the booth, marking it as theirs forever.

But forever is just a promise you make and don't intend to keep.

CHAPTER ONE

SUMMER 2000

The map in Leah's glove compartment looked well worn, but rarely got used. By now, the hills and flatlands of Garden Hills came to her like rudimentary multiplication. Every street fixed in place, easy to find by its cross street or arbitrary landmark. Out-of-season Christmas decorations hung on the corner of Plymouth Avenue, the crateral pothole on Ninth Street, or the bent "DOLE 1996" sign stuck in the brown lawn on Jacob Place. As she climbed the hills toward the northern side of town, she reached over into her passenger seat, flipped up the yellow receipt, and took another look at the address. Just within the town limits, she confirmed to herself, in one of those rich neighborhoods up the mountain. Unfortunately, the higher the taxes, the lower the tip. This commandment, written in stone at the dawn of the age of pizza delivery, remained true as ever, even at the edge of a new millennium.

Leah didn't mind. This freaky Friday night thunderstorm gave Benny's Pizza more business than a Saturday, and as the only driver on for the night, Leah would make bank. At least, make bank from the homes in more middle-class neighborhoods. These rich folks were likely to tell her to "keep the change" and put literal coins in her hand.

Homes ballooned in size, lawns stretched like football fields, and the mailboxes became more stupidly ornate as Leah drove farther into their gilded world. This house lay up a winding road, slippery from the rain splattering down from thick, gray thunderclouds. Rain fell nonstop as Leah pulled her windbreaker close, jogging up the front steps to the house. After handing over the slightly damp but still piping hot cardboard box of pizza and its accompanying aluminum tin of garlic bread, Leah received the cash for the order, as well as six dollars from a smiling woman in an apron. Probably the housekeeper, Leah surmised. Hustle recognized hustle.

"Thanks. Have a good night." Leah shoved the tip money into her jeans pocket and the order money into the waterproof pocket in her coat. Her shoes squeaked against the asphalt as she tried not to wipe out on the way back to her car. Hurrying inside, Leah glanced at the next receipt. She had three more deliveries to make before she could head back, all kept hot in the square duffel bag in her back seat.

Bobbing her head along to her killer playlist, Leah slowed down as she got to her exit. An orange streetlamp illuminated a small pond in the road, blocking the route. Not willing to risk her car through the water, she turned back onto the highway with a grumpy sigh and took the next exit instead. It was a fairly deserted service road just outside of town and she cranked up the volume of her radio, jamming to the Gin Blossoms as her tires kicked up mud and provided a stuttering backbeat. Her headlights struggled to pierce through the sheets of rain when out of the corner of her eye, Leah spotted a blue figure coasting along the side of the road. Like a ghost in search of a home to haunt, a woman in blue trudged in the mud.

Nearing closer, the ghost came into view as a girl very much alive and soaked to the bone. Inch-thick mud caked dirt-clogged heels as her hands lifted and white-knuckle gripped her dress, valiantly attempting to keep the dripping material out of the mud. She didn't even look up as the headlights shone on her and passed by—she soldiered forward, relentless. Leah pulled to the side and rolled down her window.

"Uh, lady? Miss? Are you okay?"

The girl came to a stop next to her passenger side, heaving an exasperated sigh. Without looking over, she asked, "Do I look okay?"

"No, you look like a melted candle," Leah replied. "Listen, it's like…at least another two miles to any real town from here. Do you want a lift?"

At this question the girl glanced into the car and Leah's heart pounded in recognition. Victoria Lockwood. Well, the remains of Victoria Lockwood. Her usually bouncy dirty-blond hair lay flat against her head, matching light-brown eyes rimmed red, and mascara dripped black goop like a leaky engine. Her presumably expensive dress clung to her in all the wrong places, the material ready to give up on life as water ruined the hard work of whatever sweatshop produced it.

Ahead of them, puddles overtook parts of the road, creating black voids on already treacherous ground. Peering back into the car, Victoria narrowed her eyes. "Leah? What are you doing out here?"

"You're seriously asking me that, while you're standing in the mud in a dress I assume costs more than my car?" Leah harrumphed. "Do you want a ride or do you want to swim back to Garden Hills?"

"I'm very wet."

Leah swallowed the uncouth remark on the tip of her tongue. "Yeah, no doy."

"I'll get your seats wet. And my shoes are—" She grimaced down at her feet. Her shoes, surely precious and priceless, were likely ruined. "A disaster."

"Carpets can be cleaned, seats will dry. Look, get in or don't, but make it quick, 'cause time waits for no pizza."

Tucking her lip between her teeth, Victoria let out an annoyed noise and yanked the door open, hefting her mess of a person into Leah's passenger seat. Leah waited until she buckled her seat belt to accelerate down the road, inhaling the combination of expensive perfume and heavy rain Victoria brought in with her. With her trusty steed below her, Leah confidently maneuvered over slick roadways on the outskirts of town. She focused on the road, determined not to think about the damp person in her passenger seat. Which was fine, as the person in her passenger seat didn't look over at her, either.

Eventually, curiosity won out. "So, bad night?"

Victoria attempted to huff, but a shiver caught her and she shuddered instead. Leaning into her space, Leah flicked the air vents closed and Victoria's frown lifted into a neutral straight line. "Yes."

"Wait, isn't it prom?"

With an obvious glance to her dress, then to Leah, Victoria nodded but did not comment. Clearly, whatever their prom turned out to be, she'd been right to work instead. If someone like Victoria Lockwood had a bad time, Leah probably would've died at it.

"Didn't you, like, put the entire prom together? Sucks you didn't get to enjoy it."

"Like you care," Victoria muttered.

Leah rolled her eyes. "Damn, sorry for trying to make conversation with the sponge soaking my seat." All the money in the world, and these rich kids couldn't afford a little gratitude. "Whatever, I'll bring you home. I've got like three more pies to sling, but I can make a quick detour."

Victoria sniffed. "Oh, that's why it smells like pizza in here."

"What else could it be? *Eau de fromage?*"

"I didn't think about it." Leah snuck a glance at Victoria, who shuddered and stared out the passenger window as their shared hometown passed by in watercolors. Orange streetlamps, blue homes, and gray sky blurred together in inky blackness like an abstract impressionist painting. "I'm sorry for snapping at you."

Annoyingly, her earnest apology defused Leah's temper. "Yeah, well, I guess maybe I can excuse a short fuse considering you look like someone's pool noodle that got stuck in the pool filter."

Much to her surprise, Victoria laughed. "Jerk." They shared a small smile, and Victoria bashfully looked down. "Could I just...ride with you?"

A preposterous idea. Not only did it complicate the car insurance, but she preferred the solitude. However, moved by an instinct too powerful to ignore, Leah nodded. "Yeah, sure. I have one rule for passengers—no touching the music. I have a carefully curated mix going and any interruption could be disastrous."

"Noted."

Her car slid up next to the curb and Leah threw off her seat belt. "Dope. Sit tight, I'll be right back."

The Otis family ordered a lot of pizza. They had about six kids and both parents worked full-time, so Leah frequented their home almost as often as the mail. Usually, the house exploded with the noise of young kids, but tonight only Mr. Otis opened the door when Leah knocked. Dressed in his work clothes, he offered a tired smile as he bounced the youngest Otis on his shoulder.

"Hey, Mr. Otis."

"How ya doin', kiddo?" Mr. Otis asked in a whisper, trying not to wake the slumbering baby.

"Good, thanks," Leah replied, keeping her voice low. After exchanging a pizza for payment and tip, Leah shoved her hands in her windbreaker pockets. "Enjoy the pie. Oh, and uh, skip the Yankees game tonight."

The smile on his face dropped. "Ah, you're killin' me, kid."

"Trust me. Not worth it. Watch a rerun."

Holding his baby against his work clothes with one giant hand, Mr. Otis grumbled and clearly tried to restrain his anger at the Yankees' collective failure. "Wells is a bum. Can't pitch his way out of a bag."

"Totally. Good night, Mr. Otis."

"Yeah, yeah. Good night, kid."

Mr. Otis closed the door gently, and his frustrated mutterings humored her from the other side. On her way back to her seat she grabbed a towel from her trunk, and upon reentering the car, she tossed the towel onto Victoria's lap. "I keep clean towels in case of spills or to clean my car. It's not gonna fix the dress, but maybe you'll be less cold."

"Oh. Thanks."

As Victoria wiped the moisture from her bare skin, Leah started toward her penultimate delivery for the night. Her mix playing on low, the high-pitched crinkle of her tires over the wet road created the only noise between deliveries. Victoria shivered quietly next to her, bloodshot eyes staring blankly out the window.

Whatever prompted Victoria to storm out of their prom and attempt to walk back to Garden Hills, it must've been a pretty severe turn of events. Her boyfriend, an insufferable football meathead named Carter Harcourt, asked her to prom over the morning announcements. Then, according to the high school grapevine Leah unintentionally found herself ensnared in, he brought a bouquet of roses to her homeroom. All in all, it should've been a charmed night. His and hers crowns, a limo ride, and probably a drive to the rich kids' summer homes in the lake district to lose their virginities, or the remnants of them. But instead of getting jackrabbit missionary from her insipid boyfriend, Victoria Lockwood shivered in Leah's cheesy-smelling car.

Peeking at Victoria in her peripheral vision, Leah's heart throbbed with uncharacteristic sympathy for the disaster beside her. She didn't normally reserve any goodwill for the upper echelon of Garden Hills High. "Since your dress is kind of a goner, do you want to put the pizzas on your lap?" Off Victoria's horrified expression, Leah laughed. "To keep you warm. They're in a bag, they won't get grease on you or anything."

"Oh. Yes, please."

Leah gripped the wheel with one hand and nabbed the pizza bag with the other, placing it on Victoria's lap. "There ya go. Pizza always comes in clutch."

"Thanks, Leah."

A sharp, sudden lightning bolt hit Leah between the ribs at the sound of her name spoken softly from Victoria's lips. Running in vastly different social circles, their lives only intersected during AP English, where Leah sat directly behind her in the last seat of the third row. And it's not as if they'd run into each other at Benny's Pizza or Vasquez's Auto Shop, where Leah spent most of her time. Victoria's weekends probably consisted of jetting off to country clubs, not listening to a rickety jukebox over a meatball parmigiana.

Hearing her name spoken intimately, casually, like the banter of friends, kickstarted her heart. So thrown off, she forgot to reply and drove to the next house in total silence. Leah took the top three pizzas from within the bag, running out into the rain once more with her hood pulled up over her hair. She grimaced with each step toward the home, wincing at the loud noises of a party behind the door. Leah mentally prepped herself for whatever flavor of drunk mess lay ahead. Drunk people tended to answer the door like a standup comic trying out their material for the first time. Or worse, they flirted with her.

As predicted, a drunk college-aged guy swung the door open and raucous dance music hit Leah in the face like a frying pan. "Whoa, the pizza. Nice timing, we're starved." He fished in his pockets and slapped the bills into her palm after the handoff. "Shit, I don't have tip money." He screamed back into the room at an absolutely bloodcurdling volume. "Hey! Anybody got cash? This chick needs tip money!"

"It's cool, don't worry about it."

"No! Wait one sec." The guy disappeared into a haze of pot smoke. When he returned, he held up a six-pack of Coors beer and a blunt. Handing them over with a deep genuflect, he boomed, "Get crunk, O great bringer of the pizzas."

Leah took the proffered gifts and raised them back at him. "Tight, thanks, man."

With a loud whoop of joy, the man slammed the door and Leah stumbled back. She put the six-pack on the floor in the back of her car and plunked the blunt into her empty cup holder. Victoria's eyes widened in alarm at the contraband loitering in the center console. "Is that weed?"

"I hope so. They didn't have cash so they gave me weed. Not bad, 'cause a six-pack would be at least six bucks and the blunt worth, like, twice as much." She sloshed across town and Leah caught Victoria warily eyeing the weed like it was an ill-tempered Chihuahua baring its teeth at her. "Does the weed bother you?"

"What?" Victoria snapped, immediately shifting her eyes away from the cup holder. "It doesn't bother me. It's just—it's illegal."

"It is?" Leah opened her mouth in faux shock and her sass went unappreciated as Victoria's face contorted in displeasure. "Well, the door's not locked. You can leave at any time."

"You're not scared about the police finding it?" Victoria worriedly glanced into the side mirrors like they were convicts on the lam.

Scoffing, Leah slowed down at a stop sign and rolled her eyes. "If I didn't have a blunt, they'd get me for some other invented violation."

"The police? Leah, they can't charge you with nothing."

Leah wondered briefly what it might be like to be white. Or white-passing, if she'd taken after her mother. Victoria, with her pale skin and apple-pie good looks, never had to worry about the sticky parts of dealing with small town law enforcement. "Maybe not you. Look, are you gonna be a narc about the weed, or what? 'Cause I can take you home if you're uncomfortable."

"No, it can stay," she answered quickly. "Please don't take me home."

The self-assured, popular girl Leah knew from school disappeared, and she found herself staring into sad, worried eyes. Leah nodded. "All right."

Victoria handed her the pizza and folded her hands in her lap atop the warming bag. Thankfully it was an uneventful delivery—standard tip, no weirdos behind the door—and Leah got back to the car to find Victoria's fingers brushing the CD case on the floor. "Ah, what was my one rule?"

"Sorry." Victoria retracted her hand. "I like this song. I—I got curious about what else you might have."

"Oh." Her smile hidden, Leah slowly pulled away from the curb. "Well, turn it up, then."

Victoria cranked up the volume on a late eighties power ballad. She hummed along as Leah drove to the other side of the industrial park, where Benny's Pizza sat on the end of an unimpressive, beige strip mall, anchored on the other end by a Blockbuster. She pulled into a spot right in front of the door and snatched the bag from Victoria's lap. "Uh, you want some dry clothes?"

"From—from the pizza parlor?" The genuine confusion on her face nearly had Leah laughing out loud.

"Yeah. We've got team shirts and I'm sure I can scrounge up some pants. Totally up to you, though your soaked dress is probably gonna give you swamp ass."

She sounded it out like Leah had spoken another language. "Swamp...ass?"

"Swamp ass. Hot and humid, moist ass? Right, well, you wouldn't get swamp ass because you're, like, perfect." Leah rolled her eyes, but Victoria appeared even more confused than before. "Anyway, yes, or no?"

Victoria unbuckled her seat belt. "Is anyone else in there?"

"Yes, Victoria, this has all been an elaborate prank and our entire graduating class is in there, waiting to see you." Leah gestured at the dimmed lights through the glass windows. "It's empty."

"Okay."

They entered the sepia-toned glass building together and Leah threw a quick "Hold tight" over her shoulder as she barreled through the employees-only door behind the counter. She wondered what Victoria would make of the place. Certainly, Victoria had never sat down in a restaurant without a linen tablecloth and a wine list. Even less likely she'd ever dressed out of a lost and found. After pilfering the lost and found for something acceptable, Leah changed out of her clothes as well, tossing her Benny's shirt into the restaurant's laundry and hanging up her cap near the office. From her half locker she pulled on her tank top and plaid flannel, roughly folding the sleeves up.

Emerging into the back of house prep area, Leah kicked Carlos in the shin, startling him from his engrossment in a Game Boy. "You can head home, Carlos. I'll lock up."

"You sure? It's real late. Could get thieves in here." No taller than Leah, who in her biggest boots barely scraped five foot four, Carlos would not pose much threat to an intruder.

"Dude, if someone tries to rob the place, I'll let them. I'm not gonna die to defend Benny's Pizza money. Plus, I brought a…friend. I'll be in and out once I straighten out the till."

Nosy by nature, Carlos peeked out of the port window in the swinging door. "Oh, pretty friend. What happened to her dress? She go swimming in it?"

"Go home, Carlos."

"Is it a new girlfriend? Good, I didn't like the last one."

Carlos met Hayley once for five minutes, max. How he formed an opinion in those five minutes, Leah would never know. But the men she worked with liked to offer unsolicited opinions about her girlfriends as part of their uninvited brotherly hazing. "Just a friend. Go home, Carlos."

"Okay okay, Carlos goes home. No *sexo* in the store. Benny gets really mad," he informed with a sage nod.

"Great, I hate that you know that, and I hate even more that I know you know that. *¡Vete!*"

After locking the back exit behind Carlos, Leah pushed through the swinging door with Victoria's borrowed clothes in hand: one white shirt and one pair of blue jeans in what appeared to be roughly the right size. She and Victoria had similar physiques, though Victoria's shoulders were a bit broader from swimming.

"So, I got a Benny's Pizza shirt—a rare honor to wear if not an employee—and a pair of jeans."

Victoria scrunched her nose. "Do I want to know why someone left their pants in a restaurant?"

"Nah. But they don't smell, if that helps."

Victoria hesitantly took the offered clothes and strode into the bathroom to change. Leah closed up the front of the store, leaving the rest of her receipts and money in the till in the manager's office. She turned off all the ovens but one, using it to cook a pizza for herself. Benny's Pizza functioned as a second home for her—she did homework here, had a favorite booth with her name carved in it, her band played here, her parents dined here on occasion to see her during work hours. Her first kiss with a real girlfriend happened in the back of the restaurant under a flickering floodlight, pressed against rough brick.

The squeak of a door hinge stole her attention away from the oven and she watched Victoria plod across the terra-cotta tiles, prom dress in hand. Only Victoria Lockwood could possibly make borrowed jeans and an oversized, plain cotton T-shirt attractive, and with her hair out of its intricate bun, the glistening tendrils framed her face and fell down her shoulders. A curse on the dim, golden light making Victoria look ridiculously gorgeous because Leah's gay heart could barely withstand it.

"There wouldn't happen to be any shoes in this magical lost and found, would there?" Victoria asked, wincing hopefully.

"No, unfortunately. You'll have to make the heels work for a little longer."

"That's all right." Victoria placed her items on the counter and pulled off her heels. "So, this is where you work?"

"Hope so, otherwise we're robbing the joint." Victoria smirked and Leah tried not to let it steal her breath too much. "Ah, yeah. The minute the ink was fresh on my learner's permit I basically conned Benny into giving me a job. That was…man, like three years ago."

"Wow. You must like it." Victoria leaned on the counter as Leah returned to tending her pizza. "Never would've thought you'd like the face-to-face with customers."

She slid the pizza out from the oven and onto the worktable, then gazed over the counter. "I never would've thought you'd think about me at all."

Victoria's confidence faltered and Leah busied herself finishing off the pizza and cleaning the oven. Why would Victoria Lockwood give a second thought to the kind of job Leah might have? She figured Victoria's excessive number of extracurriculars, flourishing social circle, and asinine boyfriend kept her occupied. Still, she felt bad again— her sympathy started to annoy her—and she softened as they walked outside into the balmy summer heat. Rain evanesced into humid air, periodically cooled by a constant breeze. As Leah settled into the driver's seat, she sensed a bit of awkward tension from Victoria. Surely, she wanted to get on with her life. But instead of offering to bring her home, she surprised them both by asking, "Hungry?"

"Yeah, actually. I left before they served dinner."

"Well, we've got some not cold but relatively room-temp free beers. Made a pizza." She lifted the box in her hands before putting it in her back seat. "And the rain cleared up. Normally after late weekend shifts, I drive up to Freeman's Peak. You've been there, yeah?"

"No. Should I have?"

"I guess? I figured all you popular kids made it a point to get up there and make out as a rite of passage or something. Anyway, it'll be deserted today because of—" Leah hazarded a glance at Victoria's crumpled dress. "It's a nice night for it. Good place to think."

"Sounds good."

The ride from Benny's to Freeman's Peak was as picturesque as it got in Garden Hills, going from quaint asphalt suburbia to winding roads lined with thick, centennial trees overhanging the streets like verdant arches. Leah took the curves carefully as they climbed the steep service road toward the peak.

"Leah, why are you doing this for me?"

Using her car's dashboard to open the beer bottle, Leah shrugged and took a swig of the drink as she drove. "Does it matter?"

"A little." With a firm but forgiving touch, Victoria took the bottle from her hand and placed it in the cup holder. "I don't mean to sound ungrateful, I'm—I don't know, surprised."

Leah's hand tensed around the wheel. "Right, because I'm such an awful bitch."

"What? I never said that. I would never say that." Leah thought she detected a truth to her tone, but she just as easily could've wished for it. "You're not always the…nicest person. To be honest, I thought you didn't like me."

"Who says I do like you?"

Carefully, Leah parked the car near the edge of the lookout. Without a word to Victoria, she grabbed the pizza, beers, and blunt, and climbed onto the hood of her car. Victoria sat shell-shocked in her passenger seat, but Leah intentionally paid her no mind. Obviously, everything she'd done since agreeing not to take Victoria home indicated she did, in fact, like Victoria. But everything in Victoria's life came easily—she needn't add herself to the list. She snagged a slice of pizza and lowered it into her mouth as she waited for Victoria to join her.

Freeman's Peak's reputation as a make-out point detracted from the natural beauty of its cliffside—the entire town, even most of the county, lay at your feet from the edge of the cliff. They'd put up a railing about fifteen years ago when some idiots got drunk and tumbled down the embankment. Despite the obstacle, the county sparkled below. From up here, Garden Hills could be beautiful. The right amount of distance could bring beauty to anything.

Finally, Victoria unsteadily shuffled across the hood, sitting on the other side of the pizza box. Watching as Victoria extracted a slice of pizza, Leah wondered, not for the first time, if popularity followed beauty or the other way around. Nobody she knew came even remotely close to how pretty Victoria looked every day. Even now, hair soaked and makeup ruined, she'd be the prettiest girl on any block. Of course, pretty and popular couldn't keep away the pitfalls of being a teenager, depending on what happened at prom.

"If you don't like me, then why go through all this trouble?"

Leah snorted derisively. "Why do you care if I like you or not? Is the entire school liking you not enough?"

"The entire school doesn't like me." Victoria took a dainty bite of the end of her slice of pizza. "Sorry I asked. I'm not ungrateful, just—"

"What, suspicious? Worried the class lez is going to try and put the moves on you?"

"God, are you always such a dick? Don't you get tired of assuming the worst all the time?" Victoria snapped at her, eyes ablaze. "'Put the moves on me,' please. You wouldn't dare."

Leah drank more of her beer and cursed her genetic resistance to drunkenness. She wanted the buzz, but this cheap crap wasn't doing the trick. She met Victoria's challenging gaze with her own. "You don't know what I would or wouldn't dare to do."

"I know you keep dodging my question," Victoria replied, not looking away as she tipped back her beer. "Big Bad Leah Vasquez, but she's afraid to answer a simple question."

"Damn, Lockwood." Chuckling through her response, Leah rested her elbows on her knees. "You looked like you needed a hand. 'Do not withhold good from those who deserve it when it's in your power to help them.' Proverbs."

"Oh." Visibly surprised, Victoria looked away and took another bite of her pizza. "I didn't know you were religious."

"I'm Mexican, Victoria. I was born with a rosary in one hand and a wallet-sized photo of *la Nuestra Señora de Guadalupe* in the other." When Victoria looked over again, Leah grinned at her. "I could never tell my parents, but I'm not devout like them. The Catholic Church itself, the institution, the people? I can't get down with that. People are too corrupt. Jesus I dig, though. And I do believe in God. You don't?"

"Um, no." Victoria winced as if she'd said something highly offensive. "Does that bother you?"

"Why do you care if it bothers me?" Victoria hardened her stare again and Leah held up a hand. "For the record, it doesn't bother me at all. But like, why do you care what other people think?"

Victoria gazed off into the distance and Leah lost her to her thoughts. The breeze rustling the trees became the only noise around them, other than the clink of the bottle against her car's hood. "I always have. It's how I was raised. You're only as good as everyone thinks you are."

Her resignation tugged at Leah's much unused heartstrings. "Caring about the opinions of people who don't give a shit about you sounds exhausting."

"It is." At a no-man's-land in their verbal sparring, Leah leaned back against her windshield and looked up at the stars. One of the benefits of living in a small town—the number of stars in the sky outnumbered the population by the thousands. Drawing invisible lines between constellations, she heard shuffling as Victoria laid down beside her. "Are you going to ask me what happened?"

"Do you want to tell me?"

"Not really. I want this cliff to give way and swallow me whole."

"Unfortunately, it isn't mudslide season." Leah smirked and Victoria gave her a small smile back. The dumb stutter of Leah's heart forced her to blink away, back up to the stars. "Your biz is your biz, dude."

"Why didn't you go to prom?" Victoria asked abruptly, taking a second slice of pizza from the rapidly cooling box. "I know it isn't your scene or whatever."

Leah pried off the label on the beer with a blunt thumbnail. "No date."

Victoria blinked, evidently not finding this believable. "Did you ask anyone?"

"Of course not."

She prodded. "Did anyone ask you?"

"Not anyone I would've considered going with."

Victoria drank more lukewarm beer and stared out into the city again. "Plenty of people go to prom alone."

"Plenty of losers. I mean, I know I'm a loser, but I do have some dignity."

"You're not a loser," Victoria replied immediately.

"Yeah, I am, and I don't need you to pity me or tell me otherwise." The last thing Leah wanted was to be on the receiving end of Victoria Lockwood's charity.

"I don't pity you. I envy you." Victoria turned her attention away from Leah and lowered her voice. "Whatever. I'm sure you don't care."

Leah slid her forearm under the back of her head, laughing up at the stars. "Envy me? For what? I mean, I have good skin and great hair. And I have a higher GPA than you. But otherwise, I ain't got much to envy."

Victoria shook her head. "You get to be yourself all the time," she said softly. "I envy that freedom."

"Well, I'm sure if you can't find that freedom, you could buy some."

"Right. The answer to all my problems. Money." Victoria sighed, and Leah didn't think anything in Victoria's life could be heavy enough to elicit a sigh like that.

"I guess money couldn't buy you a better boyfriend," Leah said. "Or better friends. I may be a bitch, but at least I would've done you the courtesy of telling you Carter Harcourt is a prick and you're too good for him."

"He's a raging fucking asshole," Victoria snapped. "And I hope his tiny penis shrivels and dries up, falling off like a baby's umbilical cord."

Leah winced. "That is some powerful imagery, Lockwood. Is his dick small?"

"Contrary to popular belief, I have no clue what his dick looks like. I'm assuming it must be microscopic, otherwise I don't know what all his pompous jerk-off behavior is compensating for."

Victoria shimmied off the car and stalked toward the edge of the cliff. Leah watched from the hood as her classmate inhaled deep breaths and stared out over their shared hometown. She finished the pizza and folded the box into the trash can, recycling their finished beers. Retrieving the blunt, she flicked the lighter as she approached Victoria from behind, her boots clomping in the grass.

Exhaling a dense cloud of gray smoke, Leah wordlessly offered the blunt to her. She watched Victoria debate it for a second before snatching it and taking a deep toke of the cheap weed. "Whatever happened, everyone is gonna forget about it in a week," Leah said, her voice rough from the smoke. "High school sucks, but at least it's brief."

Victoria took another long toke. "Maybe you've got the right idea, keeping everyone at a distance. You'd never let someone humiliate you at prom."

"Can't humiliate you if you don't go," Leah replied, tapping her head like she'd had a great idea. "If only you'd picked a different crowd, huh? But then you wouldn't be captain of the swim team and yearbook editor and class vice president and whatever other school spirit shit you're into."

Undeterred by Leah's rudeness, Victoria's lips lifted into a smirk. "I'm surprised Leah Vasquez, school rebel, even knows I'm class vice president. What an honor."

"How could I not? Your face was all over the hallways with your 'Lockwood's on Lock' posters." She motioned for the blunt. "Plus, I voted for you."

"Oh. Thanks."

Leah handed her the blunt. "Sure. Well, whatever Farter Barfcourt did to you at prom, I hope you socked him. God, his stupid face just needs one good punch."

"I wish I had. I also wish I'd heard 'Farter Barfcourt' before today because that's hilarious," she said, giggling as she gave Leah back the weed.

"Again, wrong crowd."

Victoria leaned on the railing, hanging her head. "God, I feel so stupid. I just want to forget prom ever happened. Throw this stupid dress and these stupid heels right over the cliff."

"That would be pretty rad." Leah propped her boot up on the railing. "But it would also be littering, which is not rad."

"So, you can skip class and smoke weed on county reservations," Victoria said, plucking the blunt from her hand and inhaling it. "But not litter."

"I'm a rebel, not an asshole." Gazing at the lit end of the blunt in Victoria's mouth, Leah's eyes sparked with an idea. "You wanna burn the dress?"

Victoria took the blunt from her mouth and turned it around, placing it between Leah's lips. The intimate gesture surprised Leah, but she coolly sucked in the smoke, waiting patiently for an answer.

"Yeah. I wanna fucking burn it."

CHAPTER TWO

The pattern of Victoria's life imitated the seam on her dress, the one she stared at as Leah Vasquez drove her to the other side of town. A neat row, not a stitch out of place, flawlessly matched to the satin and running down the side of the material and into the abyss of sapphire fabric between her legs. Perfect. Easy. Expensive. Pinned so tightly most times Victoria wanted to scream. She nabbed a blue thread between her fingers, the brave little tendril that escaped the neat seam, and she gave it a sharp tug. Satisfyingly, she liberated the thread bit by bit, freeing the hem to unravel.

Yanking and twirling the thread around her finger like a tourniquet, she gazed out the window as they bumped over the tracks into south Garden Hills. Uncharted territory for Victoria, and disorienting on any other night. But not tonight. She welcomed the change from the familiar. The last house on a dead end, the acreage of Leah's house stretched back farther than Victoria could see in the dark. Glinting car parts sparkled like an ocean of glass, waves upon waves of discards. Not really a junkyard, Victoria noted as they pulled into the driveway. It wasn't junk, just cars. Lots of cars.

So, like an idiot, she said, "That's a lot of cars."

"Pot's really hitting you, huh?" Leah rolled her eyes, leading Victoria around the side of the house, tiptoeing on a paved pathway next to a chain-link fence. One could nearly touch the house next door from here—Victoria wondered how anyone lived in such close proximity to their neighbor without going insane. She didn't even like that proximity to her family. Behind the house lay a cement patio with a white plastic set of furniture haphazardly placed in a circle, and a rather excessively large grill. An uneven lawn, thick bristles interrupted by the soft crawl of crab grass, squished beneath their feet as they walked toward a metal dome sitting farther back in the yard.

Victoria frowned, devastated at the pile of sodden wood inside the fire pit. "Leah. The wood is wet."

"I see that. Gimme a minute." Victoria flopped into a nearby lawn chair and waited with her dress and heels in hand as Leah produced a pocketknife from her jeans. Brow furrowed, Leah focused on shaving small pieces of kindling. "Gotta find dry pieces."

The sudden appearance of a switchblade fascinated her. "You always carry a knife?"

"I deliver pizza," Leah replied, as if this connection should be obvious. "Weirdos open the door sometimes."

"And, what, you threaten to shank them?" Victoria snatched the knife from Leah's hand and mimicked stabbing motions. "'Hey, pal, don't try no funny business, I got a little knife.' I bet that scares them pretty bad."

"Do you think I turn into a Victorian street urchin when I deliver pizza?" Leah scoffed. "Give me back my knife."

"Say please."

The barely restrained frustration in Leah's eyes delighted her. Leah's reputation at school set her high and above everyone else, as if the trappings snaring other high schoolers couldn't touch her. She simmered with anger most of the time, but never—to Victoria's knowledge—let the tormentors get to her. Until now. "Please give me my knife."

Victoria danced it out of her grasp. "I don't know, that please didn't sound very convincing."

Leah turned away to resume lighting the fire, passing the lighter beneath the wood. She chucked the wetter pieces into the yard, and it didn't take long for the fuzz stick to catch fire. The flames rose nearly as tall as they were. Temporarily distracted by the increasingly large flame, Victoria didn't notice Leah advancing on her until Leah's fingers grasped her wrist. "Give me the knife. I'm polite, but I don't beg."

Their close physical contact unnerved her, and Leah's voice sent a bolt of lightning to the pit of her stomach. Distracted by the sensation, she let Leah slip the knife from her hand. "Have you ever used it?"

"No," she said, hefting the switchblade in her hand before tucking it back into her pocket. "But I could fuck a dude up."

"Not if they were stronger than you," she replied matter-of-factly.

Leah raised an eyebrow. "I'm pretty strong."

"I'm stronger than you, Vasquez."

"On no planet, in this solar system or otherwise, are you stronger than me, *Lockwood*."

With only a slight wobble, Victoria got into Leah's face again with two big strides. "I've practiced tae kwon do since I was six. If you hadn't gotten me drunk and high, I could kick your ass. You should be very afraid of me."

The look on Leah's face moved from indiscernible to amused, and she chuckled airily. "Shouldn't you be afraid of me?"

"Why? Nothing about you is scary." Victoria snorted. "What? Because you're kinda mean and broody, people should be afraid of you?"

"There's also the rumor I killed a guy."

"Please, like you didn't start that rumor."

Leah gaped, playfulness dancing along with the flames in her eyes, drawing Victoria closer. In that moment she understood how moths find their doom in twinkling lights.

"You should be afraid because being seen with me can ruin a girl's reputation."

"Oh yeah?" Victoria licked her lips, and Leah's gaze followed the movement. "Like Hayley What's-Her-Face from Brookstown?"

Leah blinked in obvious surprise. "What? How do you know Hayley?"

"She swims. We compete against Brookstown all the time. Which you'd know if you ever went to your girlfriend's swim meets."

Leah didn't appear bothered by the accusation. "People go to swim meets?"

"Jerk." Victoria pushed Leah, causing her to stumble back a few steps. "Yes, they do. But, anyway, she asked me lots of questions about you last time our teams met. It was weird. It was like she didn't know you at all. You'd think you'd know someone better if you sucked their face off every day after school in the parking lot."

Eyes narrowed in irritation, Leah inquired, "Don't you have better things to do than watch me make out with my ex-girlfriend? Run a club? Wash a teacher's car? Touch your boyfriend's muscles or something?"

Maybe if she were less inebriated, she'd be more embarrassed or possibly angered at the mention of Carter, but Victoria shrugged it off. "Everyone saw you. She made such a show about it. Wait. Ex-girlfriend?"

Leah picked up a short branch and snapped it, tossing it into the fire. "We broke up two weeks ago."

Again, Leah didn't look too upset about this event, just annoyed. For whatever reason, this brought Victoria a measure of relief. Leah backed into the lawn chair and sat down clumsily, planting her feet wide apart. She sat next to Leah and stared at the fire. "Why?"

Leah relit the blunt, exhaling smoke up into the sky. "She wasn't real."

"She wasn't...real?" Victoria repeated her as if she'd misheard. "Like she's a poser, or she's a ghost?"

Midway through handing the blunt to Victoria, Leah retracted her hand. "Maybe you better lay off the weed." With a huff Victoria snatched it from her and took another deep toke. "I mean...she wasn't real. We dated but it felt like just two people hanging out. Kissing her, hooking up or whatever...didn't feel like anything. Maybe you're right, maybe it was like dating a ghost, because if she wasn't around, I didn't think about her. I want to be with someone I can't stop thinking about. I want to be with someone whose kiss makes me feel...makes me feel..."

"Like God is a heartless tyrant for making us choose between kissing and breathing." She handed the blunt back to Leah—plainly stupefied by Victoria's words—and stood, gathering her dress in her arms. "Yeah. I want that too."

Curtailing the strong impulse to throw herself on the pyre, she bundled up her designer dress and heaped it on top of the flames. It smothered the fire almost completely, and Victoria worried she'd snuffed it out. Then, bursts of flame licked around the sides and poked up through the dress, hissing as they voraciously consumed the material. Victoria stared into the orange blaze, almost unblinking as the fabric crackled and smoked, polluting the air. It did not smell very good, and Victoria briefly worried about the environment and the possible hole in the ozone layer they'd created.

"My mom is going to be so mad about the dress," Victoria murmured.

"So, lie to her." Leah shucked off her boots, stretching her socked feet near the fire. "Tell her somebody else ruined it. Spilled a drink on you or something."

The shriek of a screen door snapped their attention to the house, where a yellow spotlight buzzed on and cast a blanket of light over the yard. Out of the back door a tall, darkly beautiful woman barreled toward them in slippers and blush-pink robe. Black hair flew behind her, held back from her face by a headband. "Leonora Renata."

"Uh-oh," Leah sing-songed quietly. Lolling her head to the side, she grinned at the approaching tornado. "You know, every time you use my full name it summons a *bruja*."

"I'll show you a *bruja*. What are you doing out here? It's past midnight!" The woman, apparently Leah's mother, aimed her steely gaze at Victoria. "Who are you?"

"I'm Victoria. I'm a—I go to school with Leah."

Leah's mother raised two unimpressed eyebrows and Victoria shrank to about half her size. Older women intimidated Victoria generally, and Leah's mother's tall stature and stern features straightened her spine immediately and rendered her speechless.

"And why are you burning God knows what in my yard?"

Before Victoria could respond, Leah piped up. "I invited her over for a bonfire. And I...dared her to throw her old dress into the fire? You know me, always...pulling pranks. Sorry."

It took all of Victoria's strength not to laugh. For someone who'd just encouraged Victoria to lie to her own mother, Leah's ability to deceive fell quite short. It charmed Victoria to see Leah's misanthropic attitude did not extend to her home life. "I'm sorry, Mrs. Vasquez. We should have asked first. Leah tried to cheer me up, it's not her fault. I—I should go home. I've taken up enough of your daughter's time. I'm so sorry if we woke you up."

"Young lady, you are not going home at this time of night. Not with another storm on the way. Do your parents know you're here?" Victoria shook her head. Leah's mother crept a bit closer, inspecting Victoria's haggard appearance in the garish light from behind them. Her features softened, probably at the pitiful picture Victoria made in her borrowed clothes, puffy eyes, and half-removed makeup. "We'll talk about it in the morning. Leah, put out the fire and clean this up. And do I smell weed? I better not smell weed."

"What? No? It's probably skunks." Leah's mother sniffed the air and narrowed her eyes at Leah, whose shoulders sagged at the nonverbal inquisition. "Okay, fine. I didn't buy it. Someone gave it to me as a tip for a delivery."

"Get rid of it and get inside." Leah's mother turned her attention to Victoria. "Do you need to shower, sweetheart?"

"Yes, ma'am."

"Okay. I'll get you settled up in Leah's room as well as some clothes to sleep in."

"Dear God, not one of your muumuus, spare her," Leah remarked with a groan.

"They're called night dresses."

Leah rolled her eyes at her mother, who corralled a wide-eyed Victoria toward the house. Ushered in through the screen door, Victoria ended up in a small, clean kitchen with a yellow linoleum floor. She couldn't see very much in the dark, other than a cat clock on the wall and a tiny table shoved into a corner. From there, Mrs. Vasquez led her into a cozy family room and up a flight of carpeted stairs. Only one room took up the upper floor, evidently a converted attic space with sharply slanted roofs. Leah's room.

Leah's mother unhappily ruffled through Leah's clothes in her dresser drawers. "I buy this girl pajamas every year, and every year she sleeps in ratty T-shirts."

"Honestly, I can sleep in this," Victoria offered.

"No, you will not be sleeping in clothes that smell like pizza and weed." Her mother produced a T-shirt and a pair of cotton shorts from Leah's dresser. "Because I do not live in a frat house, despite Leah's attempts to make it one."

"I don't do drugs," Victoria blurted out. "Leah offered, but she didn't pressure me."

Leah's mother relaxed a touch, huffing out a sigh. "I know Leah smokes pot occasionally, and I've told her I prefer she do it at home where she's safe. Just not cigarettes." Then, Leah's mother narrowed her eyes. "You don't smoke cigarettes, do you, Victoria?"

Victoria straightened up. "No, ma'am. Never."

"Good," she said, her shoulders dropping their tension. "I don't mind the recreational pot, as long as it doesn't interfere with school or her work. What I don't like is when she lies to me about it."

"Wow. My mom would've already had me on a train to a boarding school by now." Victoria couldn't even imagine the haranguing if she'd come home smelling like weed. "Thank you for letting me stay here, Mrs. Vasquez."

"Not a problem, sweetheart. There are fresh towels in the closet next to the shower. She should have extra toothbrushes under her sink, God knows I buy her enough of them. I'll leave something out for you to wear in the morning, okay?"

"Okay." There didn't seem to be any arguing with this woman. Not the same, strict, unilateral decision-making her own mother employed, but a gentle, well-meaning firmness. Victoria didn't question it.

"Do you want me to call your parents and tell them you're here?"

She tried not to look stricken at the idea. "No, I can call them in the morning. They aren't expecting me home tonight anyway."

"All right." She didn't appear convinced at all, but Victoria must've looked desperate enough for her to let it slide. A mother with a maternal instinct—what a concept. "Good night."

With a pitying smile, Mrs. Vasquez left her alone in Leah's room. Though she wanted to snoop, she circumvented the urge in favor of a hot shower. Setting the pajamas to the side, Victoria turned on the shower and got herself clean. Hairspray, makeup, and sweat swirled down the drain along with the rest of the night. Her perfume, the one she'd happily sprayed on her neck and arms this afternoon, was replaced with the scent of Leah's bar soap. Something light and springy—Irish Spring? Closing her eyes beneath the water, Victoria pictured her boyfriend's smug, sneering face as he devastated her in front of their class. The horrified, titillated looks of the girls she called her friends as they stared at her. Victoria sobbed underneath the sound of the overhead spray. She finished up quickly so as to not use all their hot water, and dried and re-dressed. Only one bare foot out of the bathroom, she stopped as she caught sight of Leah staring at her with wide eyes from the middle of her room.

"Your mom said it was okay if I wore something of yours," Victoria said in a rush. "And she let me use your shower. I can change if you want."

"No." Leah choked out the word like it had lodged itself in her throat. "You're fine. You look fine. It's fine."

"Is it? You're turning really red."

Her deeply sepia cheeks went redder, and Victoria watched Leah inhale a deep breath before asking, "This is weird, right?"

"Really weird," Victoria replied, chuckling as some of the tension in the room dissipated. "But not like, that weird? Which in and of itself is…weird."

"Right. Weird but also not." Victoria smiled hesitantly and Leah's slightly nervous energy returned. "Uh, did she get you a toothbrush and stuff?"

Victoria nodded. "Yeah. I'm…all set."

"Cool. Cool, cool. I'm just gonna…" Leah bustled around her room, haphazardly tossing clothes into drawers and straightening up a pile of papers on her desk. Her bed, desk, and dresser took up most of her room; the angled ceilings didn't help make it seem roomier. Leah had only a single shelf with a few trophies on it, and posters covered every available inch of her burnt-orange-colored walls. "Sorry, I never clean my room. I mean it's clean, like, I clean it, but I didn't straighten up or anything."

"It's not like you expected to board a classmate you barely know."

Leah kicked her shoes into a corner and gave her room a once-over. "Yeah. Ah, anyway, gimme one sec. I need to shower quick." She grabbed her pajamas from the end of the bed and hurried into her bathroom.

Once she heard the shower turn on, Victoria felt confident enough to poke around Leah's room. Like an explorer belaying into an uncovered tomb, Victoria hoped it might reveal the mystery of Leah Vasquez. As class vice president, the general activity of other classmates fell within her purview, but Leah opted out of most activities. Leah's intelligence could spin heads—wall-to-wall AP classes filled her schedule and she was the best player on the chess team—but Victoria's knowledge of her ended there. If Leah had a social circle, Victoria didn't know any of them aside from Billy Reade, an affable slacker dating her friend Jenna. She'd seen Leah hang out with the chess team, particularly Fatima Singh, but otherwise she chose to stay on the periphery of their class and therefore remained an enigma.

The posters on her walls came as no big surprise—alternative rock and most of them women, including an almost movie poster-sized portrait of Selena. Her desk housed a big PC and a landline telephone with a transparent casing, and a handful of photos pinned to a small corkboard. A weathered portrait of the Virgin Mary, a snapshot of Leah with Billy outside their elementary school, and one of her now ex-girlfriend Hayley kissing her on the cheek. Tucked almost behind the monitor, a CD Victoria didn't recognize leaned against another framed photo. On each side of her chair stood short cabinets without doors, crammed full of assorted books. No room for a bookshelf, Victoria realized as she turned to check out the other side of the room.

She scanned the trophies along the wall and counted three for chess and one for pee-wee soccer. A rather large stereo set somehow squished against one wall, the equipment packed next to its speakers and a truly ungodly number of CDs. Stuffed in the corner next to a small amplifier, a Y-shaped stand held a shiny black bass guitar and an old acoustic guitar. Stroking the ribbed guitar strings, she looked up as Leah padded out of her bathroom in pajamas. Normally, Leah wore a lot of black, flannels and plaids, ripped jeans, and big boots. Heavy eyeliner and dark lipstick; a grunge look Victoria didn't understand, but suited Leah. Here, she had on a faded New York Dolls T-shirt and a pair of heather-gray sweat shorts cut off at mid-thigh. A much softer and less intimidating version of Leah Vasquez. Jet-black curls hung limply around her face, framing bronze-colored skin with nary a blemish to be seen. By any social metric, Leah could be considered a misfit, but most misfits looked the part. Awkward, too short or too tall, too loud or too quiet, but not Leah. She acted more comfortable in her skin than anyone Victoria knew. Even this version of her, in cotton shorts with dinosaurs on them and not a smidge of makeup to obscure her natural beauty, still exuded a confidence eluding most teenagers.

Without reason, Victoria felt like she had to explain why she'd been caught skulking in the corner of the room. "I didn't know you play guitar."

"Of course you don't. You don't know me," Leah replied quickly. Stung, Victoria's face fell and she pulled her hand away from the instrument. "I mean, like, we only know each other from school."

"If you're a musician, why aren't you in band?"

"How do you know I'm not?" Leah asked, crossing her arms.

Smirking, Victoria canted her head. "I'm the yearbook editor. I know the clubs people are in."

Swiping a neon orange paper from her desk, Leah handed it over to Victoria. "This is my band. We're not...hella legit or anything. We get together and jam, sometimes we play at Benny's. It's...it's dumb, it's nothing."

Leah tried to snatch the paper back but Victoria kept it out of her reach. "It isn't dumb." The flyer boasted a grainy, photocopied picture of their band, their name, and the date and time of their next gig. "'The Temple of Athena.'"

Finally nabbing the paper, Leah tossed it into the wastebasket beside her desk. "I dropped E one time and thought I communed with the goddess Athena. It turned out to be our drummer's really tall mom in a robe, but the name stuck."

Victoria attempted to not be a dork but couldn't hold it in. "Wait, you really do drugs?"

"Whoa, pack a little more judgment into your question next time." Defensively postured, Leah shot back, "I do way less of them than your friends do."

"What? My friends don't do drugs." Leah laughed immediately, evidently surprised by Victoria's naïveté. "Who does drugs?"

"All the jocks are on steroids, including your shit boyfriend. The nerds pop uppers. Your girl Gabby buys pot from the same dealer Billy does."

Victoria blinked. "This is such a weird way to find out I'm the only one not doing drugs."

"If it's any consolation, I don't think Riley does them, either. And…I don't, not really. I can't afford to spend money on stupid shit like drugs."

Overwhelmed by an influx of new information, Victoria couldn't let the subject go. "Are…are drugs expensive?"

Eyes alight, Leah laughed and nodded her head. "What a night. Educating Victoria Lockwood on the economics of the drug market. For you? No, I imagine they're not. For me? I can't go dropping twenties like that, so, yes."

Yawning, Victoria stretched and glanced at the clock on the nightstand. Nearing one a.m. now. All her friends would be at the Lake District, partying in Gabby's or Carter's family's lake house, and apparently doing drugs. She'd bet money Carter already jammed his tongue into some other girl's mouth.

"I'm pretty beat," Leah said through a yawn. "I'll pop downstairs and sleep on the couch. You can have my bed."

Blinking out of her stupor, Victoria vehemently disagreed. "No, no, I couldn't. Look, you gave up your entire night. You don't have to give up your bed, too. I can sleep on the couch. Or on the floor or something."

"It's no biggie." Leah reached for a blanket from the end of her bed, but Victoria snatched her wrist.

Her eyes, chromatic like the Earth from afar, snapped to Victoria's. She'd never noticed how beautiful Leah's eyes were up close. Without the thick charcoal eyeliner and dark eyeshadow, they freely sparkled on their own merit. "If you're not against it, we could share your bed."

Of all the firsts she'd experienced tonight, witnessing firsthand a flustered Leah Vasquez ranked as the single most surprising, and endearing. "Oh. Uh, okay. I don't mind if you don't mind."

"I don't mind, that's why I suggested it."

"Cool, then, we're good." Detouring to her light switch, Leah stopped and turned, smirking. "Don't get any ideas, Lockwood. You're not my type."

Victoria stuck her tongue out at Leah and slid under the blankets. Soft and plush, Victoria nearly groaned at the comfort of Leah's bed, thankfully large enough for them to fit without bumping as she got in beside her. Within minutes, rainfall cascading down onto the roof appeared to lull Leah into a light sleep.

Victoria was not as fortunate. The rain picked up, smacking against the roof tiles in an unforgiving torrent, much like it did when she left prom. A roar of thunder startled her, and she curled into a fetal position on her side, facing away from Leah. Outside the only window in Leah's room, the sky opened up and poured a relentless sheet of rain. Another round of thunder came accompanied by a loud clap, and Victoria gasped.

"Victoria?"

"Yes?"

"So, no judgment, but...are you afraid of storms?"

Victoria had said she wasn't religious, but she silently begged a higher power to let the next lightning bolt strike her dead. "Yes."

As if this night wasn't mortifying enough, now she had confessed to a casual acquaintance her childhood phobia of thunderstorms stuck around into pubescence. Wincing, Victoria prepared herself for the inevitable, piercing rebuttal.

But no rebuttal came. Instead, a gentle hand warmed the side of her hip. "Would it help you if I moved closer?"

"M-maybe."

Behind her Leah shuffled until she lightly pressed against Victoria's back. Wrapping her arm around Victoria's side, she patted the bed until she found her hand. Victoria held it immediately.

"Is this okay?"

"Yeah." Victoria's breath caught in her lungs. Strange bedfellows didn't begin to cover the oddness of feeling wholly protected by someone she barely knew. "Thank you."

"*De nada*," Leah replied softly. Another roll of thunder boomed across the sky, and Victoria trembled less with Leah so close. "I'm sorry to inform you cuddling a lesbian means you're gay now too. It's in the rule book."

Grateful for the emotional reprieve, Victoria spilled into giggles that escalated into full-blown laughter. "Uh-huh. Well, don't get any ideas, Vasquez." She pitched her voice low in an attempt to match Leah's naturally smokier tone. "'You're not my type.'"

A lull in the storm created space for Victoria to breathe, and she relaxed her death grip on Leah's hand. The cozy confines of Leah's room radiated comfort, like a blanket fort you make as a kid with couch cushions and throw blankets. Her photos and posters, the hand-woven blanket on her bed, the tiny leftover touches of her childhood added to the homey feel that soothed Victoria almost more so than being in her own bedroom.

After a few minutes of silence, Leah whispered, "That was a terrible impression of me."

Unseen, Victoria smiled.

When Leah rolled up in her car and offered shelter from the storm, Victoria felt like the waterlogged equivalent of "out of the frying pan and into the fire." Out of the boiling pot and into the scalding bathtub, perhaps. In the moment, she'd angrily cursed the gods for putting her most difficult classmate in her path. But if given one hundred chances, she'd never have guessed underneath the misanthropy lurked a gentle humanitarian.

Lightning struck close to the house and Victoria nearly jumped off the bed. She quickly turned over and hid beneath the blanket, tucked against Leah's chest. "I'm so sorry," she said, muffled against the cotton of Leah's shirt. "This is embarrassing."

"Yeah, it is," Leah replied. Victoria peeked up from the blanket and glared at the smirk on Leah's face. "I was afraid of storms for a while as a kid. I'd hide under my parents' bed anytime the weather was bad." Leah released Victoria's hand in favor of reaching around her, rubbing soothing circles on her spine. "One day my parents had enough and my mother sat me down and explained to me very carefully the science of a storm. What happened at each exact moment—she actually put me outside our front door and had me watch a storm come in."

Victoria shuddered. The storm, the touch on her back, the rumble of Leah's voice in her chest, the smell of fabric softener and Irish Spring in her nose—it affected Victoria in ways she couldn't describe. In ways she was not prepared to describe. "Did it help?"

"Not really. After she finished explaining the science, my dad told me what my grandmother used to tell him: the thunder and lightning is God bowling. And when the big claps come, that's Him getting a strike. The littler noises are spares, other times He whiffs it. For whatever reason, that's what made me feel better. Even now, I sometimes entertain myself during storms by trying to keep God's score for Him."

The low drone of Leah's voice settled her, and she felt herself finally succumbing to sleep. The exhaustion of the day weighed heavily on her, and she desperately needed the reset. Thunder clapped farther away, but Victoria didn't move. Lowly, she said, "Maybe three pins."

"At best."

The storm moved out as quickly as it moved in, and the constant patter of rain against the roof provided a tranquil background for their slumber. Reflecting on the past few hours, Victoria's exhaustion-addled mind surged with questions and racing thoughts. In the back of her mind, a little monster wondered what Leah could want from her in exchange for this kindness. Since birth, she'd been trained to sniff out the intentions of others. On Leah, she smelled nothing. No ulterior motives, no suspicious intentions, nothing to indicate what kind of reciprocity she might desire. The lack of scent disturbed her most.

However, she overlooked it in favor of the immediate comfort. In just a matter of hours her life turned upside down, and yet the upturned place she found herself felt like exactly where she should be. Not at Carter's lake house, not even with her friends. Here—in the quiet solitude of Leah's arms, in her tiny bedroom in her tiny home on the opposite side of town.

Eyes closed and drifting further into unconsciousness, she murmured, "Why do I feel safe here?"

The hand stroking her back stopped. A spark of fear woke her from the descent into sleep. However, the ministrations against her spine resumed, and Victoria let out a breath of relief.

"Because I would never hurt you."

Victoria woke up to the very unfamiliar sound of soft snoring. Light filtered in through the lone window, dappling orange light across the wood floor. Songbirds chirped their early morning tune as Victoria attempted not to fidget. Leah remained sound asleep with her arms wrapped around her, and Victoria wanted to enjoy what she assumed were the last few moments of Leah's uninterrupted company. Certainly, once she woke, she wouldn't want to waste any more of her weekend with a classmate she barely tolerated.

Controlling her breathing and keeping her morning breath away from Leah's face, Victoria quietly waited for her to wake up. This tiny peek into Leah's life awakened an insatiable curiosity about her. She'd known Leah since they were eleven, when the two elementary schools combined into their junior and senior high. But Leah didn't hang out after school or join clubs. Partly, no doubt, because Leah endured a lot of homophobic bullying, but Leah clearly also chose solitude, and Victoria wanted to understand. It baffled her why someone this smart, this funny, this kind, would hide those qualities from everyone.

Leah slowly woke up and sleepily blinked. She didn't immediately leap out of bed, so Victoria stayed quiet. An unexpected, hard strike hit Victoria square in the chest when their eyes met, and the puzzlement on Leah's face melted away into recognition. "G'morning."

"Morning."

"Sorry, I must've cuddled you in your sleep." Leah pulled away and Victoria immediately missed the heat of her.

"It's okay. Thank you for last night."

Eyebrow up, Leah smirked. "They'll never believe me on Monday when I tell them I woke up in bed with Victoria Lockwood and she thanked me for last night."

A cold dread spread through Victoria's blood, rendering her immobile as Leah turned to check the time. Any warmth and goodwill she'd accrued for Leah evaporated, leaving her disappointed and angry. Victoria climbed out of bed and looked around nervously, as if she were lost. "I need to use the bathroom."

Their connection from last night vanished, and now Leah would make Victoria pay for enlisting her help. Rushing into the bathroom, Victoria dressed in her borrowed clothes and quickly brushed her teeth. She avoided making eye contact with herself in the mirror—no need to make visual confirmation of how shitty she felt inside.

Once she'd finished and allowed Leah time to use the bathroom, she fidgeted near Leah's bedroom door. "I should go," she said, voided gaze looking anywhere except at Leah. "You don't have to drive me. I can walk."

Evidently angered, Leah stood up and planted her hands on her hips. "Yeah, I guess I wouldn't want to spend any more time with me if I were you, either. Don't want anybody to know you rubbed shoulders with the class queer."

"What?" The coldness in Victoria boiled into indignant anger at her accusation.

"I get it. Can't have anyone thinking the princess of Garden Hills High is a big lez."

They squared off, angry and hurt, and Victoria became even more confused. "Leah, literally what are you talking about? You just said you were going to tell everyone we slept together on Monday."

"No, I said…" Staring down at the floor, Leah visibly puzzled through the last few minutes of their interactions. "Oh. I was being sarcastic, dude. You gave me the perfect setup with the 'thanks for last night.' I'm not gonna tell anyone. Take a chill pill."

Victoria inhaled and exhaled a series of deep breaths. So, maybe she'd overreacted. In her defense, her emotions had yet to level after this weekend's series of unfortunate and unexpected events. "What happened at prom…was humiliating. Going back to school on Monday is going to suck really hard for me. I swear this isn't about you being a lesbian, but I would be grateful if we kept this between us."

Leah's expression turned unexpectedly pensive, and after a few beats, she exhaled softly and her cheek dimpled in a half-smile. "Right, so I'm hearing you don't want me to tell our class we're girlfriends now even though we cuddled and I told you the rule."

Victoria pursed her lips, mostly to cover a laugh. "Leah."

"I dunno, I feel like we're missing out on some star-crossed, wrong-side-of-town, *Wuthering Heights* stuff here."

Ice firmly broken, Victoria's face brightened and she let out a long laugh. "Yeah, right. *Wuthering Heights* is a stretch. *The Notebook* might be more accurate."

Leah's nostrils flared. "Ugh, that schmaltzy nonsense?"

"Totally a 'Noah' thing to say," Victoria replied.

"I'm Noah? Why, because I'm poor and you're rich?"

"No, because you're an asshole."

"Damn, Lockwood." Whether she meant to or not, Leah looked impressed, and Victoria preened at the praise. "Who would I tell? I make it a point to talk to our classmates as little as humanly possible. Trust that I'm not going out of my way to tell anyone what I did over the weekend. Even if it means keeping your dark secret."

Victoria tensed. "My d-dark secret?"

"About how your good-girl persona is an act and you're actually a rebellious deviant who burns clothes in fires."

"Rebellious deviant?" Victoria huffed. "I burned one dress. At your suggestion."

"And a pair of heels, and drank beer, and got high. Pretty deviant behavior. Trust me, I would know."

She couldn't let Leah win every verbal sparring they engaged in, so she drew back for the big guns. "Fine. I'm a deviant and you're a softie."

Leah glared at her, mouth open. "I am not."

"First of all, yesterday proved that's a lie so you can't deny it. Second of all, you basically admitted to having read *The Notebook*. So, yeah. I know your dark secret too. The bad-girl persona is an act and you're really a softie at heart." At this, Leah blushed even deeper, coloring her dark skin an adorable shade of crimson.

"Mutually assured destruction is it then." Leah grinned and Victoria's heart stuttered. When had she become so instantly weak for something as transient as a smile?

She smiled back, despite the unease growing in her stomach. "I should probably go, though. You've got a life to get back to without me moping around in it."

Shrugging, Leah shoved her hands in her pockets and rocked back on her heels. "I work most weekends, so you're not interrupting much. I've got a one-to-ten shift at Benny's today, and I'll spend most of tomorrow in the shop with my dad. But, uh, you're more than welcome to ride along with me on my deliveries. Not like anyone will care. Plus, who knows? Maybe I'll need someone who knows tae kwon do to back me up."

Her heart swelled to think perhaps Leah wanted her around longer. Over the last twelve hours, it became very important to Victoria that Leah like her. "My parents think I'm at the lake all weekend, so they won't expect me home. I'd like to change into my own clothes, though. No offense. I just want to feel comfortable."

"None taken. Though I'll say you're rocking the grunge look. If you ever want to change scenes, you'll do fine." Inwardly Victoria was extremely pleased, but outwardly she rolled her eyes. Leah sat down on the edge of the bed to put on her sneakers. "I can swing by your house on the way to Benny's?"

"Great, thanks. Except…my mom can't see me. I don't want to explain last night until I absolutely have to."

"All right, then we'll sneak in."

"Sneak in? To my house?" Victoria found it preposterous to insinuate her home could be as easily infiltrated as Leah's dismissive tone implied. Preposterous and also irritatingly titillating. Could Leah really access her that easily? And what would she do if she could?

Thankfully, Leah's annoyed voice halted her increasingly alarming train of thought. "What, like it's the White House or something? Every house can be snuck into. But first we'll eat breakfast, because we're not gonna walk out that door before my dad feeds us a giant plate of *chilaquiles* and my mom asks you a million questions."

"As long as they're not about prom, not a problem."

Leah nodded. "I will pass that along."

"What's a *chilaquiles*?"

"Oh, Victoria." Leah threw her arm over Victoria's shoulder. "It's a breakfast you'll never forget."

Leah hadn't exaggerated. The giant plate of *chilaquiles* instantly seared itself into her memory as the biggest, most interesting breakfast she'd ever eaten. She picked at it while she observed the dynamic of Leah's parents. Her father, Hector, supplied Leah her looks—black, curly hair, deep bronze skin, and twinkling eyes—but not her personality. Hector laughed loud and hard, smiled constantly, and treated Victoria like his own daughter, even for the short time they spent eating breakfast. Her mother, Loretta, represented Leah's shrewd, introverted side with her guarded personality and analytical gaze.

How easily they got along impressed Victoria more than the breakfast. Not just the baseline love of parents and their kid, but they actually enjoyed each other's company. It didn't embarrass Leah when her father cracked a terrible joke, nor did she grimace when her mother chided her for last night's bonfire. It was respect, Victoria realized. Leah respected her parents, and startlingly, they respected Leah too.

"So, Victoria, are you going to college in the fall?" Loretta asked, sitting back against her chair and crossing one leg over the other. Her posture radiated both intimidation and motherly comfort in equal measure; she fascinated Victoria instantly.

"Yes, I'll be attending Harvard."

"*Mira*, Leah, you'll have a neighbor!" Hector exclaimed, ruffling Leah's black curls. Wrapping his arm around her shoulder, he leaned across Leah to address Victoria directly. "Leah is going to the Massachusetts Institute of Technology."

Leah blushed. "Everybody calls it MIT, *Papi*."

"Congratulations, Victoria," Loretta said gently.

"Yes, yes, congratulations! I have never been there, Massachusetts," Hector continued. "But I looked it up on the map. And I saw 'MIT' and so many *universidades*! Boston University, Tuft-y University, Harvard University. I can't wait to see them when I bring *mi hija* to college."

Leah glanced at Victoria. "He's more excited to tour Boston than to send his only child to school, so."

Victoria felt about ten steps behind the conversation. "You're going to MIT? How come I didn't know?"

"Because I didn't tell anyone." Leah pointedly narrowed her eyes at her father, who sheepishly backed off. "I didn't want to be on the cheesy 'Oh, The Places You'll Go!' board by the administration office."

Of course, Leah couldn't have known Victoria and her friends put up the board. Or maybe she did. "Well, congratulations. MIT is a tough school to get into."

"Says Harvard," Leah replied, nudging her on the shoulder.

"Very sorry, *señoritas*, but I must leave to open the shop," Hector said, bringing his plate to the sink. Their home didn't have a dining room; they ate at a Formica table pushed up against the wall in the kitchen. Victoria looked up from her plate to the cat-shaped clock swinging its tail on the far wall.

"It's nearly nine, isn't that late to open?" she asked, tipping back her red frosted glass of orange juice. Everyone else at the table drank espresso, and rather than admit to not knowing what espresso was, she requested orange juice. She felt like a toddler with her plastic tumbler of juice, but nobody seemed to care.

"I open late on Saturdays." Hector washed his plate and plunked it into their dish rack. "I open too early to see Leah before school days, so on Saturdays we eat breakfast together. Otherwise, one day I will turn around and be too old to enjoy her."

The same part of Victoria touched by the adoring look shared by father and daughter, also ached at it. Their warmth gnawed at the cold void inside her. It was so easy, so loving and natural. No guarded looks, no passive-aggressive taunts, no pointed glares. "Oh, that's nice."

"Ah, *mierda*, the garbage men are coming." Distressed, Hector peered out the kitchen window over the sink. "I didn't bring the cans out last night because of the rain."

"I got it." Leah gave her father a pat on the arm before pushing open the screen door and jogging outside.

"So, what's the plan today?" Loretta inquired, swiping a dish towel from the cabinet handle to dry the dishes Hector washed. This, too, amazed Victoria—not only these people doing their chores, because though she had a housekeeper, she wasn't an idiot—but nobody bickered. Leah's parents didn't tolerate one another, they loved each other's company. Preferred it, maybe.

"I'm tagging along on Leah's deliveries."

Loretta raised her eyebrows. "Is that so?"

"Wow." Hector shared a smile with his wife. "Surprising."

Victoria looked between them. "Why?"

"Leah is adamant about enjoying the solitude of her delivery driving," Loretta explained. "That's her 'me time,' as she puts it. Last year, Benny asked her to train an employee and he lasted about three blocks before Leah kicked him out and made him walk back to the restaurant."

Victoria ducked her gaze to the table, snickering. "That does sound like Leah."

On cue, Leah burst in through the screen door, her boots clomping into the room. "What sounds like me?"

"The loud crashing of someone stomping through my home with their shoes on," Loretta replied, glaring down at Leah's feet.

"My bad. Anyway, ready to roll?" Leah looked expectantly to Victoria, who nodded and got up from her seat. "We've got some errands to run before my shift."

"Thank you for letting me stay over, Mr. and Mrs. Vasquez, and for being so generous with your home and the delicious food."

Hector waved from the sink. "*De nada*. Any friend of Leah's is a friend of ours. You can come around anytime for my *chilaquiles*."

"Have a good day, girls," Loretta said. "Don't start any fires today, okay?"

"No promises!" Leah called as she strolled out the door, leaving Victoria to turn around and mouth an apology on her way out.

Listening to another of Leah's mixes, Victoria quietly gave directions to her home. It took them through the south side of Garden Hills, past Mr. Vasquez's shop downtown, bumping or swerving around potholes. As Leah's car rumbled over the tracks, her quiet chuckling caught Victoria's attention. "Thinking about the incredible cliché this town is, having a literal wrong side of the tracks."

"I think that's sort of a dying concept," Victoria replied. "My little brother Durward is ten and he's had the same friends since kindergarten from all over. They redistricted the elementary schools to better combine the town. It isn't like when we got to middle school and all of a sudden you realize there's an entire side of town you've never seen."

Both eyes back to the road, Victoria didn't see, so much as she heard, Leah's snorting. Out of her peripheral vision she saw Leah's lips form into a tight line, as if on the verge of combusting. Sucking in a quick, deep breath, she asked in a slightly high-pitched voice, "Your brother's name is Durward?"

"It's a family name." She sighed. "He hates it…he goes by Ward."

"I just—" Leah cut herself off with laughter, wiping her eyes with her free hand. "I'm sorry. Your parents looked a baby in the face and named him Durward. It's not even cruel. It's straight-up disrespectful."

She caught Leah's contagious laughter and giggled uncontrollably in the passenger seat. Though at the expense of little Ward, it delighted her to hear Leah laugh so unabashedly. It felt like being let in on a great secret. "Poor Ward. He's a good kid too. He doesn't deserve it."

They entered the neighborhood of clean streets, smooth pavement, yards trimmed and sparkling green like golf courses. Home. Victoria rode these blocks on her pink cruiser as a child, sold lemonade on the corner one intrepid summer when she was ten, did all the things children do when they grow up privileged and unattended. Riley lived two houses down, Carter one block away, Gabby around the block. The friends she'd accumulated by proxy or by accident, simply by living in a home on this side of town. She wondered what her life would be like if she'd lived in Billy Reade's house, a literal stone's throw from Leah. Would they be friends? Would she be tougher, stronger, like Leah? Or would Leah have softened, like she appeared to do this weekend, in proximity to Victoria?

Leah parked around the block from Victoria's home, almost directly behind it. "Here's the plan. We go through this side gate and hop the fence into your yard. From there, we sneak in your back door, go to your room, and get whatever you want. Okay? Now, *vamos*. I don't want your neighbors calling the cops because a brown girl parked her car in front of their house." Quietly closing her car door, Leah led Victoria through the backyard, past a massive in-ground pool. The fence proved easier to scale than Victoria imagined, and they landed safely in the grass of her backyard. Sticking close to the fence line, Victoria followed Leah toward the back door to her house. "Lead the way."

They tiptoed through the kitchen and snuck up the staircase, then scurried down the carpeted hall. Victoria breathed a sigh of relief as she closed her bedroom door behind Leah. Not wanting to waste any time, she darted into her closet to quickly change and shove new clothes into a duffel bag.

The idea of Leah Vasquez freely roaming her room spiked Victoria's already frazzled nerves. It felt like too much leverage to give a girl who always had the upper hand. Unimpressive and standard, her bedroom did not harbor any deep, dark secrets to uncover, other than the book of poetry she kept well hidden. No posters because her mother forbade them. Instead, trophies lined her wall, and she had a few scattered photo frames of her family and her friends. Still, she hoped Leah wouldn't look too closely at anything.

Victoria paused at her bookcase to select a book and Leah flopped on her bed behind her and did a snow angel on the bedspread. "Holy shit, this is a comfortable bed. What is this, Egyptian cotton?"

Chuckling, Victoria shoved a book into her bag on top of her clothes and shrugged. "I don't know, probably. It's not like anyone lets me pick out the linens."

"'The linens,'" Leah parroted with a grin, stretching out like a sunbathing cat. If Mother caught her alone, she'd have a lot of explaining to do, but she wouldn't be in trouble. But Leah, a girl she'd never seen, splaying herself on Victoria's bed, would set off her mother. Somehow, Leah made it different. More illicit. Strangely, Victoria imagined it would be like getting caught with a boy in her room, rather than one of her friends.

"Yes, the linens. Anyway, I think I'm set so we can—" Her door opened and Carmen strolled in with her vacuum in tow, startling Victoria enough to throw her bag across the room. Carmen shrieked in response, her hand on her heart. Leah sat up, a big grin on her face, eyebrows nearly to her hairline. Victoria rushed to the door and closed it as quickly as she could. "Jesus, Carmen, you scared me."

"I scare you?" Carmen asked, incredulous. "Nearly gave me a heart attack! What are you doing here? Señora Lockwood say you are at the lake house."

"As far as she knows, I am," Victoria replied, widening her eyes. "Please, don't tell her."

Finally, Carmen spotted someone else in the room and narrowed her gaze at Leah. "Who is this?"

"Leah Vasquez. I go to school with Victoria." Leah stood up, reaching out to shake the woman's hand. A spark of recognition widened her eyes. "Wait. Señora García?"

As if Leah had cast some sort of spell, Carmen's suspicion lifted and she smiled widely. Victoria suddenly felt like the other in her own room, as Carmen and Leah eased into conversation like old friends, laughing and talking so fast her head spun. Their easy banter made Victoria a tad jealous of her housekeeper. She stood like set dressing until their conversation came to a natural close.

"Okay, Señorita Victoria, I won't say nothing." Carmen turned an imaginary key over her locked lips and shuffled out of the bedroom. "Have a good time."

With Carmen out of earshot, Victoria sharply pivoted to Leah. "What the hell was that? What did you tell her? Did you tell her about prom?"

"I don't know what happened at prom, Einstein." Leah rolled her eyes. "Are you always this neurotic, or is this a special show for me?"

"She tells my mom everything," Victoria insisted.

"Trust me, she's not going to tell your mom she saw you. She's my people." Despite Leah's confidence, Victoria wasn't sure, and Leah looked annoyed that Victoria didn't immediately surrender to her convictions. "Lockwood, get your panties out of a knot."

Lifting her duffel bag and hoisting it over her shoulder, Victoria glared at her. "You don't tell me what to do with my panties, Vasquez."

"*Aún no*," Leah muttered.

She sharpened her glare even further. Even on her home turf, Leah still unnerved her. Not helped by how attractive she found Leah's seamless bilingualism. "What does that mean?"

Shrugging, Leah strode to the door and peeked out. "Maybe you should've taken a practical language like Spanish instead of a bourgeoise language like French."

"*Taisez-vous*," Victoria sneered.

Instead of instigating Leah, or at the very least making her curious as to what she said, Leah snickered and took one step toward Victoria, sizing her up from head to toe. "*Je te défie, ma chérie.*"

Stunned, Victoria remained in the room long after Leah determined the coast was clear and headed down the hallway. Since when was Leah trilingual? Not enough for her to be smarter and cooler, no. Leah also had to be more confident, more talented, and more…alluring in the most frustrating way possible.

She caught up with her on the staircase, but Leah held out her hand and pointed around the corner. Near their precious exit, her mother hummed to herself in the kitchen. Victoria's heart pounded as she begged any listening higher power to grant her this reprieve. The inquisition Leah would be victim to if Mother saw her had to be avoided at all costs. Not only because of the implication of sneaking a girl into her room, but Mother's passive-aggressive racism would repulse Leah and she'd never see her again.

Fortunately, her mother took a glass bottle of water and retreated back to her office on the other side of their home. She and Leah ran for the exit, sprinting across the yard and hopping the fence as fast as they could. Not until seated and safely buckled into Leah's passenger seat did Victoria unclench her jaw.

"Jesus Christ. I've never snuck out before. That was terrifying." Tossing her duffel bag into the back seat, Victoria panted to try and catch her breath.

"Not too bad for your first time, Lockwood. We'll make a badass of you yet." With a carefree laugh, Leah started her car and carefully turned out into the street. "Under your seat, could you grab the CD case and pop a disc in?"

Eyebrow raised, Victoria reached beneath the seat and pulled out a thick black binder. "I thought the rule is no one touches the music?"

"Guess we're both breaking rules today." Leah didn't look over, clearly uninterested in elaborating.

Victoria didn't push it. She knew when to take a win. Doing as told, she plucked a CD and loaded it into the player. A bluesy song from the seventies started up and Victoria finally relaxed. From driving with her last night, Victoria understood Leah as a calm, confident driver whose focus stayed on the road. However, not long into their journey, Leah shifted in her seat and tapped on the steering wheel intermittently, as if distressed.

"Why do you have that look on your face?" Victoria mentally filed through what Leah could've seen in her home or her bedroom to embarrass her. "Was it something in my room? Oh God, is it my Communion photo? It's not my fault, Mother did my makeup. I had no control over the blue eyeshadow."

"No, no," Leah replied. "You're not going to want to hear it."

"Okay, you can't just say that. What is it?"

Leah paused, glancing at Victoria before planting her eyes on the road. Her face split into a grin. "Your mom is hot."

Mortified didn't cover it. Victoria wanted to change phases and become a liquid, then possibly a gas, and disappear into the air. "Oh my God, never say that again. That is appalling. Horrific and appalling. That is a war crime. That is an atrocity."

"Fine, fine, I'll never say it again. Scout's honor." Music filled the silence again until Leah piped up once more. "I am gonna think about it, though."

CHAPTER THREE

The synchrony of woman and machine was sacred to Leah—outside of church, driving brought her the most peace. Even in chaotic or stifling traffic, nothing could permeate the bubble of relaxation between herself and the vehicle she controlled. This made her delivery time precious, as her only uninterrupted alone time. Most of her time she spent crammed in a school she hated or stuffed between her parents on their small couch, but the open road represented freedom, space, and solitude.

But not today.

Today, Victoria replaced her normal companion of a passenger seat filled with pizza boxes and takeout tins bursting with baked ziti. Dressed in her own clothes—a boat-neck striped T-shirt and crisp beige shorts—Victoria idly flipped through the binder of CDs in her lap. Each pocket held a white CD-R with the date written in felt marker, upon which Leah had burned playlists spanning the genres from traditional Mexican to metal, country to Cambodian surf rock.

"Is there a rhyme or reason to these CDs?" Victoria asked as she popped a CD from the player and exchanged it for another.

Leah rolled down her window to allow in the summer breeze. "Not really. I get in a mood and want to listen to certain music, so I make a

CD of it. I put the date on there and it reminds me of when I made it. Like a journal, in a way."

"So, all these…" Victoria skimmed through the binder like a book. "Reflect the inner mind of Leah Vasquez?"

"Sometimes it's just tunes to jam to. But if I was pissed off in May of 1997, the playlist would reflect that, yes."

"Are you ever not pissed off?" Victoria eyed Leah out of her peripheral vision. "Feels like that's your baseline."

"If everyone stopped acting like assholes, I could stop being pissed off," Leah replied. "My baseline, for the record, is completely neutral."

Evidently amused, Victoria prodded further. "So, will you make a playlist about this weekend?"

"Maybe."

"I'd like to hear it, if you do."

Leah glanced over. Truthfully, she'd already started building it in her head. "I'll consider it."

"I wonder what it will be. Which side of you will the playlist reflect? The secret softie, or the brooding, scowl-y side?"

Leah didn't scowl, she merely didn't smile as default. If more people understood that, she wouldn't have to scowl at them. "I'm not scowling now, am I?"

"True. I haven't seen your classic Leah Vasquez scowl since at least…this morning," Victoria teased, poking Leah in her thigh. "Gosh, that must be a record."

"You're about ready to see it again."

"I'm not worried," Victoria replied breezily, withdrawing her book from the duffel bag. "It's far less intimidating up close."

A busy afternoon meant Leah couldn't stop for lunch as planned, and worked right through until midafternoon. Victoria didn't complain, content to read her book in the passenger seat and hand Leah her deliveries. Famished by her last delivery before lunch, Leah pulled into the driveway, eager to get in and out.

"Are we going to eat pizza for lunch?" Victoria asked warily.

"God no." Leah reached behind her for the box of pizza. "I love Benny's, but a girl can only eat so much Italian food. I usually go to the deli over on Oak and get a sandwich or something. Sound okay?"

"Sure."

Popping out of the car, Leah jogged to the door via the short walk. She rang the doorbell and waited patiently with the pizza clutched in both hands. A woman, maybe college-aged, opened the door and took a step, leaning against the doorframe. "What's up?"

"Uh, not much? This is your pizza. The total is…" Leah paused, checking the yellow slip. "Nine dollars and fifty cents."

"Cool." Withdrawing her wallet from her back pocket, the woman fingered a couple bills. "What's your name?"

"Leah."

She smirked. "You have a pretty name. Almost like a princess."

"Thanks," Leah replied, a bit impatient. She'd heard better lines. "I bet you say that to all the pizza delivery drivers."

"Only the cute ones with gorgeous eyes." Blushing, Leah took the twenty-dollar bill and handed over the pizza. The girl watched her closely as she withdrew a billfold to give change. "How about…you keep the twenty and give me your number?"

Exchanging her number for an almost eleven-dollar tip seemed like a good enough deal, especially with an attractive older girl on the other end of it. "Bold ask."

"Faint heart never won fair maiden, princess." Leah scribbled her number on the receipt for the pizza still hanging from the box. "Sweet. My name's Dana."

"Do you always pay girls for their number, Dana?"

Dana laughed, a little self-conscious. "Ah, no. But hot girls don't usually show up on my doorstep like this, and I'm not someone who misses an opportunity. Assuming you're single, of course."

For some stupid reason, Leah thought about Victoria. "No, yeah, definitely single."

"Good. Me too." Tearing the receipt from the box, Dana fiddled with it between her fingers. "Is this your cell phone?"

"No, it's my home line." Leah didn't know what about her obvious occupation as a pizza delivery driver invited the assumption she had personal cell phone money. "I'm usually up pretty late."

"Dope. I'll call you later?" Dana bit her bottom lip and popped it out. "And if I ask you out, you'll say yes?"

Again, Leah thought about Victoria. She thought about the duffel bag in her back seat, indicating Victoria intended on spending the night again. "Guess you'll have to call me and find out."

Dana grinned, evidently pleased with the challenge. "Okay, Princess Leah. I'll talk to you tonight."

"Enjoy the pizza. Later." Leah gave her a short wave and walked back to the car, very much aware of Dana's lingering stare on her retreating form. Backing out of the driveway, she let out a long sigh and drove toward the deli.

Not until she'd parked and started walking toward the deli did Victoria speak again. "Did that girl ask you for your number?"

She opened the door for her and ushered Victoria inside to the jangle of the door's bell. "Yeah."

After putting in their sandwich orders, Leah perused the metal carousel of chip bags, searching for the perfect complement to her sandwich. She chose corn chips, then browsed the cooler for a beverage. Beside her, Victoria seemed less interested in a soda and more interested in gawking at Leah. "And you just…gave her your number?"

"Sure, why not?" She nabbed an orange soda and backtracked to the cashier with Victoria on her heels. "Besides, she tipped me eleven bucks and she's cute. Win-win for me, really."

"Oh." The cashier rang them up, putting their chips and sandwiches into the same plastic bag. Victoria shoved Leah to the side, opening up her hand-sized coin purse and taking out a few bills. "Let me pay for lunch."

"If you want my number, Lockwood, you don't have to pay for it." Leah took the bag with a shit-eating grin. "Thanks."

With an embarrassed glance at the disinterested cashier, Victoria hurriedly paid for their lunch and scrambled after Leah, who happily popped corn chips into her mouth. "Does that happen a lot? People flirting with you? Giving tips for your number?"

"The tip thing not so much. The flirting? Yeah, occasionally. People expect a grungy-looking dude to deliver their pizza, and then I show up and they're surprised and they flirt with me." Leah got into the car, plunking the bag of sandwiches into Victoria's lap, except for her corn chips, which she kept at hand. "That's not like a brag, either, because I don't think they think I'm hot. It's the novelty factor—a girl delivery person. Plus, I deliver to a lot of dudes and they always have enough unearned confidence to take a swing."

Victoria went oddly silent as they drove up to Freeman's Peak, staring down at the bag in her lap for most of the ride. Far be it for Leah to intrude on someone else's brooding, so she parked near the cliff edge and wordlessly gathered her lunch from the bag. Settling on the hood of her car, she unwrapped the sandwich and inhaled the sweet summer air. More people wandered the grounds on a weekend, but Leah parked far enough away from them to have peace to accompany the view. The humidity from yesterday's storm evaporated and the day cracked open into a beautiful, breezy summer afternoon.

A breezy summer afternoon spent with the most popular girl in her school—a curveball Leah tried not to bumble. Victoria sat beside her, carefully unwrapping the white paper around her sandwich. "I don't think it's a novelty factor."

Mouth full of egg salad, Leah cocked an eyebrow at her. "No? You're right, it's probably my sparkling personality."

"It's definitely not that," Victoria replied, picking at the bread of her sandwich. "They flirt with you because you're cool and really confident. The combination is kinda killer."

Leah swallowed an inordinate amount of sandwich in surprise. Knowing Victoria Lockwood considered her cool, it was a miracle she didn't choke. "It is?"

"Like you don't know that." Rolling her eyes, Victoria intentionally took a bite of her sandwich and scoffed. But Leah didn't know that. At school kids either ridiculed or ignored her, so she didn't have an idea of her own attractiveness in the context of anyone her own age. "Come on. How many girls asked you to prom?"

"Three."

Eyes wide, Victoria gestured like the answer stood before them. "That's not proof enough? How many kids are even gay at our school?"

"Getting invited to prom is not a gauge of hotness," Leah replied. "Two of the girls who asked me were underclassmen, and the third was Jessie. She doesn't even like me, she's just desperate for the class to think she's bi."

"She's not? God, it's all she talks about."

"Trust me, I know. She messages me on AIM all the time like we're friends, asking advice on, like, how to be gay." Leah cringed. "It's just… different for gay girls."

"How so?"

"'Cause there's so few of us," Leah said. "And I'm out, so I become like a lightning rod for girls who are questioning, just coming out, or want to experiment. They're attracted to the idea of me—the idea they, too, could be out. So, you know, it's hard to tell who is attracted to me as a person or me as an idea."

The burden and the blessing of being out included having any consenting girl at her fingertips, but knowing they'd slip from her grasp just as easily. Between the fluidity of sexuality and hormones flying crazy, Leah couldn't rely on anyone interested in her to be truthful in their intentions.

"I can't imagine your exact experience, but I can relate to being suspicious of people's motives."

"Because you're hella neurotic?"

"Because I'm popular, butthead. I'm not trying to say I got dealt a bad hand, but it's hard for me to tell if people genuinely like me, or if they think being near me will make them popular too. Plus, my dad's well connected and sometimes people are nice to me so they can get invited to dinner with him. It's gross." Leah listened intently, as she imagined Victoria was rarely this honest out loud. "Doing school activities is great and I do like it, but it's not who I am. I don't feel like I can ever really be myself with anyone, because I'm never sure what version of me they're looking for, or what they want from me. Do they want Popular Victoria? Do they want Vice President Victoria? Do they want Victoria Lockwood, daughter of Victor Lockwood, Senior? Or do they just want…me?"

Nodding along, Leah reached over and positioned her sandwich for a cheers. "To being irresistible for all the wrong reasons."

Victoria threw back her head in laughter and tapped her sandwich against Leah's. "Cheers."

As Victoria finished her lunch, Leah stretched her legs out by doing lunges on the hood beside her. "I guess if I hadn't broken up with Hayley, I could've gone to prom with her. It seemed…too much, you know? Like, no offense, you worked hard on it and I'm sure it was really cool, but it's not my scene."

"What is your scene? Punk rock concert date?"

"Oh yeah, getting slammed around in a mosh pit by sweaty dudes is my ideal date." The more Leah thought about it, the clearer the reality became. "I don't know. Nobody's taken me on a date."

"What?" Victoria whipped her head to the side. "What about Hayley? You guys never went on dates?"

"We went on dates, but I planned them. Nobody's ever taken me out to more than a dinner or something. A lot of the time we just hook up and I—" Leah sighed. "Sometimes I want to do something normal, like go roller-skating or something. Do date stuff other kids get to do."

"Well, that's surprisingly wholesome and adorable."

Huffing, Leah planted both feet on the ground and glared at Victoria. "Don't make fun because you don't get it."

"I do, I do get it," Victoria replied through light laughter.

"Do you? Do pretty straight girls have that problem? 'Cause I doubt it." Leah took Victoria's silence as thoughtful agreement, but when she caught her gaze, her oak eyes glinted in mischief.

"You called me pretty," Victoria singsonged. "Yet yesterday, you said I'm not your type. Which is it, Vasquez?"

"You don't have to be my type for me to objectively understand your attractiveness." Leah fumbled her car keys out of her pocket and swore under her breath. Acting casual required a lot of energy. "Plus, you're like, everybody's type."

Victoria raised an eyebrow. "Not an answer."

"Why? Thinking of changing teams?" Leah never understood the straight girl obsession with knowing whether or not you were attracted to them. If someone had a gun to her head and demanded the thing she cared about least in the world, it would be her attractiveness to men.

"You're presumptuous. How would you know what team I'm on?" Peering over the top of her car, Leah's heart leapt at the teasing smile playing on Victoria's lips. That instinctive reaction had to be stopped. She could not allow those kinds of feelings to take root, not for a girl like Victoria, who would never grow those feelings for her in return. But Victoria's coy smile took a spade to her heart and buried the seed anyway.

They leisurely finished their lunches and so long as Leah's beeper remained silent, she was content to relax on the hood of her car. Sleeves rolled up, Leah sunned herself as Victoria lay beside her, engrossed in her novel.

"Good book?" She peeked at the cover. "*The Perks of Being a Wallflower*. What's it about?"

"Mostly the perks of being a wallflower," Victoria replied, slowly smirking as she looked up from the text. "A coming-of-age story about a kid coming to terms with getting older and confronting his repressed childhood trauma."

Leah rolled her eyes. "Sounds like a blast."

"Oh yeah, it's a hoot." Victoria chuckled and flipped a page. "Good, though. I think you'd like it. It's angsty, like you."

Leah swatted her. "Isn't being mean my job here?"

"You're not doing a very good job then, are you? One of us has to pick up the slack."

Victoria playfully stuck out her tongue and Leah's world condensed into a single moment. The blue of the sky, the heat of the car, the scent of grass, the sound of faraway cars, and the hammer of her heart. Rubbing her sweaty palms against her jeans, Leah pulled herself back from the brink. Victoria was on loan, she reminded herself. Only here because of extenuating circumstances rendering it inconvenient for her to go home. Not out of want, but necessity.

"Leah?" Victoria's gentle voice drew Leah back from the edge of her self-loathing spiral. "If I ask you why you're doing all of this for me…is that a stupid question?"

Leah's immediate answer was she couldn't help herself. Victoria disarmed her in the most literal way possible, leaving her without a defense against her unintended charms. Unable to divulge any inch of that truth, Leah stalled to come up with something less desperately gay. "No, it isn't stupid. Do you think I have ulterior motives?"

"I don't know," Victoria replied, her tone fragile. "I hope not."

Instinctively Leah drew toward her anger the way a warrior reaches for their weapon. But the wet hurt in Victoria's voice smothered it instantly. Victoria's question came from a place of ignorance: she plainly didn't know Leah well enough to understand her motives. "Because you've always been nice to me, even though I'm never nice to you. Whatever happened at prom, you didn't deserve it."

Resting her book on her chest, Victoria placed her sunglasses on the top of her head and stared up into the sky. She went silent for so long Leah thought she might've fallen asleep with her eyes open. "I didn't want to go to prom. I know I was on the committee and I planned it, but I couldn't get excited. There's so much pressure on one night to be memorable or fun, and all I could think about was how bored I'd be."

Leah didn't hold back her shock. "Really? I figured you lived for that kind of crap."

Victoria glared at her. "No offense taken? I wanted everyone to have a good time, but I knew I'd spend the whole night crammed between Gabby talking nonstop and Carter showing off. He's done nothing but brag about being prom king for, like, two months."

"Barf."

"Anyway, prom was nice. Nice enough. But, um, halfway through, Carter made me slow dance with him and he talked over the music, as always. He told me how excited he was about the party. About how excited he was we'd finally be alone so we can..." Victoria gulped. "So we could have sex."

"I take back my first barf. I'd like to barf now, thank you."

"God, he just went on and on and finally I stopped dancing and told him I didn't want to have sex with him. And he...lost his mind. He got so angry. I'd never seen him get like that before."

Leah's stomach turned sour. "Dick."

"Then he—I told him I was sorry, and the music stopped and he just...he accused me of having sex with Steve Barsiak and Dylan Lopez and Denny Douglas. How I'm this huge slut and too loose for him anyway. He said the only reason anyone likes me is because my parents are loaded. And—and people *laughed* at me, Leah. Even my friends... they stood there and let it happen. A teacher tried to intervene, but I stormed out."

The sheer amount of rage coursing through Leah took her by surprise. Normally it required a lot of effort to get her this angry. Her temper could flare, but digging deep for real rage was harder. But not today. Not with that story. "Fuck, I'm sorry. You never should've had to go through that. The things we let boys get away with is disgusting."

Victoria sat up, wrapping her arms around her knees, both pulled into her chest. "I don't know who put those rumors in his head, either."

"You know who: Steve Barsiak, Dylan Lopez, and Denny Douglas. Instead of just saving us all the trouble and taking out the measuring tape, they have to compare masculinities by pretending they have any game at all."

"I didn't have sex with them," Victoria said adamantly. "With Carter, or any of my boyfriends, I never did anything more than kiss."

"And? Look, I believe you. Even if you had sex with half the class, it doesn't mean you wanted to have sex with Carter Harcourt or that it was anyone's business but yours. For what it's worth, you can do much better than a sad sack like Carter or his posse of douchebags."

Victoria laughed softly, wiping her eyes with the back of her hand. "Sorry, I didn't mean to unload on you. I guess I don't want you to think I'm overly suspicious of you. I'm shaken on who I can trust."

"And until yesterday, I was a classmate who barely tolerated your existence." Victoria didn't have to agree, Leah knew the truth of it. She knew her classmates perceived her as mean and antisocial. But she only doled out barbs to those who tried to hurt her. "So, I'm guessing you guys broke up."

"Yeah, we're done." Sniffling, Victoria glumly added, "I think he only dated me for bragging rights anyway. Not that I'm much better… I've never told anyone this, but the only reason we dated is because he kept other guys away from me. It kept my parents off my back too."

Leah raised both eyebrows, impressed. "Okay, you're kind of a diabolical genius."

Again, Victoria laughed, and Leah couldn't stop the pride puffing out her chest. "Well, thanks. I'm sure you're the only one who doesn't think I'm an idiot for dumping the hottest boy in school."

"You were always too good for him. Too smart, too kind, too talented for that asshole."

A small, half-smile dimpled on Victoria's face as she narrowed her eyes at Leah. "Who knew you thought so highly of me?"

"I'm just being honest." *Not entirely honest, but close enough.* "Victoria, you can trust me if you want to. Star-crossed lovers might be off the table, we could make decent friends."

Victoria nudged Leah with her knee. "You know, you're the only person who uses my full name, besides my parents, or my brothers when they're being jerks."

"What should I call you? 'Vicky'? I'd sound like Gabby Friedman. 'Vicky, oh my God, did you see what she's wearing today?'" Leah flipped her hair dramatically and scoffed in her Valley Girl impression.

"Fine, what do you want to call me? Lockwood? That's what my swim coach calls me. You'll give me kick drill flashbacks."

Leah paused. "What about Tori? Does anyone call you that?"

"Nope. Tori, huh? I like it. Well, I like the way you say it." The slightly affectionate look in her eyes caused Leah to blush and turn her attention away. "Can I call you Leonora?"

"Sure. If you want me to throw you off the cliff."

"If you had the upper body strength I might believe you, Leonora."

Swiftly Leah slid her arms beneath Victoria, one under her back and the other under her knees and lifted her up off the car's hood. Though it took a bit of effort, she trudged them over to the edge of the cliff near the safety rails. "What now?"

"Okay, okay, no Leonora. Only Leah. I got it." Leah gently put Victoria on the ground. She straightened her clothes and Leah felt her scrutinizing gaze give her a once-over. "It's a beautiful name, though. Leonora Renata Vasquez. It's rhythmic, like a song."

"Well, I hate it," Leah replied curtly, taking a step back. "I should get back to Benny's. Dinner rush soon."

"Whoa, hey." Victoria touched her forearm and halted her step. "I'm sorry, I won't call you that."

"It's fine, I don't like it 'cause…well, that's a story for another time. I really do have to get back before my beeper starts going nuts."

"Sure thing." Victoria threw her arms out wide. "Carry me to the carriage, big strong hero!"

"*Dios mío*, you're walking, Tori."

The mad dash of Saturday night had Leah doing sprints from her car to homes around the county for a few hours straight. Tips and payments piled up in the center console, sorted by her companion who handed her food or read quietly. Victoria kept the mix CDs going without more than a few beats of silence, allowing Leah to concentrate on making quick, accurate deliveries. They worked in perfect tandem, like a piano and drum duet. Percussive and melodic—the same, but different. Leah kept her enjoyment close to her chest—no need to advertise to Victoria that her secretly wicked sense of humor made

Leah smile more than she had in her whole life. The smiling alone was embarrassing enough.

Orders dwindled as Benny's neared close, and Leah drove up a dead-end road to her last delivery. Uneventful, thankfully, and Leah returned to the car, and Victoria, to organize her delivery receipts. As she fiddled with the papers, Victoria cleared her throat.

"You're square."

Leah balked. "What? I am not. If anything, you're the square."

"The receipts, you dork," Victoria said, gesturing to the pile between them. "I've been keeping track for you. The left pile is the delivery money and it matches your receipt total. The right pile is your tips."

In her center console two piles of money sat side by side, neatly stacked and in ascending order of value. "Well, shit. Should bring you more often."

"Oh, yeah. My ability to do simple addition is a real windfall for someone going to MIT."

"You have other uses," Leah replied. "Adequate playlist shuffling. Superb delivery organizational skills. Excellent passenger etiquette. I give you five stars."

"I'm honored." Victoria smirked, but as they drove away from the last house, her expression turned serious. "I'm glad to come along, you know."

Glancing sidelong at Victoria, Leah smiled softly. "I know."

Their sleepy suburb slept quietly as Leah drove through it toward Benny's. Surrounding roads and towns bustled with streams of cars, people heading to the city, but their own town had naught but the occasional shift worker. Nighttime in Garden Hills was one of the few parts of her hometown she enjoyed. Quiet roads, loud stars, and room to breathe in between.

"What will you major in at MIT?" Victoria asked when they paused at a stoplight just outside the town limits.

Leah snagged her bottle of water and took a sip. "Civil Engineering."

"Wow. That's...not what I expected."

"You've thought about my major before? Exactly how much of your free time do you spend thinking about me, Tori?"

Visibly flustered, Victoria managed a feeble glare at her. "It's a philanthropic job for someone who actively avoids other people."

"I can make better roads and infrastructure to get people away from me faster." The look on Victoria's face indicated her answer would not satisfy. "I'm good at math, physics, and building. Sophomore year,

Fatima and I were the only students to build a popsicle stick bridge sturdy enough to hold any weight. It held fifty-five pounds."

Victoria rolled her eyes. "Uh-huh. You yelled 'fuck' when it fell, and Mr. Barnes docked six points from your grade."

"Ugh, he's such a dork." And by some magic, Victoria's captivating eyes prompted her to elaborate a step further. A step she'd never admitted out loud. "I want to be successful enough to never have to come back to Garden Hills. I feel like if I don't get a degree in something practical, something high-earning, I'll end up in this stupid town forever."

"Aw, come on. You won't miss our little hometown?"

"It would take you ten Hubble telescopes to find an iota of my affection for this place. I'll miss my parents, but if they don't wanna leave, that's on them. The minute I graduate college, I'm not coming back."

Victoria turned down the volume and pivoted as much as she could with her seat belt on. "I'll have to come back. Lockwood Industries is based just outside Garden Hills."

"So? Can't you do something else?"

Victoria's eyes lost a bit of their shine. "If I refuse to work for them, they won't pay for me to go to college."

Stubbornly, Leah refused to allow Victoria to place her future squarely in the hands of her parents. "Tori, you're really smart. You could get a scholarship."

"Based on what? Maybe my academics, but my parents make too much for me to qualify for most of them, and the money should go to kids who need it."

Kids like herself, Leah thought. Poor kids with more smarts than generational wealth. However, Leah didn't see much honor in sacrificing your future for people you didn't know. "What's your major?"

"Computer Science," Victoria said, and it sounded like a curse word. Leah raised an eyebrow. "I didn't get a whole lot of say in it."

Leah turned into the lot, parked the car just outside the doors, and cut the engine with a flick of her wrist. "Do you even want to go to Harvard?"

"No. I want to go to Northwestern. I got in, too." Victoria smiled sadly. "But Liberal Arts degrees don't have much practical application, so, Harvard it is. And, look, it's fine. I can't complain about the privilege I have."

"Yeah, you can." She never expected to sympathize with someone whose allowance could probably lease a new car, but here she was. "Everyone deserves a chance to do what they love, Tori. Even spoiled brats like you."

"Gee, thanks." Genuine gratitude marbled through the sarcastic slab of her reply. "I snuck in an additional field of study in English and a minor in Creative Writing. Not all is lost. I just…wish I had more control over my own life."

"Why don't you ask for it?" Victoria tilted her head in apparent confusion. "Do they know you want to write? Do they know you don't want to work with your dad?"

"I wish it was that easy. Nobody listens to me, or cares what I think."

Leah paused. "So, you're going to live the life they want you to live? Forever?"

"Not everyone can be like you and say and do what they want all the time," Victoria replied. They'd drifted into murky waters, but Leah's principles wouldn't let her back down.

"Yeah, everyone can, but they don't because they're scared." Hands in the air as a white flag, Leah backed off. "I'm not telling you what to do—I'll let your hot mom keep that job—but I hope you realize at some point what you want is worth fighting for."

With Victoria behind her, probably still miffed, Leah shouldered open the door to Benny's. Inside, patrons sat in the booths, finishing up their meals to the tune of a loud Aerosmith song crackling out of the ancient jukebox. Leah's manager, Jake, stood at the register, counting out the till. He looked up, first with his greet-the-customer face, then his normal one when he recognized her. "LV, what's good?"

"Hey, Jakey." Leah slapped the money and receipts on the counter, sliding them toward him. "Solid night. How was dining?"

He nodded toward the dining room. "Not bad. Steady." Moving his gaze from the dining area to Leah, he did a double take at Victoria by her side. "Who's your friend?"

"Tori," Victoria replied, and Leah felt a warmth blossom out from her heart, making her ears burn. It went unnoticed as Jake and Victoria sized each other up.

Jake stretched his hand over the counter, grinning like he always did at pretty customers. He was handsome by any regular standard, Leah figured. Like the second- or third-most popular member of a boy band. "Nice to meet you, Tori. Leah doesn't usually bring her dates here."

Every cell in Leah's body ceased to move. Before she could open her mouth, Victoria angled in. "Usually? Do you mean to tell me she sometimes brings dates to her job?"

"What? I've never. How could you even—?" Her words left her in a desperate rush as she glared at Jake. She turned to Victoria. "I've never."

"I guess it makes sense," Victoria continued, clearly eager to embarrass Leah further. "You wear that cute hat, you get free food. I can see the appeal."

Dramatically flopping both arms on the counter, Leah glanced up at her boss for mercy. She found nothing but his laughing face and the sting of betrayal. "Oh, Tori, you made her blush. I don't think I've ever seen Vasquez turn that red before."

"Can I take my money and go now, please?" Leah ripped off her hat and narrowed her eyes at Victoria, who, like Jake, appeared alight with glee.

"Yeah, yeah." He slid her pile of tips toward her. "I'll square up the receipts later, but I'm sure you're good."

"Never been a penny off in two years. Good bet." She shoved the money into her pocket. "See you, Jake."

"See ya, LV. Oh, wait. Dad asked me to make sure you guys were good for the next gig."

"Yeah, we're good. We'll be ready." Benny really wanted to know how many sweaty minors would pack into his family restaurant and to remember his cut of the meager ticket sales. "Set's not much different from last time."

"Set?" Victoria looked between them expectantly.

"Her band." Jake leaned on the counter like a gossiping mother in a tenement window. "You didn't tell your girlfriend you had a gig coming up?"

Contemplating the easiest way to shove Jake into a pizza oven, Leah grumbled, "Hardly a gig. Just playing Benny's with my band."

Victoria gawked. "And you weren't going to invite me? Some girlfriend you are."

"*Dios mío, ayúdame,*" Leah said, making the sign of the cross. "I'm leaving. You're leaving. We're leaving."

"Treat Tori here to somethin' nice with that fat stack of tip money, cheapskate."

Leah flipped him off as they left and piled back into her car. Evidently pleased with herself and the act she put on, Victoria giggled in the passenger's seat as she buckled in.

"Oh, yeah, that's real funny. Keep laughing, see what happens."

"What's gonna happen, Vasquez? You'll blush to death?" Cackling, Victoria slid another CD out of the case pocket and switched out the one in Leah's radio. "I can't believe I have to go to school on Monday knowing Leah Fucking Vasquez is a softie who blushes when her boss teases her and I can't tell anyone."

The heartbeat of the road, a yellow pulse of light illuminating the interior of the car, kept rhythm as Leah drove the short distance home. Out of her peripheral she caught Victoria staring at her a few times with a curious expression on her face. Leah parked in the driveway and threw off her seat belt. "What?"

In the darkness of the car, Victoria's hand grabbed her arm and stilled her before she could open the door. "I like it, you know."

"Being a jerk, or ganging up on me with my boss at my place of employment?"

"That you're soft. That you're kind. That there's this real, human, embarassable, endearing person beneath the dark makeup and sarcasm. Don't get me wrong, I like the makeup and the sarcasm too. But…" Neither girl moved, suspended in the moment like slowly falling snow. A moment so delicate a whisper could break it. "You're so much more."

Now the blush on her face would be worthy of ridicule, but the heat in her cheeks didn't compare to the heat in her belly, stirred to life by Victoria's words and touch. The absolute last thing she needed was to fall for the least attainable girl in her school. Pulling away from her, Leah smiled and attempted a casual, "Thanks."

Victoria's light brown eyes dropped to the place where they'd been touching, then back up to Leah. "Welcome."

An emotion crept into the cabin of the car, indiscernible and stifling, worsened by Victoria staring down at her lips, then up into her eyes. Leah swiftly exited the car and took deep breaths of the night air. No way Victoria Lockwood wanted to kiss her. More importantly, she was not going to kiss Victoria Lockwood. Leah resolved to undo these impulses before she did something stupid, like act on them.

CHAPTER FOUR

Armed with her own hair care items and pajamas to change into, Victoria felt less intrusive in Leah's bathroom than the previous night. She took her time, fingering the makeup strewn across the sink's off-white porcelain: a tinted ChapStick, mascara, black liquid eyeliner, and an eyeshadow palette only in shades of black and gray. These were the tools Leah used to construct the mask she wore at school—dark and disinterested, calculatedly aloof. Victoria had peeked beneath this mask to the beautiful, expressive face she hid. A face full of mirth and cunning wit, of softness and empathy. A face that hardened into lines when angry, waves across her forehead like rumpled bedsheets. Victoria couldn't decide if she wanted to smooth them out or crawl inside.

After twenty-four hours with Leah Vasquez, Victoria became dissatisfied with the way things were. They could make good friends if given the chance. But something more brewed between them, something enormous and obscure. Something Victoria wanted to taste. Reaching for the doorknob, Victoria paused as she heard Leah talking on the other side. When she didn't hear a response, she realized Leah must be on the phone. She didn't have a cell phone, only an ancient beeper, so she must've been on her personal landline.

"Cool, yeah. Well, listen, I gotta go." Victoria pressed her ear to the door, feeling stupidly gossipy but unable to help herself. "Yeah, I've got someone over and I don't wanna be rude." She paused again as the person on the other line must've spoken. "Nah, it's not like that. She's just a friend…Yeah, I don't know, but it's nothing to worry about." An ugliness snuck into Victoria's heart. The distaste curled her lip. "All right. See ya."

Victoria waited a respectable couple of seconds before coming out of the bathroom to sit casually on the edge of the bed and run a comb through her damp hair. "Is that your own phone line?"

"Yep. I pay my folks each month so I can have the line for my phone and the web."

"Must come in handy when your girlfriends call," Victoria replied, allowing the little green person inside her heart to speak for her.

Visibly surprised, Leah stopped short. "Uh, I guess? I use it more for surfing the web without getting kicked off if my dad needs to talk to clients on our home line."

"Oh, right." Feeling foolish, Victoria climbed into Leah's bed and left an exaggerated amount of space between them. Leah flicked off the light and padded to the bed. Intentionally or not, she kept clear of Victoria as she slid under the covers.

They were, after all, just friends. Barely friends.

Sleep wouldn't come despite the metronome of Leah's breathing. The churning sensation in her stomach migrated into a nagging in her brain. Leah considered them friends, which delighted Victoria in a small way, but it didn't satisfy. The enormous, obscure thing between them rapidly came into focus. She liked Leah. She *like-liked* Leah. What a very stupid thing to do.

"I had a good time today," Leah said suddenly, facing away from her. "I hope you did too." How could she respond to that? Honesty was out of the question, because then she'd have to admit this was the best weekend she'd spent in a long time. Leah's hand cupped her hip and gave it a gentle squeeze. Like an echo, her heart ached in response. "G'night, Tori."

"Good night, Leah."

In the most bizarre groundhog day imaginable, Victoria again woke up in the arms of Leah Vasquez. Though they'd fallen asleep at either side of the bed, in the night Victoria had snuggled into Leah's back and she awoke with her arm around Leah's torso and her nose buried in the soft, delicate curls of her hair.

No graceful exit possible, Victoria slid her hand away and the movement roused Leah from sleep. Turning over beneath their shared blanket, she blinked groggily into the sun. Light poured in from the window behind Victoria, making every fiber and speck of dust come alive in the air like interstellar clouds. It brightened Leah's face, and though she winced at it, the kaleidoscopic beauty of Leah's eyes struck her in the heart. An ever-changing refraction of green, brown, and blue. They sparkled in the sun, as if created for the light like precious gems.

"Another day," Leah grumbled in a sleep-laden voice.

Victoria struggled to find words, so she used Leah's. "Another day."

"Time to face the music, huh?" Leah rubbed her face roughly with her hand. "Unless you want to go to church with us."

Attending church with the Vasquez family sounded much better than going home. Though not strictly religious, she'd take any number of sermons over the haranguing awaiting her. "No, that's okay. You've put up with me long enough."

Leah snorted. "That vice comes with a whole lot of versa. But I could put up with you as long as you'd like." She lifted her arm to tuck a rogue strand of Victoria's hair behind her ear. "You're not so bad, Lockwood."

Before Leah could pull away, Victoria snagged her hand in her own and cradled it. "You know, when I realized it was you who pulled over, I was so mad. I thought, 'God, anyone else in the entire class, because Leah Vasquez is going to eat me alive.'"

"You wish."

"I am trying to give you a compliment," she replied, rolling her eyes.

"Then get to the compliment already, geez."

Victoria arched an eyebrow. "Aren't lesbians supposed to be into foreplay?"

The sleepiness in Leah's expression vanished and she turned over, cackling toward the ceiling. "Oh my God. Wow, okay, I'm so sorry, take all the time you need."

"I was just going to say, I was wrong. I'm so glad it was you and not anyone else."

Leah narrowed her eyes, searching Victoria's face. She didn't know what Leah hoped to find, and all she could offer was a small, earnest smile. Leah ran her tongue along her lips and for a second, a single moment, Victoria anticipated a kiss. Just as Leah's eyes dropped to Victoria's mouth, Hector's voice boomed from downstairs, startling them apart.

"*¡Mija!* Is your friend coming to church?"

"No, *Papi*, I have to take her home," Leah called back. Moment gone, Victoria rolled out of bed and planted her feet on the shag rug beneath Leah's bed, nabbing her clothes and gunning for the bathroom.

"*Bueno*, hurry back. We want to make the ten o'clock Mass. Your mother says the one at eleven has too many people."

"Okay!"

Victoria promised her mother she'd be home by noon on Sunday, with her brother due back from college in the afternoon. The return of the prodigal son meant a big dinner and mandatory attendance at said dinner. And, of course, she would have to explain why she left prom and destroyed her dress. Re-dressed and dejected, Victoria waited on the edge of Leah's bed for her to finish getting ready. She would miss this room. Their sanctuary against the world.

Lost in thought, she didn't see Leah exit the bathroom until she stood right in front of her. Then, her throat ran dry. From the ground up, Leah had transformed into a different person. Shiny black dress shoes, pressed navy-blue slacks, a tucked-in, crisp baby pink button-down shirt, and a blueish tie with slim pink stripes. She'd rolled up the sleeves to mid-forearm and stuck her hands in her pockets. "Ready?"

The speed at which Victoria sailed from "Leah is the prettiest of my friends" to "I am attracted to Leah Vasquez" could've created a maelstrom in its wake. But here she sat, staring up at Leah's dashing, androgynous figure, drowning in her sudden desire.

"Uh, yeah." Standing up with an awkwardly rigid posture, Victoria attempted to return to Earth. "Wow, you look…spiffy."

"Thanks. Don't like it, but don't have a choice."

"Why?"

Without answering, Leah scooped Victoria's duffel bag and led them downstairs. Her parents sat at the kitchen table, each engrossed in a newspaper, but they looked up from their contented domesticity to say goodbye.

"It was nice to meet you both," Victoria said. "Thank you for everything."

"Not a problem, Victoria." Leah's mother smiled, her demeanor gentler in the warm morning sun. "You're welcome here anytime."

Hector nodded. "*Sí, sí.* Come back for Vasquez Karaoke Night."

"Karaoke Night?"

Groaning, Leah stepped between them. "I bought my dad a karaoke machine for Christmas last year, and every day of my life I regret it."

"She loves it," Hector said conspiratorially. Leah did not appear to agree, the tips of her cheeks growing red. "She loves to sing with her *papi*."

Victoria grinned at Leah's discomfort. "If you sing half as well as she does, I think I'd be too embarrassed to join you."

"Okay, great, I'll give Tori the 4-1-1 on karaoke in the car. Bye." Leah rushed her out, but called behind her, "Love you, see you at church."

More humid than days prior, the morning heat stuck to Victoria's skin on the short walk to the end of the driveway. What she wouldn't give for another day in Leah's car, heat coming in from a cracked window as cool AC blew across her face. Leah tossed her duffel bag in the back seat, closing the door and leaning her palm against it. "To answer your question from before, our church has a pretty strict dress code for whatever reason. Women usually wear dresses, but who would want me in a dress when I make a tie look this good?"

Victoria laughed, if only to hide how thoroughly she agreed. "Okay, Vasquez."

Choosing a CD for perhaps the last time, Victoria buckled in and waited for the telltale roar of Leah's engine turning over. When it didn't come, she noticed Leah's pensive expression. Her curiosity at Leah's sudden melancholy must've been written across her face. "How did you know I can sing?"

"Oh. From seventh grade choir when you did that Christmas solo. You were incredible. I...remember it really clearly."

Finally turning the car on, Leah loaded the CD Victoria held in her hand. "Ah, right. You haven't heard me sing any other time, right?"

"No, why?"

"No reason. Just curious."

It struck Victoria as an extremely flimsy fib. But she let it rest, keen on enjoying what may be the last couple minutes of real friendship. Flipping through the CD binder, Victoria caressed the discs wistfully, as if tracing the letters of a long-lost lover. With nothing to commemorate this weekend other than a secret attraction and a Benny's T-shirt, Victoria eyed the glistening CDs like war booty. "Could I borrow one of your mixes?"

They pulled away from the Vasquezes' home, carefully avoiding potholes back toward the center of town. "Yeah, sure. Knock yourself out."

In just a short weekend they'd gone from "don't touch my music" to "take it home with you" and Victoria couldn't pinpoint when. Her burgeoning attraction to Leah explained her end, but what Leah got out of it, she didn't know. It fell within the realm of possibility that Leah was attracted to her, too, but Victoria doubted anything she could offer would suffice for someone as complex as Leah. A rowboat in deep waters, she hoped not to drown.

Parked at the end of Victoria's block, Leah turned down the volume and cleared her throat. Levity escaped out the open windows, trapping Leah and Victoria in the car with the reality of their situation. Tomorrow, Victoria would have to deal with the fallout of breaking up with Carter, pretend like Leah Vasquez wasn't the only person she wanted to talk to, and ignore the sudden, inescapable attraction to her class's resident curmudgeon.

"So, I guess I'll see you tomorrow." Leah didn't look over as she spoke, only reached behind her and grabbed the duffel bag to heft it into Victoria's lap. "And, to be clear, I'm not going to tell anyone about this weekend. I won't…I won't approach you at school like we're friends or something."

"I don't want it to be like that," Victoria whispered.

"But it has to be." Leah's voice, normally low and controlled, tightened. "It's what you asked for, isn't it?"

The duffel bag's strap gripped in both hands, Victoria fought the headache creeping up her temples. She stared out the windshield, down the road toward her house, then looked to Leah, her arms taut as she clenched the steering wheel. "Do you want it to be like that?"

"You made it crystal clear you don't want me to make things more difficult for you, and I respect it. What I want doesn't factor in." She grunted in frustration. "Why are you asking me? What do you want, Tori?"

"I don't know," she replied. "I don't want you to be mad at me."

"I'm not mad. Or…I'm not mad at you. Maybe mad at myself for…" She trailed off, apparently collecting her thoughts. "For letting my guard down."

Victoria found herself unprepared for how much that crushed her. All this time believing she had to learn to trust Leah, never considering Leah may not trust her. "I hurt your feelings, didn't I?"

Leah pulled her sunglasses down over her eyes. "Don't worry about my feelings." She nodded toward the door. "Go on. I can't be late for Mass."

The furrow of hurt between Leah's brows gutted her. So, she did the only thing she could think of to relieve it and took Leah's chin between her fingers, bringing them face-to-face. Without taking a moment to second-guess her decision-making skills, she leaned over the console and kissed her. Kissing Leah wasn't like letting Carter jam his tongue down her throat, or the sloppy, stubbly kisses of her other boyfriends. Not only because of Leah's soft lips and smooth jaw, but also because Victoria's entire body rushed with a want so great it nearly burst from her skin. A short and sweet kiss, lips barely moving, just long enough to leave a thin sheen of gloss on Leah's lips. But Victoria's entire world capsized.

Leah's eyes widened through her sunglasses and the furrow on her forehead didn't go away. "Get out of my car."

"I—I'm sorry, I—"

"Go home, Victoria." The tendons in Leah's neck strained. "Please."

Her brusque tone left no room for argument, and Victoria didn't have one. She hurried out of the car, not chancing to glance behind her. Adrenaline fueled her speed, if only to outpace the dread and fear on her heels. Once when she reached the threshold of her house, she looked back to see Leah's car still parked near the curb. It slowly made a three-point turn before creeping in the opposite direction.

A hot lump formed in her throat, increasing the heat behind her eyes. No, no, she couldn't cry here. Not with possibility of her parents home, ready to grill her. Collecting herself as best she could, Victoria slung her duffel bag over her shoulder and pushed open the wide wooden door.

Thankfully, the foyer was empty and quiet, save for Carmen's melodic whistling. Mother forbade whistling in the house, so Victoria drew the conclusion she wasn't home. Hastily retreating to her room, Victoria slammed the door, pressing her back against it. She slid to the floor with her face in her hands, finally allowing the tears to fall. Stupid, she thought. Clearly, Leah wouldn't want anything to do with her now. Kissing her without consent and not considering her feelings? She ruined it. She ruined the only good thing to come out of this dreadful weekend. Classic Victoria.

Once unpacked and undressed, Victoria sank into a hot, fragrant bath in her en suite. Carmen stocked the best bath soaps, and Victoria had greedily dumped several of them into the water and turned on the jets. She rested her head on the bath pillow. Perhaps a good soak and she'd drown these feelings for good. However, instead of letting them drown, her senses threw her feelings a life preserver. Her tongue remembered the taste of weed and beer, and her lips felt the brush of Leah's own. The scent of petrichor and bonfire lingered in her nose. And when she opened her eyes, Leah appeared in full, dazzling Technicolor, the phantom sensation of arms wrapped around her slid into the bathtub. Her ears recalled the comforting whispers spoken softly over downy blankets.

Because I would never hurt you.

Victoria had vowed no such reciprocal promise. Submerging herself in the steaming water, she held her breath and squeezed her eyes shut. Vic would be home soon, and with him, some semblance of normalcy in their home. Normalcy in the sense that his presence sucked all the attention away, allowing Victoria to live her life less scrutinized by their mother.

"Victoria." *Speak of the devil.* Victoria popped her head up from the water, gasping. Her mother's voice was easily recognizable, even under water. Cassandra Lockwood didn't have a lot of talents, at least none Victoria knew of, but she did know how to freeze a room with a single word. Like the spirit of every terrible headmistress spoke through her. "Where are you?"

"In the bath," Victoria called to the other side of the door. Within moments, her mother barged in and gave her a tired, disapproving stare.

"Hello, Mother."

"Why aren't you dressed?"

Victoria peered down at the water. "Because it would get my clothes wet?"

Her mother remained unamused. Tough crowd. "Your brother will be home soon, and I want you downstairs, ready, when he arrives."

"What is he, Captain von Trapp?" Her mother's double eyebrow raise prompted her to raise her hands out of the water. "I'm kidding. I'll be downstairs for the return of the prodigal son, I promise."

"Very well." Cassandra turned toward the door, then pivoted back. "How was prom?"

Could it be that she didn't know? Had the universe seen fit to throw Victoria this single bone? "Fine."

"Good. Were you voted prom queen?"

"No." Victoria hoped her tone came off as remorseful. In reality, she probably had won prom queen, but in her absence someone else would receive the crown. With any luck, it would be Gabby. Otherwise, Victoria would have to hear about it on Monday.

"Hmm. You know, your brother was prom king." Her mother sighed wistfully. "He looked so handsome in the crown. I hoped to add your prom queen photo to the wall, but I suppose I dared to dream."

Victoria wanted to fling herself down the drain, and with any luck, get swept directly out to sea. "Sorry to disappoint."

"Mm-hmm." Victoria dipped a little lower in the bath. Would her mother even notice if she slipped below the water and never returned? Maybe when she had to call a plumber. "Who was that who dropped you off?"

Victoria tried not to sputter. "Who? Oh, that was…nobody. Just someone from school."

"Wasn't Carter supposed to drive you home from the lake?"

"I left early."

"Very well." Her mother sighed, having spent the last bit of her interest in Victoria's life. "Don't be late, dear. And put some cucumbers on your eyes. You look like a drug addict." Dropping her parting advice like a grenade in a trench, Cassandra pivoted sharply and left the bathroom.

It didn't take Victoria long to get ready—clothes, makeup, hair—it was mechanical, like breathing. Every day she put on the uniform of a regular high school girl, a teenager on the brink of womanhood, and every day she felt like a fraud. Leah's perception of her popularity wasn't entirely wrong, but despite her over-involvement in school, she never felt like she fit. It took her such an incredible amount of effort to be Vicky Lockwood. Spending time with Leah, being "Tori," she felt both different and the most herself she'd ever been. Her looks hadn't changed. Still the same eyes as her grandmother, her mother's hair, the matrilineal constellation of freckles, and her body—thin but muscular from swimming. However, she felt changed. Evolved, like a creature shedding its shell and growing a new one.

Victoria logged into her password-locked journal on her desktop computer. Nobody else used her PC, but she knew leaving a digital trail of her thoughts invited her mother to snoop. So, she hid the journal like porn, buried in a nesting doll of random program files. Fingers flying over the keys, Victoria furiously filled up digital page after page with her thoughts and feelings about prom, about Carter, but overwhelmingly about Leah. How she looked, talked, smelled, moved. The softness of her lips. Her intelligence, her unexpected kindness and tenderness. By the time her fingers cramped from typing, she'd filled nearly ten pages with a rambling ode to Leah Vasquez.

A swift knock on her door had her scrambling to save the file and close out the program. She swiveled in her desk chair to see Carmen peeking her head in. "Miss Victoria, Miss Riley is here."

Riley appeared behind Carmen, waving to her.

"Hey, Riley. Come in, come in. Thanks, Carmen."

Her friend stepped into the room and the door closed behind her. They'd been in each other's lives since Pre-K, and Riley was about as natural in her room as her bed, her desk. But she stood awkwardly with Victoria's purse and cell phone in one hand, her weekend bag in the other. "I took your stuff with me to the lake. I didn't want it to get lost."

Victoria collected the items from Riley, spilling them onto her desk. A purse that perfectly matched her dress, home to a tiny portable camera with which she took no photos, and makeup she never applied. Her weekend bag she'd filled with clothes and a bathing suit and books to read. Both items felt like relics belonging to a person she no longer was. "Oh, wow. Thank you. I didn't even think about it."

"No, I'm sure you didn't." Sitting on the edge of Victoria's bed, Riley smiled wanly at Victoria. They looked enough alike to be mistaken for sisters, and for the first time, Victoria wished it were true. Only a bond that close would allow for her to spill the thoughts in her head. Instead, she flipped open her cell phone and stared at the screen blinking urgently with missed calls and texts from various friends.

"I thought everyone was coming back later tonight?" Victoria asked.

Riley shrugged. "I left. It was weird without you. People partied really hard and I didn't have anyone to talk to. I left this morning while everyone was still asleep. I thought I'd come check on you. Prom was…well, you know what it was. I'm sorry about what happened with Carter."

Victoria pulled up her legs to sit cross-legged on her chair and attempted indifference. "It's whatever, I guess."

"It's not whatever. He shouldn't have said those things. Especially not in front of everyone. He's an asshole." Riley's unexpected use of salty language made Victoria laugh in surprise. "What? He is. He always has been. I never understood why you were with him to begin with."

Channeling Leah, Victoria replied, "Damn, Riley. Tell me how you really feel."

"Honestly, I'm kind of relieved to tell you the truth. I wish the circumstances were better, but at least you're rid of him." She eyed the duffel bag Victoria had stashed in the corner of her room. "How did you get home? Billy drove Jenna and I around to find you, but the teachers told us we could only leave for twenty minutes."

"Actually"—Victoria scoffed—"if you can believe it, Leah Vasquez found me walking on the side of the road and picked me up."

The shocked look on Riley's face relaxed and gave way to regular confusion. "Wow, really? I guess it's not that surprising. I've always gotten the impression Leah's a lot less, um, grouchy than she wants people to believe."

"She's definitely a little grouchy. But she let me in her car even though I was soaking wet, and she..." Made me feel like a human for two days, is what Victoria couldn't say. She couldn't say that Leah made her feel more in those two days than she'd ever felt in her life. That Leah took hold of her cookie-cutter world, turned it upside down, and now Victoria was infatuated with her. "Brought me home."

A lie by omission, but her Leah sphere and her friend sphere couldn't overlap, not while she still needed to graduate.

"That was nice of her. Did she say anything? Did you tell her what happened?"

"No, not really. We listened to music while she finished her pizza deliveries."

"She didn't ask why you were soaking wet in your prom dress?" Victoria shook her head. "Gosh. Either she really doesn't care or she's way nicer than people think and tried not to hurt your feelings."

"I think it's the latter," Victoria replied. "You're probably right, she's not as mean as she wants people to think. But I guess I'd have a defense mechanism too if I had to deal with all the crap she's dealt with at school."

Riley nodded in agreement and glanced away. "People can be really cruel."

Commotion downstairs reached Victoria and Riley in the bedroom, and Victoria sighed heavily. "My brother is back from college."

"Oh, cool. Maybe your mom will lay off you." Riley suddenly looked panicked. "Does she know about prom?"

"Not yet. I imagine once Carter gets home and tells his mom I dumped him, she's going to call here."

Riley rolled her eyes. "She'll be so upset her son isn't going to be the next Lockwood heir. Ugh, his family is gross. Like, I realize all our families are pretty gross, but the Harcourts are so tacky."

"They are. The inside of their house looks like how a six-year-old imagines rich people live. All this gaudy gold crap, marble floors, and these horrendous, thick curtains on all the windows." Victoria scrunched her face in disgust. Her mother called for her and she shared a look of resignation with Riley. "The bell tolls."

Riley stood up from the bed and pulled Victoria into a hug. "I'm sorry you didn't get to enjoy prom. I'm sorry Carter ruined it. And I'm sorry your mom is about to go turbo because Vic is home."

Victoria laughed into the hug, returning it with a squeeze. "Thanks, Ry. I'll walk you out so I can prepare myself for the arrival."

"Have to practice your genuflect for the prince," Riley replied with a grin.

They descended the stairs together, Victoria retracing the steps she'd taken sneaking out with Leah the day prior. How illicit it had felt to have Leah there, as if she'd been sneaking out a paramour. With no Vic yet in sight, Victoria trudged to their den to await his arrival. Ward had already stationed himself on the carpet, eyes glued to the television. Her father sat on the couch with his newspaper, barely registering her presence while Mother's voice boomed from the other room, directing Carmen to do some menial tasks in preparation for Vic's return. Victoria sat on the floor next to Ward, who appeared enthralled in a NASA documentary.

"Have you seen this one before?" Victoria asked.

Ward nodded without a glance in her direction. "Yeah. I taped this one a couple weeks ago. But nothing else good is on and Mom yelled at me for staying in my room."

"You know how weird she gets about Vic. Soon enough she'll get weird about you too."

"Ew, I hope not."

Just before the show ended, their mother blew into the room in a tizzy. "I heard the car! He's coming! Get up from the floor, you two. Really, Victoria, you're not a child. Sit in a chair like an adult."

As Vic made his entrance, their mother skittered across the floor of their cavernous foyer and embraced her firstborn as if he'd been overseas at war for years, and not a few hours from home. Vic rolled his suitcase a few feet away from them and hugged their mother, patting her on the back. "Hey, Mom."

"Are you hungry? You're hungry. Carmen, bring Victor something to eat." Carmen nodded, about to scurry away when Vic pulled himself from their mother's grasp.

"I'm fine." He stepped around their mother to hug Carmen. "I'm sure she's driven you insane and I'm sorry."

"It's no problem, Mr. Victor Junior." But the secret look she gave him indicated otherwise.

Their father stood and folded his newspaper under his arm, regarding Vic with the same scrutinizing gaze he used on subordinates. Measuring them up with the intent to always find them lacking. "How was the semester, son?"

"Good, sir. Aced my exams. Treasurer of the frat. Rowing team did well too." Victoria rolled her eyes behind their father's back, knowing all too well the kinds of reports their father asked for. His stilted, quarterly check-in with his own children, as if they were stockholders in their own last name.

"Glad to have you back. Once you're settled, I'll take you into the office and get you set up for the summer. It'll be nice to have another Lockwood in the building again." Victoria watched her brother die inside as he wordlessly nodded and let their father aggressively pat him on the shoulder.

Ward broke formation and ran to Vic, hugging him around the torso. Her little brother stood about three inches taller than his classmates already, but he looked shrimpy next to their brother, who'd been six foot four since his sophomore year of high school. He smiled down at Ward, giving an affectionate tousle of his hair. Despite their height differentials, all three of them resembled each other quite clearly. Same brown hair, same light brown eyes, same easily tanned white skin. In fact, they were each practically carbon copies of their mother, but thankfully, none of them inherited her personality.

"Sister! Join the hug!" Vic demanded, grinning from ear to ear. Victoria dragged her feet and reluctantly joined Ward in his effusive hug. "Lockwoods, assemble!"

Ward dissolved into giggles and Victoria extricated herself from their grasp. "You're an idiot. I'm going back to my room."

"Dinner is at seven," her mother said from behind them. "Carmen made your favorite, Victor."

Their mother peeled Vic away to interrogate him on the last six months of his life, so Victoria returned to her room. She hibernated for the better part of an hour with Leah's playlist in her stereo and a book in her hands, but she hadn't read past the first page. The ink bled and warped into smudges, coalescing into a graphite rendering of Leah. Her thick, straight eyebrows above two glorious, color-changing eyes whose penetrating stare haunted Victoria's soul. Wide-set cheekbones slanted sharply to her chin and culminated in a shallow dimple. The three vertical lines between her eyebrows, the ones she conjured when frustrated, confused, or sad. And, of course, the two angle brackets on either side of her mouth when she deigned to smile.

This newfound obsession threw Victoria for a loop. She had ascended into puberty without so much as a peep from her so-called raging hormones. Boys disinterested her and dating bored her to tears. Focused on academics and extracurriculars, Victoria left the boy-crazy teenage stuff to her friends. It never occurred to Victoria she might be a lesbian. Everything else about her was so average, why wouldn't her sexuality be the same? But, then…Leah.

Admittedly, Leah crossed her mind more often than her other classmates, despite Leah's antagonism toward her and her friends. Victoria looked forward to the throaty, intelligent criticisms grumbled behind her during AP English. And, well, Leah was pretty. She always knew that, though an appreciation for her beauty never clocked as attraction. But something about Leah glinted in Victoria's mind like sea glass catching sun. It drew her toward the loner, who she inadvertently kept tabs on throughout their shared years at school. Generally, Leah hung back from activities and didn't do much to draw attention— aside from the criminal act of being unapologetically herself in the unforgiving, homogeneous atmosphere of high school—but one memory of her stood out among the rest. Middle school, seventh grade, when they were twelve or thirteen years old, Victoria and Leah sang in the same school choir. As a taller girl, Victoria stood in the back row, but Leah stood near the front, so she'd never heard her sing and assumed Leah joined choir for the credits like she did. However, on the night of their Christmas pageant, their choir crammed into the music room to find out the girl selected to sing "O Holy Night" got strep throat and could not attend. Victoria remembered that night in vibrant detail—the smell of popcorn and feet in the choir room, the school's overzealous heaters boiling the pubescent students packed into their nice clothes—and she remembered Leah sitting in a chair backward near the piano at the front of the room. Their choir director shushed the rambunctious preteens and fretted over having to omit the number. Calmly, Leah raised her hand and volunteered to sing it.

With no time to practice before the show, Leah confidently strolled to the front of their risers and waited for her cue. She sang the song perfectly, note for note, her voice soaring over the audience with a maturity belying her twelve years of age. The sheer amount of soul she fit into the traditional song sent chills down Victoria's spine. It was the closest she'd ever gotten to church.

So, now Victoria had her first real crush on the pretty, angry, queer girl with a voice of an angel.

A light, rhythmic knocking on her door broke her from Leah-filled reverie. "Come in, Vic."

Vic let himself into the room and inspected it with his hands behind his back like a drill sergeant. Still dressed in his stupid polo and khaki pants, looking like one of their father's interns, he relaxed his posture. "How's it been? Senior year going okay?"

Victoria shrugged. "It's fine. Almost over, thank God."

"You said it." He flopped on the edge of her bed and Victoria bounced, chuckling. She tossed her book to the side. "Mother said you were not voted prom queen. I'm sure you're devastated."

"I'm not sure how I'll recover," Victoria replied. "Always a joy when she shares my accomplishments."

"She said you're still dating, ah…what's his name? Carson? The airhead football player?"

The grin fell from Victoria's face. "Carter. We broke up. I…didn't tell Mom."

"Oh, good. He sucked." Vic had their father's gift for brutal, accurate summations. "At least you're getting the hell out of here soon enough. You'll like college, I think. Where are they sending you?"

He knew the drill. Lockwood kids don't choose their own futures. "Harvard."

"Right. Grandfather's alma mater," Vic announced in an imitation of their father. "The legacy child."

"You're the legacy child," Victoria reminded him. "Victor Lockwood, Junior. Heir to Lockwood Industries. The one who will give Mother the grandchildren she so desperately requires."

"Ugh, her and the grandkids." Vic grabbed one of Victoria's small stuffed animals from the end of the bed, perching it on his stomach. "Can't you do the grandkids thing?"

"Mom wants your progeny, not mine."

He frowned around the sizable stuffed pony. A song change pulled his attention away from their conversation and toward the stereo on her desk. The music on Leah's mix changed genre from track to track, and it currently played a fairly heavy rock song Victoria hadn't ever heard before. "Whoa. I didn't know you listened to this."

"It's a mix I borrowed from…a friend." Her hesitation didn't go unnoticed, and Vic glanced at her, eyebrow raised.

"A friend, huh? A friend with sick taste in music."

Flustered, Victoria grabbed one of the decorative pillows and held it over her stomach, clenching it as if to protect herself from a maiming. "A new friend. Or…sort of a friend. I don't know, actually. It's complicated."

Catching on to her seriousness, Vic turned over and faced her on the bed, placing the stuffed animal between them. "Sounds like a Real Talk is coming."

Her entire body heated up in embarrassment. However, if she could tell one person, it would be Vic. "So, prom was a disaster. I'll tell you another time, but the short story is I broke up with Carter and left in the middle of it."

"Ohh, drama." Victoria glared at him. "Sorry."

"Walking back toward Garden Hills, a girl from my class found me and picked me up. I asked her not to bring me home…I didn't want to face Mom or Dad." Vic nodded in understanding. "She was really nice to me, took care of me, didn't ask for anything in return. Just…we got along really well. Which is so weird because we're not friends, you know? She's, like, basically famous in our class for hating everyone."

"But not you, huh?"

"Maybe? I felt a connection with her. Something I've never felt with anyone before. I…well, now I think I have a crush on her."

Vic's thick fingers scratched the faint whispers of a beard on his chin, and he thoughtfully considered her confession. "Okay. How does it feel to say that out loud?"

"How does—" She hadn't thought about it, but it was kind of a relief. "It feels terrifying but also kind of nice?"

"Sounds about right." He tucked one of his legs under the other and faced her entirely. "First, let me say it's great you got rid of that idiot. If you're going to date some guy as a beard, you can do better. That boy is so supremely stupid, he'd need quadruple the brains to be a half-wit."

"I know, I know." Victoria paused. "What's a beard?"

"You'll learn in time. Second, I'm in one of the only LGBT-friendly frats on campus. Not on purpose, but it's nice. Lots of gay guys pledge to us because they know it's a safe space and most frats aren't. For anyone. So, like, they would tell me their coming-out stories, the couple of them that are out, and you could feel the struggle. But those guys, the ones who were out, were the happiest. And they smelled good, which helps in a frat that smells like one cohesive fart all day and all night."

Victoria laughed and tossed a stuffed animal at his head. "Men are gross."

"Right? This is why cool people dig chicks. Can I get it up top?" He put up his hand and Victoria grudgingly high-fived him. "I guess that's not totally true. My roommate, Kyle, likes dudes and he's definitely cooler than me. Outside of Kyle, men are gross." Suddenly, he sat up ramrod straight. "Wait. Does this mean I can help you cruise for chicks? Please, please, please? My whole life I've been preparing to force myself to be friends with your dumb boyfriends but instead we can cruise the town for chicks. This is an outstanding development."

Though grateful for his enthusiasm, Victoria killed his dreams with a shake of her head. The big, boyish smile on his face turned into an exaggerated frown. "'Cruising for chicks' makes us sound like we're in the T-Birds or something."

"Ugh, I wish, but I can't pull off a plain white T-shirt to save my life. I look like a flagpole."

"Also, I…don't want to look for girls. I only like the one. I like her a lot, I think."

"Right, right, your mean-girl hero." Leaping off her bed, Vic shuffled to her bookshelf and scanned the spines until he found a thick, blue book and yanked it from the shelf. He thunked her yearbook down onto the comforter. "Show me her photo. Oh no! Better! Show me a club she's in and I'll find her."

Smiling and blushing like an idiot, Victoria thumbed through the yearbook until she came to the club section. She bypassed the sports and stopped on the chess team, then spun the book to face him. "Chess team."

"Chess team. Hmm. Means she's smart. Already an upgrade from the previous one." Once Vic zeroed in on the photo, he gave her a droll look. "There's only two girls here and it's clearly the one in the flannel mean-mugging the camera."

Victoria chuckled, replying with a wistful, "That's Leah."

"Leah…" He ran his finger along the text. "Leah Vasquez. Does she like you too?"

"I don't know," Victoria admitted, tracing the seam on her comforter. "I don't know how she feels at all, actually. We weren't friends before this weekend, and then I kissed her in the car like a total idiot and—"

"Slow down. You're at 'I think I like her' but you already kissed her?"

Victoria smothered her face in her pillow and groaned in embarrassment. "She was not happy about it."

Vic yanked down the pillow and stared at her, aghast. "What did you do? Lay one on her and tuck and roll out of the car? I know your boyfriend was trash, but we have more decorum with ladies, Victoria."

"I don't know what I'm doing!"

"That's apparent."

"Ugh. Leah knows exactly who she is and she's had girlfriends and she's so much cooler than me." Victoria sighed, sharp and dramatic. Her burgeoning feelings for Leah made her feel every inch seventeen and confused in a way her many years of careful planning did not appreciate. "I don't...I don't know where to begin. Or if I should begin. I mean, Mom and Dad will never be cool with it."

The smile playing on his lips fell, and Vic turned unexpectedly pensive. His happy-go-lucky personality buoyed them through their shared, complicated childhood, but he knew better than anyone the intense pressure within their family unit. "Mom and Dad don't have to live your life. You do. Do what you want."

"You know it's not that easy. I'd have to hide her from them to avoid all their racist, homophobic crap, and that's not fair to Leah."

"Maybe let her make that choice, then." Vic scooted closer and set aside the pillow. "You're an incredible person, Vicky. Really. You're worth loving. You're worth being patient for. And if she can't do it, that's her loss and her choice."

A single tear escaped and she quickly swiped it away. "She might not even like me."

"Then Plan B is we hop in the nicest car Dad owns, cruise for chicks, and find someone who does."

"I'm not going to cruise for chicks."

Melodramatically flopping over on her bed, Vic groaned. "Ugh, Victoria! You're taking all the fun out of having a lesbian sister."

"Is it supposed to be fun?"

"It could've been!"

CHAPTER FIVE

A chorus of hymnals lifted Leah in the pew. Not literally, but her voice soared and mingled with the others, their combined melodies echoing off the domed interior of the church, cascading back down to them in harmony. The beauty of a church—its intricate carvings, peaked ceilings, vibrant stained glass, aroma of incense and floor cleaner—text could never replicate the spirituality of the construction. Men were fallible in the text. Sinners and zealots, unreliable narrators and glory-seeking scribes, they did not hold a candle to the mathematical beauty of a church. To Leah, architecture was the one thing those self-important men ever got right. The cavernous room provided her both the space to fill with her prayers, and the intimacy required to commune directly with God.

But an insistent beeping cut in on her line. A third caller in the form of Victoria Lockwood, breaking her connection with God with a series of sinful thoughts for which Leah added in a few extra prayers. Leah's long dormant feelings for Victoria fought to emerge, eager to awaken from their years of forced hibernation. Her heart struggled to be heard, but her brain drowned it out with the known realities of her situation. Victoria was straight. Victoria was rich. Rich, straight, white girls did not fall in love with poor brown girls from the literal wrong side of the tracks.

But she kissed you, Leah's annoying inner monologue reminded her. Sure, she silently reasoned, but how many times had she been made a fool by the fleeting romances of a straight girl? Even God in His infinite patience probably tired of hearing Leah complain about straight girls. Especially ones as audacious as Victoria, who kissed her without understanding how one soft brush of her lips could be a hard strike of thunder in Leah's heart.

So, with this heart full of thunder and her mind wrestling with indignity and excitement, Leah ghosted her tongue across her lips to savor the fading flavor of strawberry lip gloss. The faint taste belied something much stronger: the idea that Victoria might like her back. She didn't want to consider it too seriously, but she said an extra prayer to the Big Guy just in case. Guide Victoria's heart to the truth, Leah asked of Him, and keep mine safe.

As her parents spoke to the priest on their way out, Leah waited by their car and ignored the looks from passing churchgoers. While the church itself preached progressive ideals, the reproach from other parishioners was tangible. She disengaged from their pointed stares and tugged on the knot near her throat, loosening her tie until it unraveled and hung in a U-shape around her neck. Leaning back with her head against the roof, she noted with a smile her favorite clouds, cumulus, floating above her head. The wind shaped them like hands on clay, graduating from one puffy design to another. She wondered if Victoria ever looked up and saw the clouds as a mirror. Breezing through life, changing shape with the wind, being whatever she needed to be to keep moving, unaffected. Not grounded to reality, not one thing or another. Vicky one minute, Victoria the next. Tori in secret.

Later that afternoon, changed out of their church clothes and into sweats, Hector and Leah sat side by side on the couch, glued to the Yankees game. She caught her father sneaking glances at her until he finally, and gently, asked, "Everything okay?"

"I'm fine," Leah replied evenly. Too much or too little resistance and she risked him digging further. Every teenager perfects the balancing act of assuaging worry while avoiding a disaffected tone.

Her mother cleared her throat from the chair beside the couch and Leah stiffened. *Papi* was a soft touch but her mother could be a surgeon with words. "I liked your friend Victoria. She's smart. Polite, too, especially for a teenager."

Leah mounted a weak and singly syllabic defense of her species. "Hey."

"Regardless, she's welcome to come by the house again. As long as there's no more ozone-destroying dress burnings in my yard." Leah saw her own glare reflected at her from her mother. The edges of her eyes crinkled and Leah let out a breath, nodding in agreement. Their oblique phrasing kept the door open: if she wanted to talk about Victoria, they'd listen.

"Okay. Thanks."

Eager to escape another awkward conversation, Leah excused herself on the fib of leftover homework and retreated to her room. On her way to face-plant into her bed, she picked up the book Victoria left behind. Her wallflower book. Though she should practice her bass for their next gig, or call Dana back, Leah didn't have the motivation for either. Instead, she lay on her bed, turning to inhale the lingering scent of Victoria's body spray on her pillow.

Don't be so stupid, Leah thought, squeezing her eyes shut. You can't miss someone you barely know. This wasn't Romeo and Juliet, she said to herself as she opened the book. Nobody falls in love over a weekend.

Once she'd pulled into the parking lot of Garden Hills High, Leah gripped her steering wheel and sat in her spot for a few minutes. The school, like most schools in the US, looked like a repurposed prison. Fading brick façade, small, sad windows with fat AC units sticking out every ten feet, and blue doors made of weird textured plastic. Between each painted line sat a car varying from expensive foreign SUVs to beat-up hoopdies with enough miles on them to get to the moon and back. The cohesion of rich and poor lasted only to the threshold of the school—inside, a dog-eat-dog hierarchy of rich kids ruled the school and the middle-class kids stayed out of their way. Except for Leah. Even her car didn't fit in—not a disaster on wheels, but not one of the glitzy cars the northern kids drove, whose sticker price cost more than what her father made in a year.

Methodical and ritual, she adjusted the air freshener, cracked her windows, and turned off the engine. Her religious cleaning of her car, as well as weekly deep cleans, kept it fairly clear of pizza odor. She vacuumed her seats and carpets every other day, conditioned the leather with wipes, and cleaned the windows to a streak-free shine. As a point of pride—maybe cultural, maybe socioeconomic—Leah knew the only way to keep nice things was to pour her energy into them.

Loath to leave her mobile sanctuary, she nabbed her backpack from the passenger seat and trudged across the parking lot toward the east entrance. The crashing of locker doors, chatter of kids, and skidding of sneakers filled the concrete walls of the wing as Leah entered. She kept her sunglasses on and plunked her headphones on her head, bumping through rowdy students to get to her locker. With their lockers assigned alphabetically, she stood no chance of accidentally seeing Victoria prior to their shared AP English class. It gave her at least seven periods to prepare herself for acting totally normal in front of the girl who had kissed her less than twenty-four hours ago.

However, when Victoria walked into the classroom just shy of the bell, Leah realized quite quickly she wasn't prepared. Headphones in and head down, she smelled Victoria before she saw her. A plume of her perfume wafted under her nose as Victoria sat in the seat directly in front of her. Something heavily floral and a little musky, but distinctly Victoria. She wore a boat-neck tank top, accentuating her shoulders, athletic and broad from swimming. Eyes glued to the desk, Leah ignored the way her pulse sprinted, and when she sensed Victoria look at her, didn't dare look up.

Their teacher, Mrs. Knight, signaled the start of class and Leah packed her headphones away. Down the rows, photocopies of a poem were handed over shoulders to each student. Victoria turned to hand Leah hers and their eyes met, causing Leah's breath to catch in her throat. Victoria formed a tiny, secret smile with an outsized ability to stop Leah's heart. She snatched the paper and pretended not to see Victoria's smile fall.

After giving them about ten minutes with the poem, Mrs. Knight poised her chalk over the board and asked, "Okay, who would like to give me their idea of what the poem is about?"

A few hands went up. The stars, someone said, and the teacher scribbled it on the board. Love, Victoria suggested, and Mrs. Knight wrote the word in all caps in the center of the board. "I agree, Miss Lockwood. Above all the metaphor, this is a poem about love."

Leah cleared her throat and raised her hand from the back of the classroom. "Mrs. Knight?"

"Ah, Leah?" Leah didn't begrudge her teacher the trepidation in her voice. She did have a well-earned reputation for being combative in class.

"It's not about love."

Chuckles reverberated through the room and Mrs. Knight paused. "It's not? I think Mr. Auden would be quite interested to hear you say that."

"It's about unrequited love," Leah replied. "And that isn't love at all. It's a ghost in an empty house."

Mrs. Knight turned away from the chalkboard, her flowing red skirt swishing against the tile as she perched on the edge of her desk.

"Wonderful observation. The poem is about unrequited love. Auden says if you are to be in a situation as such, it would be better to be the one who loves and has their feelings unreturned, than the one who does not love at all."

"Unrequited love is love," Victoria interjected. "You still feel it. If you feel it, it's real."

"I disagree." Victoria turned around and Leah met her challenging gaze and elaborated, "If you don't share that love, if you bottle it inside and keep it hidden, it doesn't exist."

Victoria shook her head. "Your whole premise is flawed. If a love is unrequited, you'd only know that if you attempted to share it and found out the other person didn't feel the same."

"Not necessarily. Auden has no way of confirming if the 'stars' return his love, he assumes they don't because of their supposed indifference. But maybe they, too, are keeping it hidden. And therefore, what do they have? Nothing. Just some kind of Schrodinger's love that exists and doesn't exist."

A red wave crawled up Victoria's neck from beneath her shirt. Her oak eyes lit like the cradle of a forest fire. "A hidden love is still love."

"A hidden love is bullshit. If you can't speak the love aloud, then—"

"Maybe he can't," Victoria shot back. "Maybe he doesn't know how to express it. Maybe he doesn't…understand it."

Leah scoffed. "He probably didn't even ask the stars how they felt."

"How do you ask a star how it feels?" Victoria's friend Riley, who sat perpendicular to them, inquired softly from her seat, her eyes pinging back and forth between them. "Maybe Auden feels it's easier to assume he would not be loved back than to risk expressing his love and having it go unreturned. He says at the end he could get used to inky nothingness, but I don't think he would. He's trying to convince himself because above all else, he's scared. Being vulnerable to love, unrequited or not, is scary."

At the head of the class, Mrs. Knight appeared near tears. With a hand on her chest, she sniffed and heaved a dramatic sigh. "What a lively discussion, ladies. I think you've all made salient points worth considering."

A baseball player Leah assumed had been assigned to their advanced class by clerical error slowly raised his hand. "So, it's…it's not about space?"

Leah didn't speak for the rest of the class period, instead turning inward as she read the lines of each stanza over and over. The merciful bell rang and Leah shoved her materials into her backpack, slinging it over her shoulder and leaving before anyone else had gotten out of their chairs. Truthfully, her notes on the poem had been about God. She hadn't even considered it much of a love poem until Victoria mentioned it, and then couldn't resist the opportunity to get under her skin. The intellectual equivalent of tugging on her hair like a grade-school boy.

After that somewhat revealing emotional close call, they avoided each other for the rest of the day and for several days after. Leah kept to herself during English and tried not to seek Victoria around every corner. When they passed in the halls, they exchanged clandestine looks packed with a meaning Leah didn't understand. Still, it took a lot of strength not to reveal herself in these passing glances. Could people see in her eyes she knew what Victoria sounded like when she slept? How she'd felt the pliability of the tops of her hands? Could they sense she had seen what the soft wash of first light looked like against Victoria's pale skin? Did they know Leah had tasted the strawberry sweetness of Victoria's lips? Probably not. Most kids were too busy frothing at the mouth in anticipation of the end of the school year to notice her gay longing.

Getting through the week was like living inside a Cure song. Monday blue, Tuesday and Wednesday gray, Thursday didn't even start, but by Friday, she'd gathered the courage to actually speak to Victoria again, under the guise of returning the book she'd left at Leah's house.

Swallowing her anxiety, Leah approached the boisterous circle in the hallway outside Victoria's locker. She needn't open her mouth—her mere presence near Garden Hills High royalty abruptly ended their conversation. Leah ignored the awkward silence and cleared her throat. "Uh, hey. Just…returning your book. I finished it Monday, but I didn't have time to give it back 'til now. Obviously. Uh, anyway, thanks. You were right, I really liked it."

Leah handed over the book and Victoria took it with a silent nod. Gabby raised her eyebrow. "Why did she have your book?" she asked, addressing Victoria, but staring at Leah.

"She lent it to me?" Leah answered quizzically.

"Oh my God, were you tutoring her?" Victoria struggled to respond, but Gabby spoke again before she could get a word out. "You're such a star student. Like, taking time out of your life to tutor the less fortunate. Wow."

Leah scrunched her face. "What? Tutor *me*? I have a higher GPA than she does."

Gabby gawked. "How do you know Vicky's grade point average? What a stalker." The boys, two twin jocks named Jack and John, laughed. Leah didn't know a thing about the twins but disliked them on principle. The other friend, Riley, edged behind Victoria as if afraid Leah would bite her. Leah didn't mind Riley—unassuming and quiet, unlike loudmouth Gabby—though anytime Leah caught her eye, she thought Riley might rocket into space out of pure terror.

"The grade point averages of the top ten students in our class are posted every month," Leah replied. "But of course, you don't know that because your GPA is as low as your IQ."

A faint smile twitched on Victoria's lips, and Riley snickered into her fist. Gabby sniffed, but quickly turned her demeanor from affront to attack. "And? I'm still going to Stanford."

Leah snorted. "As what? The new mascot?"

"For your information," Gabby replied in her nasally voice. "I got a lacrosse scholarship. Some of us actually do things after school besides smoke weed and deliver garlic bread."

The barb stung and Leah gripped her backpack strap closer to her chest to soothe the pain. "A scholarship? You're not even the best player on the team. Riley is, despite the fact she runs like a baby giraffe."

"What the fuck?" Gabby made a noise of disgust. "Whatever, it's not gonna matter when I've got an Ivy diploma and you're still tossing pizzas in your beat-up tuner."

"Jesus, Gabby, chill out," Victoria said, finally. She aimed a sharp, imperious look at her friend. "Quit being a bitch."

"What?" Leah winced at Gabby's shrill squeak, sharp like a boot stomping on a rubber chicken. "Tell her to stop being a bitch!"

"You started it," Riley piped up from over Victoria's shoulder. "Also, just for reference, Stanford isn't considered an Ivy League school."

Gabby pivoted to her. "You're taking her side? She called you a baby giraffe."

"I said she runs like one but she's also the best player on the team," Leah corrected. Riley smiled shyly at her, still half-hidden behind Victoria. "Two things can be true."

"Thanks for returning my book, Leah." Victoria slid the thin paperback into her messenger bag. An ache gripped Leah's ribs at the soft, fond look in her eyes. "I'm really glad you liked it. I'll see you around."

Watching after Victoria like a lovesick puppy as she walked away, Leah leaned against a locker and let the butterflies flutter. She'd liked girls before. Sometimes a lot, in fact. The knot of yearning she felt in her stomach had tangled itself before. But never, ever, did Leah Vasquez get butterflies.

A presence beside her forced the look off her face, and she collected herself before half turning to see her chess teammate Fatima approaching from a nearby classroom. "Hey."

Fatima nodded in greeting. "Hey, you ready? You look a little... distracted."

Leah shored up her personality and evicted the butterflies. "You wish. Maybe you'd win our match if I was."

"No way, you're still gonna kick my ass today. You've been demolishing everyone since we started the tourney." Demolishing everyone as silent, petty revenge for Fatima being chosen over her for the statewide friendly chess tournament. "So, who were you looking at? I don't think I've ever seen you look dreamy before."

"I do not look dreamy."

"I would absolutely describe your look as dreamy. I half expected hearts to start shooting out of your eyes." Leah glared as they walked, hoping the curtain of her curly hair blocked Fatima's view of her blush. "Well, whoever they were for, I hope she's better than Hayley."

Leah stopped short of the door to the classroom in which they held their chess meetings. "What the hell was everyone's problem with Hayley? She didn't even go here."

"Every time we went to a party, she spent the entire night shooting daggers at any girl that looked at you. Even me." Leah couldn't help but laugh at Fatima's withering stare. "The sentence 'I'm asexual and I don't want to bone your girlfriend' meant nothing to her."

Chess team met in the math wing in one of the freshman classrooms, where Fatima and Leah tossed their backpacks into a corner. "Right. Well, no dreamy look. No girl. Just...lost in my thoughts about what move I'm going to use to beat you."

Fatima rolled her eyes at her apparent transparence. "Uh-huh."

Leah mentally prepped, ignoring the influx of students who'd come to watch their final matchup. It wouldn't be many people outside of the chess team, but with most clubs winding down for the year, they were one of the few clubs still going for anyone with nothing to do after school. In the seat across from Fatima, Leah rubbed her palms along the material of her shorts and stared down at the chessboard. She mentally moved the pieces until a familiar voice snapped her attention to the door. With a silent groan, she realized Victoria and Riley had entered the room, squished next to other kids waiting to spectate.

The shift in her demeanor caught the attention of her opponent, and Fatima scanned the line of kids. She lowered her voice to a near whisper, under the din of their chatter. "Lockwood, or Myers?"

"No, nobody. Nothing."

Their adviser droned on about the rules as Leah squirmed in her seat, now watched by both Fatima with her stupidly knowing grin and Victoria from across the room. All week, Leah mapped out how to play Fatima slow and methodical, but the adrenaline in her system wouldn't allow it. Fatima moved her first white piece and hit the buzzer, and Leah began her attack. She watched her opponent's eyes widen in surprise at the move, but she calmly responded. Though over the thirty minutes of play Leah got sloppy due to the Victoria Lockwood-shaped distraction in the room, ultimately her desire to impress trumped Fatima's skill. Leah would have mate in two. Fatima could resign. But her opponent seemed to understand Leah needed the win, and she intentionally began the sequence of her undoing.

They shook hands over the board as her teammates cheered. The spectators mostly filed out, including Victoria. Leah sighed, relieved. "Good game."

"That was a great game, Leah," Fatima said, following her from the table to the corner where their backpacks lay heaped in a pile. "You should've gone to state. You might've even won."

Leah shrugged as she hefted her backpack over her shoulders. "Maybe, maybe not. The good thing is you went and not one of these dorks." She eyed the group of boys staring at their finished chess game, analyzing the moves. "If not me, then you."

"I agree. And—if there's something going on I can help with, let me know. You've seemed…broodier than normal this week."

"I have?" It surprised her more to know someone noticed her at all.

"Yeah. Just not yourself. You haven't sassed Mr. Zoetz once in AP Calc all week. That's got to be a record."

"Guess it's just…hard to care with graduation coming up."

As Leah fiddled with her backpack's strap, Fatima took pity on her and let up. "Whatever it is, it didn't stop you from kicking my ass at chess. But you know you can always message me on AIM if you want to talk."

"Thanks. I'll see you Monday."

Leah followed the well-worn path from the side exit to the student parking lot, where her "beat-up tuner" waited for her. Backpack tossed into the trunk, Leah soothingly rubbed the bumper of her car. "The fuck does Gabby Friedman know? She wouldn't know a tailpipe from her own ass. You're not beat-up at all. You're loved."

Scuffling a few yards away caught Leah's attention, and she outwardly groaned at the sight of Victoria jogging across the lot toward her car. "Wait up a second," Victoria called as she got closer.

"Why?" Leah asked, scowling. She peered around Victoria. "Got any other friends you want to bully me with before the weekend?"

"No, Leah. Look, I'm sorry about Gabby. She…sucks sometimes."

"Sometimes?" Leah laughed, throwing in a scoff for good measure. "Sure, whatever. Is there something you wanted?"

"I…" Victoria looked lost and crestfallen. Leah tried hard not to let it get to her. A week's worth of restrained yearning had her short on patience. "I want to hang out with you this weekend."

In one breath she'd removed the wind from Leah's sails. Leah stared into Victoria's eyes as they searched her own. As Victoria's gaze dipped to her mouth, Leah wondered if her lip gloss tasted the same today. "I want to hang out with you, too, but I'm confused as to what this is."

"That makes two of us," Victoria admitted softly. "I know I want to hang out with you more."

"But not if your friends know about it." Leah raised an eyebrow. "Because I'm not good enough for them."

"It has nothing to do with my friends. It's my parents I'm worried about." Chewing on her bottom lip, Victoria leaned against Leah's car. "Gabby tells her mom everything because she's annoying. Her mom will tell my mom, and then she'll ruin this somehow. She ruins everything. And this—you—mean a lot to me. I don't want my parents to ruin the one thing in my life that's good, a-and mine. So, please, I know it's a tough ask. And I'd understand if it wasn't worth it for you."

Leah peered up from her shoes, only to get an eyeful of Victoria's dramatically protruded lower lip. "Jesus, Lockwood, what a pout."

Her pout did not relent. "Is it working?"

"Yes, it's working." Victoria brightened and Leah rolled her eyes, annoyed at the sensation of her insides going soft. "Fine, let's hang out this weekend. What did you want to do?"

"Are you working on Saturday?"

She lolled her head to the side. "Dude, I'm always working."

"Benny's, or the shop?"

"Shop."

"Okay. I have to go to some gross public family dinner because my brother is home," Victoria said, making an annoyed face. "But that's not until seven."

Now it was Leah's turn to pout. "What, no sleepover?"

By the sharpness of her exhale, Victoria didn't find the comment nearly as funny as Leah intended. "If I'm with you, who's going to bow at Vic when he walks by?"

"Damn, Tori."

"Sorry," Victoria mumbled, visibly embarrassed. "We can do our AP English homework together when you don't have customers. Is that cool?"

"Is it cool to make me do homework at my job? No. But, yes, we can do homework. I'm so grateful you can take time out of your busy schedule to tutor me."

"Yeah, I know. Gabby is an idiot, you can't expect her to have read the list of top students in the class. I don't know why you didn't just tell her you're going to MIT."

"'Cause fuck her. She's not invited to my future. That's mine."

Victoria nudged her, flashing her stupid half-smile and making Leah's heart skip. "You told me. Am I invited?"

"Maybe. Don't make me regret it." Scowling and blushing, Leah coaxed Victoria away from her car door so she could get in and drive far, far away from Victoria Lockwood and the stranglehold she had on Leah's good sense. "I'll see you tomorrow. Eleven?"

"Ten," Victoria said, stepping back to allow Leah room to get into the car. "Don't try to squeeze me out of Vasquez Time."

"I wouldn't dream of it."

Fixing cars came naturally to Leah, like riding a bike or doing long division. Any activity living in the waters of mathematics and creativity, Leah swam them without fear. Music, mechanics, or math; when her brain and her hands combined, she could make magic. She and her father worked in tandem, tuned to one another like dueling violins, engrossed in their diagnosis as her father's old cassette player blasted Linda Ronstadt's Spanish-language album. Their harmonies, perfected over road trips and long days at the shop, filled the cement-walled warehouse in clear acoustics. Leah didn't hear the bells jingle when the door opened, and she only realized they weren't alone when her father's voice ceased to sing along with hers.

Leah popped out from under the hood to see Victoria walking in with her book bag slung over her shoulder. Flushing beet-red, she dropped her wrench and heard it thump as it hit her father. "*Mierda*, sorry, *Papi*. Hey, Tori. I uh, didn't hear you come in."

"How much do I owe for the concert?" Victoria wiggled her eyebrows and Leah wished to melt into a pool of oil.

Hector slid out from beneath the car on the creeper. "Tori! Good to see you!"

"Hi, Mr. Vasquez," Victoria said with a cheerful smile. "Thanks for letting me hang out in your shop. Is there a place for me to put my stuff?"

"The break room is to your right. We have some snacks and drinks in the fridge if you want." As Victoria nodded and followed his directions, Hector rolled back under the car. Suddenly, he appeared between Leah's feet where she stood hovering over the engine. "Another weekend with 'Tori,' huh?"

Leah blushed at the insinuation. "It's not like that, *Papi*. She's just a friend."

"Okay, okay." He slid back under, leaving just the top of his head exposed. "Your mother was 'just a friend' too, until she could no longer resist me."

"You mean until you got her pregnant and had to marry her," Leah said, glaring down at him.

"See? *Cuidado*, *mija*. Tori won't be able to keep away from you. It is not her fault; the Vasquez charm is hard to resist." Chuckling to himself, he continued, "Every Sunday at church I say prayer you can't get anyone pregnant. I'm too young to be an *abuelo*."

"Doesn't stop me from trying." Hector abruptly stopped chuckling, grew somber, then burst into hysterical laughter, grabbing her ankle and shaking it. Her mother would've had her head for that joke, but for she and Hector, the rules were different.

"Okay, I don't tease you anymore. But be careful with Tori, yes?"

Leah placed her boot on the end of the creeper and fondly shoved her father under the car. "*Sí*, *Papi*, now go away."

Once her father no longer required her assistance, Leah washed her hands and joined Victoria in the break room. Atop the table, where Leah had already placed her books, Victoria sat cross-legged with a notebook open in her lap. When she looked up, Leah could've sworn she did a double take. With an almost imperceptible swallow, Victoria managed a smile. "Is that…is that one piece?"

"Have you never seen a jumpsuit before?" Leah looked down at her jumpsuit. She'd unbuttoned the front down to her waist, pulling out her arms and exposing her white tank top she'd worn underneath. "Like not even on TV?"

Cheeks flushed, Victoria huffed out a laugh. "No, I have, I was just curious. I've never seen it worn in half. Does it come off all at once?"

Leah planted her hands on her hips and cocked an eyebrow. "Are you trying to figure out how to undress me, Victoria Lockwood?"

"No!" Leah took great glee in the flaming embarrassment on Victoria's face. "I—I was wondering how you pee."

"Out of my vagina like every other person with a vagina?"

"Oh my God, I hate you."

"You have to take off the whole thing to pee. Like everything else, they built it with men in mind." Leah sighed as the front door bells jingled. "Now, if you'll excuse me, I have to get that. But then you can 'tutor me' when we're done."

"You know, the more you say it, the more it starts to sound like a euphemism."

Leah threw her a wink. "You wish."

Quiet traditional Mexican music floated in from the bay, and Leah attempted to focus on her homework. However, between a serious bout of senioritis and the tops of her knees brushing Victoria's, the finer parts of *A Doll's House* were lost on her.

"Hey, what did you get on the AP exam?" Victoria asked suddenly.

Leah didn't look up, continuing to jot down notes. "In English? A five."

"Wow, you really are smarter than me."

"Maybe," she replied. "It's just a stupid test."

Victoria's hand came down between them, pushing Leah's notebook down into her lap. "Why do you do that? Insist you're not smart?"

"Is that what I'm doing?"

"It sure seems like it." Victoria sighed, clearly irritated. "It's annoying when you diminish yourself."

Leah pulled her notebook out from under Victoria's hand. "I'm not. I'm just not going to gloat about a meaningless AP exam."

"It's not meaningless," Victoria replied. "Do you know how small the percentage is of people who score a five? Less than ten percent. You know why I know that? Because my mother called the test people and asked. I got a four and my mother found it important to know just how many students did better than I did."

Part of Leah felt sympathetic about Victoria's overbearing mother, and part of her resented the course this conversation took. Leah quelled her instinct to antagonize and took the middle road. "Well, I'm sorry your mom is a dick about it, but it doesn't matter. You're going to Harvard. Friedman is going to Stanford. That alone should show you AP tests are a scam and don't matter."

When Leah finally looked up, Victoria stared at her with intense scrutiny. Like an idiot, she blushed under the attention, going even redder when Victoria smiled. "You shouldn't ever hide how smart you are, Leah. It's one of your less annoying qualities."

"Right. Like you're not annoyed I'm smarter than you."

"I'm not," Victoria replied immediately. "I think it's hot."

Unable to respond, Leah returned her attention to her thesis. She'd picked a relatively easy topic as a final essay—AP exams were over and Leah didn't want to tax her brain any more than she had to. She read the same sentence over and over, feeling Victoria's eyes on her. "What?"

"You have a smudge of car grease on your face." Without asking, she plucked a handkerchief from Leah's lap and dabbed the fabric against her tongue, reaching across to wipe Leah's cheek. Victoria's playful brown eyes bore directly into Leah's, and her heart fluttered so hard it could've lifted her from the table like a helicopter.

Leah gulped. "Did you get it?"

"Not all of it," Victoria replied in a whisper.

"Any chance you think that's hot too?"

Huffing out a short laugh, she nodded. "Honestly? It's kinda cute."

"Yeah?" Victoria lingered near her face, close enough for Leah to feel the cool wash of her breath against her skin. "What are you doing?"

"I don't know," Victoria answered softly. "Is it okay?"

"Yes." Energy crackled between them and the thump of Leah's heart pounding in her ears drowned out the ambient noise of the shop. The moment begged for a kiss, it ached for it.

But the moment, and Leah, were left wanting.

"Ladies!" Her father's voice boomed from the other room and Leah jumped back so quickly she tumbled off the table and onto the floor. Hector rounded the corner and came upon Victoria looking shell-shocked on the table, and Leah sprawled on the floor. "What happened?"

Blushing furiously, Leah got to her feet and rubbed her elbow, which, along with her ego, had taken the brunt of the fall. "Nothing. What's up?"

"It's lunch time, *señoritas*." Hector rubbed his belly. "Thought we'd head to the truck."

"Lunch is in a truck?" Victoria inquired with an innocent blink.

"Oh, yeah. There is this absolutely amazing taco truck parked a few blocks from here, near the industrial park." Leah gestured in the general direction of the park. "The food is, like, ridiculous."

The quizzical look on Victoria's face persisted. "That's where Lockwood Industries is. I've been going there since I was a kid and I've never seen a taco truck before."

"Uh, no offense, but uh…"

Victoria immediately turned haughty and Leah held back a laugh. "What?"

Hector backed away, a mischievous look on his face. "She thinks maybe you're too fancy for the taco truck."

"I'm not fancy!" Victoria hopped down and huffed indignantly. "I've just never seen it."

"Maybe because the limo you take brings you right to the door? And you probably eat on-site catering?" Leah ventured a guess, and Victoria did not deign to respond, instead sticking out an imperious chin. "You're a little fancy, Lockwood."

"I'm not," Victoria whined. Leah and her father chuckled at her impetuousness, and Victoria gestured ahead of them. "Lead the way, Mr. Vasquez. Apparently, I need to prove to your daughter that I'm not a snob."

He clapped his hands in excitement. "¡Okay, *vamos!*"

Leah and Victoria followed about three paces behind Hector as he walked them through downtown toward the industrial park. Side by side, the hair on Leah's arm raised in proximity to Victoria. Hyperaware of their touch, Leah put space between them and hoped those few inches might give her space to breathe. It was nothing short of magnetic, how Victoria intangibly drew Leah close. Intentionally keeping away from Victoria exhausted her, like she was pushing her body to do something it wasn't meant to do.

After ordering and receiving their food, they took a seat at a picnic bench on a grassy section of the parking lot. Mostly men and women in business attire surrounded them, but a good chunk of people had traveled from town to patronize the truck.

Delicious tacos temporarily distracted Leah from her almost-kiss with Victoria, who leaned over to peek at her lunch. "What did you get?"

"Two *hongos* and one *nopales*," she replied. "Mushroom and cactus. I got you a cactus, a *carnitas*, which is pulled pork, and *barbacoa*, which is beef."

Hector nodded toward his daughter. "Leah and her mother are vegetarian. So, I'm vegetarian, too, at home. But at the taco truck, I maybe indulge a bit."

Victoria blinked. "Oh. I didn't know you were vegetarian."

Mouth full of *elote*, Leah shrugged and washed it down with a pineapple Jarritos soda. "Why would you? It's not like I go around telling everybody."

"Right, true. Will it bother you if I eat the meat? I can get something vegetarian."

Leah waved her off. "Nah, don't worry about it. I've seen Billy scarf down much worse."

They ate quietly, save for the small talk between Hector and Victoria. It came as no surprise to Leah that Victoria and Hector got along; each of them alone had enough good-natured charm to seduce a whole village. They bantered about baseball, and Victoria politely inquired about Hector's work as a mechanic. Leah thought Victoria's genuine curiosity about her dad's life was sweet. Lots of people, especially white people, marginalized him because of his thick accent and sometimes broken English. Very little angered Leah more than the casual condescension of white people toward her father. However, Victoria respected him, and Leah became a tiny bit smitten with her because of it.

Her dad left to buy another taco and talk with the owner of the truck, leaving Victoria and Leah alone at the bench. With each day growing hotter they'd luckily snagged a bench under the shade of a giant maple tree, swinging its leaves above their heads. While she still wore her mechanic jumpsuit with the top half hanging down, Victoria wore a midriff-baring tank top and low-rise shorts, with a peek of her soft, tanned belly in between.

Victoria pointed to the glass bottle on the bench. "What kind of soda is that?"

"Jarritos. It's a sweet Mexican soda that's been my favorite since I was a kid. Do you want to try some?"

Victoria nodded, so Leah handed her the soda and watched her take a long sip. It passed her strawberry-flavored lips and Leah followed the bob in her throat as she swallowed. A small trickle of sweat dribbled down Victoria's neck. The image of flattening her tongue against the rogue droplet and trailing its path back upward struck her with the force of a high-speed taco truck.

"Wow, that's really good."

"Yeah, it is," Leah said roughly, taking back her drink and resisting the urge to put her lips where Victoria's had just been. "They used to sell the Goya sodas here, but I convinced the owner, Jorge, to switch to Jarritos."

"How did you manage that? Are you friends with the owner?"

"Eh, sort of. The Hispanic community here is pretty small so we all went to each other's *quinceñeras* and stuff. Everybody's *abuela* is everyone else's *abuela*." Scratching the back of her neck, Leah elaborated, "And I kind of dated Jorge's daughter sophomore year. Only for a couple months."

"Does she go to our school?"

"No, she lives in Kowahoke." Kowahoke buttressed Garden Hills and Leah spent one lazy summer between the two towns, casually dating Jorge's daughter Maritza. Outside of a couple intense hookups it never went anywhere, especially when Maritza started dating a senior at her own school. It didn't break Leah's heart so much as fractured it, and the fissures healed quickly. Their entire relationship lay based upon the small dating pool for LGBTQ teens in the county. Queer kids in small towns do not find big love. "It wasn't much. It wasn't like, Julia Roberts Love, you know?"

Victoria chuckled softly. "Right. Like, 'just a girl, standing in front of a boy, asking him to love her.'"

"Or a girl standing in front of another girl, asking that girl to love her."

"Right." Victoria's voice rose barely above a whisper. "That too."

Leah's father approached their table, planted his hands on Leah's shoulders, and beamed his smile down at them. "Did you like the tacos?"

With an enthusiastic nod, Victoria dismounted the bench and gathered their trash. "They were amazing, Mr. Vasquez. Thank you for treating me to lunch."

"Anytime!" As Leah got up, he wrapped one burly arm around her and the other around Victoria, jostling them. "Any friend of *mi torita* is a friend of mine."

Rolling her eyes in embarrassment, Leah shoved her dad away. "Dad."

"Is that Leah's nickname?" Victoria inquired, evidently very amused. "*Torita?*"

Hector snickered at Leah's obvious discomfort. "Yes, it means little bull. We gave her the nickname because she's always been very stubborn, yeah? Even when she was not as tall as my boots, my wife and I say it was like trying to tame a bull to get her to do anything she didn't want to do."

"Sounds about right," Victoria said with a giggle.

Leah stuck out her tongue. "You're both extremely rude."

"Ay, but you love us," Hector replied. "Isn't that right, *Torita*?"

Placing her hands on either side of her head, Leah made horns with her fingers and jabbed them into her father's side. He yelped and pretended to scurry away, waving an imaginary flag for her to charge. Just before she did, she caught Victoria's eye and went nearly breathless at the conspicuous endearment in Victoria's eyes.

Maybe God had heard her prayer after all.

CHAPTER SIX

Victoria despised little more than public family dinners. Private family dinners were their own special hell, carefully crafted in dysfunction, but tolerable, as Victoria could bail to her room. A public dinner offered no such escape. They put on airs and pretended to tolerate one another, which exhausted Victoria. At least Vic and Ward would be there. Her brothers were annoying by default, but their presence usually diluted the alkali of her parents.

After finishing up her homework with Leah, Victoria returned home to prepare for the family dinner. As she put away her backpack, she saw the book Leah had returned to her. Plucking *Wallflower* from her bag, a white envelope fell out onto her carpet. Not an envelope, she realized with a smile, but a crinkly white sleeve with a CD in it, FOR TORI scribbled in black felt marker in Leah's choppy handwriting. With a smile she placed the CD in her player and pressed play. A somewhat familiar song struck up and Victoria put her hand over her mouth, giggling. As it got to the chorus, she burst into laughter as the singer crooned about how much he loved a rainy night.

She got ready to the playlist, regretfully ending it once she'd put on enough makeup for her mother to find her presentable. Descending the stairs in heels she despised, Victoria waited with her brothers in the den for their father to return home from work.

"Do you know where we're going?" Vic asked, propping his designer sneakers up on the coffee table. Only he could get away with that move. "I specifically asked Mom not to pick something upscale."

"I don't think she did," Victoria replied. "She made a big deal about having to scout a 'normal' restaurant."

Ward, reclined on the carpet staring at the ceiling fan, chimed in. "She said something about a Mexican American place nearby."

"Wow, Mom is really branching out these days," Vic replied, rolling his eyes. He was right, of course, and again Victoria envied his ability to speak so freely about their overbearing mother, especially when she might be hovering within earshot. "That's good, though. You like Mexican American, don't you, Victoria? I heard you're a big fan of Mexican American."

"You are?" Ward asked, innocently blinking his big brown eyes. Victoria's cheeks burned hot and she lobbed a throw pillow at her older brother. Ward paused. "I mean, I guess I like tacos."

Vic nearly burst. "Victoria absolutely loves tacos."

"I hate you with an unquenchable fire."

He grinned. "You do not."

Once their father arrived and changed into his "dinner clothes," the family piled into their luxury sedan and drove through and out of Garden Hills. Victoria, squished between her brothers, played with her bracelet mindlessly on the ride there. Spending the day with Leah only served to worsen the crush Victoria struggled to hide. After admitting it to Vic, she felt the affection come to her more easily. Affection she could somewhat handle, but the stupid, uncontrollable lust gave her a hard time. The mere idea of kissing Leah again consumed her. It factored into all of her daydreaming, and she knew it was only a matter of time before she lost the ability to restrain herself, either in public or privately. All week at school she fought the urge to pull Leah into a dark classroom and find some measure of relief in her lips. But she still didn't even know if Leah really liked her like that. How do you ask a star how it feels?

Crowded on a Saturday night, the restaurant teemed with people as their family of five entered. Not nearly as upscale as the places her mother had forced them to go in the past, but it wasn't quite Benny's, either. Their father's clout got them seated right away at a round table far enough from the kitchen to make her mother feel important. Cassandra sat next to Vic, presumably to incessantly nag about college. Victoria barely looked at the menu, ordering a vegetable fajita before handing the menu to the waiter and folding her hands on the table.

"Vegetable fajita?" Her mother snorted, shaking her head in obvious disappointment. "Eat some protein, Victoria."

"Beans have protein," Victoria replied. "I'm trying to eat less meat. It isn't good for the environment."

"You'll become anemic," her mother said, quite matter-of-factly considering Victoria was sure she never gave a shit about nutrients before. "Get an iron deficiency. Bring her a side of steak as well."

"Please, do not bring me a side of steak," Victoria said to the waiter in the sternest voice she could drum up.

Glancing between Victoria and her mother, her father tiredly gestured to the waiter. "Bring the steak, son. Leave it on the side."

The waiter thanked them for their order and vacated swiftly, hustling into the kitchen, no doubt glad to get away from their dysfunction. Victoria wished she could follow him there, maybe just dunk her head into a pot of boiling water and put an end to this misery.

"I knew we shouldn't have sent you to public school." Her mother sipped her wine, not even looking at Victoria as she demeaned her. "You'd never find a *vegetarian* at a private school."

"I've met lots of them at Brown. It's become very elitist, being a vegetarian. One might even say posh. Victoria's just getting ahead of the game before she goes to *Harvard*," Vic said, emphasizing the last word with a terrible Boston accent.

"Now, Victoria," Cassandra began, and Victoria deflated in her seat. Even Vic's attempt at humor couldn't put her mother off. "I got a call from Mrs. Harcourt saying you and Carter are no longer dating? Is that true? What happened?"

"She told you we broke up, but didn't tell you why?" Victoria scoffed, staring down at the tablecloth. "Because he's a dirtbag, that's why."

"Victoria, let's not use salty language at the table," her father said. "Though I'm not inclined to disagree."

"Victor." Her mother's admonishment breezed by her dad, who shrugged and gave Victoria a knowing look across the table. "Carter is a fine young man. He would've made an excellent husband."

"The boy's an idiot, Mom," Vic replied. "Victoria's smarter than him by several nautical miles. She can do way better."

"His family is reputable and he's good-looking. He has a successful future ahead of him. Victoria should be so lucky to date a young man like him."

"It sounds more like you want to date him," Victoria snapped.

Cassandra gasped. "Victoria. He received the Garden Hills Hometown Hero award for his Eagle Scout philanthropy. We don't just hand that award to any miscreant off the streets. He's a fine young man."

Vic gave their mother a droll look. "We sponsor that award, Mother, and we all know you nominated him after they started dating."

"Carter called me a slut in front of our entire graduating class at prom. He accused me of sleeping with several of his friends, which I think part of my class actually believes. Are you happy now? Is that what you wanted to hear?" Trembling in her seat, Victoria held back the hot tears forming behind her eyes. "I was humiliated at my own prom by my idiot boyfriend because I refused to sleep with him."

The briefest flash of surprise blinked on her mother's face, then vanished. "Oh, you know how boys are. Jealous and ridiculous. It's the hormones. I'm sure he didn't mean it."

"No one should talk to you like that." Her father's face turned cold as he looked to his wife. "Our daughter will not tolerate boorishness and disrespect from anyone, no matter how allegedly handsome he is. I don't care if he meant it or not. I'm going to call George Harcourt in the morning and give him a piece of my mind."

Cassandra frowned. "Victor, don't act rashly."

"Go for it, Dad. And while you're at it, tell him his knock-off Armani suits aren't fooling anybody," Vic said. "Even I think he looks cheap, and I don't have any style at all."

"Did he ever speak to you like that before?" Victoria hadn't expected this inquisition from her father, but then again, she rarely spoke to him about her personal life. He appeared genuinely bothered by this information, which almost affected Victoria enough to let her tears fall.

"Uh, no," Victoria replied. "To be honest, we didn't talk very much."

"I will speak to George in the morning, first thing. Disgusting behavior." As the waiter brought their food, her father held up his hand at the small plate he attempted to place in the center of the table. "Sorry, can you take the steak back, son? She's not going to eat it."

Victoria smiled weakly at her dad. Just behind him, Victoria caught sight of a familiar flash of curly black hair. A voice, raspy and lilting, pinged Victoria's brain. Directly diagonal from her seat—Leah. Her presence instinctively put a smile on Victoria's face, until she let her eyes wander across the table. With Leah, making her laugh, sat a girl Victoria didn't recognize. Certainly not someone from their school, a few years older at least. Dark hair and dark makeup, she looked like the white, goth version of Leah. Pretty, though, Victoria admitted reluctantly to herself. And clearly, she didn't have any issues making

Leah comfortable. The smile slipped from Victoria's face, and the extremely unpleasant combination of jealousy and anger settled on top of her stomach.

So busy staring at them and letting ugly emotions roil, Victoria didn't immediately notice Vic following her line of sight to the other table. But when the girl reached over and stroked Leah's hand, Victoria tore her eyes away and saw her brother raise his eyebrows in silent question. She stared down at her fajita, now the most unappetizing meal in existence, and tried hard to keep her attention at their table. But Leah's voice cut through the din, piercing the drone of her mother gossiping, and ran through Victoria's chest.

"Excuse me." Victoria tossed her napkin down on the table and rushed toward the bathrooms. Bypassing the marble sinks and high-end hand dryers, Victoria barged into a stall and locked the door. Perched on the edge of the toilet seat, she put her face in her palms and breathed through the obstruction of her fingers. It shouldn't hurt this much, she told herself. They were friends. Victoria was glad they were friends. Leah represented the only pure thing in her entire life. But when she'd kissed her, a hallway full of doors burst open in Victoria's heart. All this time, staring down the barrel of being Mrs. Carter Harcourt, or whatever well-bred son they wanted her to marry, and Leah threw it into doubt. Suddenly a different future opened— one where she was happy, loving the person she wanted to love.

In the midst of her lavatory existential crisis, Victoria heard voices from outside the bathroom. One, a man's voice, seemed to be agitated with the other, a woman. "Why are you creeping around the women's bathroom?"

What became obvious as Vic's voice sighed, exasperated. "I'm not creeping."

"Oh? Where you come from it's totally normal to stand outside a woman's bathroom and not say anything?" Victoria smiled. It was Leah.

"Jesus Christ, I was about to knock on the door when you barreled over here and started reading me the riot act like you caught me looking through a peephole!"

"Why are you creeping outside the women's bathroom?"

"I'm not creeping! My sister is in there."

"That's not creepy? I'm sure she can go to the bathroom without you. Unless she's, like, four or something."

"Can you just?" Victoria held back giggles as Vic grunted in frustration. "Wait, are you Leah? Leah Vasquez?"

Then, Victoria froze. "Ew, yes? Why do you know who I am?"

"You're friends with my sister, Victoria, right? And you left your date to come see if she's okay?" Vic asked, intentionally loud.

"Why are you shouting?"

"Sorry, sorry. Go ahead. I'm sure she'll feel *much better* after she talks to you."

Contemplating fratricide, Victoria hung her head. Leah obviously hadn't caught on, replying with a highly suspicious, "Um, okay?"

The door opened and closed and a pair of boots clopped across the tile floors. Leah must've hoisted herself onto a sink, as the boots levitated a few feet in the air. Leah didn't say anything, so Victoria felt compelled to break the silence first. "That was Vic."

Leah snickered. "Yeah, I know. He looks just like you. Did your dad even have anything to do with your conception? It's like your mom cloned herself."

"God, I hope that's not true." Sighing, Victoria leaned her head on the cool stall wall. "I'm okay. You can tell him I'm fine."

"Tell him yourself," Leah replied. "And are you okay? You stormed across the restaurant like you were about to barf."

"So, you came in here to what, listen to me barf?"

"Yeah, dingus, I wanted to hear you barf. I just can't get enough of listening to chicks barf." Hopping off the sink, Leah slapped her open palm on the stall door. "All right, then. If you're not barfing or taking a big poop, come out."

She swung the door open and glared at Leah with a full blush spread across her cheeks. "I am not 'taking a big poop.'"

"Victoria Lockwood never takes big poops," Leah mocked in an affected, 1940s-era Transatlantic accent. "She takes dainty, ladylike poops."

"Please stop saying poops."

She held her hands under the automatic faucet and soaked them in the rush of warm water. Leah observed quietly, her hazel eyes scrutinizing and narrowed. Victoria used the mirror to appraise Leah's outfit. She looked really nice, dressed in dark-wash flare-leg jeans and a slim, button-down shirt. Her hair was pulled back with only a headband keeping it away from her face, otherwise flowing freely. So simply and stupidly beautiful, Victoria wanted to cry.

"What happened? Did your mother say something out of line? God, why are the hot ones always so mean?"

Victoria flicked water from her hands at Leah's face. "I'm her clone, so am I hot and mean too?"

"No." A smirk curled on her painted lips. "You're not mean."

"Oh." Victoria stepped around Leah to stick her hands under the dryer. "Not as hot as your date, I guess."

Leah rolled her eyes and stood in between Victoria and the door. "That's how it's gonna be? I gotta say, green isn't your color."

"I'm not jealous," Victoria shot back, so unconvincingly she may as well have admitted to everything instead.

"No?" Victoria's train of thought left the station without her as Leah drew closer, eyes searching Victoria's face. Darting her tongue out to quickly moisten her lower lip, Leah's nearness nearly made Victoria pass out. "Don't play games with me, Tori."

"I don't even know how to play games," she replied, exasperated.

"Not being honest is playing games. But I'll lay it all out right now, okay? If you're not interested, I'll walk away. No harm, no foul, no hard feelings." Leah waited for a response, so Victoria nodded once. "I like you. I really like you. What's going on between us feels good, like we're onto something...big. I know you feel it too. Not because you kissed me, but because every time we're together it's like all the air leaves the room. I can't make that happen alone."

Victoria processed that information as best she could, fighting the shell shock paralyzing her muscles. "But...but then why did you get mad when I kissed you?"

Leah blinked and pulled backward, and Victoria ached all over at the sudden loss of her. Why did it feel like this? Why did it only feel okay with Leah close to her? Those little lines appeared between Leah's eyebrows and Victoria frowned. "Because you didn't mean it, and as far as I can tell, you don't know what the hell you want."

"Geez, I'm sorry I don't have a better handle on emotions I'm feeling for the first time." Leah didn't appear impressed by this answer and Victoria groaned in frustration. "You are...more than I expected and these feelings appeared practically overnight. In the car, you were so upset with me and I couldn't bear it. I needed you to know the weekend meant something to me. That I feel...something."

Somewhere in her ramble she'd landed on a sentiment that resonated with Leah, whose face ran the gamut of several emotions before she responded. "I can't do anything with 'something.'"

Victoria grabbed the lapels of Leah's shirt and shook her. "Jesus, fine, I like you too, okay? I like you so much I haven't thought about anything else but you in days. I've never liked someone like this before, ever."

"Really?" The lines between Leah's eyebrows smoothed, and the slightly hostile expression on her face melted into something like affection, or at least Victoria hoped. She was counting on Leah having a weakness for her. For her, not her date. For her, and for no one else. "You're not messing with me?"

"Leah, I would never. God, I—the reason I stormed in here was because I saw you on your date and I hated it. I hate seeing someone else make you laugh, or shooting fucking heart eyes at you across the table." She hadn't let go of the lapels of Leah's shirt and the instinct to draw her in grew stronger, like a rogue wave trying to keep from the shore. "Nobody has ever made me feel this way, like I'm not in control of my heart."

Leah's hands came up to cover her own, but she didn't remove them from her shirt. She skimmed the tops of her hands with her fingertips, tracing the bones of Victoria's wrists. Tenderly, Leah asked, "What do you want?"

Victoria's lungs constricted and her words came out in a rush. "Don't go home with her. Don't date her. Date me."

She detached her grip from Leah's shirt and smoothed out the wrinkled material. Though naturally she stood at least an inch or two taller than Leah, they were often the same height due to Leah's boots. But in her heels, she had height on her, and she gazed down into Leah's eyes, which simmered with heat before she spoke. "I wish we were not in a public bathroom because I would really, really like to kiss you."

Lost in what the moment could be, Victoria hadn't really given any thought to what it actually was. Two girls in the bathroom of a restaurant, standing close enough to kiss between the stalls and the sinks. "I wouldn't stop you."

Like she'd pulled a trigger, Leah's expression exploded in desire. "Jesus. Fuck, okay, well, I would like to do that but I…I've already been gone a suspiciously long time and Dana's probably going to think I ditched her."

"Maybe you should ditch her."

"C'mon. I know I'm from the other side of the tracks, but I do have some class," Leah replied, to which Victoria pouted. "Trust me, it's very hard to go back to her knowing there's, well, you."

"Oh, there's me. There's a…whole lot of me." Victoria grimaced at herself and took a step backward. "I get it. You should go. Just don't…"

"I won't. I'll see you soon."

"Okay."

Victoria watched her go, filled with a renewed sense of hope and lungs inflated with wistfulness. At the door, Leah stopped and sighed, loud and dramatic. "Fuck it."

Leah approached her with fast steps, took her face in her hands, and kissed her soundly and softly. She backed Victoria against the sinks and leaned into her, possessing all of Victoria's senses at once. Victoria didn't know where to put her hands, so she settled on Leah's hips, holding on to the top of her leather belt. It ground her to the world as Leah slid one hand around her neck and the other around her waist, keeping them pressed against one another as her tongue snaked into her mouth. Every hitched breath, every press of lips, every gentle meeting of tongues, verified Leah's claim. All the air really did feel like it had been taken from the room.

Her sole breath came in a short gasp and unlocked something feral in Leah—Victoria felt the change from soft affection to desire—and her only coherent thought was why she hadn't done this sooner. Leah bit her bottom lip, then licked across the small hurt. Victoria wrapped one leg around the back of Leah's knee and pulled them flush. A groan filled her mouth—whose groan, she didn't know—and Leah's hand gripped her thigh to keep her in place. Heavy arousal clouded her mind, and she would've sold her soul and half her family for Leah to drop to her knees. However, it was just as good for them to keep kissing, especially as Leah's lips pressed against the sensitive skin of her neck.

When Leah pulled back, her eyes were glazed and full of awe, and Victoria smiled shyly at her. Slightly out of breath, Leah stilled with her hands wrapped around Victoria. Despite the unfortunate reality of standing in a public bathroom, Victoria wanted to pause this moment and curl up inside of it.

"Of course you'd be a good kisser. You're so annoying." Despite her whine, Leah didn't appear to be suffering too much.

"Thank you?" Victoria faltered for a moment. "You're also...very good at kissing."

She plastered an infuriating smirk on her face. "I know."

Rolling her eyes at this arrogance, Victoria ran her fingers along the leather of Leah's belt. "Do you want me to give you space? O-or time? I know this all happened pretty fast."

"Ah, no. I know what I want." Her intense stare caught Victoria's breath in her throat. Leah knew what she wanted, and she wanted Victoria. The anticipation grew so strong it made her fingers hurt.

"Is it…it's me, right?"

"Yeah, dummy, it's you. But listen, I won't go back in the closet at school. If it's important to you that people don't know about us, then…there can't be an us."

Internally, Victoria panicked. She couldn't be out. She couldn't come out. She didn't even know if there was an out to come to. "You don't want to date me in secret? Steal me away during class and get up to sexy hijinks?"

"No," Leah replied, with a thud of finality. "I want to date you so loudly it rings in people's ears for miles."

Leah's words rendered her breathless and Victoria took a moment to collect herself. Feeling valued, feeling wanted without motive, heat grew behind her eyes as she fought to keep her feelings in check in front of Leah. "Would you wait for me until graduation? I won't ask you to go back in the closet, I would never. But if you could wait until summer, my mom usually gets off my back."

Leah released her waist in favor of tucking Victoria's hair behind her ear. She used her thumb to wipe smudged lipstick off Victoria's bottom lip. Tiny touches, tiny gestures of affection like seeds, bloomed inside Victoria's chest. "I can be patient. I understand you're overwhelmed. Despite how it looks, I'm overwhelmed too."

"You are?" To Victoria, Leah looked to be totally in control. An anchor of lesbian confidence.

"You're the prettiest, most popular girl in school, Tori. And I just kissed you in a bathroom. This is an insane turn of events in my world."

Victoria leaned down to kiss Leah once more. "You think I'm pretty."

"Yes, well, I've been blessed with eyeballs that work." Victoria bit Leah's lower lip for her sassy remark. "I can be patient, but we have to be careful for the next few weeks."

"Careful? Why?"

Leah ghosted her lips along Victoria's as she spoke. Each syllable tingled down Victoria's spine. "You think you can keep your hands off me for the twenty days until graduation? Twenty days, at minimum, until you can kiss me again?"

Her smile curling into a grin, Victoria tugged Leah by the belt loops and watched with glee as the desire flashed in her eyes. "I can be patient too."

"Yeah? Wanna bet?" Victoria waited for the proposition. For an only child, Leah was disproportionately competitive. However, Victoria had two brothers and a perpetually unimpressed family, so she met the challenge. "Ten bucks says you break first and kiss me before the twenty days are up."

"I'll take that bet. Shake on it?"

"We can do better than that." Leah captured her lips again, swallowing Victoria's gasp of surprise. When Leah's pliant, warm tongue slid into her mouth, Victoria had an epiphany. This was why kids liked to play Seven Minutes in Heaven. Seven minutes of this? Of this amazing kissing that turned her insides into marshmallows? Even if it was just Seven Seconds In This Public Bathroom, Victoria would've signed up immediately.

"Wait." Leah didn't move, and Victoria slid her hands up Leah's arms to grab the collar of her shirt. Leah's breaths came out long and soft as she waited for Victoria to speak. "When can I see you again? Are you busy next weekend?"

She put her hands over Victoria's wrists. "Why? Want to barge in on another date of mine?"

"I didn't barge. I'm here with my family." Victoria poked Leah in the shoulder with a petulant grunt. "I just thought we could hang out."

"I'm busy next weekend," she explained slowly. "My band is playing Benny's."

Eyes wide, Victoria lit up. Knowing Leah played music was cool enough, but seeing her play live would be an invaluable piece of Leah's inner world. An inner world to which Tori desperately wanted a key. "Your band! I forgot! Can I come watch?"

Victoria's heart warmed at the coyness on Leah's face. Making Leah Vasquez bashful ranked up there with making her flustered, in terms of Victoria's new favorite hobbies. "I can't stop you. It's a free country, in theory."

Toying with the hem of Leah's shirt, Victoria glanced up at her. "Do you want me there, Leah?"

"I...wouldn't mind," Leah replied, biting her bottom lip. Victoria envied her teeth, how they could bite that plush, crimson lip and she couldn't. "If you wanted to."

"I want to."

It only took a fond quirk of Leah's lips for Victoria to want to kiss her again. She might lose that bet.

"I'll see you then."

Aside from once with Leah, Victoria never had to sneak out of her house. The chances of her parents being home and interested in her whereabouts were slim to none. So, she had no qualms about walking out her front door past ten p.m. and driving across town to Benny's. Instead of taking her own car, with GHHS CLASS OF 2000 and Ron Jon Surf Shop stickers affixed to her bumper, Victoria took one of her father's nondescript cars to the restaurant to reduce the chance that someone she knew would see her car and try to find her. She checked her makeup in the rearview mirror and reapplied her lip gloss once more, rubbing it between her lips. She'd chosen the shortest skirt she owned and a pink striped polo T-shirt, as well as gleaming chunky white sneakers with tiny rhinestones on the side. Victoria didn't know if there was a dress code or the type of music they played, but she wanted to look hot. She wanted to look like someone Leah would want. All week at school, she'd worn slightly more risqué clothing than normal on the off chance she might attract Leah's attention. The wolf whistles from gross boys were tolerable only because when she did secretly catch Leah's eye, the yearning on Leah's face thrilled her from head to toe. This silly game of chicken they played at school extended to their nights, where Leah would instant message her and they'd chat well into the early morning. But it wasn't enough. Victoria needed Leah's undivided attention and touch, not just words and passing glances.

Which is how she found herself at a strip mall on a Saturday night. Leah's band could be heard from several storefronts away, heavy bass rattling the windows. Jake stood just outside the door, smoking a cigarette with his arm around a girl. He watched her approach with narrowed eyes, then grinned as he recognized her. "Tori, you came! I thought for sure Vasquez was gonna puss out and not invite you. Babe, this is Leah's girlfriend, Tori."

"Not her girlfriend," Victoria said, shaking the girl's hand.

Jake scoffed. "Not yet. I've never seen her make those googly eyes at anyone before."

"Well, you're missing your Not Girlfriend's concert," Jake's girlfriend said, snapping her gum. "They started like fifteen minutes ago."

"Oh, geez. I should get inside. Who do I pay the cover to?"

Laughing, Jake waved her in. "Leah covered you. And hey, uh, don't mind the groupies. They always come to LV's shows, but they're harmless."

"Groupies?" Victoria asked as she pushed the door open, wincing at the volume of music violating her eardrums. Any table not bolted to the floor now barricaded the windows, and the wide dining room area served as a packed dance floor. On a small, elevated stage where the four-piece band held everyone's attention, Victoria had no problem finding Leah. She stood in front, her bass guitar slung low around her hips, lips brushing the edge of the microphone as she sang.

She looked incredible. The same button-down shirt she'd worn on her date, now left open from the collar to just above her belly button, exposing her stomach and a bit of her bra. Ripped jeans fit snug, and a pair of high-top Converse stomped the carpet on the stage. Every inch a rock star, swinging between cool detachment and crowd engagement, hamming it up any time she saw a camera emerge from the throng of people near the stage. Victoria didn't dare try to get close, but instead swooned from the sidelines. Leah's voice remained as transcendent as Victoria remembered from middle school choir. No headband tonight to tame her hair, it flowed freely and whipped around her head as she sang, tossing sweat onto anyone within about three feet of the stage.

Leah stepped away from the mic to allow someone a guitar solo and Victoria watched her scan the audience as she rapidly plucked her bass. The swelling sea of concertgoers thrashed and bounced to the music but Victoria stood still, eyes locked with Leah's as she smiled, throwing Victoria a wink before sliding back up to her microphone. Her self-assured, seductive drawl captivated the audience and made Victoria lightheaded. She spotted the aforementioned groupies in the audience, nearly as besotted as Victoria with the swaggering lead singer.

The band sounded good, Victoria thought. Not so much punk as pop rock, somewhere between Letters to Cleo and Green Day, with catchy hooks and good lyrics. Victoria bopped along for the better part of an hour, as they never took a break and seamlessly segued from one song into the next. Her chest rumbled with each pound of the bass drum, each pluck of Leah's strings. Leah looked directly into her eyes as she sang, and Victoria's heart could barely stand it. Sometimes when she attended Carter's football games, he'd point her out in the crowd and people cheered. Victoria would wave and she knew she should feel something, maybe pride, but ultimately, their interactions left her hollow. Leah's looks, packed with meaning and unresolved tension, were different. They ignited her from below like a kettle about to scream.

The set concluded to clapping and whooping and Leah thanked the audience, her natural rasp strained by the vocalizing. House lights came back on and the band began to break down their instruments. Most of the audience filed out, but the groupies were harder to shake. A circle of girls, barely legal by Victoria's estimation, vied for

Leah's attention. Victoria watched Leah politely deter them, and Billy corralled the more compliant girls toward the exit. One girl, older than the others, stayed behind and started to stroke Leah's arm. For a moment Victoria considered jealousy, but the look on Leah's face was pure disinterest and discomfort.

When the girl trailed a fingertip down Leah's exposed abdomen, Victoria abruptly stood, walking over with confidence and sliding her arms around Leah's middle. "Hey, babe. Great show." Leah's head swiveled to her, surprised, and Victoria kissed her hard. Her altruism had an ulterior motive, but nobody needed to know that. Nobody needed to know how desperate every inch of her body was to touch Leah again. "You ready to motor?"

Poor Leah tried not to sputter, but did in fact stutter before replying, "Oh, uh, yeah, yes? Yeah. Just need to pack the bass."

The touchy girl with flaming red hair stepped back and glared at Victoria. "Oh. Didn't realize you're dating Preppy Barbie."

Victoria didn't let go of Leah, holding her tightly and straightening her back to appear taller. "Yeah, she is. Turns out she's not into, what do you call that, Extra Raggedy Ann?"

The girl sized Victoria up, then looked at Leah. "You could do better."

"Not with you," Victoria replied. She dismissed the girl with a "run along" gesture. "Why don't you run back to whatever drug store dye box you crawled out of?"

The girl flipped off Victoria and stalked toward the door, barreling past a confused Billy on her way out. Leah appeared impressed. "Whoa. Guess I was wrong. You are hot and mean. That was like the Valley Girl version of turning into The Hulk."

Victoria internalized the praise with a giddy thrill. Outwardly, she remained somewhat cool, and chuckled. "Are you into mean girls, Leah Vasquez?"

"No," Leah replied, grinning widely. "But you are."

"Please, you're not mean. You're grumpy, there's a difference."

"Oh, really?" Leah hadn't let go of her, and their torsos fit together seamlessly. The heat from Leah's body seeped into her clothes and Victoria would've dishonored any and all of her ancestors to remove the fabric between them. "I think most people would beg to differ."

"Most people haven't seen you in your cute little pajamas." Victoria leaned in closer. "Don't worry, I'll keep your secret."

Leah let go of Victoria to pack her bass into its soft-shell case. "Right. Thanks, *babe*."

Victoria blushed and put distance between them, finding a seat near the door to wait. After speaking briefly with Jake, Leah sauntered over. "Didn't take you for a groupie. Do you want an autograph?"

"Oh, gosh, would you?" she asked, her voice breathless. Victoria pulled her shirt to the side, exposing the top part of her breast above her bra cup. She batted her eyelashes for good measure. "Could you sign right here? I'm your biggest fan."

With a visible gulp, Leah's eyes wandered down, then respectfully shot back up. "You play dirty, Lockwood."

"You started it," she said, leaning against the cool window to escape some of the heat packed into the restaurant. "Coming out here, sweaty and half-naked. No wonder those girls can't keep their hands off you."

Leah glanced down at her open shirt, and Victoria's knees grew weak at the bashful smugness. "My cross to bear."

Victoria smacked her arm. "All right, hot stuff. What are your plans now? Big after-party?"

"For everyone else, but I have to get home. Early Mass and then a full day at the shop." Leah gestured toward the door and they walked through it together, with Leah's guitar bag bouncing against the side of her leg. "If we gig on a Friday I usually go, but not Saturdays. My folks would kill me if I missed church. And I would definitely miss church. Those parties are killer. One time I woke up on a swirly slide outside Barton Elementary at, like, four a.m. I don't know how I got there, because we found my car parked at the McDonald's on George Street."

"Oh my God, Leah. Those are miles apart!"

Leah shrugged. It never ceased to amaze Victoria how disparately two people from the same small town could live their lives. Planting her guitar on the ground in front of her car, Leah rested her forearm on it and in doing so, lifted one half of her shirt away from the other. The way it drew Victoria's eyes was nothing short of magnetic.

"My eyes are up here, Lockwood."

Embarrassed but indignant, Victoria's eyes scrolled upward. "Like you didn't wear this outfit to be ogled."

"I still can't believe you even want to ogle me." Perhaps because they were out in the open, humid summer air and not in the crowded restaurant, the adrenaline and its accompanying swagger rolled off Leah like steam, dissipating into the air. "I never thought in a million years you'd like me the same way."

"Neither did I." Then, her words caught Victoria's attention. "Wait. Are you...are you saying you liked me before all this? Before prom?"

"Crap." Gaze firmly planted on the ground, Leah struggled openly with her divulgence. "No?"

Victoria reached up, gently holding Leah's chin with two fingers and pulling her gaze up. "Leah? No games, remember?"

"I…" Huffing, Leah shook her fingers through her messy hair and let out a grunt of frustration. "I've had a crush on you since eighth grade."

Eighth grade, Victoria thought, astonished. A lifetime ago. Eighth grade passed as a blip in her memory. She had braces then, and hated them. Gawky and awkward, somewhere in between her girlhood and the throes of puberty. Hard to believe anyone would've liked her back then. "No way."

"Way." Rubbing the crease between her eyebrows, Leah appeared reluctant to elaborate, but thankfully went for it. "One day after gym class, I was in the locker room. I'd just finished getting changed and I didn't think anyone else was in there. I started singing because the acoustics were amazing. You walked out of the bathroom and looked at me, and you said, 'I love that song. You sound really good.' I've pretty much had a crush on you since then."

Victoria canted her head. "Why didn't you ever ask me out?"

"Are you kidding?"

"Do I look like I'm kidding?"

"For real? Okay, let's list the reasons. One, up until recently, you thought you were straight. Two, you've dated a parade of nauseating boyfriends since freshman year. Three, you have a ruthless social circle. Four, our tax brackets are light-years apart, and your mom would probably turn me away from your house with a hose." Leah faltered on the last one, blinking away. "And five, if you'd said no, it would've crushed me."

How heady to know she had power over someone like Leah Vasquez. She never considered herself a person who inspired deep feelings in others. "I wish you'd have let me make that decision for myself."

"When? How embarrassing for me to be like, 'Hey I know we barely know each other, but I have a big, gay crush on you because you were nice to me for ten seconds five years ago.'"

"Except that's exactly what happened."

"Yes, but telling you is more embarrassing than its existence as the truth," Leah shot back. "And after what happened to you at prom, I didn't want you to think I helped you out because I wanted something."

"But you did want something." Victoria gasped and slapped Leah on the shoulder. "I am your type! You lied!"

Leah snickered and relented. "Okay, that's fair. I didn't expect anything, though. I would've been okay being friends. But the truth, is I've liked you since we were thirteen."

Dare she hope? If hope was the thing with feathers, Victoria hoped it could withstand her tight fist grasping. She dug into her purse and withdrew her wallet. Sliding out a ten-dollar bill, she grabbed Leah's hand and slapped the money into it.

Leah peered down at her hand. "You don't owe me yet. I play fair, I won't count the rescue back there."

"It's not for that."

Victoria grabbed Leah by the face and kissed her. Pinning Leah against her car, she deepened their kiss immediately and forced Leah to steal air in between passionate embraces. She wondered, as her fingers tangled in the damp, warm locks of Leah's hair, if it would always feel like this. If kissing Leah would always feel like spinning on a teacup ride, exhilarated and dizzy, spiraling into oblivion. Could anyone else in the universe make her feel this way? Or did they simply belong, having exploded into stardust billions of years ago, only to coalesce right there, right at this moment, to be together again?

Starry-eyed as they broke apart, Victoria placed one hand on Leah's cheek, leaving the other in her hair, never looking away from Leah's awestruck gaze. She felt Leah slide the bill into the band of her skirt and wrap her hands around her back, stroking the base of her spine through her shirt. "Six days."

"Don't be smug." Victoria patted Leah's cheek in mock admonishment. "But thank God there's only fourteen more."

CHAPTER SEVEN

Since childhood, Leah treated happiness the way people treated the weather—out of her control, and mostly inconvenient. It couldn't be sought or bought, it either was or wasn't. Wake up, check the forecast. Will there be happiness? Who could tell? Not Leah, whose life pendulated between tragedy and pleasure. When joy came into her life, Leah cherished it but also held the conviction that maybe the universe owed her one.

Maybe that wasn't fair to God. The Bible wastes a lot of trees and ink on the idea of fairness, of overcoming adversity, of accepting your burden and knowing you never shoulder more than you can bear. However, the Bible was written by men in a desert who never had to stay late after school to scrub the word "dyke" off their locker. So, with all due respect to Big G, she had a debt to collect.

Victoria's affections could be interpreted as the universe seeing fit to throw her a single bone. Years of pining after her from afar, of shoving her feelings down deep because of the sheer improbability of Victoria Lockwood being even tangentially queer, years of watching boys like Carter hang all over her and ogle her during swim meets. Now, Victoria was hers to touch, to appreciate, to turn over in her mind like a warm nickel in her pocket. During the long days from her gig to graduation, they found ways to be together. Nothing particularly intimate—watching movies in Leah's room, Tori tagging along on deliveries or sitting on a tool chest in the shop and bantering with Hector, eating takeout on a park bench in another town—but the happiness Leah had in those hours couldn't be measured. They exchanged nothing more than looks or a casual hello at school, but even those fleeting moments filled her cup drop by drop. At home, her mother had strict rules about girlfriends. Leah's door had to stay open, and they could not stay past eleven p.m. She did her best to convince her mother Tori wasn't technically her girlfriend, but goody-goody Victoria insisted they obey her rule regardless. At the very least, it prepared them for what being under Loretta's roof as a couple might be like after graduation.

Graduation felt surreal as it approached. The plans made in abstract freshman year—she and Billy would walk together in the procession, party after—were nearly a reality. But before they could get to the arches, take their photos, and throw their caps, they had four more days of school left. The onset of summer already lengthened the days into never-ending, humid loops. Classrooms burst with noise and excitement, teachers having long given up on trying to control anxious seniors. Lunchtime, three periods stretched over about two hours, was particularly rowdy. Kids sat atop tables, hacky sacks bopped on the sides of skate shoes, and conversations bounced down the halls.

Leah stood in the hot lunch line behind a few obnoxious jocks, and in front of Victoria and her friends. Ahead of her stood Denny Douglas, loitering with his idiot friends near the cashier. As they held up the entire line, Leah churned, remembering his name as one of the people who claimed to have slept with Victoria. Finally, Gabby yelled at them. "Stop fucking around and pay, Douglas."

"Who was that? Gabby?" Denny peeked over the heads in line to spot Gabby, with her hand on her hip, glaring at him. "Why don't you do something useful and show us your tits?"

"Because you can't afford to see them and I don't do charity work," Gabby retorted. Leah hated her guts, but she respected a solid comeback game.

"Yeah, right. We know you sluts put out." Victoria shrank back. Leah felt her hands cramp as she gripped her tray. "Carter told everyone."

The lunchroom quieted down at this proclamation, presumably since most of the seniors sitting at the tables had attended prom as well. When she hazarded a glance back to Victoria, she saw tears well in her light brown eyes. Rage coiled in her stomach.

"Shut up, Denny," Victoria said, her voice quiet and furious.

"Poor Vicky. Did it hurt when Carter dumped your ass at prom?" He and his friends laughed, and the plastic of Leah's tray creaked in her grip. "I heard you blew a trucker for a ride home. That true?"

Unable to stand by any longer, Leah shoved Denny, hard, and his tray smashed into his chest, clattering to the floor. The tension in the cafeteria eased as a few kids snickered. Covered in mac and cheese and undercooked peas, Denny grew red in anger.

"What the fuck, Vasquez?"

Leah shrugged. "I tripped?"

Just as Denny opened his mouth and Leah squared up defensively, Coach Billings peeked into the cafeteria. "Douglas, clean up your mess." Denny tried to respond but the coach's booming voice clamped his mouth shut. "Now, Douglas. Or you and your buddies aren't walking at graduation."

Grumbling, Denny sank to his knees and pulled the strewn items onto a tray. "Fucking clumsy dyke."

Leah stomped her foot down on the dropped tray and glared at him. "What did you say? A little louder, Denny."

"Vasquez, I'm warning you. Leave Douglas alone to clean up his mess," Coach Billings said, adjusting his windbreaker over his portly belly.

Denny looked up. "I said you're a fucking clumsy dyke."

"Hmm, thought so." As their classmates watched on, stunned and amused, Leah reached over and grabbed a cup off the tray of the girl behind her. "Sorry, Riley. I owe you a Coke." She dumped the contents of Riley's drink on Denny's head. The lunchroom erupted into gasps and laughter, the combination of which appeared to infuriate Denny.

Fuming, he rose and snarled into Leah's face, all impotent rage and misdirected masculinity. Unmoved and unimpressed, she stared up into his enraged blue eyes with intentional disinterest. "The fuck is wrong with you? You think 'cause you're a girl I won't kick your ass? I'm a boxer. I could lay you out flat with one punch, bitch."

"That's it. Douglas, clean this up and report to the principal's office when you're done." The coach's patience for their teenage squabbling was clearly spent, if he ever had any at all. "Vasquez, with me. Principal's office, now."

She'd gladly accept the consequences of her actions, but you don't leave the ring before delivering the knockout punch.

"Sorry, Denny, my tray just slipped right out of my hands. Gosh, I don't think my fingers have been this wet since your girlfriend came all over them during the Just Say No assembly." With a low, humorless chuckle, Leah shook her head and aimed her gaze at him. "Hilarious, right? Because everyone is learning to 'just say no' but she just couldn't stop saying yes."

A chorus of gossipy *oohs* erupted from the cafeteria. Denny yelled, "Liar!"

"Ask her," Leah replied, leaning in to deliver her threat in a low voice. "Watch who you step to."

"Why don't you fuck off, Vasquez?"

"Why don't you ask your mom why you don't have a neck, Douglas?"

"Vasquez, enough." Coach Billings advanced toward them and Leah put her hands up in surrender, allowing herself to be escorted out of the lunchroom.

No stranger to detention, Leah picked her favorite seat by the window and settled in for the hour. After receiving a tired chastisement from the vice principal, she'd given Leah detention every afternoon until graduation. Not the worst punishment, as Denny got banned from walking at graduation for his part. Notebook out and headphones on, Leah sat back and doodled as the clock spun slowly.

"Mrs. Vauxhall?" Leah perked up from her meditative doodling and spotted Victoria timidly walking into the room.

"Miss Lockwood, what a surprise. You don't have detention, do you?" Mrs. Vauxhall asked with a teasing smile. Nobody could feasibly think Victoria Lockwood would get detention. Not the Garden Hills Poster Girl.

"No, I just need to speak with you." Briefly eyeing Leah, she approached the desk. "We're having fittings for cap and gowns, and the kids in the Honor Society are getting special ropes."

"Oh, that's lovely."

"It is," Victoria agreed with an enthusiastic nod. "Um, but unfortunately, they need the person to be there to size them. You don't want the strings to be too long or too short."

"Ah, and you need this penitent young woman, I presume?" They both looked at Leah, who saluted from her seat. "I suppose I can count today as time served."

"Thank you so much," Victoria replied in a fake voice she used for teachers. Leah heard it every time she gave her class council speeches. "I hoped you'd understand."

"Yes, very well. Run along, Miss Vasquez." She didn't need to be told twice. Leah gathered her things, shoved them in her backpack, and burst into the hallway with Victoria hot on her heels.

"Where are they doing the fitting?"

Victoria laughed, high and gentle. "There's no fitting for the strings. They're all the same size."

"Victoria Lockwood." Leah stopped short and spun on her heel. "Did you just sneak me out of detention?"

Victoria glanced up and down the empty hallway before backing Leah into a darkened classroom with one hand on her chest. She closed the door behind them, advancing toward Leah until she was backed against the teacher's desk. "You didn't have to do that to Denny. That no-neck idiot isn't worth detention."

"Fuck Denny Douglas. I'd take ten detentions just to tell him I fucked his girlfriend again."

The teasing smile on Victoria's face fell. "Wait, that's true? You and Katie Bauman?"

"Yeah." Victoria's face smoldered with jealousy. Leah watched her nostrils flare and her throat bob as she swallowed saliva, and the darkened classroom suddenly felt incredibly small. Only an inch or two taller, Victoria imposed upon her as she trapped Leah against the teacher's desk. "It was...just the once."

"Yeah?"

Victoria dropped her book bag to the floor and kissed Leah without warning. Evidently this was Victoria's new thing—backing Leah into kisses she couldn't deny and making her heart beat out of her chest. Her urgency and desperation flooded Leah's good sense, and she energetically accepted the drowning by way of passion. Victoria's hands met around her and she skimmed them across the small of her back. Her fingertips skirted under Leah's shirt, tracing her skin and Leah shuddered into their kiss hard enough to break them apart for a moment.

"How do you make me feel like this?" Victoria asked against her skin, kissing her cheek, her ear, and down along her jaw. "All of a sudden...I can't stay away from you."

Having been taken by surprise at Victoria's advance, Leah used the brief reprieve to switch their positions and pin Victoria to the desk. She reveled in Victoria's tiny gasp and kissed her again, hungrily, deeply, allowing everything else to fall away. Leah lost herself in the feel of Victoria's hands squeezing the top of her butt, the way she'd whine if Leah tugged on her hair, and the sweet chemical taste of her lip gloss. Her roaming touch drifted under Victoria's skirt just a few inches, caressing the soft flesh of her thigh. She growled into Victoria's ear. "These skirts drive me fucking crazy."

Victoria chased Leah's lips, taking the bottom one between her teeth and biting it softly. "Why do you think I wear them?"

When Leah opened her eyes, she stared right out of one of the windows into the eastern courtyard. While she didn't spot any students, it reminded Leah they were still, in fact, on school grounds. Regretfully, she pulled away. "Shit, Tori, wait. We can't do this here."

"Why not? School is almost out," she replied, pressing kisses down the side of Leah's neck. Each one robbed Leah of a bundle of neurons, but eventually her propriety won out.

Leah backed out of her reach, and Victoria pouted. To soothe the petulant look on her face, Leah took Victoria's hands in her own and kissed the knuckles. "Not here."

As if finally coming back to reality, Victoria blinked many times and smiled apologetically. "Sorry, I—I got carried away."

"Yeah, me too," Leah replied breathlessly. Victoria's lips, puffed up with rushing blood from their kiss, only made her want to kiss her more.

Humming, Victoria ran her fingers through Leah's curls and nodded, giving her one final kiss. "Nobody's ever defended my honor before. It was incredibly sweet, even if it did include finding out some unfortunate information about you and Katie."

"It was nothing. I'll always have your back, Tori," Leah replied, leaning into Victoria's hand cupping her cheek. "But next time, I'll try not to name-drop a girl I fucked in a closet."

Victoria's eyes bulged. "There are more?"

Glancing up at the clock behind Victoria's head, Leah bent down to grab her bag and hurried toward the door. "Geez, look at the time. I really got to get to work."

"Leah Vasquez, you get back here right now."

"Sorry, gotta go!" Leah opened the door and waved from the hallway. "Talk to you later!"

Fiddling with her honor cords, Leah waited in the sultry heat for her and Billy's chance to walk in the processional. The grass on the football field wilted in the heat, further flattened by the feet of graduates walking in pairs toward the rows of folding chairs on the forty-yard line. Billy looked like a giant next to her and used his exceptional height to swivel around and find his girlfriend in the line of waiting graduates. Tall and objectively handsome, Billy had punched above his fighting weight and landed Jenna, a popular girl tangentially friends with Victoria. That kind of rise in status could make a lesser boy turn into a jerk, but Billy remained the same affable, dopey boy who lived next door.

A few pairs ahead of them, Victoria walked alongside Riley, the two friends speaking quietly to one another as they waved to their parents in the crowd. Leah sought out the Lockwoods, attempting to differentiate them from the other white families packed in the bleachers. She found Vic first, pumping his fist for Victoria, and then Victoria's little brother, poor Durward, imitating Vic. Her mother, the hot and mean Mrs. Lockwood, stared down at her phone. No sign of her dad, Leah thought, as the families on either side of them were clearly unrelated. What a dick. Leah would've bet he attended Victor Junior's graduation.

Billy nudged her. "So, Lockwood, huh?"

"What about her?" Leah asked, not looking over.

Nudged harder, Leah finally glanced up into his puppy-dog eyes. "I saw her chase that chick away at the gig. Plus, our houses are like three feet apart. I've seen her by your place every weekend for a month."

"I need to build a fence."

Mr. Brannon, a pudgy, red-faced teacher in the English department, anxiously signaled them to walk. Billy confidently strode through the grass several paces before realizing Leah had not budged. Mr. Brannon frantically waved at her. "Miss Vasquez, let's go. Let's graduate before we die of heat stroke."

Leah caught up to Billy, who slowed down his long gait so they could walk in tandem. "Just...keep it down, okay? It's a little complicated right now and she doesn't want anyone at school to know. Or her parents. Who, I assume because they're rich and white, are probably homophobic and racist?"

Billy nodded, his brown hair bouncing and falling into his eyes. Sweeping it under his cap, he smiled. "You must really like her."

"I do?"

"Yeah, to put up with all that? When I told you Jenna's parents didn't like me 'cause I'm poor, you told me to dump her and egg her house." Leah had forgotten about that, but it did sound like a suggestion she'd make. "It's not a bad thing to take your time. Not everybody can be a badass like you. Fully out, fuck the haters, gay as fuck."

They paused at the arches, smiling for their sets of parents in the audience. Leah found her parents easily, seated directly next to Billy's mom, waving ecstatically. She waved back, and she and Billy continued their journey to their seats. "I guess so. She's...she's really cool. I like her a lot."

"Hey, I'm all for it. Vicky Lockwood is really nice, not to mention super cute and hella smart."

Leah adjusted the gown so she didn't drag the grass as she took her seat. "Speaking of super cute and hella smart, how is it going with Jenna?"

"Real good," Billy replied, a dumb smile on his face. "Sometimes I get sad 'cause I think about how much smarter than me she is. It's like…she's not gonna want to be with such a dummy. Not after she meets smart, suave college dudes."

Leah frowned. Billy's intelligence lay rooted firmly in the social and emotional, but he'd never been insecure about not being traditionally smart. Jenna, like Victoria and Riley, came as one of those gifted rich kid packages, bundled with good looks, intelligence, and money, and sent off to a university Billy couldn't even name, never mind attend. "She'd be an idiot to trade you out for some preppy brain at UNC. Plus, she's crazy about you, dude. It's gonna take way more than a kid with a good report card to steal her away from you."

He nodded, clearly trying to absorb her confidence about it. "Yeah?"

"For sure. If she breaks up with you, I'll kick her ass. And egg her house."

Billy swung his arm over her shoulder and gave her a side hug. "What am I gonna do when you go to MIT? Are you even coming back over breaks?"

"If I can't find a job in Massachusetts," Leah replied. "And if my dad is okay at the shop. He said he will be. I'd just…" Leah gave a disparaging look at their high school campus. "You know I don't wanna end up here my whole life."

"I know. You got big dreams, bigger than all these dumb mountains can hold. I love it here, though." Billy inhaled a deep breath, as if appreciating the sticky and hot Garden Hills air. "This town's too small for Leonora Renata Vasquez."

"Call me that one more time, William Barnabas Reade."

He winced. "Ouch."

Billy eagerly tried to find his paramour in the sea of their graduating class, and Leah smiled at him, unnoticed. All things considered, he had to be her best friend. They didn't have a typical friendship. They didn't do long talks and pinky swears. Their friendship was Billy giving her the courage to come out to her parents, and Leah sharing her bed with him when Billy's dad came home drunk. They didn't plumb the depths of each other's hopes and dreams, but they shared a bond being two outcasts in a hometown that never felt like home.

The great irony of Garden Hills was, as a garden, it sucked. It confined and didn't nourish and nothing could grow, nothing that wasn't specifically designed for it. Leah wanted to put down roots and expand, reach deep into the soil and soak in. She could never do that here. Despite her best efforts to the contrary, Billy reminded her there were a few good things about this place. There wouldn't be any Billys at MIT. There would be smart kids, rich kids, but no Billy. No goofy, guileless boys to make the tough days a little better.

"I'll probably come back in the summer," she said, out of the blue. She hadn't planned on it. "My dad can always use the help. Besides, we're two flowers in the same pot, right?"

Billy smiled. "Buds for life."

Leah never attended a high school graduation before, but she was sure hers ranked as the most boring of all time. Administrator after administrator droning from prepared statements in front of a lectern until she nearly fell asleep in her folding chair. Most of the speeches sucked, but Leah tuned in for Fatima's valedictorian speech. With their grade point averages identical, Leah graciously and without hesitation let Fatima be valedictorian. That mattered to Fatima and her strict parents; Leah just wanted to get the hell out.

Near last alphabetically, Leah sat in the heat and waited patiently as the principal called up each student from a list on the podium. The jocks—the annoying ones on the football team—insisted on having their team nicknames announced as well, perpetuating an already ponderous process. Leah spied Carter waiting at the base of the steps to be called next and finally tuned in.

"Vanessa Gorofolo." Pause for applause. Leah smirked. "Carter 'Small Dick' Barfcourt." Carter, mid-jump-for-joy, landed on the stage with a thump to the raucous laughter of their graduating class. Their flustered principal did a double take at the roll call sheet, dabbing his forehead with his tie. "Not funny. Whoever adjusted the roll call sheet, I will find you. Sorry, Mr. Harcourt. Please, step forward for your diploma. Carter Barf—I mean, Harcourt, congratulations."

Beside her, Billy dissolved into tearful laughter, clutching his stomach. Though she could feel a particular set of eyes on her, Leah kept her gaze forward and watched Carter dejectedly make his way across the stage. Eventually, the principal calmed them down and sputtered another vague threat about finding out who did it, but he'd lost the crowd and appeared to give up as he hurried through the rest of the names. They threw their caps in the air and hugged to the sound of graduation processional music. Leah broke away from Billy to find her family on the field.

Her father hugged her tightly, lifting her off the ground and spinning her in the air. "¡*Felicidades, mija!* We are so proud of you."

Kissing them both on their cheeks, her mother rattled the disposable camera in their faces. "Okay, time for photos. One of just Leah. Then one of Leah with her *papi*, then one of Leah and me, then one of all of us." She rolled her eyes, but Leah entertained their excessive photo-taking. Her *abuelos* loved to receive photos of her, and it would no doubt go on the braggy Vasquez Christmas Card they'd send to her father's cousins. Plus, as their only child, they'd never do this again and Leah understood its importance.

Once they'd taken nearly the entire roll of photos, including just one of her and Billy, her father stood on his tiptoes and looked around at the football field full of families. "Where is Tori? Doesn't she want a picture?"

"Oh, no, she's got her friends to take photos with," Leah replied easily.

Her father took this with a nod, but her mother narrowed her eyes in scrutiny. "She's not one of your friends?"

"Are you kidding? Tori is really popular." She put as much confidence in her tone as she could, as if this would shut the issue down. They didn't possess some delusional notion that Leah was popular, or even well-liked, but they also didn't understand the fragility of the high school ecosystem. Leah was like an outdoor cat, disrupting the local wildlife of preppies and jocks with her invasive presence and snapping jaws. "I don't want to get into it."

Her mother took Leah into a hug she returned tightly. "Okay, baby. Now go on. Curfew is waived, tonight only. Just call and tell me where you'll be. And don't drive drunk."

"Promise. Love you."

"Love you too, baby. Be good." Her mother dropped a kiss on her forehead, while her father again wrapped her in an excruciating bear hug. Once released, she jogged across the grass toward Fatima and their chess team. Their excited chatter bounced all over the place but eventually settled on discussing the party at Fatima's house.

Passing around a flask, Fatima handed it to Leah and smiled brightly. "Are you coming to my party tonight? All the honor kids are invited, plus the chess team and the robotics team."

"Sounds like a rager," Leah replied drolly.

"My parents won't be home." Fatima raised both eyebrows and Leah gave her an impressed nod. Though her mother eliminated curfew, Leah hadn't committed to attending any after-grad parties.

Billy's girlfriend, Jenna, invited them to her house, but Leah knew popular kids would go to that one. Victoria would go to that one. "Door's open if you want to come."

"'Kay. Thanks, Fatima."

Leah navigated around the exterior of Garden Hills High one last time, her sneakers skipping across the gravel toward her usual parking spot near the back of the lot. Gazing upon the red brick of her school, Leah took off her cap and gown and chucked them in her trunk alongside her diploma. Would she miss walking those halls? The intrusive ring of the bell every forty-five minutes? The bustle of kids going to and from class, frantically searching their lockers or leisurely leaning against the cool metal? Maybe, but college sounded like a dream. A bunch of like-minded people from all over the country, even the world, coming together to learn engineering. Learning the streets of Cambridge, just over the bridge from Boston. No longer would her life be confined to the geography of her stupid hometown.

She stretched, the fabric of her tank top riding up her stomach. They'd been instructed to wear formal clothes beneath their cap and gown, but once Leah realized nobody would check, she opted for her tank top, ripped black jean shorts, and trusty Converse sneakers.

Other graduates filled the lot, hollering to their friends and families as they left in different directions. Some Leah would probably never see again. If she never had to see Denny Douglas or his stupid big head ever again, it would be too soon. Never mind Carter Harcourt and his smarmy grin. Billy intended on staying in Garden Hills, maybe be a contractor with his ne'er-do-well dad, so she'd keep in touch with him. But just about everyone else could fall off the planet and Leah wouldn't miss them in her orbit.

As she considered Fatima's offer of a party, a familiar face bounded toward her from around the building. Leah leaned back against her car and put her foot up as she waited.

"Hey."

Breathless, Victoria beamed at her. "Hey. Fatima just told me about the honors party tonight. Are you going?"

"*You're* going to the honors party?"

"Yes? I am on the honor roll, Vasquez." She put her hand on her hip and Leah rolled her eyes at the impertinence.

"I'm well aware. I didn't think it would be your scene."

With a sigh, Victoria crossed her arms over her chest and ducked her gaze. "Yeah, so, I'm thinking maybe it's time for me to get a new scene."

"Is that right?" Leah asked, raising an eyebrow. "They won't miss you at Jenna's?"

"Only Riley will care if I'm gone, so she's coming too."

Leah deflated. "Uh-huh. You want to get drunk with me and stay a platonic distance apart? No thanks."

Pouting, Victoria prodded Leah's shoulder with two fingers. "C'mon. Riley won't stay late anyway, and she won't care about us hanging out."

"As friends," Leah clarified. "You really want me at this party? Because I know for a fact I can hold my liquor, and I know for a fact I can keep away from you. But I don't think you can do either."

"You think you're irresistible, do you, Vasquez?"

"I don't think that about me. You think that about me, Tori." Leah rolled the 'r' in her name just to see the arousal flash in Victoria's eyes.

"Just come, okay? I'll see you tonight."

"I'll think about it."

But she didn't have to think about it.

Around ten that night she waited outside Fatima's house, one hand in her pocket and the other one holding tequila. While she kept her Converse and shorts, she'd switched her tank top for a loose, short-sleeved button-down. Fatima's family had a lot of money, maybe from jewelry or something, and it showed in their professionally landscaped lawn and heavily ornate door. It was like the entrance to the Beast's castle in *Beauty and the Beast*, all big golden hardware and polished wood. Skipping the ridiculous lion's head knocker, Leah pressed the bell and waited.

"Leah!" Fatima exclaimed as she opened the door, smiling ear to ear. "I'm so glad you came. Come in. Oh God, is that tequila?"

Entering the cavernous foyer, Leah let the obvious packaging answer Fatima's question. "It's the only thing I can smuggle from my dad's liquor cabinet he won't know went missing—he'll think he drank it."

"Right on, okay. Well, the party is in the backyard mostly. Everyone's been drinking since we left graduation, so people are pretty—"

"Leah!" Again, someone happily shouted her name. Victoria had also changed outfits, and it short-circuited Leah's poor, gay brain. Jean short-shorts with a Minnie Mouse patch on them, a lacy white tank top, and a yellow and green flannel tied around her waist. Visibly drunk, her eyes glassy and gait less graceful than usual, she approached Leah with a smirk. "I knew you'd come."

"I didn't think either of you would come." Fatima glanced between them, narrowing her eyes in what Leah took as light suspicion. "I figured Leah would skip the parties, and you'd be with your friends at Jenna's."

"Ew, with Carter Barfcourt?" Victoria tilted her head back and guffawed, then clamped her hand on Fatima's shoulder. "Here's the thing, Fatima. Most of my friends suck. And you, and Leah Vasquez, and Riley—where is Riley? I lost her. Anyway—" Victoria hiccuped. "You guys don't suck. And I wanna be around people who don't suck. Unless...do you think I suck?"

"Nobody thinks you suck, Victoria." Leah rolled her eyes as Victoria detached from Fatima and dramatically slung herself around Leah's shoulders. "You good?"

"I'm great. I'm finally free of that prison and I'm ready to party. Are you ready to party, Leah Vasquez?"

Fatima opened the tequila and wordlessly handed it to Leah. Taking a few painful gulps, Leah exhaled sharply and nodded. "Yeah, I'm ready to party."

She was not, in fact, ready to party.

By midnight, more classmates caught wind of the honors party and Fatima graciously let them crash. Music pumped from speakers both inside and outside the house, with a couple of kids having shucked off their tops and bottoms to swim in their skivvies. Victoria, however, hadn't left Leah's side all night, spending most of her time with a drink in one hand and the other arm wrapped around the back of Leah's shoulders. Not that Leah minded the proximity, but the possessive and needy clinginess caught her by surprise. She, Riley, and Victoria sat near Fatima's pool, watching a few kids race each other from one end to the other.

Victoria heckled them from the lounge chair. "You guys are so slow."

"Put your money where your mouth is, Lockwood," one of them challenged from the water. "Twenty bucks says I beat you."

"Make it fifty," Victoria shot back, already up and removing her shirt. Instead of handing it to anyone she draped it over Leah's shoulder and kicked off her shoes. She tied back her hair with the scrunchie from her wrist. "I'll race you both. Fifty each. If I lose, I'll give you both a hundred bucks each."

Never having seen Victoria in this state of undress, just a bra and her jean shorts, Leah accidentally crushed the red Solo cup in her hand. Her eyes flitted like Plinko to each exposed bit of skin and the modelesque smattering of freckles and moles speckled across like flicked ink. As Victoria negotiated the terms of the agreement, Leah drank the small amount of alcohol remaining in her cracked cup and placed it on the concrete patio.

"She's very competitive," Riley said softly from her side.

Glancing over, Leah laughed. "She do this a lot?"

Riley appeared surprised by the attention and blushed, blinking her wide doe eyes. Under normal circumstances Riley wouldn't speak to her at all, but judging by the strong scent of liquor from her cup, she had found some liquid courage. "My birthday was last week, and somebody brought up how fast they could eat a slice of cake and she insisted she could win that too."

"Did she?"

"No," Riley replied, chuckling. "She lost badly and got mad about it."

"Damn." The competitors dove into the pool and it quickly became apparent the challengers had gotten in too deep, so to speak. "Happy belated birthday, by the way."

"Thanks. When's yours?"

Leah tore her eyes away from Victoria's swimming and raised an eyebrow. "My birthday? November first."

"Ah. Scorpio. Suits you." They watched Victoria swindle the others into a double-or-nothing bet and Riley sighed. "Do you want to get new drinks? Looks like she's gonna be a while."

Though taken aback by Riley's boldness, Leah nodded and helped her up from the low-slung lounge chair. They weaved in and out of classmates toward the makeshift bar just outside the home: three kegs and assorted liquor and soda bottles along with a ridiculous number of plastic cups stacked on a gray folding table. "What do you like to drink?"

Riley looked stricken. "Oh, I don't know. I just…drink whatever, I guess." She scanned the table of liquor bottles and pointed to the gin. "I liked that one. It was really strong on its own, though."

"You drank gin straight? Damn, Myers. I'm impressed. Disgusted, but also impressed."

Riley blushed furiously. "I didn't know what it was. I liked the man on the label with his fancy little hat. Why, how am I supposed to drink it?"

"Come." She grabbed the gin in one hand and Riley with the other, escorting her into the house proper. Surely a rich family like the Singhs had a liquor cabinet somewhere. With Riley tagging along behind her by the hand, she led them into a game room where Leah finally spotted the prize. "Here we go."

She opened the cabinet doors and nabbed vermouth. Mixing it with the gin in unscientific amounts, she garnished it with an olive and presented the makeshift martini to Riley. "Martini. A little vermouth and some gin. Sometimes they add bitters or whatever but, we make do with what we have."

Riley took the drink with big, wide blue eyes. Every one of Victoria's popular friends was pretty in their own way. Even Gabby. Riley was no exception, with aquamarine eyes and fair skin. Taller than Leah—though most people were—and athletic from her years on both the lacrosse team and the school's soccer team. Mixing her own drink, Leah watched as Riley tentatively sipped from the cup. It took a moment to settle, but then she smiled. "This is really good."

"Hey, there you go. Maybe that'll be your signature drink." She raised her beverage and touched their cups together in cheers. "*Salud.*"

In the relative quiet away from the majority of the partygoers, Leah sat on the edge of the pool table and nursed her drink. The distraction from Victoria helped clear her mind, even as the alcohol continued to blur her good sense. Riley approached, staring down at her cup. "You know, I…I always wanted to tell you how much I liked the posters in your locker. You listen to cool bands."

When Leah lifted her gaze, a layer of Riley's shy girl persona had peeled away. Her eyes were open, expressive, and somehow deeply knowing. "Oh, yeah? Which ones?"

"I'd never heard of The Cardigans but I ended up really liking them," Riley said, hopping up on the pool table to sit on the green felt. "I bought the *Romeo and Juliet* soundtrack because a couple of the bands you liked were on it."

"Wait, you'd never heard 'Lovefool' before?" Riley shook her head. "That's incredible, that song was everywhere a few years ago." She idly sang a couple lines of the chorus and Riley watched her with rapt attention. As her voice trailed off, Riley took a long, purposeful swig of her martini and the nervous energy she normally radiated returned in smaller vibrations. "Not my favorite off the *Romeo and Juliet* soundtrack, though. I like 'Kissing You.'"

Riley spit out some of her drink, coating Leah's leg in warm vermouth and gin. "Oh my God, I'm so sorry."

Leah grabbed a napkin from the liquor cabinet and wiped her leg, laughing at Riley's horrified expression. "Chill out, Myers. I mean, it's not my preferred way for a girl to get me wet, but it's not the worst."

"I thought it would take me longer than five minutes to act like an idiot," Riley mumbled as Leah returned to the pool table and sat with her leg pulled up and brushing Riley's own. "If it wasn't obvious…I'm intimidated by you."

"I got that impression, but I don't know why. I'm really not that bad, you know."

"No, no, it's not you. You're not—not bad, you're good. I'm just—" Riley sighed like the entire world rested on her shoulders. Intrigued by what caused this sudden weariness, Leah reached over and cupped Riley's knee. Riley looked down at the point of contact, then back up into Leah's eyes. "I'm not afraid of you, I'm afraid of how comfortable with yourself you are. Like, your confidence is contagious, and I'm afraid of what would happen to me if I caught it."

Leah wished she was less drunk. Trying to will sobriety into her bloodstream, she put down her drink and scooted closer to Riley. People didn't often confide in her and she didn't know how to continue. So, she went with honesty, because that's what she did best. "What would happen is you'd be more yourself, but sometimes being totally who you are, you lose the people in your life who only liked a part of you. And for real, dude? That's not the worst outcome. Anyone who doesn't like you—all of you—isn't worth your time."

"You're just being nice."

"Fuck no I'm not. You know me, I'm never nice. I'm honest. We don't know each other well, but I know you're a good person. You're smart, you're hot, and you have every reason to say fuck it and be yourself. And once you do, and you unlock Riley 2.0 or whatever, somebody like me isn't going to intimidate you at all. You'll walk into a room and people are just gonna—" Leah dramatically fell back onto the pool table, as if flattened by Riley's mere presence. "You'll floor 'em, Myers."

Giggling, Riley reclined on her side and propped her head up on her elbow, her entire neck and cheeks flushed from alcohol and intense blushing. It was kinda cute, Leah admitted to herself. "I can't imagine a world where you walk into a room and I don't turn into a massive dork."

"I never said you wouldn't be a dork. The Lord works in mysterious ways, but miracles are pretty hard to come by." They dissolved into laughter together, with Riley poking Leah in her stomach in retaliation. As their laughter died down, the look on Riley's face turned peculiar, and Leah couldn't identify the emotion. Riley opened her mouth to say something but the door to the game room opened, letting in not only whoever interrupted them, but a big influx of music and noise. Abruptly sitting up, Leah watched Victoria pad into the room on bare feet with a drink in her hand. Someone had given her a towel, which draped over her shoulders. Her hair, down out of its scrunchie, cascaded in ringlets around her face.

"Hey, Vicky," Riley greeted in an inebriated slur. "Did you win your races?"

"I did." Victoria advanced on them, surveying the scene she'd come across with her almost girlfriend and her best friend lying together on a pool table. Leah wanted to laugh.

"I've never seen someone be a literal pool shark before," Leah replied, and Riley burst into giggles. Both she and Victoria looked at her in surprise, but only Leah smiled. Victoria's face grew dark.

The dip in the pool hadn't sobered Victoria, not to mention the drink she downed as they spoke. Three hot chicks in one room and Leah suddenly wondered what the statistical likelihood was that they'd both want to sleep with her.

"What're you doing in here?"

"Riley drinks like an amateur, so I crashed Fatima's liquor cabinet to help her out. Turns out your girl likes a martini. Probably something in those preppie north Garden Hill genes."

By the look on Victoria's face, the likelihood of the threesome dropped to below zero. Despite Riley being her best friend, and straight as far as Leah knew, jealousy flared in Victoria's eyes. Victoria scrutinized them, but it appeared only Leah understood they were being analyzed. "Uh-huh. Well, people are pretty much leaving. Courtney is a designated driver and offered to take people home."

Riley slid off the pool table, wobbling on her feet as she set the cup down. "Oh, I should take her up on that. I can come back for my car tomorrow."

"Good idea," Victoria replied, but the ice in her tone slid right past Riley.

Throwing her arms around Victoria's shoulders, Riley hugged her friend tightly and swayed them back and forth. "I'll call you tomorrow, okay?"

From over Riley's shoulder, the look on Victoria's face softened into reluctant affection and she hugged her back. "Okay. Get home safe, Ry."

Riley pivoted and took a step toward Leah, then stopped. "I feel like maybe you're not big on hugs."

"That would be a good guess," Leah replied. "But the sentiment is noted and returned. I'll see you around, Myers."

"See you, Leah." Her gentle tone brought back the stern angles on Victoria's face, though Riley didn't appear to notice as she hurried out the door in search of her ride home.

"Fuck, I either need way more liquor or way less," Leah said, hopping off the table and rubbing her temples. "I'll slow down, I can't be driving drunk. You good?"

Victoria didn't say anything at first. She only approached on slow feet, deliberately pinning Leah against the edge of the pool table. Everything about her smoldered. Leah wouldn't have been surprised to see steam rise from her body. "Come upstairs with me."

Leah cocked an eyebrow. "Why?"

Victoria didn't explain, and Leah let herself be dragged upstairs to Fatima's second story, where a loft area led into a few bedrooms and bathrooms. She opened a door, revealing two of their classmates making out in a rather large bedroom. They broke apart, panting and shocked. "Oops! Sorry, boys, don't mind us."

They found the next free bedroom, and Victoria closed the door behind them. "Do you have a thing for Riley?"

So that's where this was going. Leah crossed her arms. "Define 'thing.'"

Victoria's eyes blazed. "You know what I mean."

"Do I? Are you asking me if I want to fuck Riley Myers?" Leah met Victoria's deliberate steps with ones of her own. They stood at an impasse in the middle of the room. "Or are you asking me if I like her? Or if I like-like her?" Leah asked in a mocking tone.

"Don't be an asshole."

"Don't ask me asshole questions."

Brown eyes bored into her, digging for the honesty Leah always kept right at the surface, and Victoria stalked toward her. "I just want to know."

"You already know."

Victoria took another step closer. "So, say it."

"Say what?"

With Victoria's hazy gaze dipping to her lips, anticipation prickled across Leah's skin. In the time it took Leah to blink, Victoria pushed her flat onto the bed and straddled her waist. Her kiss was hard and urgent, tasting of tequila and rum, and Leah's head swam as if she could drink the liquor right from her tongue. None of her fantasies between eighth grade and now could've prepared her for the real thing—the real taste of Victoria, the real sound of her intakes of breath, the real feel of her skin—it blew Leah's imagination away. Victoria grabbed

Leah's hands from where she'd placed them on her hips and entwined their fingers, pinning both of Leah's hands above her head.

"Say it, Leah," Victoria warned in a lilting voice directly into her ear.

Leah lost all resistance. "I don't want her."

"Good." Victoria kissed a line down the side of her neck. Her lips and tongue prodded the soft flesh until she bit hard and Leah's hips bucked at the twin sensations of pleasure and pain.

Leah allowed Victoria to finish her work on the hickey before rolling her onto her back. Victoria took hold of her shirt, bunching the material and tugging Leah farther on top of her. This dominant, desperate move combined with Victoria's sweet, surprised little gasps, caused a sudden wave of helplessness to crash over Leah. Slowing down with shorter, more chaste kisses, Leah pulled back to look at Victoria's face. Flushed, smiling, pupils dilated, lips puffy. The want and awe sparkling in her light oak eyes sent Leah's stomach tumbling. She possessed no defense against the concurrent onslaught of Victoria's innocence and passion.

"You're going to ruin me." It was the helplessness talking, but it felt truer than math to Leah in the moment. Pythagoras could only have wished his theorem to be as true as Victoria Lockwood equaling the demise of Leah Vasquez.

Victoria looked at her strangely, searching Leah's face as if deciphering a map. She didn't understand, and of course she didn't. Victoria was sweet, kind, lovely, and all the things Leah could've ever wanted in a girlfriend. But of the truthiest truths of the universe, one truth loomed larger than all: girls like Victoria didn't spend their lives with girls like Leah. There would be an end, and it would hurt. The only unknown was by what degree.

Nipping her jaw and her throat, Victoria's hands came to her jeans and popped open the button.

"Wait, wait, Tori. Stop."

"What?" Victoria pulled back only a touch, slowly inching Leah's zipper down. "We graduated, right? So, we can do this now."

Leah nabbed both Victoria's hands and stilled them between her own. "It's not that we can't. It's that we shouldn't."

"Why not? You don't want to…you don't want to have sex with me?" Victoria asked, bewildered.

The size of the absurdity of her question could've been seen from space. "It's not about want. It's about consent. You're drunk."

Surprisingly, tears sprang into Victoria's eyes and panic gripped Leah's heart. "You don't…you don't even like me that way, do you?"

"What? Slow down, dude. You're spiraling."

"How could you?" One palm on each of Leah's shoulders, Victoria shoved her over and Leah landed on her back with an *oof*. Victoria got to her feet and spun, aiming her inebriated ire at Leah. "How could you? You're just like them, aren't you? Like—like Carter and all of them."

The blunt edges of Leah's fingers dug into her palms in restrained anger. "Are you fucking kidding me? You're gonna compare me to Carter Harcourt because I won't take advantage of you? Geez, sorry, Victoria. Why don't you lay down and I'll dry hump you with my little dick and then tell everyone you're a slut, hmm?"

"Like you're any better? You'll finger Katie Bauman in the fucking janitor's closet but you won't touch me?" Leah stood up and buttoned her pants, ready to dig into whatever stupid fight this was about to be. "Is it because I'm a virgin? Want me to get my belly button pierced like her and wear that stupid dangly piercing? You know she *cried* when they pierced her?"

"Look, you're drunk, you don't know what you're saying."

"Don't patronize me," Victoria replied, jamming her finger into Leah's chest with every syllable.

Leah swatted her finger away. "Don't compare me to Carter fucking Harcourt."

Face flushed in anger, in embarrassment, and definitely from the alcohol, Victoria fumed. "No, you're right, you're nothing like him. You're worse."

Leah bent over, as if Victoria had physically knocked the wind out of her. She didn't leave time to retort as Victoria bolted out the door like a spooked horse, and Leah heard the front door slam before she could even move out of the bedroom. Dazed, she slowly crept down the stairs, finding Fatima at the foot of them, staring up at her with raised eyebrows.

"You two okay?"

"Uh, no? I don't know," Leah said haplessly.

"She forgot her shirts." Fatima handed over Victoria's top and flannel. "I don't know where her shoes went."

Sighing, Leah looked toward the front door. "For someone that put-together, she really is a mess."

"Are you guys, like, a couple?"

"Not officially, no. She just tried to have sex with me in your guest room, but I told her she's too drunk and now for some reason she's mad." Meeting Fatima's mildly shocked gaze, she shrugged. "Safe to call it complicated. Thanks for the party, I gotta go catch up to her because she's hella wasted."

"Sure. I'll see you in a few months." Leah froze, and Fatima smiled. "I'm going to MIT too."

"Oh, cool. Okay, great. If I don't see you this summer, I'll see you there." She waved as she hurried out. "Later!"

In the dead of night, on Fatima's lovely suburban cul-de-sac, Victoria stood out prominently under the cones of light from the streetlamps. Jogging to catch up, Leah was almost out of breath by the time she got to Victoria's side. "Hey, Tori, come back."

"Don't touch me," she said, ripping her arm away from where Leah had attempted to stop her. "You're a jerk."

"Oh, I'm a jerk? You just told me I'm a worse person than Carter Harcourt, so right now, I think you've got the jerk thing covered."

Victoria whipped around. "You are worse!"

"Cool, great, keep saying that. It definitely doesn't suck to hear it again."

"No, you're worse because…because I should have seen it coming from him. The whole thing at prom…I should have seen it coming. Carter is a huge asshole, but everyone knows it. He doesn't pretend to be anything else. But you? You say all the right things and do all the right things. You spent all this time making me feel…making me feel like you liked me, like you cared about me, but you tricked me! So, yeah, it's worse. It's worse because I really believed you."

"I'm not tricking you." Each time Victoria tried to step around her, Leah matched it. "Quit fucking around!" Her harsh tone of voice caused Victoria to stop short. The whole night—the relentless heat of Victoria glued to her side, the jealousy, the casual intimacy—all of it wore down Leah's patience. "I don't have sex with drunk girls, okay? Even when they're my dream girl, I don't, and I won't. That's it, period."

"Oh." Victoria looked down at her bare feet. "And you don't…you don't like Riley, do you? 'Cause you guys looked really cozy and she was looking at you weird and you were being nice to her."

Leah handed Victoria her shirts and waited for her to resume eye contact to ensure Victoria understood her completely. "So, I can't be nice to other girls now? Listen, Riley's cute and she's nice, but she's not you, Tori."

"So, it's 'cause I'm drunk and not because I don't have my belly button pierced or—or because I'm a virgin?" Victoria's dopey, watery eyes implored her with an earnestness that would've made Leah laugh had she not found the whole thing equally adorable and annoying.

"Never, not in a million years, would either of those be the reason." Reaching out, she straightened Victoria's flannel and took each of her hands in her own. "I like you a lot. I like you so much it makes me very, very stupid. For real. I think my IQ plummeted because all the blood in my brain has gone elsewhere."

Victoria looked horrified. "Oh no, where did it go?"

"*Dios mio*. Never mind. If and when we decide to have sex, I want it to mean something. I want it to matter, to be special. I want you sober because I don't want you to have an excuse to go back on it. Okay? So, there's no tricks. There's just me, just Leah, and all the crazy-stupid feelings I have for you."

Victoria smiled, peering down at their joined hands. The tizzy she'd twisted herself into unwound, and the tension in her body left her as Leah saw her visibly relax. "Did you call me your dream girl?"

Leah swung their hands to buy time before she threw herself headfirst into vulnerability. "Uh, yeah. I think you're perfect, Tori. I always have."

"Gosh. That's really sweet." Victoria's face twisted into a peculiar expression, before she abruptly took two steps backward, pivoted, and barfed into the street.

"Damn, Lockwood. Too sweet, I guess."

Victoria held up a hand as she bent over, retching. "So sorry," she managed to eke out between vomits. Leah strode to her side, pulling Victoria's hair from her face. "Thank you."

"*Papi*'s tequila is not for the faint of heart," Leah replied with a sympathetic grimace. "Can I drive you home now?"

"Oh God, please don't take me to my house." Victoria groaned, using her flannel to wipe under her nose. "Can I sleep at yours? I won't try anything, I promise."

"Like I can't handle you." Victoria tried to look pouty, but with flecks of vomit on her chin and her face void of color, she just looked incredibly pathetic. Her dream girl. Leah huffed out a laugh. "Let's go home."

CHAPTER EIGHT

Since time immemorial, teenage culture revolved around sex. Victoria never grasped the concept of it—the overwhelming need to be close to someone, to touch them, to see them naked. She'd gone to enough parties, watched enough movies, to know her lack of obsession with sex put her in the minority. Even Vic, otherwise a paragon of levelheadedness, went girl crazy during high school. It appeared to be a rite of passage she'd circumvented.

With Leah, Victoria understood the salacious thoughts with painful salience.

Her proximity alone caused Victoria's heart to palpitate, and her touch ignited a wick inside her chest she didn't know existed. A feral gravitation puppeteering her every move, pushing her toward Leah as often as possible. Hours or days apart physically hurt, and Victoria spent that time counting down the hours until she could see her again. In between bouts of Leah, she performed a high-wire act balancing her friends' expectations of hanging out during "their last summer" and finding any excuse to be with Leah instead. Only Vic knew of her duplicity, which made her feel marginally guilty about not telling Riley. However, an innocuous remark from Riley could inform her parents, who in turn would inform Victoria's. Keeping her circle out of the loop was the best method to spend as much time with Leah as possible.

They didn't do anything particularly exciting—hanging out at the auto shop, sharing meals, stealing kisses and touches—but even the banal was more thrilling with Leah near. Still, she wanted to woo Leah in a way that made her forget about the girls who hadn't treated her well in the past. So, on a Friday night when Leah didn't have to work late, in a rare reversal of duties, she picked up Leah from her house and drove her to the single bus stop in town. She parked her car in the gas station parking lot and took Leah's hand, leading her to the bus vestibule.

Leah, who'd patiently allowed Victoria to wordlessly steal her away, finally spoke up. "What are we doing here?"

"Taking the bus."

She glared at her. "Where?"

"The city."

"Why?"

"You'll see. No more questions." Fondly, Leah rolled her eyes and sat quietly, content to lace her fingers in and out of Victoria's own. The bus grumbled down the single road into town, coming to a squeaky stop in front of them. Victoria deposited the bus fare for them into the coin receptacle, and they took their seats near the back.

Next to the window, Victoria stared out into Garden Hills as it disappeared behind them. The bus stopped intermittently in surrounding towns, each time losing more passengers than they gained. By the time they'd crossed the bridge into the city, she and Leah were two of only six people left to disembark. Taking her by the hand, Victoria weaved them in and out of the bus terminal and into the bustling city blocks. Honking and traffic and noise greeted them as they emerged from the underground terminal, and they stared up in wonder at the magnificently tall buildings.

Leah stood in the center of the city sidewalk, fitting in seamlessly with the rest of the people around her. She'd worn a plain black ribbed tank top and torn denim shorts, forgoing her usual giant boots for a more sensible low sneaker. The city had grit and character, and it never presented a false front. Victoria loved cities. And Victoria loved Leah.

"Tori, where are we going?"

"It's close. Almost there." Just a few blocks from the terminal, past the bodegas and the coffee shops, an ancient brick building stood out on the otherwise quiet block she'd taken Leah down—a warehouse left over from more industrial days, with a rather plain exterior of fading brick. Except, of course, for the twenty-foot neon sign of a pair of rollerblades, blinking back and forth to mimic movement across the façade.

Leah stopped midstep and looked up. The neons flashed in the glistening, glorious eyes of her girlfriend. "Is this…a roller rink?"

"It's not just any roller rink." As she brought her closer, they saw the line forming near the door as a bouncer let people inside in small groups.

Though she noticed immediately, it took Leah another couple of minutes to put it together. "Is…are all these people gay?"

"Maybe," she replied, smiling. "It's pride night."

They waited, hand in hand, to be let into the monstrously sized roller rink. Once they'd been given rainbow wristbands to indicate being underage, they followed the line of people toward the skate rental. The interior smelled like popcorn, liquor, and sweaty socks, and the lights barely illuminated the skaters. In a far corner, a tiny café served up soda, pizza, popcorn, and hamburgers. A massive arcade took up a good portion of the floor space next to lines of benches for skaters to lace up or wind down.

Victoria paid for their skate rental and guided Leah to the bench. "So? Is this okay?"

While she sat to pull her rollerblades on, Leah stood next to her, holding her skates in her hand like a sack lunch. "You took me on a date."

"Hopefully just one of many," Victoria replied, patting the bench next to her. "Let me woo you, Leah Vasquez."

"Thank you." Victoria could barely hear Leah over the pounding dance music, especially when her voice had gone unusually soft. "You didn't have to do this. I didn't mean to tell a sob story and make you feel like you had to go through all this trouble."

"It wasn't a sob story. You're my girlfriend. And while I can't shout it from the rooftops at home…" Around them, other queer couples happily held hands or kissed, engaging in the kind of casual PDA most heterosexual couples performed without a second thought. Girls kissing girls, boys kissing boys, people all over the gender and sexuality spectrum enjoying each other's company. "I can at least take you on a halfway decent date here, where we won't be stared at or have to worry about what anyone thinks. We can just be us."

Leah nodded along, fidgeting with the skates on her lap. "So, this is a bad time to tell you I can't skate, right?" Victoria sharply looked over at Leah, who smiled sheepishly. "Nobody's ever taken me! You just said! Remember? Sad Leah whose girlfriends never took her to gay roller rinks."

"It's fine, you'll get it in no time. I'll help you." Victoria got to one knee to lace up Leah's skates. After a wobbly detour to the lockers to secure their shoes, Victoria gently guided Leah over the carpeting and toward the rink. Leah hesitated in front of the hardwood as dozens of skaters whizzed by them. "You'll be fine."

"I feel dumb."

Couples sped by on blades and skates and music pumped in from speakers in the ceiling, played by a DJ working behind a plastic partition above the rink. Some kind of eighties music, but Leah obviously recognized it and bopped along as she stood on the periphery of the rink.

"You're so cute in your skates."

"Yeah?" Leah peered down at herself, then tentatively back up at Victoria. A rare picture of vulnerability. "I don't look stupid?"

"No, you're adorable. Now c'mon, I've got you."

Hesitantly, Leah took her first step onto the rink surface, holding both of Victoria's hands for support. She released one hand to clutch the short wall, cowering away from the other skaters flying by them. "I'm gonna fall on my ass."

"Yeah, probably," Victoria replied, chuckling. "But nobody's going to care."

"My ass will care."

Victoria rolled her eyes, pulling Leah into the rink and keeping her upright as they slowly skated in a wide circle near the wall. "I promise, I care too much about your amazing ass to let anything happen to it."

"Just don't let go of me," Leah said, gripping Victoria's hand for dear life.

"Never."

For the better part of an hour, they twirled around the rink, with Leah growing more comfortable on her skates with every revolution and every new song spun by the DJ. It did wonders for Victoria to see other happy same-sex couples with their arms around each other's waists or spinning each other in circles. Carefree, normal, infatuated teens just like them. She didn't have to hide their clasped hands or pretend like they were friends. Victoria wondered if life would ever be like this outside of these walls. Could she ever love Leah like this in the real world, without the halogens and the anonymity?

Leah cut short her reverie by leaning into her and kissing her on the cheek. "Thank you for bringing me here. I love it. Best date I've ever had."

Just as Leah finished speaking, they lowered the lights for a romantic couples' skate. A few skaters zoomed out of the rink but many stayed, glued to one another. Emboldened by their unabashed romances, Victoria pivoted to skate backward, took Leah by her cheeks, and planted a soft, ardent kiss on her lips. The song, a cheesy pop love ballad, nearly moved Victoria to tears. If this was being in love, well, Victoria could see how a poet might fill endless pages in devotion to this feeling.

She rested her forehead on Leah's and continued to skate backward, dropping another kiss on the tip of Leah's nose. Leah looked down at their feet and Victoria's eyes followed, Leah's chunky four-wheel skates leisurely gliding against Victoria's rollerblades doing small figure eights to propel backward.

"Show-off."

"Oh, yeah? Are my sick rollerblading skills impressing you?" She literally skated in circles around her as Leah cruised at a slow pace.

In lieu of answering, Leah took her hands and pulled them flush, leaning up to kiss Victoria urgently. They ceased skating and stood in the middle of the other couples, lit only by flashing strobes and darting halogens, and Leah had both her arms around her shoulders and held her tightly. "You always impress me."

Her words flooded Victoria with warmth, tingling from the tips of her fingers right down to where her toes were squished inside the rollerblades. Leah pressed their lips together again, teasing her with a warm tongue that tasted like cinnamon gum, creating a hunger inside her like she'd never experienced before. With her hands tangled in Leah's hair, neither of them noticed the house lights come back on and more skaters enter the rink.

Not until one whizzed by and bumped into them. Leah broke away from her, ready to aim her deadly stare at someone. The someone, a tall gay boy in a mesh tank top, rolled his eyes as he whipped around on his skates. "Lesbians are so dramatic. You can skate and be gay at the same time, ladies. Chop, chop!"

Victoria took Leah's hand and resumed skating with her, side by side. She thought about the other dates she'd been on with Carter or her previous boyfriends, and how stilted it felt. Like every action was performative—but she figured that was normal. They didn't make her feel alive. They didn't make her scared. Leah's honesty, her open affection, her layers of personality that Victoria had the privilege of experiencing, it scared Victoria to death. Having Leah's love frightened her because it made her feel real for possibly the first time in her life. But the prospect of losing her love was equally scary, because if Leah made her real, what could she possibly be without her?

Victoria wished it would rain. The humidity had the weather in a stranglehold, and a battalion of humungous gray clouds held back their threat of rain. Sweat beaded on her forehead as she rode shotgun on Leah's deliveries. Thankfully, Leah generously used her air conditioner in addition to keeping her windows down, but the heat would not let up. While she anxiously awaited the end of Leah's workday, this time was precious to her too. Listening to Leah sing, driving with the windows down, crisscrossing Garden Hills and its surrounding towns, talking about everything and nothing, Leah with one wrist on the top of the steering wheel, her other hand clasped with Victoria's in her lap—it brought her a calm contentment. The wonder of it almost suspiciously simple. This was why the radio played saccharine top-forty songs. This was what boy bands pined for as they danced in perfect synchronization. For what she and Leah had.

When Leah finally delivered the last pizza of the night and squared up her slips with Jake, she drove them to a park outside a high school two towns over. Between their car and the sky, the poorly maintained floodlights flickered off and only the moon glistened against the damp asphalt beneath them. The car barely in park, Victoria climbed over the middle console and settled on Leah's lap. Pressing her hips down and her lips into Leah's, she groaned into their kiss as Leah's hands ran up her back. Their kissing grew heavy, slow, and passionate. Leah dragged her tongue down the sweat-slicked skin of her neck, stopping at a tender spot on her throat. Gripping Victoria's back tightly, she bit down and suckled on the flesh there. Victoria gasped, bracing herself with one hand on the soft fabric ceiling and the other palm flat against the cool, condensation-filled window, squeaking as her hold slipped.

"Fuck, Leah." Apparently encouraged, Leah sucked harder, then popped her lips away. She lavished kisses along the bottom of Victoria's neck, dipping her tongue into the divots along her collarbone and throat. The number of hickeys she received and her skill at blending concealer had grown exponentially over the past couple weeks. With her hand around the back of Leah's head, she guided her lips to the other side of the neck. "Do it again."

Leah's chuckle vibrated against her skin, and she deliberately didn't follow Victoria's request. Instead, she pressed open-mouthed, hot kisses along the column of her throat, nipping her each time. Victoria whined at her insolence.

"Patience, *mi amor*."

A shudder ran down her spine. "Is it racist if I think it's sexy when you speak Spanish?"

"*Peut-être*," Leah replied. "*Est mon Français sexy aussi?*"

"Jesus, yeah. Ugh, it's so unfair of you to be hot in three languages."

"*Gracias*." Leah sank her teeth into the flesh of Victoria's neck, running one hand up her shirt to squeeze her breast as she did so. As Leah sucked on the skin, Victoria grabbed her free hand and forced it down between them, directly under the skirt she'd worn intentionally to tempt Leah.

As usual, Leah didn't take the bait and gripped her thigh near the juncture of her hip. However, she could feel the tension in Leah's hands as she fought the urge to put her hand between her legs. "Leah, please. Just touch me."

The lips on her neck faltered, and Leah peppered light kisses along her collarbone. "Not here."

"Then where? I'll go anywhere you want to go." Both of them panting hard, Victoria leaned back and rested against the steering wheel. Sure, maybe Leah's car in a parking lot wasn't where she wanted to lose her virginity, but every day it got harder and harder to resist. "Is it something else?"

"No, it's…" Sighing, Leah's face flushed in embarrassment as she glanced away from Victoria sitting in her lap. Leah's chivalry came from a good place, but Victoria wanted more. She didn't know what the obstacle could be; she'd given Leah every green light. "I want it to be really nice for you. My first time was…not great. I want you to have a good experience, not a quickie in my car."

Victoria would've killed for either of those options at the moment, arousal-addled as she was, but she appreciated Leah's reticence. The warmth of Leah's hands on her and the heat of their bodies crushed together made thinking difficult, but Victoria paused. "Yours wasn't good?"

"Not really. It didn't feel right." Her eyes dropped to their laps. Heart aching, Victoria pecked kisses as balms along her forehead. "It became all about how fast she could get in my pants, as if that was some show of skill. Half the time I wasn't even wet. It wasn't until my next girlfriend that I learned how it was supposed to feel."

"I'm so sorry, babe." With Leah's cheeks cupped in her palms, she rubbed her thumb along her cheekbones. Two gorgeous eyes, swirling like galaxy centers, blinked back at her. "I'm sorry that happened to you. I know you'd never do the same to me."

"And I...I don't want you to think sex is all this is to me."

"I don't think that, Leah. I promise. And it's not why I'm here, either, despite the fact that all you have to do is look at me and I get wet." Leah tucked a kiss-swollen lip between her teeth, her chest rising and falling slowly. "I don't need any special treatment, roses or candles or whatever. I just want you."

"I know. We'll find the right moment, together, okay?" Adjusting Victoria's skirt so it lay flat again, Leah inhaled a deep breath. "So, I planned a surprise for you."

Victoria toyed with the bottom of Leah's shirt. "What kind of surprise?"

"A surprise. All you have to do is come to my house on Saturday. Dressed up."

Victoria's curiosity piqued. Leah didn't do "dressed up." Only for church did she wear anything other than jeans and boots. "Dressed up? How dressed up?"

"Formal."

"Whoa." The coy look on Leah's face put a wide smile on her own. These softer, romantic sides to Leah came as a surprise, but Victoria adored each of them. "I know lesbians have that U-Haul stereotype, but it's a little early for proposals, don't you think?"

Leah cocked an eyebrow. "You wish I'd let you gay-wife me."

"I dunno, Leah Lockwood does have a cute alliteration to it."

"Kinda like Victoria Vasquez?"

"Oh, right. I hear Tori so much now I sometimes forget." She leaned down and kissed Leah softly. "Eventually, everyone will call me that...and then I can be reminded of you all the time."

Leah nuzzled into the crook of her neck, darting her tongue out every so often to taste her skin. "That's extremely cute and super, super gay." A short, electronic whir signaled the end of the current playlist in Leah's CD player. She nabbed a CD from the binder next to them, and used one hand to pop the old one out and insert the new. "Another one?"

"If you're asking if I want to make out with you for however long it takes to get through your next playlist, I think you know the answer."

"Is the answer super, super gay?"

Victoria grabbed the seat adjustment lever below the seat and pulled it up, forcing Leah to recline. The shock and wonder on her face gave Victoria the fortitude to ignore the seat belt receptacle digging into her thigh, and she leaned down to skim her lips across Leah's neck. "You're obnoxious."

"Yet here you are."

"Yet here I am."

Victoria knocked on her brother's door and waited in the hallway as the volume of music decreased. "Enter!"

Rolling her eyes, she walked in and closed the door behind her. Like her room, Vic's was void of any personality aside from trophies and personal photos. His looked even emptier since he went away to college and got rid of many of his childhood possessions in the process. Deep green walls and a plush crimson carpet scrunched under Victoria's bare feet as she walked in. Music played quietly from the boombox next to his bed, some obscure indie artist Leah would probably know.

"I need a favor."

Vic placed his book on his bed and sat up. It smelled like a boy in his room, like body spray and feet, but it made Victoria nostalgic for their childhood. Sneaking away into Vic's room to play video games with him, asking him for help with her homework, or just bugging him because that was her right as his little sister.

"I will give you this favor, on the day of my daughter's wedding," Vic replied, dropping his voice low and raspy. Victoria stared at him blankly. "*The Godfather*? Been 'watching movies' with Leah for weeks now and never got around to that one, huh?"

"I think you know the gender ratio in *The Godfather* means Leah is never going to watch it."

"So true," he lamented with a dramatic click of his tongue. "But, uh, what can I do for you?"

"I need you to drive me to Leah's on Saturday."

Vic tapped his finger against the stubble on his chin. "And why, pray tell, could you not use one of the dozen vehicles we own?"

"First, I have to dress up and I don't want Mom and Dad to see me. Second, I won't be back 'til the next day, and if one of the cars is missing, Dad will know something's up."

Her brother raised his eyebrow. "Wow, that's a lot of subterfuge. Can't one of your friends drive you?"

"I also don't want them to know," Victoria admitted. "I'm afraid if they know about Leah, Mom and Dad will find out and ruin it."

"Have you considered coming out to your friends? I mean, you're not in high school anymore. If they're cool about it, great. If they suck, you never have to see them again."

Victoria sat on the edge of his bed. "Riley might be cool about it, but Gabby would snitch. If it got back to Mom or Dad, I'd be screwed. Dad's a homophobe and Mom hates me."

Vic crossed his legs and scooted toward her on the bed. "You know Mom doesn't hate you, right?"

"Sure, she's just disproportionately bitchy to me for the fun of it," Victoria replied. "You're her favorite and Ward is a close second. I'm a distant fifth or sixth."

"She's just fucked up and doesn't know how to show affection like a normal person." Sighing, he placed his hand on her shoulder. "I wish she was less tough on you."

"I wish she'd just leave me alone entirely, but whatever. So, will you help me?"

"Of course. You know I'm always game to fool the 'rents. How about this? I'll get dressed up too. Throw on a suit or whatever. If they see us, I'll tell them I'm bringing you to meet college friends of mine. They'll love that stupid networking shit and think I'm setting you up with some yuppie loser."

Victoria brightened. "Really? You'd do that for me? You hate suits."

"Might as well get used to it," he said, rising from his bed to pad over to the closet. "Once I graduate, I'll be in suits until I die. And then after I die, they'll put me into one last suit, just to really drive the point home. But for you, dear little sister, I will."

"Thank you!" Victoria leapt up from the bed, hugging Vic around his neck. "And thank you for…everything else. For being here. It's nice to tell someone about Leah."

"It's nice to hear about," he replied. "She seems cool, even though she's kinda scary and she yelled at me."

"I would say 'she's not like that,' but she is. But she's also a lot of other really good things." Nothing could stop the smile from bursting on Victoria's face.

It must've been contagious, as Vic smiled back at her. "Then go put on your finest pearls, missy. We have a date with a young lady to attend."

They'd gotten out of the house unscathed thanks to Vic's deflection and presence. As they pulled up beside the curb, Vic peeked around Victoria to take a look at the house. "Wow, that's a lot of cars for such a tiny house."

"Her dad runs Vasquez's Auto Shop over on Washington. Leah says he buys crappy or totaled cars and fixes them up, and then sells them really cheap to people who can't afford a new car, or might not be able to have their credit run." Vic craned his neck to see the breadth of the acreage covered in cars. "He has a lot of clients at the auto shop and doesn't get around to this as much. Hence the big sea of projects."

"Dang, sounds like a good dude. If he's ever looking to get out of that business, we should get him to manage the fleet of cars for the company. The guy who does it now is a scumbag and definitely scamming us out of money."

"Ugh, who would want to work for Dad?"

"Good point." Vic scratched his chin and peered at the house. "Is it always so dark?"

"Actually, no," Victoria replied, looking down the driveway. "Hector's truck isn't there either. Just Leah's. Weird, her parents never go anywhere."

"Damn, the whole house to yourselves?" Vic slid his arm around the back of her headrest. "Seems I need to give you The Talk. Now, Victoria, when two people really like each other, they sometimes want to express that love by smushing their bottom parts together."

"Oh my God. Okay, thank you, I'm leaving now." Hastily, Victoria got out of the car, making sure not to let her dress drag on the ground. It wasn't as nice as her prom dress, but her mother had picked that dress out anyway. This was her favorite dress, the one she often wore to weddings or her father's fancier events. Lower, more sensible heels as well. She'd gone less heavy on her makeup, gathering her hair up into a braided bun. Wherever Leah planned to take her, she hoped she wasn't overdressed.

As she knocked on the door Vic drove away, the tires of their father's expensive sports car squealing. Nobody answered her knock, and Victoria pouted. Keeping her dress from touching the grass, she walked around the side of the house toward the backyard. Nothing out there but the fire pit, lawn chairs, and the abandoned car projects in the distance.

Just as she began contemplating breaking into Leah's house, a pair of headlights shone down the dead-end street. Standing at the edge of the yard, Victoria realized it wasn't a car, but rather a limo. A limo making an extremely awkward K-turn in front of Leah's house. When it finally straightened out and pulled to the curb, Leah stepped out of the back seat dressed in a dashing black suit with a single royal blue flower boutonnière. All her curly hair was flipped to one side, cascading over her shoulder opposite her flower. The suit fit her like she was born in it, and Victoria forgot how to breathe. Her pearly whites flashed at Victoria, and she produced a plastic box from behind her back.

Leah approached slowly and held out the corsage. "May I?"

"Leah, what is all this?" Victoria asked, holding her wrist out for Leah to place the corsage on.

"Tori, will you go to Not Prom with me?"

Victoria's brain felt like her dial-up modem—slow to connect. "This is my surprise?"

"There's more than this, obviously," Leah replied, gesturing at the limo. "But you only find out when you accept."

"Oh." Then, Victoria smiled. "Yes, Leah, I'll go to Not Prom with you."

With a dramatic sweep of her arm, Leah escorted Victoria to the limo and opened the door for her. Carter had hired a ginormous Hummer limo with enough room inside for the entire football team for their prom. Like Carter, the limo was expensive, useless, and mostly empty inside. This limo didn't boast nearly as much, shorter and more reasonable for two people. The privacy screen rolled up and the unseen driver whisked them away.

"So, um, I thought…I don't know, your prom was shitty. You worked on the committee all year and never got to reap the benefits. And while that put you in my path, which turned out hella good for me, it also sucked for you." Leah shrugged and attempted to be casual. An adorable feat for her to try, considering the epically romantic adventure they were on.

"Wait, so we're really going to a prom?" Victoria tried to look out the windows, but the tinting prevented her from seeing much other than the basic shapes of buildings and lights. "How? Where?"

"You'll see. We're almost there."

They didn't drive for very long, less than ten minutes by Victoria's estimation. And when Leah extended her hand to pull her out of the limo, she understood why. They were at Benny's. It appeared the lights were out, and heavy blinds were drawn over the large windows.

"Benny's? Did I get dressed up to eat pizza?"

Leah rolled her eyes. "Come on." She held out her elbow and Victoria slid her arm through it, letting Leah take the lead. As they entered, Leah stepped away from Victoria as she took in the spectacle before her. It wasn't Benny's any longer. Streamers hung from the ceiling, garland strung from corner to corner like glistening stalactites. The tables were pushed to the edges, similar to the layout for Leah's concert, and a disco ball hung in the center, refracting squares of light all over the floor. A fog machine under a table puffed out breaths of white fog, just enough to turn the terra-cotta tiles into a dreamlike dance floor. Pink and blue strobe lights crisscrossed the dance floor from precariously hung positions on the walls.

A rather excessive speaker setup sat on the stage, wired to a dinky CD player in the center. Music played low, quiet enough where she could hear the clack of Leah's polished shoes coming up behind her. She'd even set up a photo booth in the corner, like the one Victoria arranged for prom.

"This is incredible."

"You like it?" Leah pivoted on her heel, walking backward toward the center of the dance floor. "I know it isn't the Marriot…"

"No, Leah…" The lump in her throat choked the words she wanted to say. "How did you do all this?"

"Benny wanted to throw me a going-away party, and I asked him for a favor instead. To let me have the place for the night. He asked why, and once Jake and Billy got involved, uh, we all sort of went nuts with the decorations."

Along a table near the jukebox, Victoria spotted platters of hors d'oeuvres, and champagne and cola chilling in an ice bucket. It really was like a mini prom, complete with balloons and white tablecloths. Bouquets of flowers stood proudly in vases of all different shapes and sizes. "I can't believe you. This is beyond romantic."

"Don't cry yet, because we haven't taken our pictures." She grabbed Victoria's hand and they skittered into the photo booth. Not quite a professional setup, but a camera on a tripod and a fairly standard off-white background for them to pose in front of. Leah set the timer and jogged back to her, wrapping her arms around Victoria from behind. They took a few more photos this way, changing poses every so often. "Okay, one more."

Victoria grinned, grabbing Leah by the face and turning her around, kissing her fully and deeply as the flash went off. She didn't stop, wrapping her arm around the back of Leah's neck and keeping her there for a couple more blissful moments. "You're amazing, Leah Vasquez."

"We've barely started, baby." Leah hopped up on the stage and tapped on the CD player, increasing the volume of the dance pop hit blaring from the speakers. "Let's dance."

Victoria came to the bittersweet conclusion she'd never had this much fun in her life. She buried that depressing nugget lest it escape and sour the room like a gas leak. Twirling in manufactured fog to an endless stream of music, Victoria let go of the negativity and let Leah's energy and affection soak in. Unlike prom, Victoria didn't have to worry about decorations or attendees. She didn't have to take care of some baby-boyfriend or listen to gossip. The shackles of expectations snapped; Victoria was free to be herself. To say it was better than prom would've undersold it. This night made her prom, her Sweet Sixteen, and any birthday party she ever attended feel like a funeral in comparison.

They didn't bother much with the food platters, opting for generous flutes of champagne between dances. As the night spun into the very early hours of the morning, Victoria danced cheek to cheek with Leah in the center of the dance floor, gently swaying to the music. Victoria rested her head on Leah's shoulder as Leah sang softly into her ear. "This is the best prom ever."

"Not Prom," Leah corrected. Suddenly, she pulled back. "I almost forgot." She scurried away in her socks—they'd long since abandoned their fancy footwear—and retrieved two homemade paper crowns from behind one of the tall speakers. Leah plunked one crown on her head, a spiky gold one with hilariously large gems, and got on one knee to offer the other to Victoria. "For my queen."

Giggling, Victoria took the crown and secured it atop her head. "Wow, I won the vote."

"Fuck the vote." Leah stood up, easing Victoria back in for the remainder of their slow dance. "I got mine by proxy, but you earned yours. Everything you did at school, all the work you put into making everyone else's experience better? Maybe it went unappreciated, but it never went unnoticed. Even by me, as much as it may not have seemed so."

"Well, of course you noticed. You and your big gay crush on me." She heard Leah scowl into her ear and she chuckled. "But, really, Leah. Thank you. This is way more than anyone has ever done for me...I don't even really know what to say."

"You deserve this. You deserve way more than this, more than I could ever give you. I'm...I feel very lucky to be your girlfriend."

Victoria freed her hand from where it clutched Leah's and touched her cheek. Gazing into the ever-changing depths of Leah's eyes, she inhaled a deep breath and went for broke. "I love you."

It felt like forever before Leah responded. In rapid succession, she watched surprise, desire, and affection all pass over Leah's face. "I love you too, Tori."

Pressing their lips together softly, Victoria stopped swaying to pour her energy into their kiss. It astounded her to feel this way about Leah. About anyone, really. A passion lurked deep inside her, lying in wait like a predator, waiting to sink its jaws into a worthy love. The overwrought romantic poetry she read junior year suddenly made sense. She finally understood why Neruda so badly wanted to do to his lover what spring does to the cherry trees.

"Did we find the right moment?" Victoria inquired in a low voice, keeping her eyes closed as she rested her forehead against Leah's.

"Yes." Leah's instant reply thrilled her. "Let's get out of here."

A short limo ride later, helmed by Leah's friend Billy as Victoria had discovered, they arrived at Leah's darkened house. Normally her parents greeted them from the couch, but as Leah unlocked the door, Victoria glanced around the empty home. "You didn't...tell you parents about this, did you?"

Leah barked out a laugh, closing and locking the door. "You think I asked my parents to get lost on the off chance I might get laid?"

Blushing, Victoria shrugged as she took off her shoes, leaving her heels next to their coat rack. "No, I just...they never go out. I don't think I've ever been here when they weren't around."

"I planned it that way. They're at my *abuelo*'s for the weekend. I usually go, but I told them I wanted to pick up more shifts before I go to college."

Up the stairs and back in the comfort of Leah's room, Leah shucked off her jacket and threw it over the desk chair. She lit a single, scented candle, and turned on only her desk lamp, giving the room a golden, warm glow. It wouldn't be Leah without a playlist, and she bent over her desk to cue one from her computer. Soft, mostly instrumental R&B thumped from the speakers.

She padded across her rug to Victoria. "Nothing has to happen tonight. And once you say yes, you can say no."

"I don't think I will, but thank you." Suddenly full of nerves, Victoria wrung her fingers in front of her. Her lack of experience toppled her with insecurity. Leah knew what to do, where to put her hands, and how to create pleasure from touch, but Victoria...she wanted to be good. "What do we do first?"

In place of a barb or wicked grin, Leah smiled softly and took Victoria's hand, leading her to the bed. They sat down next to each other, knee to knee, and Victoria exhaled a long breath. "I know this feels overwhelming, but it'll be okay. It's just kissing and touching.

There's no schedule, there's no right way or wrong way. We do what feels good, all right?"

"What about our clothes?" Victoria asked, slightly panicked. "Do we take them off all at once? Or is it a one-by-one situation?"

"We take them off when we need to. Or we don't, plenty of things to do with clothes on. But first." Leah brought Victoria's hands to her lips, pressing a soft kiss on the back of her hand. "First, we kiss. We're good at that."

They were good at that, Victoria reasoned. Weeks of practice made them great at it, actually. She let Leah take the lead, gently and tenderly kissing her with slow, soft purpose. Her hair came tumbling down from its updo as Leah snaked her hands into it and unclipped the barrette keeping her braid together. Steadily, like one coaxes a fire to flame, Leah pushed their desires forward, faster, higher, until Victoria panted so hard she nearly passed out.

Her ratio of anxious to aroused slid in favor of the latter, especially when Leah's hand began roaming beneath her dress. Grazing her inner thigh with blunt nails, grabbing it with her whole hand, and squeezing her in bursts of desire. Suddenly, Victoria hated clothes. "Take off my dress."

She hadn't meant to sound demanding, but by the wide, smoldering look she received, she decided not to go back on it and stood up. Leah gently gathered her hair, throwing it over her shoulder to expose the zipper. Victoria gasped as Leah kissed along the top of her back, running her tongue very quickly up the vertebrae along the nape of her neck. Agonizing and annoyingly slow, Leah pulled down the zipper until it reached the end near the small of her back. She started to turn, but Leah gruffly held her still by the waist. Leah kissed her back, her shoulders, every bit of exposed skin she could, before sliding her hands beneath the dress fabric and hugging her from behind. Her embrace made Victoria feel safe as houses, but also like a home on fire. The top of her dress folded over and Leah's hands trailed upward. Up the abdominal muscles of her stomach, grazing her ribs, then cupping her bare breasts.

Not wearing a bra had been a product of the dress not allowing for it, and now she thought it might've been the best decision she ever made. Leah groaned into her neck, kissing and biting as she fondled Victoria and swiped eager thumbs over her nipples. She'd always fended off Carter's attempts to grope her and she was very glad she did. None of his awkward, fleshy hand fumbling could've compared to the slightly coarse, nimble, reverent ministrations of Leah's hands.

Leah turned her around by the waist and kissed her with ferocious passion. She shimmied the rest of her dress to the floor and Victoria stepped out of it. Leah's eyes glanced at her in question from her kneeled position, tracing around the elastic of Victoria's underwear. Victoria nodded her consent. Feeling exposed, Victoria sat down on the bed and Leah was on her in an instant, guiding her to lie down and positioning herself above Victoria.

Victoria blushed at Leah's admiring stare, and for perhaps the first time ever, Leah Vasquez looked out of her depth. "Do you have any idea how gorgeous you are?" Leah didn't wait for an answer, peppering kisses from Victoria's neck down her chest, some light and some hard enough to leave marks. "Beautiful. Perfect. Every inch of you is perfect."

Victoria's stomach swooped in response to the praise, the pull between her legs growing stronger with every kiss and swipe of Leah's tongue. Leah lavished more praise on her, and suddenly she stopped moving as she hovered over Victoria's lips, poised to kiss her. "What's wrong? Do you want to stop? Are you okay?"

She fisted the material of Leah's shirt and drew her nearer with a sharp tug, trying to give back the passion tenfold. But Leah drew back, bracing herself on one arm to use the other to wipe a tear from Victoria's cheek.

"Sorry, I didn't—didn't…"

Puzzlement and concern darkened Leah's face. "Tell me what you need. Did I hurt you?"

"No. Just keep going." Leah's movements all but ceased as she searched Victoria's face for an answer. Frustrated, Victoria huffed and glanced away from her, mumbling, "It's what you said, okay? It was really nice and…you sounded like you meant it. Can we please keep going?"

Leah blinked away her apprehension and smiled, dimpling her cheek. She kissed her again, slowly increasing the heat of their embrace until Victoria started clutching at her, desperate for something more. A whine escaped her as Leah pressed a leg between hers, providing pressure directly where she needed it. Reaching between them, she unbuckled Leah's belt and popped the button on her dress pants. Next came her shirt, with Victoria attempting to undo all the buttons as Leah rocked into her and kissed her senseless.

"You're wearing too many fucking clothes," Victoria said as she struggled with the dress shirt and its trillions of buttons. "You could help, you know."

"I could, but you're really cute when you're frustrated." She did her best to glare, and Leah chuckled but acquiesced, removing her tie and motioning to throw it. Victoria caught her wrist.

"Keep that handy."

With an impressed look, she dropped the tie next to them but wasted no time in divesting herself of the rest of her outfit until she was down to just a pair of tight black boxer briefs. Their kissing began anew, and the feeling of Leah's overheated skin against her own sent her reeling. Everything became heady and real, and Leah's boobs became real, and they bewitched her. This enthusiastic appreciation went appreciated, with Leah writhing and moaning at every touch. A thin gold chain hung from her neck and the dainty gold cross on the end dangled near Victoria's face. She wasn't religious, but Victoria understood the devotion. She wanted to learn Leah's body like a holy scripture and worship at the altar of Leah Vasquez.

However, at seventeen and horny she wanted the patience to worship but needed gratification now. She gracelessly worked her hand into Leah's briefs. Her proactivity surprised Leah, based on the Spanish expletive hurled at her. "Is this okay?"

"Yes." Holding herself up with one arm, Leah used the other to free herself from her briefs and widen her knees apart. Victoria explored this newly exposed part of her with eager, curious touches. Even with Leah on top of her, Victoria stayed in control, feeling her way around what made Leah tick. Her fingers dipped into dense curls, explored the wetness there, and slid around the bundle of nerves she'd discovered. Leah's reaction was immediate—a sharp gasp as hips chased the contact. "Fuck, Tori. I was...I was supposed to...you first."

"I thought there wasn't a schedule?" Victoria tried to keep her tone light, but Leah's actions mesmerized her. The rocking of her hips, the clenching of her stomach, the tension in her arm muscles. It reminded her of the ocean, and Victoria the moon, creating the tides. "You are so pretty."

Leah bashfully ducked her head into Victoria's chest. "You don't have to say that."

She used her free hand to push Leah's head up and level their gazes. "It's true. You're gorgeous, Leah. You're the prettiest girl I've ever seen in my life." Victoria leaned up and kissed her hard, letting her fingers slide inside Leah and reveling in the gasp she released against her mouth. Leah hungrily returned her kiss, driving her hips against the rhythm of Victoria's inexperienced hand. She found leverage on Leah's back, splaying her hand on the dip near the end of her spine and skimming the sweat there with her fingertips. The angle allowed her to completely submerge her fingers inside Leah, dragging them out against her textured front wall with each thrust.

"Jesus, you're surprisingly strong."

Victoria faltered. "Am I hurting you?"

"Fuck no. It's really hot. Don't stop." Emboldened, Victoria changed angles and received a moan so guttural it shook her to her core. They kissed clumsily and ardently, punctuated by Leah's whines and pants of breath. She felt Leah's insides squeeze her fingers and she looked up into her eyes. The raw, unfiltered adoration stole her breath away, leaving her with the aching realization nobody had ever looked at her that way before. Leah came with a short cry, and Victoria felt the pulsing on her fingers. Erotic and profoundly intimate, she watched the pleasure ripple its way across Leah's face. She slowed down but didn't stop, reveling in the silky feeling on her fingers. Leah lazily rolled her hips against the waning rhythm, bracing her weight on her knees so she could reach a hand between them. Her fingers slid easily through Victoria's folds, and Leah's awestruck look lessened how bashful Victoria felt about her abundant arousal.

"That was amazing. You're amazing." The truth of Leah's feelings sparkled back at her from those prismatic eyes, and Victoria knew if she could plumb those depths, she'd get lost forever. "Are you ready? Or do you want to stop?"

"Ready." Victoria exhaled sharply. "Very, very ready. N-never been this ready. A little embarrassed about how ready I am. I think I ruined your sheets."

"Kind of hoping you did," Leah replied with a grin both lecherous and adorable. She leaned down and captured Victoria's lips, a stutter in her breath as Victoria slipped out of her. Leah's skilled fingers worked between her legs with finesse and confidence. The arousal in her stomach spread out, and she quickly began losing control. She silently begged Leah for something she couldn't put in words and her girlfriend obliged, applying the exact amount of pressure in the exact right place to send Victoria into a stratosphere of pleasure. Leah gradually slowed her movements, but Victoria continued to pant hard, even as Leah placed gentle kisses around her chest and neck. "Breathe, *mami*. Are you okay?"

"I'll—I'll be okay. Just need a second." Leah hummed in response and appeared content to lazily kiss her neck as Victoria's breath gradually returned to normal. "That felt incredible."

"Good," Leah replied, nuzzling her nose up Victoria's jaw to gaze into her eyes. "Because I'd like to do that a few more times. If you're up for it."

"Yes, please."

The candle's flame licked the rim of the glass jar, flickering just above a pool of melted wax threatening to overtake it. Victoria leaned over and blew it out, its light no longer needed as the blue wash of early morning flooded over the floor. A buzzing air conditioner circulated a cold breeze to cool their overheated skin. Tangled sheets, mingling aromas of sex and candle, the sound of Leah's music and percussive cadence of her breathing, wove into an Elysian blanket Victoria curled into.

The endless computer playlist droned on, and Victoria tuned in for the first time all night. A cheesy pop love song crooned at her from dual speakers on Leah's desk, and she smiled to herself. With all her alternative music posters on the wall and her punk band, Leah had top-forty schmaltz on what Victoria assumed was a sex playlist. Yet another facet in the never-ending prism of Leah Vasquez. Lying next to her multifaceted wonder of a girlfriend, Victoria breathed in the scent of her and the cocktail of sweat, cologne, and perfume lingering in the air between the bed and the crossbeams. This little attic, unassuming and modest, became a nexus for the rerouting of her destiny. Strange how the biggest moments of lucidity happen in the tiniest of spaces, as if the revelation cannot escape and must be reckoned with.

"So, I'm a lesbian."

Leah snorted into her pillow. She turned just enough to peek one eye at her. "Yeah?"

"Yeah."

"Damn, what an endorsement. Wish I could've used that on my college applications." Victoria slapped Leah's bare butt, shifting on her side to lie partially on Leah's back. "Kidding. Kind of."

"I think maybe I've always known, to some extent." Tracing the lines of bones and muscle on Leah's back, Victoria spoke her truth aloud. "I knew I wasn't interested in guys, not in the way most girls are. I made myself believe I hadn't met the right guy yet."

"Society conditions us to believe heterosexuality is the norm and anything else is a deviation. You're probably not even the only 'straight' girl in our graduating class who thinks that. And with the caliber of dumbass boys in our school, who could blame you?"

Victoria chuckled, lazily kissing Leah's shoulder. "Not you, though."

"No, not me. I always knew. In kindergarten, I'd get jealous when a boy would steal the attention of one of my female 'friends,'" she explained. "It never crossed my mind to be any other way. Plus, my dad took me to see *Jurassic Park* and Laura Dern pretty much made it official."

"Really? Laura Dern?"

"Yes, Laura Dern. We don't disparage Laura Dern in this house, Tori." The deadpan expression on Leah's face grew tight into consternation. "What's fucked up is, I knew to hide it. Just as easily as I knew I only liked girls, I knew nobody else could know."

"Then you came out, though," Victoria said sleepily. "In middle school, you were out. We all knew."

"Not by choice."

Curious, Victoria rolled over onto her side, poking Leah until she mirrored her position. "What do you mean?"

Leah turned completely onto her back and sighed. "I kissed a girl at summer camp between sixth and seventh grade. By the time school started in September, everyone knew. And I...I didn't know what to do so I leaned in to it. I acted as if I was already out, like the rumors didn't bother me. But I was horrified. Here was this dirty little secret I tried to hide from God, and suddenly it was the only thing about me anybody knew."

Victoria never heard any rumor about Leah kissing a girl. Leah's sexuality was common knowledge, like her extraordinary math skills. Discovering the origin of how it became public knowledge brought her incredible sadness. "I'm sorry you didn't get to come out on your own terms. That sucks."

Leah shrugged. "Thanks."

"I always thought you were so brave," Victoria whispered. "Anytime I saw you in the hallways, I just...admired you and your courage. I never realized you had to wake up every day and make that choice. You woke up every day and chose to be brave."

"What other choice did I have?"

To be weak, Victoria thought, and a coward, like me. Die-cast by the pressures of her family and her friends into the person they wanted to see when they looked at her. Only here, in this unassuming and modest attic, did Victoria feel real. Only with Leah did the pieces fit together. Only with Leah did she feel whole.

CHAPTER NINE

Morning-afters usually felt like wearing a shoe on the wrong foot. Leah didn't have a ton of experience, but she knew that mistakes the moonlight made look soft, the garish morning sun would reveal. That did not apply to waking up with Victoria Lockwood.

Leah could've leapt out of her bed and started singing like she lived in a musical. The intruding sunlight only served to cast an angelic glow over her sleeping girlfriend. A spotlight on her pale skin, isolating the golden hues of her hair, made her so real. Really Victoria Lockwood. Really her girlfriend. Really her whole heart curled up in her blankets. Nothing about this felt like a shoe on the wrong foot. It felt like a Cinderella's-slipper type of love.

Her alarm blared early, and she turned to slap the snooze. The noise roused Victoria from her slumber and she sleepily harrumphed, thunking her arm over Leah's torso.

"Don't go. Warm."

"Babe, it's a million degrees in here, why would you want to be warmer?" Despite Leah's portable air conditioner doing its best, her attic retained a lot of heat, especially in the summer. Now, beneath a thin sheet and the weight of Victoria Lockwood, Leah was sweating. "We already took showers, I don't wanna do it again."

"I wouldn't mind doing it again," Victoria replied, batting her eyelashes to try to look seductive. Realizing she failed, Victoria instead latched herself to Leah's back and curled around her arms. She shuddered as Victoria laced kisses across her back, nuzzling into her hair. "Don't get up. I don't want to stop touching you. Don't ever wanna stop."

Leah tilted her head back to grant Victoria access to anywhere she wanted to touch. After evidently tiring of her roaming caresses, Victoria pressed flush against Leah's back and dipped into the slick heat between her legs. "This is why my mom doesn't allow sleepovers," Leah joked breathlessly. "Open doors really put a damper on morning sex."

"Uh-huh. Stop talking."

"You didn't mind dirty talk last night," Leah replied, attempting smugness despite being played like a violin.

"Talking about your mom isn't dirty talk." Victoria shifted so she could pin Leah flat with one hand and undo her with the other. Staring up into her eyes, Leah fought her release just to be an asshole. "Anyway, I don't think that will stop me. Every house can be snuck into, isn't that right?"

The low, threatening rhetorical question aroused Leah to an embarrassing degree. Victoria caught on to her deliberate self-denial and she cocked an eyebrow at the unspoken challenge. Leah smirked. "Victoria Lockwood loves rules. She loves being a good girl."

"Not where you're concerned." Leah struggled to stay afloat, teetering on the brink of insanity. Victoria redoubled her efforts, though she didn't try as hard. She learned very quickly how to use her strong hands to unravel Leah like thread. "She can't keep me away from you."

The dichotomy of Victoria's tough touch and soft voice edged Leah closer to her climax. "Fuck, ah. Jesus, you feel so good. Keep going."

"Yeah?" Victoria asked, breathless from exertion. "How does it feel?"

"I—I don't know." She struggled to speak as her pleasure took over. "It's never felt like this before."

Foolishly and recklessly in love, the tender look in Victoria's eyes sent her over the edge. Victoria drew it out for long, liquid moments and kissed Leah deeply, filled to the brim with adoration. "Really?"

"For really real." She regarded Victoria with narrowed eyes. "You're really going to try and sneak into my room?"

"If you want me to. I respect your mom's rules, but I draw the line at the rules which prevent me from defiling her daughter." She grinned wickedly as she leaned down to press a kiss against Leah's lips. Smirking against Victoria's mouth, she drew her into a hot, open, dirty kiss she never wanted to end.

"Rebellious deviant."

"Mm-hmm. Softie." Leah let out an unhappy snarl and glared as Victoria chuckled at her. "Besides, what's the rule even for? You're eighteen and a lesbian. It's not like it's illegal, and you won't get pregnant."

"Yeah, it's not that." Considering Tori's propensity for jealousy, Leah carefully admitted, "She walked in on me having sex two years ago and we were both scarred for life."

Victoria stopped kissing her. "What? With who?"

"Oh, sure, that's very casual," Leah replied. "You don't know her."

"Uh-huh."

Victoria grew quiet and Leah watched her descend into her thoughts. Propped up on her elbow, she traced her finger from one freckle or mole on Victoria's torso to another. She spent her entire puberty jealous of every boy who courted Victoria, every boy who put his arm around her in the hallways, all the boyfriends Victoria had. So, she allowed herself to enjoy a bit of smugness at Victoria's perceived envy.

"You've had so many more partners than me," Victoria said, to which Leah nodded.

"And? What have I told you? I don't lie. It feels different with you."

This appeared to be A Thing now, as Victoria's face became pensive. "How? How is it different?"

"The obvious difference is I love you." The discontent abated a bit, and Leah could've laughed at the thought that Victoria Lockwood needed this much positive reinforcement. Her mother really did a number on her. Cupping between her legs, she rubbed slowly and kept talking. "Being with you makes me feel warm. A good warm, safe. And then sometimes a burning kind of warm, like I'm on fire when you touch me."

Victoria whimpered, and Leah knew she'd broken through whatever insecure shell into which Victoria had receded. She took her time, gradually building the pressure for Victoria and watching the flush spread across her pale skin. Her heart filled to the brim, as if it could burst any moment. Victoria's shallow breaths gave way to gasping, and she clutched Leah with both hands. "Keep talking."

"You make me feel…endless. Nobody in this world could make me feel like you do," Leah said, as much to Victoria as to herself. "I'll never want someone else like I want you. I'll never love anyone like I love you."

The vibration in Victoria's legs intensified, shaking until Leah felt her reach her climax, her eyes screwed shut, gasping and digging her nails into Leah's skin. She forced Leah into a warm, slow, indecent kiss.

Leah had a lot of partners in the past, and a few assorted girlfriends, but none she could remember loving like this. With them, she couldn't imagine loving them for five, ten, or even twenty years like her parents. But when she looked down at Victoria, smiling at her with a dopey, post-orgasm grin, she knew no number of years would ever be enough.

Over the next few weeks, their routine shifted from hookups in cars to Victoria sneaking into Leah's house after her parents fell asleep. They were addicts, routinely feeding each other's addiction for one another with an exhausting amount of sex. Leah suspected her mother knew, as Victoria's "sneaking" lacked finesse. For an unspoken reason, her mother permitted this. Maybe she liked Victoria. Maybe she knew summer neared its close anyway, and soon they'd be out of her house. Whatever the reason, Leah was grateful. Because while they often filled those sultry, late nights with debauchery, they just as often didn't. Carnal pleasures turned emotional, talking until blue midnight melted into the gray hours of morning. Sharing dreams and memories, exchanging their pasts and futures while cozied together in their present.

Most mornings, just before sunrise, they'd scurry to the diner around the block from the shop. Tony's Diner never had a lot of patrons, so they could be together without the fear of running into one of Victoria's friends. With kitschy décor and a cheap menu, only truckers and lost tourists ever patronized the restaurant. But its proximity to their shop meant she and her father frequently stopped in for coffee or lunches, and now she shared this hidden gem with Victoria.

Leah slid into their favorite booth, pulling Victoria in beside her. With her arm thrown over Victoria's shoulder they leisurely enjoyed a pancake breakfast, taking turns feeding each other generously syruped bites.

Victoria sighed dramatically, and Leah raised her eyebrows in silent question. "I didn't know dating could be like this."

Leah snagged a bite from the fork. "Like what?"

"Good. Safe. Fun. It was such a chore with Carter." Victoria leaned back, turning contemplative. "It's like, we never talked, you know? He didn't talk to me about anything but school. Most of the time I spent fending him off."

"Gross. Now I spend my time fending you off." Unimpressed, Victoria stole the fork from Leah and ate the bite of pancake she'd intended to serve herself. Leah pouted. "Like, I get relationships take work, or at least effort, but you shouldn't have to try so hard to like the other person."

"Exactly. It should be easy enough that you can do it in secret for four years." Evidently satisfied with herself, Victoria smirked and dipped a piece of pancake in syrup. Not one to be outdone, Leah dabbed her finger into the syrup and smeared it over her lips. Without warning she kissed Victoria hard on the cheek, leaving a sticky imprint on her face.

"Quit being a butthead, Tori."

"I'm your butthead, though," Victoria replied with a grin that dimpled beneath the syrup kiss print.

"Yes, *cariño*, my butthead."

The patrons of the diner, few as they were, ignored their existence for the most part. Even their canoodling—and Lord knows it was canoodling, though Leah would deny it to her death—didn't faze them. For a fleeting moment, Leah felt normal.

"Will it always feel like this?"

Leah turned toward the sound of Victoria's soft voice. "What do you mean?"

"I mean, you and me. Will it always feel like this? What if we drift apart?"

"What's the alternative? We're together forever?" Leah shrugged. "I don't believe in forever."

Victoria slowly pulled away from her, knitting her eyebrows together. "You don't?"

"No. I think forever is a promise you make and don't intend to keep." Leah paused, attempting to collect her thoughts in a less abrasive way. "Look, you know I love you and I would do anything for you, but I also see reality. We're going to different colleges. You don't want to come out of the closet. I'm not trying to stamp an expiration date on us, but the outlook is what it is."

She watched Victoria's face, and her heart sank when Victoria's lip quivered. "It sure sounds like you're trying to stamp an expiration date on us."

"No, no, come here." Using her superior strength, Leah pulled Victoria closer to her. "I'm sorry, that's not what I mean. We don't have forever, none of us do. We have limited minutes, hours, days, weeks. Every single one of those I want to spend with you, for however long I can. I can't promise forever, but I can promise my best, always."

Victoria worried her bottom lip and pivoted in her seat to face Leah completely. "So, you're not going to break up with me to hook up with smart, hot, older college girls?"

Leah tapped her index finger against her chin. "Hmm, I don't know. How hot are we talking? We talking dimes? We talking tens? Nines?"

"Ugh, now who's the butthead?" Victoria shoved her before sliding out of the booth. "I'm going to use the bathroom. Try not to pick up any 'dimes' while I'm gone."

Watching her go, Leah turned around once she'd disappeared behind the door. Truthfully, Leah feared the end of their relationship the way a child fears dark. It gripped her when she was alone, when she didn't have the reality of Victoria's skin on hers to keep her from tumbling into anxiety. Rubbing her thumb on the bench seat to try and calm her fraying nerves, Leah traced gouges in the wood. She peered down, reading the name someone scrawled deep into the seat. HANK or maybe HONK.

"Why would someone write 'honk'?" she asked under her breath. Nevertheless, the indentation gave her an idea. Leah heard Victoria coming up behind her and cast a wary glance over her shoulder. "Hey, keep watch for Tony. I'll be just a second."

"Why, what are you doing?" Leah felt Victoria's breath on her neck, and soon after heard her scandalized gasp. "Leah! You're defacing private property! It's vandalization. You're a vandal."

"*Dios mío*, don't be a dork. Just make sure nobody is looking over here." Leah finished her work and wiped the bits of wood from the bench. Her dorky girlfriend anxiously bounced on her heels behind her, as if they were heisting and not committing small-time vandalism on a bench that had been vandalized almost as many times as it had been sat on. She slapped a twenty on the table and shooed Victoria away from the bench. Unable to be cool at all, Victoria conspicuously leaned back into the booth as Leah hurried out the door.

Two storefronts down, Victoria finally caught up and squeezed her from behind. She'd never admit it out loud, but she preferred to be the little spoon. Feeling Victoria's weight against her back flooded her body with a sense of relief. "I can't believe you just committed a crime for me."

"Generous use of the word 'crime,' but okay." Leah chuckled as Victoria hung off her shoulders. "I thought about what you said and…"

well, at least our initials can be there forever. Forever, in that moment, you and me. As long as the booth exists, our love exists."

Victoria took her hand, swinging them together as they neared the shop. "So, our entire relationship rests upon Tony's Diner never going out of business?"

"Listen, two things can survive the apocalypse: roaches, and Tony's Diner."

"Is it because the roaches are in Tony's Diner?"

"Entirely possible."

Rounding the entrance to the shop, Victoria reached out and stopped them from walking any farther. "Do you hear that?"

Leah only heard the dim sound of highway traffic, but she stayed quiet and listened as best she could. Years of working in an auto shop and playing in a loud band meant her hearing probably lagged behind other kids her age. "No?"

Victoria, following a sound only she and perhaps dogs could hear, tiptoed around the shop toward the alley. Once past the dumpster, Leah heard the noise. Crying, very faint, like someone's baby but from far away. Halfway down the alley, they spotted it: a tiny, lone kitten cowering in a shoebox. "Oh no! Kitty!"

"Tori, don't touch the cat. It might be sick." Victoria ignored her, walking slowly toward the kitten, who bravely inched out of the box to investigate her with a sniff. It cut a pathetic picture with its haggard, tortoiseshell fur matted in places, one eye glued shut by gunk, and one ear shorter than the other. "Weird, we don't get a lot of stray cats here. *Papi* feeds them sometimes, and trapped a few to neuter, but not in a while. I wonder how it got here."

Victoria scooped the kitten into her arms, cooing at it. The pitiful creature shook from head to tail, but otherwise appeared friendly and alert. "Poor angel. We need to get it to the vet."

Torn between needing to open the shop and the anguished look on Victoria's face, predictably she and the kitten won out. "All right. I'll get a towel from inside and we'll take it to the clinic. But we can't keep it, okay?"

"I would take it home, but Ward is allergic and my mom would probably think it was her familiar."

Leah laughed, inching toward where Victoria cradled the kitten in her arms. One arm stretched out, she allowed the kitten to sniff her hand. It immediately started purring, obscenely loudly, and affectionately rubbed its dirty cheek on Leah's hand.

If there'd been a battle, she immediately lost. "Oh, Goddamnit."

With the kitten in Victoria's arms, wrapped in a towel, they walked the few blocks to the vet clinic together. It blinked one eye at her, observing the world with its big pupil. Leah gave it a wary look. "What do cats even eat?"

"Cat food." Victoria lifted the kitten up to eye level. "She's so cute. She needs a little love and she'll be okay again. We'll get her a litter box and some food. Ooh, some toys."

"We're not keeping the cat. You don't even know it's a her."

"It's definitely a girl," Victoria replied matter-of-factly, though there was no way she knew that. "And of course you're going to keep her. She's a grumpy kitten, just like you."

"What the hell? I'm not a grumpy—" So enthralled with the kitten, neither of them looked up as they nearly collided with someone else on the sidewalk. Victoria froze, and the kitten curiously peeked out of its towel to see what stopped them. "Hey, Myers."

"Riley." Victoria's voice, more like a squeak, shot out of her. She looked between Riley and Leah so quickly, Leah thought her eyes would fall out of her head. "Hey."

Riley smiled. "Hey, guys. Is that your cat? It's really cute."

"It is a cat Victoria just found in a shoebox," Leah replied tiredly. "It belongs to no one, but she is trying to force me to rescue it."

"Aw, what a teeny sweetheart." Riley leaned down to be level with the kitten, who stared back with her one good eye. She pet between the kitten's eyes just above her nose and received a quiet purr. "You should keep her if you can. Her eyes look just like yours. Well, her eye. She's in rough shape, it's a good thing you guys found her."

"Yeah, I, um, I was going for a walk. You know, just like I do sometimes. I heard this cat crying and it happened to be behind Leah's dad's shop? So, I asked her if she wouldn't mind getting me a towel for the cat, and then she offered to come and help me with the cat, so, here we are. With the cat." Torn between laughing at Victoria's horrible attempt at lying and being disheartened by it, Leah settled on shrugging.

Glancing between them, Riley's gaze lingered on Leah a moment before nodding along. "Oh, that's nice. I was on my way to the bookstore. I won't keep you. Good luck with the kitten."

"Thanks, Myers."

Victoria smiled in a way Leah could only describe as maniacal. "Good luck...with your...books."

Victoria practically ran toward the clinic and Leah had to power walk to catch up with her. Once around the block and out of the eyesight of Riley, Victoria let out a long breath and didn't wait for Leah as she burst into the veterinarian's office. The office was nearly as old as the town, with outdated carpeting and a stale, antiseptic smell. Each wall was nearly covered with pet safety or pet-related encouragement posters, and the far, long wall held a giant corkboard jam-packed with a chaotic collage of pet photos thumbtacked to it. As Victoria signed forms and gave the kitten to a vet technician, Leah plopped into one of the maroon vinyl seats below the corkboard. She didn't look over when Victoria sat down, practically hyperventilating. Across from them, a little girl sat next to her mother, with a guinea pig snorting around inside a pink cage on her lap.

"So, you made that hella awkward."

Victoria looked at her sharply. "I did not. I just…didn't expect to see Riley here."

"She does live in town. Maybe she has a secret girlfriend too." Apparently, she'd said the wrong thing because Victoria scowled. "What's wrong?"

"What if she tells someone she saw us together?" Shrill panic clipped her worried whisper. "Fuck, do you think she suspects anything?"

"Like what? That we might be, perish the thought, friends? It's not like she caught me with my hand down your pants."

"It's not funny, Leah," Victoria shot back hotly, each of her words a dagger poking at Leah's heart. "If she says anything and it gets back to my mom? I'm dead. She'll tell my dad, and then they'll both freak out."

"Because you made a friend?"

"No, because you're—"

And at that, the ice in Leah's heart spread to her blood. Victoria clamped her mouth shut. "Because I'm what, Victoria? Finish your sentence."

"Ugh, Leah, no. I wasn't going to—I'm just freaked out right now, okay? I'm not making any sense."

Leah fought the tears burning her eyes and pushed herself out of her chair. She looked down at Victoria with her practiced façade of indifference. "No, you're making sense. I'm gonna wait outside."

On a bench in front of the clinic, Leah sat down and rubbed her face in her hands. She wondered if she stood a chance against the architecture of the life Victoria had been promised. Where did a poor brown girl from the poor side of town fit in the gilded life of Garden Hills royalty? In the margins, in the periphery, in a place easily accessed—and easily hidden. Of course, Leah knew what she'd gotten into. She agreed to be patient, to have empathy for Victoria's inability to come out, but she'd underestimated how much it might hurt to be continuously seconded to the fake life Victoria was living.

About an hour later, Victoria emerged with the kitten in a small carrier. She sat next to Leah, placed the carrier at their feet, and stared out into the hot morning sun. Shops around them began to open their doors, local business owners planting sandwich boards onto the sidewalks to bring in foot traffic. A weekday, so not many people walked the streets, but soon it would have that sleepy town bustle of retirees and stay-at-home parents strolling the sidewalk.

"She's going to be fine. They said it looks like an animal bit her ear, so they bandaged it and she'll have to get it checked again in a week or two. They cleared up the gunk in her eye and gave me some medicine to give her to help clear the infection, but they didn't seem sure she'd have full eyesight in that eye. But, otherwise, she's a healthy kitten. They think she's about seven weeks old." Victoria looked down, clearing her throat. "Uh, they also said she was very aggressive toward the male vet they had in there but seemed okay with the women."

"Smart kitty."

"If you don't want to keep her, the vet offered to take her to the county shelter."

Leah picked up the carrier and turned it so the wire opening faced her. The kitten blinked sleepily—perhaps they drugged her—and stretched out a tiny paw toward the grate. Leah met the paw with her finger, pressing into the multicolored pads of her feet. "Who's gonna love you, huh? A misandrist gremlin with one good eye and a bitten-off ear?"

Victoria smiled gently, leaning toward Leah to get a glimpse at the kitten. The kitten kept its one good eye locked on Leah, blinking it once slowly. "She likes you. That's the way cats say they love you. Slow blinks."

"We gotta teach you not to trust people so easily," Leah said to the cat, reaching her finger into the crate to pet her tiny head. "You'll only get hurt."

Eyes on the kitten, she felt Victoria's stare on the side of her face. Victoria tucked Leah's hair behind her ear, drawing close to press her forehead against Leah's temple. "I'm sorry."

"Tori, are you ashamed of me?" Victoria pulled back and appeared horrified at the suggestion. "I know you're scared of people knowing you're a lesbian, and I get that. I don't get you being afraid of people knowing we're friends. That makes me feel…really shitty."

"God, no, Leah. I'm so, so sorry I made you feel that way. I'm not ashamed of you. Not even a little. I panicked, that's all." Victoria took the carrier and placed it on the ground to capture Leah's full attention. "Look, my parents have controlled my life since the day I was born. I mean, who names two children after their dad? But it was made very clear to Vic and me that there were specific paths for us to take, and any other paths would not be supported. You know like how at an arcade, dummy coins get automatically rejected into the coin receptacle? That's my family. If you don't have the same stamp as all the others, you're not worthy. My cousin Dan decided not to go into my great-uncle's business and instead became a chef. And he's a great chef. He's got a restaurant with a Michelin star. Nobody in my family speaks to him."

"What? Why?"

"For a while they tolerated him, especially at first when he got successful really fast. Then one Christmas, he brought his Japanese boyfriend to my grandparents' house. The looks on their faces..." Victoria looked stricken. "My uncle and his boyfriend didn't stay for dinner, and he was never invited back. My mom made it apparent, in no uncertain terms, that Lockwoods who don't fit the mold are not considered part of the family." Victoria sighed and placed her head on Leah's shoulder. "I love you, Leah. That's not up for debate, I hope you know that. I'm not ashamed of you. Most of the time it's the opposite—I can't believe you want anything to do with me. But...my mom won't accept you. And if I tell her about us, or she finds out, she'll do anything she can to ruin it. She tried to get my cousin's restaurant closed by paying off the food inspectors. She's heinous."

Leah understood, acutely, the trembling fear of coming out. Even though deep down she knew her parents would never reject her, the possibility never went away until she told them, and there was collateral damage despite their acceptance. She drew her arm around Victoria's back. "That's a lot of fear to live with."

Victoria sandwiched Leah's hands between hers and sighed. "It is, but...you make me less afraid. Being with you gives me hope that things can be better."

"I have always considered myself a beacon of positivity and light," Leah replied, and Victoria burst out laughing, tightly curling her arms around Leah's. "I wish our happiness didn't scare other people. I wish it didn't scare you. But that's not saying I don't understand, because I do. I wouldn't be here with you if I didn't get it."

Victoria placed a soft kiss on her cheek. "I know it's been hard on you, dating me in secret, and I don't want it to be that way forever. I'd like to make it up to you, at least a little. Can you take time off work?"

Leah paused. She could always take time off from Benny's; she practically made her own schedule there. Her dad would understand if she needed time away, as he already prepared to be without his apprentice when she left for college. "Sure, why?"

"My parents are going away to Europe for the week." Leah snorted. "Yeah, I know, it's a thing they do every year. I thought...you know how we're always trying not to get caught by your mom at your house? And how it's hard for us to find places to, uh, be together?"

"Like the dressing room at JC Penney? Or behind the carnival at the Kowahoke Fair? Or my car...a lot?" While being with Victoria felt incredible beyond compare, the places in which they acted on those feelings were inglorious and inadequate. Leah ached to have a place they could enjoy each other without interruption or requiring gymnastics.

"Right, exactly. Well, Vic is taking Ward to some nerdy convention, and I thought maybe you'd like to come to our lake house with me." Victoria's eyes, lightly brown and flecked with soft yellows, gazed at her hopefully. "We can stay there for as long as you can take off work."

Leah glanced at the carrier. "I'd have to make sure my parents are cool with handling her for a couple days."

"Aw, I'm so glad you want to keep her."

"Want is a strong word, but I feel bad for the pathetic thing."

"So, you want to go? We can go out on the kayaks, and there's a really cute downtown. The house is huge for no reason—it has a jacuzzi and a giant patio overlooking the lake." Victoria beseeched her, "Say yes, please. It'll be so nice for us to have time to ourselves. We're both leaving for college soon and we should, I don't know, have a getaway before we have to go."

"Okay, okay, don't break out the pout." Throwing her arms around Leah's shoulders, Victoria hugged her tightly and kissed her on the temple. "Fine, let's do it."

To the tune of a new mix Leah created, Victoria drove the one and a half hours to the lake district. In a rather podunk part of their state, at the base of a chain of ski-ready mountains, sat a glistening, freshwater lake surrounded by rich people's summer homes. Leah'd never been there, only driven through on the way to another place, but seen enough photos to know of its beauty. The Lockwood summer house appeared fairly modest for the area. Not a gaudy McMansion, but a luxurious cabin attempting to imitate being rustic. It boasted seven bedrooms—Leah counted as Victoria brought her to theirs—and at least five bathrooms. A spacious great room with a fireplace, a full kitchen, a hot tub out on a giant deck, a small, private pool, and a game room.

Truly how the other half lived.

"There are a couple kayaks down by the dock, and we own a pair of rowboats. If you felt like going out on the water while we're here," Victoria explained, pointing out of the glass back doors toward the shore. Without having to sneak around as they did at home, Victoria looked more relaxed. Of course, pictures of her family hung everywhere, including the pointed gaze of her mother, but Leah could see she'd left most of her tension behind.

Leah gently lifted Victoria's hair over her shoulder, pressing kisses from her bare shoulder, up her neck, to the outer shell of ear. "With all due respect to this big-ass house? I don't want to see any other room but your bedroom for no less than a minimum of three hours."

Victoria took her hand and pulled her up the staircase, back toward the bedrooms. "Is that so?" she asked, walking backward down the hallway. "No sightseeing, then?"

"No, *cariño*," Leah said, plastering a big smirk on her face. "Only spelunking."

With Victoria's palm flat on her sternum, she got unceremoniously shoved into the bedroom, laughing and stumbling inside. Absolutely worth saying, as the fierce blush on Victoria's face, in combination with the indignation, had her nearly doubled over with laughter. She flopped back onto the bed and Victoria vaulted her and pinned her to the bedsheets. Bracketing her arms on either side of Leah's head, she kissed the tip of Leah's nose.

"I love you," she murmured, placing another kiss on her lips. "Despite the fact that you're lewd."

"You like that I'm lewd."

Victoria hummed, sinking her teeth into Leah's shoulder. "Shut up and get to that spelunking, Vasquez."

Unsurprisingly, they did not, in fact, make it out onto any of the boats. Spending most of their time holed up in the house or lounging on the deck, only at night did they venture to the lake, sun-kissed limbs absorbing the moonlight. On their last night away, they sat on the edge of the Lockwood's dock, swinging their bare feet just above the water. Thankfully the weather held up, allowing them an open view of the stars and the bright, bulbous moon. While Leah enjoyed the weekend, every moment ached with a twinge of doom. Move-in day was just over a week away, and while they hadn't spoken about it, Leah knew Victoria's would be around the same time.

As if reading her mind, Victoria spoke up. "I wish we could run away."

Her voice was soft, perhaps afraid of spooking the calm contentment between them. "Yeah? Where do you want to go?"

Victoria shrugged, sliding over to rest her head on Leah's shoulder, and wrapped her arms around Leah's middle. "Anywhere. I just want to be with you."

"California? Alaska? Hop on a boat, get lost on a Polynesian island? You give pasty Europeans swim lessons, and I serve up sugary cocktails to tourists?" For those precious couple of minutes, Leah fantasized about that life. Her tan girlfriend with salty, beach-babe hair strolling into their cozy hut over crystal blue waters. Their own paradise, away from the prying eyes of the world. "I wish we could run away too."

"But we can't," Victoria whispered. "You can't. Your future is so bright. A civil engineer, changing the world. And I—I'll probably end up back in Garden Hills at my dad's company."

The way Victoria said it sounded like a jail sentence. Maybe it was. "What do you want to do? What's the ultimate dream for you?"

"I want to be an author," she replied without hesitation. "I always have."

Leah rested her head against Victoria's. "You'd be good at it. Your creative writing in AP was always the best in the class."

"It was?"

In fact, Leah kept a copy of one of Victoria's poems in a drawer in her room. They'd printed it in the school newspaper, and she'd read the stupid paper for the first time in her life, snipped the poem, and tucked it safely away. "Yeah. You're a talented writer, Tori. You could go anywhere with that talent."

Victoria didn't respond, only scooted closer to press against Leah's side. They watched the other lakeside residents bring in their boats for the night, some unknown curfew keeping them off the lake after dark. Water lapped at their feet, splashing quietly against the wooden dock below. "Do you want to keep dating in college? I know these past few months have been hard, us hiding and me being an idiot. I don't like that we have to lie, or hide, and that I can't show off my hot, freakishly smart girlfriend. And, well, I…maybe I'm selfish, but I want to keep seeing you. I love you. I…don't know what I'd do without you. But I'd understand if it was too hard."

How could Leah assess the difference in difficulty between dating Tori in secret and being without her? Both tore her heart in two, did it really matter how?

"Tori, you know I love you. I would do anything for you. Obviously, I don't want to hide forever. I get that coming out for you is really hard, and I'm not going to push you. For the time being, I'm cool with us being discreet when we're home. If that's the price to pay to be with you, I'll pay it." Leah inhaled a deep breath to steady herself. "But eventually, I think you're going to have a choice to make. I hope you choose what makes you happy."

After a bout of thoughtful silence, Victoria hugged her tighter. "You make me happy."

Could she ever make Victoria happy enough to choose her over the other futures competing for her attention? Leah wasn't sure how well she stacked up against the formidable monolith of the Lockwoods. But she didn't voice these concerns, because no matter how brave Victoria thought Leah was, she didn't have that kind of courage. "You make me happy too, *mi amor*. More than you'll ever know."

After returning from the lake house, Leah barely saw Victoria as they packed and prepped to make their individual moves to Massachusetts. Leah intended to drive up with her dad, who talked nonstop about his excitement over taking the Amtrak train back home. Victoria unfortunately was subjected to a family trip to Harvard, so she knew it would be a bit before they could see each other after they moved in.

So, when the phone rang at the shop and Victoria's voice came through the other line, the ache in Leah grew so strong she'd have committed treason just to look at her. The circumstances, however, were not ideal. "I'm so, so sorry, Leah. I would never ask you to come here, but I'm desperate."

Twirling the phone cord around her finger, Leah leaned against the wall of the shop. "It's not a problem, *cariño*. It's literally what I do. You're at home?"

"Yes. I can't get this stupid car to start." Leah could hear Victoria kick the car over the phone. "I think it just needs a jump but the guys my dad usually hires aren't answering and nobody is home. Not that anybody here would know how to jump a car. Maybe Ward because he's a weirdo, but he's also eleven."

"Relax, I'll be by in a minute. Okay? Love you too. Bye." Leah hung up, turning the corner of the office to see her father grinning widely with Gremlin in his hands. His giant man hands dwarfed Gremlin into a pocket-sized kitten. Of course, she was pocket-sized. Leah actually carried her in a pocket sometimes. "Yes?"

"Gremmy and I heard you talking to your *novia*. Is everything okay?"

"Tori needs a jump start. All that money for garbage foreign cars that don't start," she lamented, shaking her head. Her father placed Gremlin on his shoulder and followed her into the office where she kept the keys. Gremlin busied herself gnawing on the outside of her father's ear. Luckily it was only his ear. As it turned out, Gremlin did hate men and would hiss or hide at any man who came into the shop. Any man, of course, but Hector. Maybe he'd been right about the Vasquez Charm.

"Okay." Leah found the silence he left between them suspicious, so she stopped short of leaving and sighed. "How come we never met Tori's parents?"

"Because I've never met them." Leah swallowed, kicking at the tiles with her boots. "Her parents are homophobic, and she doesn't want them to know we're dating."

Hector frowned. "I do not like that, *mija*. Anyone who is lucky enough to date my Leah should not be ashamed."

"Yeah, well, it's complicated. I don't expect you to understand." Brushing past him, Leah climbed into his pickup truck and turned the engine over. She pretended not to see him staring after her from the door of the shop, unhappily crossing his arms over his chest.

Leah drove the couple of minutes to Tori's house, up the winding hill on the north side of Garden Hills. It felt illicit to pull her truck into the Lockwood's driveway, clandestinely meeting their only daughter in a garage. A spacious three-car garage, she noted, hopping out of the truck in front of the open garage door where Victoria's sporty white sedan sat in the center. She paced back and forth behind it and squealed when she saw Leah.

Victoria hugged her hard, giving her a quick kiss on the lips. "Thank you so much. I'm supposed to be meeting Dad at some dumbass event and I insisted on driving separately so I could come see you after, and now the stupid car won't start."

She wanted to share Victoria's enthusiasm, but her father's voice echoed in the back of her mind. "It's all good. Should only take a minute, *amor*."

"Sorry, I'm just...stressed out. My mom's been a huge dick since they got back from Europe, and this event is apparently really important and I have to attend. Plus, just, getting ready to leave for college and I...I'm overwhelmed."

Leah nodded, stroking her hand through Victoria's hair. "I get it. Let me get you out of here. Solve at least one problem for you, okay?"

Though she had to climb onto the bumper to get into the hood of her dad's truck, the rest of the jump she did with ease. Having jumped cars since the fifth grade, it didn't take more than a minute or two to get Victoria's car to roar to life. Victoria jumped up and down at the sound of the working engine. "Oh, thank God. Or, no. Thank Leah."

She disconnected the cars, tossing the cables into the bed of the truck. "We should let the car run for a minute."

Leaning against Victoria's car, she watched as Victoria slowly approached her with a predatory glint. "Oh, whatever will we do to pass the time?"

Victoria pinned her with her hips, bringing her in for a kiss Leah hungrily returned. They hadn't seen each other in days, and the physical withdrawal usurped her better sense. Eventually, her brain restarted and she pulled back an inch. "Tori, we probably shouldn't."

"Why not? There's nobody home," she said, trailing her lips down Leah's neck. "I haven't touched you in days. It sucks. I can't stop thinking about you. I can't stop thinking about how you feel in my hands...how you feel inside."

A sentiment Leah fully understood and felt similarly, so she threaded her fingers in Victoria's hair and pulled her in again for another kiss. Victoria grabbed the collar of her jumpsuit and kept them close, slotting Leah's leg between her own. "Jesus, Tori."

"Showing up here in your jumpsuit. You know it drives me crazy. You look so good in this." Leah smirked into the kiss, lifting her leg just enough to press between Victoria's legs and cull an obscene moan from her girlfriend.

The vibrating hum of Victoria's engine covered the noise of heels clicking against the cement floor until it was too late. Her zipper got yanked down by Victoria's insistent, hot hands, and just as her palm grazed the hem of Leah's tank top, someone cleared their throat.

Victoria jumped so far away from Leah she could've bounced into another county. She said one word and Leah's world crashed down.

"Mom?"

CHAPTER TEN

Fourteen years ago, Victoria attended a birthday party for one of her older brother's classmates. The family owned a pool—a big, glistening azure paradise luring Victoria like a siren. At three, she could not swim, as her parents hadn't yet installed the in-ground pool in which she'd later spend most of her adolescence. With the bravery of a toddler and no one watching, she walked into the shallow end of the pool and delighted in the way the warm water distorted her legs and feet. Slowly descending deeper, she reveled in the buoyancy of her body in the water. Bold, she ducked her head underwater and sank to the bottom. The world slowed down beneath the water. Sounds muted, her body weightless, life on pause until she'd breach the surface and gasp for air. She did it several times, each time moving deeper and deeper into the pool. A squeaky slip on the incline separating the shallow water from the deep, and Victoria descended into the dark abyss. She screamed, but her voice garbled under the surface. Water rushed down her throat. Her eyes burned from the chlorine. Fear filled her every cell.

Two strong arms yanked her up, hauling her out of the pool. She sputtered and coughed up water, blinking up into the summer sun as her father, eyes worried and linen suit soaked, blurred into existence.

Shortly after, Victoria took up swimming in an effort to never feel that way again.

However, fourteen years later, she stood above the water, drowning.

She stumbled back from Leah like she'd been lit on fire. The arousal fled quickly, and her body went cold despite the summer heat. About ten feet away, her mother waited at the entrance to the garage, purse slung over her arm. Her eyes, the cold version of Victoria's own, shot icicles at her from afar.

Then came the tired, disappointed sigh. "Really, Victoria."

"It's not what you think," Victoria replied quickly. "It's—"

"It's not what? Not you, in our garage, getting felt up by the help?"

"The help?" Leah asked, voice pitched high in shock.

Her mother huffed, unimpressed. "Is this a friend of yours?"

Leah, visibly agitated by her mother's racist assumption, appeared primed to respond. Victoria replied first. "No, no it's…nothing like that. It's…we're not…"

The irritation in Leah's eyes gave quickly to disbelief. Her mother thankfully couldn't see Leah's face; the heartbreak would've been a dead giveaway. It killed Victoria to see Leah hurt, but the panic squeezing her veins cauterized any other option.

"Victoria, I know you're prone to your cries for attention, but honestly. If you're going to try on a personality, lesbian isn't the look for you. For one thing, you don't have the hair for it."

"I'm not gay," Victoria objected in a hurry. "I'm not a lesbian."

"You could have at least found someone of your own class to have a sapphic interlude with." She sneered at Leah, lip raised in distaste. "Not dip into the south side population and go with whatever stuck to you."

"Is she for fucking real right now?" Leah turned to glare at her mother. "You're a piece of work, lady. I guess it's true what they say, you can't buy class."

"It doesn't appear you'll ever know."

"You know what, Mrs. Lockwood? Just save us the time and call me a slur," Leah replied hotly. "Go for it. I'm sure I've heard it before and it won't bother me, but maybe it'll loosen the stick in your ass to say it out loud."

"Leah, stop," Victoria pleaded, on the verge of hyperventilation. "It's fine, Mother. She was…she was just here to help me jump the car. I got…carried away."

Every word leaving her mouth visibly stung Leah until she stumbled back into Victoria's car door, reeling. "Wow. I am so dumb. I am really,

really fucking dumb. I...I need to go." When their eyes met, Victoria's chest constricted in pain. The devastation and disappointment on Leah's face shattered her heart.

"Did you pay her, Victoria?" Leah stopped in her tracks at the silky, intentional question from her mother. "It's usually customary to pay for a service."

"I don't want your fucking money." From within her designer wallet, Cassandra withdrew several crisp hundred-dollar bills and extended them to Leah. "What is this? You think..." Leah laughed humorlessly, wiping her eyes with her forearm. "You think I give a shit about your money?"

"I will not let you perform this service in exchange for my daughter whoring herself. Take the money and get off my property before I call the police. Am I understood?"

Leah looked between the money and Victoria, silently begging her to intervene. All those sweet words she'd spoken, all the promises, all the declarations of love, Victoria couldn't back it up. Tears welled in Leah's eyes, and how badly Victoria wanted to soothe her, to beg for forgiveness. Fear kept her still and silent. Leah took the money. "Sure. I understand perfectly, Mrs. Lockwood. And don't worry, you won't be seeing me again."

The door to her truck slammed loud enough to startle Victoria. Leah backed out of the driveway quickly, tires squealing in her wake as she disappeared from view. It took all of Victoria's strength not to weep. Her heart thumped fast, overwhelmingly so, as if she were about to have a panic attack. With calm, deliberate steps, her mother approached her and got far too close. The scent of expensive perfume invaded her senses.

"Victoria, listen to me very carefully. If I ever see this deviant behavior from you again, you will not only be cut off from this family, but cut out. No college, no cushy job with your father, no home, nothing."

Sniffling, Victoria stuck out her chin with the small amount of defiance she had left. "I haven't done anything wrong. You can't prove anything."

"Not a very smart bet, darling." She leaned in close. "I know, Victoria. I know everything."

A chill shot down Victoria's spine, like a shock of cold water into her bone marrow. "I—I don't know what you're talking about."

"Of your minimal talents, lying is not one of them. You mean to tell me that wasn't Leah Vasquez, daughter of Hector Vasquez, who owns the auto shop downtown? Leah Vasquez, who you paraded around our family's summer house?" The panic fully set in, and Victoria felt the beads of perspiration form on her forehead. She gripped her fists in sweaty palms. "I know you spent the summer fucking that wetback all over the county."

Victoria blinked, furious tears trickling down her cheeks. How could she know? They were so careful. Well, sure, maybe in hindsight the lake house wasn't a great idea…but everywhere else? "Don't you ever call her that again."

"Or you'll what?" Cassandra laughed, light and airy. "So quick to defend her, and yet where is she? Probably halfway to some drug den with my money. Why do you think she started up with you, hmm? You think she'd give a damn about you if you weren't rich?"

"No, Leah's not like that. You don't know her. Unlike you, she actually loves me. And I—I love her, Mother. I love her."

Eyes glinting, Cassandra cocked an eyebrow. "Really?"

"I'm in love with her." Gathering up any bits of courage she might have left, Victoria went for broke. "And I don't care what you think. You can tell Dad, take away my college money, do whatever you want. It's not going to stop me from loving her."

"I see. You're willing to ruin your life for her. You think that's romantic, do you?" Victoria didn't respond. She'd failed Leah once already today; she wouldn't fail her twice. Her mother's rouge lips curled into a knowing smirk. "Then let me ask you this: are you willing to ruin her life too?"

"What? I…I would never hurt Leah." *Not any more than I already did.*

"You don't have to do a thing. Do you want me to have her arrested for assault? You're only seventeen, and I would have no trouble convincing a judge into a statutory rape charge." Victoria trembled, eyes widening in shock. Cruelty dripped from her mother as easy as water. "Do you think she has the money to fight those allegations in court? I don't. And who knows what else they'll dig into? It'd be a shame for a young girl to see her father deported right as she enters college. And, of course, a felony means bye-bye scholarship. She'll be slinging pizza pies for the rest of her life. Is that what you want for her? Will your 'love' be worth all it will cost her?"

The thought of her mother robbing Leah of the very future Victoria so badly wanted for them…she couldn't bear it. She didn't deserve Cassandra Lockwood's wrath. She deserved the world, and if that meant a world without Victoria, well, maybe she'd be better off.

What did Victoria have to offer, anyway? A life in the closet with a toxic family, and a future chained to a desk in corporate purgatory. Nothing good enough for someone as tremendous as Leah.

"Don't...don't do anything to Leah or her family. Please." She tried desperately to control her breathing between short sobs. "I won't see her again, I promise. Just...leave her alone."

"As long as you behave yourself, nothing will happen to your precious south side dyke. Now, pull yourself together and get to your father's luncheon. We will never speak of this again."

Her mother stalked away, the clack of her heels fading into the distance. Victoria got into her car, gripping the steering wheel tightly with both hands. She let out a long, hard scream. But she'd slid underwater and nobody could hear her. She drowned, alone.

The luncheon lasted several hours, where Victoria allowed older men to attempt to impress her or throw their age-appropriate sons at her. Without Vic, who usually shielded her from these unwanted advances, she had no reprieve from the attention. This was her future, she realized as she looked around at the copy-and-paste white men in suits. A bland hotel ballroom full of rich white men, reeking of shrimp cocktail, whiskey, and imported cologne. There would be no Leah in her future. It'd been foolish to think there could be. You get money and privilege as a Lockwood, but you don't get happiness too.

Victoria snuck away into the women's bathroom, stood over the sink, and sobbed openly. Unexpectedly, a woman strolled into the bathroom and Victoria instinctively turned from the door to hide her sniffling. Not many women attended these functions, but Victoria didn't want any of them to see her cry. God forbid her parents find out.

"You okay?" The voice didn't sound like one of the rich ladies, and when Victoria turned, she realized it was a caterer. Not much older than Victoria, looking like a tall version of Leah with the same curly hair, but with brown eyes instead of Leah's green marble. "Do you need help?"

"No, no, I'm fine," Victoria replied through sniffles, waving her off. She withdrew a tissue from her clutch purse and dabbed under her eyes. "I'm obviously not fine, but it's okay."

Victoria made herself unobtrusive in a corner as the woman used the restroom. When she arrived at the sinks to wash her hands, she gave Victoria another look. "Do you want to talk about it?"

"That's really nice of you, but no, I don't want to ruin anyone's day. I just...broke up with my girlfriend. Or, well, she left and I don't know if I'll ever see her again and I…" Tears fell from her eyes again, and Victoria struggled to breathe through the constriction in her throat. Alarmed, the girl rushed to her and gave her a hug, and Victoria wept into the girl's black vest. "I love her. I've made a huge mistake."

The girl pulled back, placing her hands on Victoria's shoulders. "Hey, breathe for me, okay? Deep breaths. Why don't you call her?"

"She doesn't have a cell phone. I tried her home phone already and she didn't answer. I—I beeped her, too, and nothing." Victoria attempted the deep breaths as suggested. After a dozen of them, she could manage more coherent sentences. "I just want to tell her I'm sorry."

"So, tell her you're sorry. It's not like she fell off the face of the Earth or something, right?" The caterer smiled at her. "This thing is almost over anyway. Whose kid are you?"

"Lockwood. I'm Victoria. Uh, Tori."

"Nice to meet you, Tori. I'm Wil. Look, if anyone asks, I'll tell them you were sick in the bathroom and went home, okay? If I see Mr. Lockwood, I'll let him know. Go find your girl."

From her lips it sounded so easy. Victoria nodded, swiping under her eyes again to try and catch the dripping mascara. "Okay. Thank you, Wil."

"Good luck, Tori."

Victoria rushed out of the bathroom and managed to slip out of the hotel unnoticed. Obliterating the speed limit, she raced to Leah's home on the far side of Garden Hills. Her car came to a screeching halt outside the house, and she barely remembered to turn off the engine before sprinting out of the car.

Leah's car was missing from the driveway.

Panicked tears streamed down her face as she pounded on the front door. "Leah! Leah, answer the door! I'm sorry. I'm so sorry. Please, please answer the door."

Victoria paused, fist raised, as the door opened. Her eyes slowly tracked upward to the kind, startled eyes of Leah's mother. She'd never admitted it to Leah, but Loretta scared her. Loretta showed her nothing but kindness but remained aloof, as if she hadn't fully trusted Victoria but tolerated her for Leah's sake.

"Hello, Tori."

"Hi, Mrs. Vasquez. Sorry to knock like a crazy person. Is Leah home?" Victoria barely got the words out in her haste.

Loretta, calm as ever, shook her head. "She left for college."

Victoria gaped and lowered her fist to her side. "She…left? I thought she wasn't leaving until Thursday."

"Yes, well, she was keen on getting out of here as quickly as possible. She and Hector left about two hours ago." The news hit her like an uppercut and she stumbled, dazed, nearly falling off their front stoop. She gripped the railing to try to keep herself upright. Her mind swirled, heat building behind her eyes. Sinking to the ground, Victoria choked out hard sobs.

Leah's mother sat next to her on the steps. "I'm sorry, Victoria. I told her she was being rash, but you know how she is when she makes up her mind about something."

"Uh-huh." Her words barely registered in Victoria's mind. Leah was gone.

"Why don't you come inside for a minute?"

"No, no, I'm sorry. I should go," she said between gasps for breath. "I didn't mean...to..."

"Please, I don't want you driving this upset." Loretta didn't budge, standing up from the stoop and holding out her hand. And really, where could Victoria turn? The only other person who knew about Leah was Vic, and she couldn't go home yet. She took her hand and followed Loretta inside. Victoria hadn't spent much time in the Vasquezes' living room—it barely fit the three of them, never mind adding Victoria to the equation. She sat down next to Loretta on the worn, brown-and-orange plaid wool couch. A tiny three-seater, and three worn spots where the Vasquez family hung out together. Victoria didn't feel comfortable encroaching on their family space, especially now, and sat on the edge of the cushion. Loretta sighed. "Leah didn't explain everything to me. She was rather inconsolable, as you can imagine. I got the gist."

"I fucked up." Clearly surprised at her language, Loretta raised her eyebrows but kept silent. "I love Leah, Mrs. Vasquez. I love her so much. But I messed up so bad, and now I can't fix it. Leah's gone, and she's not going to want anything to do with me. I feel...lost."

"I think that's a very reasonable way to feel right now. At your age, love is...it's everything. It's big and deep and tough." She graciously handed Victoria a tissue. "You know, Hector and I met when we were fifteen."

Victoria dabbed her nose. "Really? That's young."

"It was. I get it, a bit, how you two feel about each other. It can feel tremendous."

"She's the most important person in the world to me and I...I failed her, Mrs. Vasquez. My mom caught us together and said such horrible things to Leah and I just stood there. I stood there like a coward. So of course Leah left. Why wouldn't she? Now she's seen me for who I really am. A big, stupid phony whose own mother doesn't accept her."

Through her tears, Victoria saw a flash of anger in Loretta's eyes. She did seem to have the same inclination for passion like Hector and Leah, but hers was a creeping intensity, like an ocean wave building. "I'm very sorry you went through that, sweetheart. Being a parent is a tricky thing, but loving your child is supposed to be the easy part. However, even that has its challenges." Loretta folded her hands in her lap, peering down at them. "Leah's always been Leah. There was never a time when she wasn't exactly the person you know. So, Hector and I had a feeling early on in her childhood about her being a lesbian. Something was always different about her. Leah was really, really into the yellow Power Ranger."

Wiping her tears on the tissue, Victoria chuckled. "She told me about the obsession she had with Vanessa from *The Little Mermaid* too."

Loretta grinned, fondly rolling her eyes. "Oh, my goodness, do you know how hard it was to find anything with her likeness? She's only on screen for like twenty minutes, and she's a villain. What little kid begs for a shirt with Ursula's human form on it? So, obviously we had an inkling. I prayed about it a lot. I asked our priest for guidance and…he didn't offer the kind of advice I sought, and instead threw more doubt at me."

"What did he say?"

"Unkind things about my child." Loretta's features hardened. "One day, Leah came into the living room with this crumpled piece of paper in her hands. She couldn't have been more than ten, maybe eleven? My little girl stands right there"—she pointed to a spot on the carpet in front of the television—"shaking so hard I thought she had the flu. She could barely look us in the eye. Just clutching this piece of paper like it was her will to live. And you know Leah, she's never scared of anything."

"No, never." Except me, Victoria thought, and she was right.

"I'm worried, because what could possibly have scared my warrior girl this much? She reads from her paper, her tiny voice trembling, and she tells us she's a lesbian."

Victoria's eyes watered. "She's so brave."

Loretta nodded. "So brave. We give her a hug, tell her we love her no matter what. And when she goes back up to her room, I nearly burst into tears because…she was afraid of us. She was scared to tell us who she is. My baby that I carried inside me, whose little knees I kissed when she fell off her bike, whose hand I held on the first day of kindergarten, who looked at me like I hung the moon her whole life… my baby was afraid of me. Afraid I wouldn't love her anymore. That gutted me."

"But you did it, though. Loved her and accepted her."

"Loving is easy, but accepting was hard for me." The guilt rolled over Loretta like a thundercloud. "I struggled with it. Privately. I never told Leah, but I struggled. I prayed, spent late nights talking to Hector, and I kept coming back to thinking I did something wrong. I worried about her life, her future. How many people would hurt my baby because of who she is? How many chances will she be denied because she's perceived as different? How much harder will she have to work because of someone else's hate? It seemed like the world got so much smaller for her."

Victoria wondered if her mother thought this way about her. Maybe. Maybe her denial, her cruel rejection, was her way of trying to keep Victoria safe. "How did you get over it?"

"Time," she replied. "And talking. We changed churches, found a priest who wasn't a bigot, and he guided me. Hector helped, too, because he never wavered. He comes from this huge, strict Catholic Mexican family, and he told them, in no uncertain terms, that if they didn't accept Leah, he'd never see them again, and they'd never see their grandchild."

Of all the shades of Leah that came from Hector, her commitment to herself and her principles might have been Victoria's favorite. "Leah is like that."

"Yes, she is." Loretta smiled softly. "At Leah's request, I told my parents, and they chose to cut us from their life. It was really hard. They put me in a place where they expected me to choose between them and my daughter. I'd…Leah is named after my mother. My mother held her and wept in the hospital when Leah was born. Her namesake grandchild, her only grandchild. Yet…when Leah needed them, they refused to be there for her."

"That's heartbreaking."

"It was. For me, and for Leah. She loved her grandparents. I told her they wouldn't be visiting anymore, and we would not be visiting them, and she apologized to me. Her big, shiny eyes blinking up at me, holding back tears, and she apologized for being a lesbian. Told me she could hide it from them if I wanted her to. She said sorry so many times I thought she needed to lie down or something. I could tell she was looking for the rejection. Putting her guard up, waiting for me to choose them over her, and it just broke me."

Victoria swallowed the hard lump in her throat, picturing Leah's betrayed, anguished eyes as she allowed her mother to tear them apart. After all she'd sacrificed—agreeing to hide, to be not herself, just so Victoria would love her.

"From then on, I didn't struggle. I never wanted my baby to look at me like that ever again. I made sure she understood I love her without conditions. Her happiness, her love, her truth, is what matters to me. I choose her, and I choose this family, my family, over everything else. Maybe one day my parents will come around. Hector's parents did. They didn't want to be cut off from their grandbaby, so they do their best, even if they don't totally understand. Last year they bought Leah a Melissa Etheridge CD for Christmas, smiling at her so big like, 'She's a lesbian, too!' So proud of themselves for connecting with her. Leah's probably never listened to it, but it meant a lot to her."

Victoria had seen the CD—it leaned on Leah's desk, with a big, bold red album cover, right next to a photo of Leah with Hector's parents. "It must've been hard to cut out your parents like that. My mom…she won't accept me. She basically told me I'd be disowned if I came out to my family and forbade me from seeing Leah again, and threatened to ruin Leah's life."

"Ruin her life how?"

"Mess with Hector and his immigration status, or get Leah arrested because we…" Victoria blushed, but the persistent look on Loretta's face forced her to continue. "Because I'm technically a minor. My parents are well connected and my mother's heinous scheming could give Rumpelstiltskin a run for his money."

Apparently much better than Leah at hiding her emotions, Loretta only flared her nostrils before she spoke in an even tone. "Victoria, you do not have to worry about protecting my family. That is not your burden. If anyone wants to try to come for my husband or my daughter, they will have to go through me. Do you understand?"

"Yes, ma'am." The familiar fire she'd seen in Leah gently roared behind Loretta's eyes. "I'm sorry about my mom. I wish I could cut my parents out like you did, but I don't have anywhere else to go. I'm not brave like you, or Leah."

"It's very hard to accept my parents' hatred. Especially because they don't see it as hatred, they see it as a convoluted kind of love. Like they're protecting Leah in some way. But, it got easier. As Leah grew up and became this strong, smart, outspoken person, I'm glad I never forced her to hide who she is." Victoria nodded, glancing away in shame. "All that to say, I'm sorry your mother said those things to you. I'm sorry she can't open up and love you for the wonderful young woman you are. For some parents, it takes a while to reevaluate who your children are and love them without conditions. Other parents, like Hector, pivot beautifully. That's a blessing."

"My brother did that," Victoria replied. "I told him I'm a lesbian and he just said okay. No hesitation. I don't know where he learned to love like that. Not from our parents."

"No, thankfully we don't all turn out like our parents. Mine didn't even like Hector."

Her eyes widened. "What? But he's so nice and he loves you a lot. How could anyone not like Hector?"

"That's what I thought. All they saw was a poor, Mexican immigrant with no education. You can imagine their thrill when I told them I was pregnant and we're keeping the baby. I thought my mother was going to have a stroke. In her defense, we were only seventeen. However, I don't think that's what bothered her most."

"Seventeen, wow."

"Yes, but we made it work. It was hard, and we sacrificed a lot. Hector wanted to be a big band leader, but we needed money. So, I didn't go to college and stayed home with Leah, while Hector went to trade school to be a mechanic. Every day we struggled, but we never gave in. My parents offered me twenty thousand dollars to divorce him. They offered to buy a house for just myself and Leah, if I would leave him."

Victoria blinked. "Sounds like something my parents would do. Try to buy love."

"It's a tough road sometimes, but a real, good love will get you through just about anything."

Victoria nodded, squeezing her eyes shut as another wave of grief washed over her. Nothing could stop the anguished cries from overpowering her senses. Loretta leaned over, collecting Victoria into her arms and holding her tightly. The loving, maternal gesture made her cry even harder.

"Oh, Tori. I'm so sorry. It'll be okay one day, I promise. But right now, we can just let it hurt, okay?"

"Is she…is she ever going to forgive me?" Victoria hiccuped, hugging Loretta as close as she could.

"It will take her some time, but yes."

"What if I don't deserve it?"

Pulling back, Loretta wiped her tears and used her free hand to grab Victoria another tissue. "We all deserve forgiveness. The first step is to forgive yourself."

"Forgive myself?" Victoria blew her nose softly, though it did nothing to clear the tear-induced stuffiness. "How can I ever forgive myself?"

"Forgive, and you will be forgiven. I believe that's true, Tori, even if it may take some time."

"How much time?"

"Oh, that I don't know," she said, rubbing Victoria's shoulder soothingly. "Timing is tricky. The only certainty is not to miss the opportunity when it comes."

CHAPTER ELEVEN

2005—CURRENT DAY

On the corkboard of Leah's life, cars were pinned directly in the center. They filled the yard of her childhood, functioning as her playground. Climbing over hoods, ducking under engines, rolling rimless tires through sodden grass. She and Billy hid in trunks, periodically getting locked in and crying for help. And as soon as she could hold a wrench, her father brought her to the shop as an unpaid apprentice. While school and life routinely spiraled into quagmires, cars remained a touchstone. Leah could lose herself in the machinations, the electronics, the personalities of each car and allow her life to take a back seat.

When she sat in their seats, Leah enjoyed the same short snapshot of people's lives she used to get from delivering pizzas. Feeling the wear on their steering wheels, or noting what dangly item they hung from their rearview. Personal vehicles, as a portable pod of semi-privacy, closely reflect the inner workings of the driver. This car smelled like money. An air freshener clipped to the vent pumped out a "new car smell" when the air-conditioning blew, but it smelled like a rich man. The cabin reeked of cologne, leather, not a speck of dirt or a hint of sweat. She caught a whiff of Tori's conditioner from the passenger seat and instantly, Leah saw them in the back seat of Tori's two-door coupe, her knees digging into the rough floor carpets as Tori writhed on the seat.

"Nope." Angry at the universe and its continuous efforts to ruin her life, Leah swiftly exited the car and slammed the door. How hadn't they discontinued the conditioner in the last five years? "Nope. Nope nope nope nope nope."

Gremlin circled Leah's legs, peering up at her as she talked to herself. She input the name of the part into the inventory computer and scanned the results. Coincidentally, they'd junked a similar car recently and had the alternator in stock. Lucky break, as otherwise she'd have to put an order in and extend this proximity to Victoria and her…fiancé. Well, not Victoria anymore. Evidently, she now went by Tori. Which was fine, of course. Hearing someone else call her that felt…fine.

The front door bells jingled, calling Leah from the stockroom toward the lobby. The fiancé, Ben, waved at her from the door. From between Leah's legs Gremlin hissed loudly, rearing back, and stuck her tail straight up in the air. Wisely, Ben stopped in his tracks.

"Sorry about that." Leah scooped Gremlin into her arms and deposited her on top of an elaborate cat tree she and Hector had built. Only food could distract Gremlin from her misandry, so she fished out a treat from her pocket and plunked it in front of the cat. Distracted, Gremlin crouched to eat and watched Ben out of the corner of her eye. "She, uh, doesn't like guys."

To his credit, Ben smiled and shrugged. "Who does?"

"Yeah, right." Leah had neither the desire nor time to make small talk with this flavorless seltzer of a man. "Did you need something else?"

"Nope, we're going for a walk, and I thought I'd stop in and see what the good word was."

"Ah." Of course, Tori didn't "stop in." Busy being extra heterosexual somewhere else. "Well, the 'good word' is that your alternator is shot."

Ben blinked. "Is…is that bad? That sounds maybe bad?"

"Nah, not really. I can fix it for you in about an hour."

"Cool. We won't be far. Tori said there are some taco trucks worth trying a couple blocks from here." He shrugged and slid his hands in his pockets. "She didn't want to stay at the diner."

Inhaling sharply, Leah reined in her emotions lest they break free and trample this man. The trucks, the diner—Leah avoided them both in the years since returning to Garden Hills. The memories they wrought were too much for her to bear. "Not as many as she might remember, but a few goods ones are left. Anyway, once you're done, I'll have the car ready to go for you."

"Great! Can I bring you anything?" Ben warily eyed Gremlin, who aimed her green stare at him with unrelenting severity. "An offering for the beast so that I may be spared her wrath?"

Scratching between her ears, Leah smirked at Gremlin. "I'm okay. I'm sure Gremlin would appreciate any scraps. She is fond of chicken."

"Chicken! Got it." He gave her an enthusiastic double thumbs-up. "Thanks a lot, Leah."

Leah nodded instead of responding, exhaling loudly as Ben left the store. Happy to be out of the presence of a man, Gremlin purred and rubbed Leah's face with her own. "Okay, Gremmy. Let's get to work."

Replacing the alternator didn't take the full hour, so Leah rotated the tires and filled them with air. She checked fluid levels and topped off anything low. Her father did this—he called it *hospitalidad*. Small efforts of little cost, but show the customer you don't just care about the problem. Their car is your car, he'd say. Well, he said *su coche es mi coche*, and gave customers his big grin. Leah didn't smile at people, but she did her best to treat the cars with the same care. His scruples were more his legacy than the shop. She dipped a squeegee in fluid and carefully washed the windshield from side to side. Methodical and precise, she let her mind wander as the bubbles appeared and disappeared with her actions. She didn't hear the bell, but Gremmy darting across the shop broke her from her reverie. Hopefully Ben did bring the chicken with him, because otherwise he wouldn't get far into the shop.

"Back here," Leah called. She dropped the squeegee into the bucket and looked up at the person who'd set off the bells.

Not Ben.

Tori.

Or, almost Tori. Back on the road where she'd towed them from, she hadn't spent any time scrutinizing her ex-girlfriend. The shock had overridden her other senses, leaving her with just enough faculty to do her job. But here, in the familiar setting, she could take a moment to really see her. It was…almost the girl she'd loved, but also not her at all. Older, obviously, with her long hair shorn into a professional woman's haircut whose ends grazed her shoulders. Makeup pristine, dressed in sensible pumps and neatly pressed pants, with a pinstriped button-down shirt tucked in. Leah, to her knowledge, looked the same as she did in high school, but with tattoos. But perhaps not. Perhaps

Tori saw the funhouse mirror ghost version of someone she loved as well.

"Hey." In her palm, Tori held a rolled-up ball of aluminum foil and extended it down to the cat. Gremlin, ever the traitor, circled Tori's legs and purred loudly, happily blinking her eyes. "Gremmy, look at you. Pretty girl, you got so big. I brought you a snack."

Tori fashioned the foil into a bowl of chicken. Gremlin happily chomped up the offering, her tail flicking in delight. Leah never moved but couldn't resist. "No snacks for me?"

With the phantom of a smirk crossing her face, Tori withdrew a yellow glass bottle from her purse and extended it out. "I thought you might want one of these. Jorge's daughter said she hadn't seen you in a while."

Leah walked like she had toothpicks for legs. She took the soda from Tori and smiled sadly down at it. Pineapple, her favorite. "You asked about me?"

"Yes." Her eyes flicked up to Tori's, searching for any remnant of the girl from years ago. The sparkle, the gleam, Leah found none of it. Only resignation, and a dash of fear. "How have you been?"

Rolling her eyes, Leah walked out of the bay and into the lobby to finish the paperwork. "Let's not."

Tori trailed behind her. "Leah?"

"Don't. Don't say my name like we're still—" Leah swallowed. "I'll ring you up and you can get back to your life with Brad."

"Ben." Despite the malice Leah spat at her, Tori's worried expression never went away. As Leah plugged numbers into the computer, Tori slowly walked to the front of the counter and put her hands on the cool Formica. "Leah, look at me. Please."

Because of fatal weakness, Leah did look up. Of course she did, because five years distance couldn't kill the magnetic pull Tori had over her. "What?"

"Where is Hector?"

"He's home. He doesn't work at the shop every day anymore. It's just me." Her practiced speech; nearly all her father's regular customers asked about him, the ones who didn't know. "I topped off the fluids and rotated the tires. The oil looked okay, but you'll want to get it changed in the next thousand miles."

A shaky hand with an expensive manicure handed over a black credit card. "I'm sorry I didn't get to see him. Please tell him I said hi. Your mother too. They were always very kind to me."

"Right, I'll be sure to pass that along," Leah said with a derisive snort.

Then, a bit of the old Tori flared with her temper. "Why are you making this difficult?"

"I didn't realize it was my job to make things easier for you."

"I just—" Tori grunted in frustration and visibly tried to will herself calm. "You could at least pretend to be civil. We were, at one time, friends."

"Hah. Is that what you tell yourself? No, we weren't."

Her slung arrow appeared to pierce, and Tori pulled back a bit. "We weren't friends?"

"No, Tori, we weren't friends," Leah said, the resignation and defeat slumping her shoulders. "I was madly in love with you, and you broke my heart, left town, and never came back."

"You left first." The anger between them fizzling out, Leah paused at the hurt in Tori's eyes. "You left first, and you didn't say goodbye."

"Yeah, it looks like you took that really hard."

"I did." A surprising honesty and anguish squeezed her words. "I was devastated."

Nearly. Just nearly, did Leah fall back into her trap. But Tori always had a gift for pretty words and empty promises. "Well, it appears you got over it, and me, just fine. Your mother won't mistake Bob for the help, good for you."

"Ben." Tears accumulated in Tori's eyes, and Leah watched her jaw flex in anger. The thing about having your heart forever fettered to another? No matter the distance, in minutes or miles, inflicting pain came just as readily as affection. Getting under each other's skin happened easily—the wound had never closed. "God, you're infuriating. You haven't changed at all. Still the same stubborn know-it-all you've always been."

"Yeah." Any fight left in Leah vacated swiftly. She shrugged. "You're probably right."

Tori blinked in obvious astonishment, clearly expecting a rebuttal. As she opened her mouth, the bells behind her jingled and Ben strolled in through the door with a smile. Unaware of the tension in the room, he stood next to Tori and peeked into the shop. "You fixed it?"

"It's fixed," she replied, tearing the receipt for Tori to sign. "You're all set."

Tori scribbled on the receipt and Gremlin crept into the shop, rubbing between Tori's ankles. Ben took a wary step back. "I knew I should've been the one to bring the chicken."

Gremlin narrowed her eyes at him but didn't hiss, instead hopping up on the counter to sit primly next to the register. Leah slid the receipt beneath the till and shut it with a short slam. "This is about as endeared to her as you're going to get."

"I'll take it." He nodded deferentially at the unamused feline.

Tori put her wallet away, rearranging her purse over her shoulder and wiping the expression from her face. Good ol' Neutral, Not Gay Tori. Must be nice, Leah thought, to turn your sexuality off and on at will.

"Thanks for your help, Leah."

For all his seeming obliviousness, Ben picked up on the intimacy in Tori's tone. "Do you two know each other?"

"We went to high school together," Leah filled in quickly. "Graduated in the same class."

This brought Ben a lot of glee, though Tori barely held back a grimace. "No way! I wish I'd known. I'd have stayed here the whole time and bugged you for stories about high school Tori. Any good ones? Any embarrassing tales?"

Leah sensed Tori's rigidity before she saw her tense. Ah, so the fiancé didn't know about prom. Still privileged information. After looking from Tori's helpless brown eyes to Ben's bright blues, Leah shook her head. "Not really. Tori was too popular for me. But, uh, it was nice to meet you. Good luck."

Ben grinned like an actor in a toothpaste commercial, all teeth and exuberance. "Thanks a lot, Leah. You're a lifesaver."

At closing, organizing the credit card receipts for the day, Leah spotted one with more writing than the others. She pulled it out and heaved a sigh.

Leah -
Here's my number. Call me.
XO
Tori

After diverting to Benny's to pick up dinner, Leah took the long way home, circling the back roads of Garden Hills, admiring the new construction going up on her side of the tracks. The mayor they'd elected while Leah was away at college actually made good on her promise to revitalize the dying parts of town, encouraging new businesses and building affordable homes. Even around her neighborhood, tiny facelifts brought them incrementally closer to the prestige of northern Garden Hills.

Her home had gotten a facelift, too, but not the kind with fancy new siding or modern landscaping. Leah built a ramp crisscrossing in front of the house, leading to the door. She'd also built a staircase onto the back of the house and cut out a door to her room. It made living with her parents at twenty-three years old less insufferable and pathetic. She entered through the front door, kicking off her boots just inside the threshold, and let Gremlin out of her carrier. Hector sat in his usual spot, in his wheelchair, parked just to the right of the sofa. A *telenovela* blared from the television near the wall. "*Hola, mija.* How was the shop?"

"Good, *Papi*. Steady." She raised the pizza and jerked her head to the kitchen. "Mom's on the late shift tonight, so we're on our own."

Hector followed her into the kitchen, pivoting to the cabinets to pull out the paper plates and napkins. They'd gotten him the most compact, lightweight wheelchair they could afford, but maneuvering around their microscopic kitchen still took a lot of effort for him. Leah arranged their meals, then opened the window to let in fresh air. About a year after she left for college, they finished installing the sound barrier along the highway, keeping the noise and pollution at bay. Finally, opening the windows felt refreshing.

They said grace and dug into their dinner, each of Leah's bites interrupted by Hector lobbing questions about the shop in his usual end-of-day inquisition. Leah understood his need to be involved, but rehashing her entire day both bored and exhausted her. Most days, the work was so laborious she simply went to sleep after, leaving dinner for her parents.

After falling quiet for a bit, Hector leaned back and gave her a quizzical look. "What aren't you telling me?"

Leah bit into the pizza crust, tearing it away and chewing as slowly as she could. Hector knew her too well. Nobody's father should know their child that well. "I saw Tori today."

His eyes bulged. "Oh, wow. She came by the shop to say hi?"

"No." Her gaze dropped to the paper plate. "Her fiancé's car died on the road in and I fixed it for them. We didn't say very much. It was…weird to see her."

Gremlin hopped onto the table, inspecting their dinner with an interested sniff. Hector shooed her from the pizza. "*Novio*, eh? *¿Gringo?*" Leah nodded. "What kind of car?"

The official metric by which he'd be judged. "A BMW."

"Ah, so money," Hector said, "but no taste."

Leah laughed and tore into another slice of pizza. Her father smiled the same high-wattage smile that never failed to lift her spirits.

She produced the receipt with Tori's number on it. "She asked me to call her."

At the production of the receipt, her father turned pensive. He slid the note toward himself with two fingers. Time smoothed the wrinkles in her memory, but Leah remembered quite vividly the long, tortuous ride to MIT. Her overwhelming sadness in duet with her father's anger. An anger he attempted to hide with cajoling and sympathy, but Leah felt it nonetheless.

"I never was so angry as I was that day," he admitted softly. "That *bruja madre* of hers...I thought many mean things about that woman. I said many prayers. For you, for Tori, but also for me, because I had hate in my heart."

"Me too." One of Leah's first lasting memories of college took place in a glorious, two-hundred-year-old Roman Catholic Church in Boston, where she'd sobbed in a pew and begged God to heal her heart. "I've missed her. I didn't realize how much until I saw her again."

"Young love, it's messy even without parents messing it up. How many years ago was that?"

"Five."

"*Cinco años, Dios mío.*" He tapped the paper against their kitchen table. "But to see her again, with a boyfriend, it hurt you like it was not five years, but five minutes."

He slid the receipt back to her. Leah traced the ink with her finger and looked up at her dad. "Do you think I should call her?"

Hector paused for a while, thoughtful. He knew she weighed his guidance more heavily than anyone else in the world. "You have to do what's right for you, *mija*. Do you want to talk to her again?"

"I've thought about what I might say to her, and it usually involved a lot of yelling. When I saw her I felt a little anger, but mostly sadness. I'm so tired of being sad, *Papi*."

Hector frowned. Her admission brought her a measure of guilt, as obviously a significant portion of her terminal broodiness had been caused by his accident. Tori, however, disturbed her to the depths of her person, lifting a tsunami of new sadness from the ocean of her past. Crashing upon her consciousness with wave after wave of grief—for Tori, and for the girl she used to be when they were in love. Would Tori ease this pain, or worsen it?

Big, calloused hands stroked her knuckles with paternal tenderness. He sat back in his seat and pointed at his head and his stomach. "Your smart brain, and your smart *estómago*." With one finger from each hand, he drew a line and met them in the middle over his chest. "They will guide your *corazón*. Trust them."

"What if all three of them say I'm an idiot?"

"Eh, then we break out the Don Julio and watch the Yankees." Hector eyed her carefully, waiting until she'd taken another bite to speak again. "Ah, so, I need to talk business."

Leah raised an eyebrow. "What happened to *pone el trabajo a la puerta*?"

"I made the rule, I break the rule," Hector replied. "We have a lot more expenses and the shop profits are no good all the time."

She bit back the immediate remark about the shop never making much profit and instead nodded along. "Okay?"

"So, I…met a man the other day and we made a deal."

Leah's heart sank. "What kind of deal?"

"He is a big businessman who has many dozen cars and trucks for his company. He wants us to do the maintenance and fixes for the cars. We will mostly do the work at the shop—he said someone will bring the cars to us—but sometimes we go to the car."

As that information seeped into her brain, Leah followed the hesitation as it rolled across her father's face like a heavy storm over a plain. "By 'we,' you mean me."

"*Sí, pero mija*, the price he is wanting to pay us? It can get us out of the debt."

"When did you do this deal? Where the hell was I?"

"You were getting us lunch." Which, of course, was code for Leah taking a long drive up Freeman's Peak for about an hour and coming back with sandwiches. "If it doesn't work, okay, no problem. But we can do this. You can do this. You are two times the mechanic I am."

Leah sat back in her chair with a huff. "Who is this guy?"

"Ah, I forget his name," Hector said, patting his chest and pockets. "I wrote it somewhere. He will come by the shop in a few days to introduce himself and we can sign the paperworks."

"You should have asked me first." Hector blinked, evidently surprised at her rising anger. She'd been careful not to get too heated around him out of concern for his heart. "You can't just make deals without me, *Papi*. That's a lot more work to take on for just me."

His dark eyes glared back at her. "I work too."

"I know that. But I already have so little time to myself as it is, and now I'll be some rich white man's *chofer*?" Abruptly Leah stood and pushed her seat back, wincing at the noise as it scraped the linoleum floor. "Find his number, call him back, and tell him no."

"No," Hector replied immediately. He pulled out from the table and rounded on Leah. "We need the work."

"I'm aware of how much work we need. I do the books. I do the tow jobs for extra cash. I take care of all your projects in the backyard." She planted her hands on her hips and glared right back at him. "I balance the checkbook, and I should be the one in charge of taking on work. You're the one who insisted on putting my name on the sign, insisted on making me a partner, and then you go and make a huge call like this without talking to me?"

"Okay, I see you are mad—"

"Don't fucking patronize me."

"*Cuida lo que dices*, Leonora," he snapped, and Leah immediately straightened up. Hector's anger struck fear in her heart. Like her, he didn't get angry often, but when he did, he was a force to be reckoned with. "This talk about Tori got you all mixed up. She shakes you like an earthquake."

She turned from him with a scoff. "Tori has nothing to do with me being angry about you putting work on me."

"We will talk later, but my decision is final."

"Sure, whatever." Grabbing her jacket, which she did not need but it added to the dramatic effect of her exit, Leah stalked toward the door. "I'm going out."

In her car, the small sanctuary she had left, Leah flipped through her CD binder. Every sleeve a tiny portion of her life, a disc with her memories and emotions at the ready, waiting to be lasered to life. She slipped one from its pocket and examined the front. JULY 2000 scribbled in felt marker. Parked at Freeman's Peak, Leah slid the CD into the player and sat back into her seat. A different car, a different time, a slightly different schematic of constellations, but the same emotions stirred inside her. It brought her to an open road, her girl by her side, the wind in her hair, the entire world out before her, unraveling and infinite. No checkpoints, no stop signs, nothing but a future waiting inside forever, the possibilities endless.

Leah pulled the receipt from her pocket. Tori's handwriting, neat and even. A secret request, scribbled in the margins, just as their relationship had always been. Crumpling the receipt in her fist, she thought about throwing it right over the edge. Let it get tangled in the tiny ravine before deteriorating and returning to the soil. The music from her car followed her to the edge of the cliff.

She couldn't throw it. Littering still wasn't rad.

Leah deposited the receipt into the rusty trash bin and sat on the guardrail, silently begging the dazzling stars to guide her like they used to do for the ancient seafarers. Unmoored and tossed about by waves, she didn't need them to point her toward safe harbor. She wanted them to point her home.

CHAPTER TWELVE

Returning to Garden Hills didn't feel like coming home. It felt like time travel. A town suspended in time, but Tori grew and changed. Harvard, Cambridge, Boston, and its spacious boundaries gave her room to be herself. The museums and libraries, nightlife and bars, the beautiful beaches, they watered her and she bloomed. For hours, she'd lose herself on the historical cobblestone streets, settling down with her notebook and a latte outside a colonial wooden building with an anachronistic drip-coffee shop stuffed inside. An imperfect city with grit and heart, Tori fell in love with its eccentricities over the course of four years. So much so, she convinced her parents to let her do a year-long internship after graduation in place of coming home. She dreaded the transition from the life she'd built in a big city and a wide ocean, to the twisting, contorting, and shrinking she did to fit inside the confines of Garden Hills. An even tighter fit to stay in the home she grew up in. Though it was a giant home with several more bedrooms than people, Tori had to be the smallest version of herself.

She circumvented her parents by spending time with Ward and Vic, or showing Ben the three things worth seeing in Garden Hills. Unfortunately, her luck ran out about the third day in, when her mother cornered them and laid out binders of wedding plans on their dining room table. Tori disassociated as her mother and Ben discussed flowers and invitations, seating charts and color palettes. She focused on the glass sculpture near one of their large windows. It drew her attention as a child—no doubt in part because of how forbidden it was to touch—but the colors calmed her. Swirls of green, blue, and brown refracting the sunlight pouring in, scattering rainbows on the floor.

"Victoria, I asked you a question. I need your opinion."

Tori blinked back to reality. "That'd be a first."

Cassandra shot her a withering look. "The bouquet. I was thinking dahlias, but it will depend on the season. Are you considering an autumnal wedding, or perhaps early summer?"

"We haven't picked a date," Tori replied absently. "We only just got engaged, Mother."

"Well, you're not getting any younger, dear." Beneath the table, Ben squeezed her thigh in what she assumed he meant as a conciliatory gesture. But she'd spiraled so far from the current conversation, she didn't feel the sting of her mother's barb. She imagined herself inside the statue, swimming in the greens and blues, untouchable. "Let's assume early fall."

As her mother talked aloud to herself about appropriate autumnal wines, Ben leaned in. "Are you okay?"

"No." She looked into his open, understanding face. "I need to get out of here."

Ben patted her leg and turned to her mother. "Cassandra, would it be possible to sneak down to your wine cellar? Maybe we could find inspiration in one of the bottles. Tori tells me you have some really wonderful vintages."

Hooked like a fish, Cassandra beamed at him in a way she'd never beamed at her. "Benjamin, that's a wonderful idea. Victoria, why don't you come down to the cellar with us and try some?"

"She's got enough planning to worry about. Perhaps we can pick out a few of our favorites and bring them up here for her?" Ben offered, and Tori would never deserve that man as long as she lived. Taking that bullet for her, it was almost worth marrying him for on its own merit.

"A sound idea. She's never been a connoisseur, not like her brother."

"Ward did strike me as a sommelier," Ben said, and her mother let out one of her truly awful guffaws at his joke. He aimed a look at Tori over Cassandra's shoulder and safely escorted the venomous python disguised as her mother to the basement.

Tori made a break for it. Grabbing the nearest set of keys, she got into whoever's car the key opened and left her house behind. Windows down and wind in her hair, Tori let the highway take her north for a while. Winding over the mountains, rushing through the major artery connecting their state to another. The blue sky fell into darker shades, like water when gradually increasing its depth. To her left, the sun trumpeted out its last blasts of orange as it dipped below the horizon, and Tori took that as her cue to turn around toward Garden Hills. During college, she would drive to the beach in the early morning and watch the sun rise over the ocean. In those quiet moments, the secret minutes between day and night, Tori belonged to the universe. The tug between the two worlds of night and day brought her a measure of understanding.

She felt the same tug inside her heart, but not as acutely since leaving for college. However, it reappeared instantly with the reemergence of Leah in her life. Three days had passed since she gave Leah her number and got radio silence in return, which did not surprise her so much as it disappointed. Leah didn't consider them friends. She considered them exes and put away Tori into the same box as her other heartbreaks. However, Tori realized, when Leah's beautiful, unnerving eyes trapped her in place, she hadn't put Leah away at all.

On an instinct she could either chalk up to self-sabotage or second nature, Tori parked outside of the Vasquezes' auto shop.

Just around the corner, she watched Leah from a safe distance to observe without being noticed. The golden hour poured its aurous light onto the streets, which caught Leah perfectly. Tori stopped to behold her. Her luscious, brown curls shimmered like glowing firewood, her dark skin glistening with sweat, refracting the light. Her physical transformation took Tori's breath away. Impressive muscle tone from her laborious work, giving her enviable, strong arms and rippling back muscles. Not the soft teenager Tori remembered grasping on dark, sweaty nights. Leah's cocky teenage arrogance had matured into adult swagger, and her patented look of distrust now clocked as enigmatic. Her immutable broodiness appeared to be tinged with more shades of sadness. From deep within her, Tori felt the tug. Tug, tug, tug, directly to the girl who never left her orbit.

Leah pulled down the garage door, locked it shut, and scooped up Gremlin into her carrier. "Time to go home, Gremmy. You did great work today. Virtually purr-fect." As Leah turned, she nearly collided with Tori, who grinned in amusement at Leah's fright. "*Jesus Cristo.* Creep much?"

"Where's your little knife, Vasquez?" Leah visibly battled to keep a smile off her face and warmth spread through Tori's veins. She could still make Leah Vasquez smile, and for whatever reason, that was important to her. Behind Leah, a giant American flag flapped distractingly loudly in the wind from a giant pole bolted to the brick. Tori narrowed her eyes at the unfamiliar sight. "That's a big flag."

Leah followed her gaze and harrumphed. "They asked 'random' businesses in town to fly it after 9/11."

"Nothing to do with Hector's Mexican flag in the window, right?"

They shared a knowing look. "It's gaudy, but *Papi* doesn't mind, he loves it. He calls himself a 'Jankee Doodle Dandy,'" she said, mimicking his accent to an uncanny degree. "So, what are you doing here? Did Bill's car break down again?"

"Ben." Tori crossed her arms. "You didn't call."

"And naturally, your instinct was to stalk me?" Leah picked up the carrier from the ground and slung the strap over her shoulder. "Couldn't call. I threw your number away."

Tori flinched at the brutal truth. She threw it away. "Why?"

"I didn't want to talk to you?"

"You're talking to me now." That patented Vasquez Glare aimed right at her, and Tori let it hit her square on. She missed the power of it. "Get a drink with me."

"Why would I get a drink with you?" Leah walked past her. "No, thanks."

"Please." Tori grabbed her forearm and stopped Leah midstep. She smiled at her, putting on the best imploring face she had. "Please, Leah?"

Leah's resolve neared its breaking point. At least that hadn't changed. "Why?"

Of the multitude of bad decisions in her life—and Tori efficiently made several in a short amount of time—reconnecting with Leah ranked high among them. She risked being shut out, or worse, drawn back in. But like the cobalt sky chases the sun to the end of the earth, Tori kept reaching for Leah.

"Shouldn't you be on the arm of your beau?" Tori rolled her eyes, letting go of Leah's arm and dropping it at her side. "Really, Tori, what do you want? What do you hope to gain from this?"

"I don't want to 'gain' anything. I've missed you." She couldn't think of anything more honest to say without betraying her selfishness. "I want to talk. I hurt you and I'd like to apologize."

Leah shifted the strap on her shoulders and the movement peeved Gremlin, who let out an unhappy mew. "I don't have the energy for this anymore, okay? My life is…small. Simple. I need it that way."

"I'm not here to hurt you," Tori replied.

"I don't think you wanted to hurt me the first time, and yet." Rubbing the crease between her eyes, Leah appeared to contemplate the offer. "You can't just turn up all this dirt and bail. How long are you even in town? A week? Two weeks?"

"I can stay as long as I need to." Growing desperate, Tori stepped closer. "You don't have to forgive me, but at least hear me out."

Visibly torn, Leah considered her request. In the same way she couldn't help but return to Leah, she knew Leah wouldn't turn her down. "One drink. Meet me at Hillside Tavern. Just give me a half hour so I can shower and feed Gremlin."

"Deal."

Hillside Tavern could not have been more aptly named—a tavern located on the side of Garden Hills. Tori remembered it as a hole-in-the-wall, the kind of place minors could get served with terrible fake IDs. However, in the past five years, Hillside Tavern underwent significant improvements. Instead of sticky floors and smoke-stained walls, Tori sat at a respectable, if overly trendy, bar surrounded by offbeat décor. Light alternative rock played from speakers affixed to the ceiling, underscored by the percussive clack of pool balls on the billiard tables in the corner.

Nursing a beer—though she preferred Cosmos, she didn't want Leah to know she'd become a full-blown cliché—Tori waited for Leah to arrive. Her nerves collected into a beehive of buzzing insecurities, and even the dark stout in her hand couldn't calm them down. The methodology of her apology changed over the years—from grand, romantic gestures to intimate talks—but her desire to be understood prevailed. And, when she felt really greedy, she wanted to be forgiven.

Mercifully, Leah strolled through the door and the constriction in her chest loosened. Out of her jumpsuit, she'd changed into a low-cut tank top and ripped jean shorts, as well as her usual combat boots. While the aesthetic still screamed Leah Vasquez, she no longer wore her dark eyeliner and goth-adjacent makeup. She'd traded it for a swipe of mascara and tinted ChapStick, her skin now decorated with tattoos. Gorgeous red, blue, and black inks in various designs on her arms, as well as two on her thighs. It suited her perfectly. Tori wondered what they tasted like and almost dropped her beer.

"Vasquez, how's it going?" The bartender slapped a napkin down next to Tori, and Leah straddled the barstool. "Usual?"

"Please and thank you, Dan." Leah nodded approvingly at her choice of beverage. "Wow, a Guinness, huh? You can take the girl out of Boston..."

Sipping the nearly black beer, Tori shrugged and placed it carefully on the coaster she'd been provided. "It's an acquired taste."

"I bet." Dan the Bartender placed Leah's drink down in front of her, Well, drinks. A beverage resembling a Bloody Mary, and the other a shot glass of clear liquid. "Thanks, Dan."

"You got it. First one's on me."

Leah raised her eyebrow. "Why's that?"

Dan smiled. "Saved our asses getting my van up and running. Never could've taken that catering job."

"Oh, well, it was no sweat, but thanks for the drink."

Tori watched the bartender toss a towel over his shoulder and shuffle down the bar to another patron. "Friends with the bartender, huh? This your usual haunt?"

Leah downed the shot, which Tori could now clearly smell as tequila. "Maybe once a week. Beat a few idiots at pool, throw darts. Couple years ago you'd have to watch your drink for roofies or steer clear of a bar fight, but it's cleaned up. And, due to my positive influence, Dan now makes the best *michelada* in the state."

Leah took a long sip of her beverage, running her tongue along the rim to collect some of the flavored salt. Tori gazed into the abyss of her dark beer. "I'm surprised. You seem...comfortable here. Not, you know, just in the bar, but in Garden Hills. I never thought you'd come back."

"I never wanted to," Leah replied. "I had to."

"Why?"

Leah wagged a finger at her. "Nope, not doing that. You wanted to talk. So, talk."

"Ugh, fine." Tori chugged the last of her beer and signaled for another. "I've tried to figure out for years how to tell you how sorry I am."

A bloated silence followed. Leah's eyes never left her drink. "Well, at least you didn't try to kiss me. That always was your preferred method of apologizing."

"Even if I could, it wouldn't suffice. I never should've let my mother say those things to you. I'm sorry I let you down. I'm sorry I let things between us end that way. You deserved better."

Leah nodded along with her apology. The skepticism in her face remained, but her smirk had disappeared. Recalling that day, just those few minutes, turned Tori's stomach immediately. She couldn't begin to imagine how Leah felt. "Okay."

"I did go after you, you know," she said, to which Leah raised her eyebrows. "Your mom never said anything?"

"My mom?"

"Yeah, I—I had to go to a stupid luncheon, but then I drove to your house and your mom told me you and Hector already left. I…had a breakdown on your porch and your mom talked me through it."

Clearly Leah hadn't heard, based on the surprised and mildly pissed-off look on her face. "She never told me. Then again, I didn't ask."

"Oh. Well, I…have a lot of regrets about that day. I have a lot of regrets about the whole summer. Not about us, just…me."

"Right." Leah placed her drink on the bar as Dan brought Tori her second beer. "Our colleges were five minutes apart. You could have apologized at any time over those first few years, but you didn't. So, I don't know what to do with your apology now."

"I wanted to find you, Leah. I wanted to see you so badly, but I…I couldn't."

"Why not? Hmm? 'Cause from where I'm sitting, this is the same old Victoria Lockwood. Lots of promises, lots of apologies, just talk and talk and talk, with nothing to show for it." Tori winced and sipped on her dark beer, trying to figure out how to recalibrate the discussion. Resistance she expected, but the splashes of acid hurt. Leah knew exactly how to wound her. "I know you felt bad. Maybe you still do, but it was different for me. It wasn't only that I loved you and you broke my heart. I trusted you. Losing the person I trusted most hurt more than everything else."

The noise of boisterous talking snapped Tori's attention from Leah to the door. Gabby entered in a flurry of designer clothes and high-pitched giggling, followed by a much calmer Riley. Tori quickly ducked away.

"Shit, the reunion. I totally forgot. God, I'm so stupid."

"Reunion of what?" Leah asked, turning to follow Tori's gaze to the door. "Your gaggle of friends?"

"You didn't know our five-year reunion is this weekend?"

"The fuck would I know that for?" Despite Tori's obvious discomfort, Leah didn't seem bothered. Back in school, just Gabby's voice would've set her off, crunching into her defensive posture, waiting to strike. Now she looked at them with amused disinterest. "Have you kept up with them at all?"

"Only Riley. I try to keep Gabby at a distance."

"Can't blame you." Since Leah continued to casually sip her drink, Tori relaxed as well. They didn't have anything to hide, not this time. "Gabby lives on the West Coast now with her husband and their organic dog biscuit business."

"How do you know?"

"Small town, Tori. Everyone knows everything." She let out a short laugh. "Except about us. We're the last secret this town has."

"Oh God, they've seen us." The familiar pang of panic she remembered from teen-hood clanged in her chest. She had nothing to worry about, she reminded herself. Just two former classmates out for a drink. Not so different from Gabby and Riley.

Except it was different because Riley and Gabby were friends, but she and Leah were not. They'd never been friends. Friends don't yearn. Friends don't lust. Friends don't know the feeling of each other's pulse on their tongues.

Gabby, head to toe in designer clothes and absurdly tall heels, bounced toward them with an ear-piercing squeal and embraced Tori hard, which she attempted to return. Riley stood quietly, smiling politely and casting a glance at Leah. Tori plastered on a fake smile. "Wow, I haven't seen you two in forever."

"Oh my gosh, you silly ghost," Gabby gushed. "Riley told me about your engagement, congratulations."

"Thank you." Tori subtly shifted away from Leah. "You remember Leah Vasquez. From, um, from school."

"Formerly Friedman." Leah tipped her drink in Gabby's direction. Gabby performed a halfhearted, disingenuous wave. "Myers."

Riley smirked. "Vasquez."

As Gabby chatted away about their upcoming reunion, Tori zeroed in on Riley and Leah. They seemed too comfortable in each other's presence. Through college, she'd only kept in touch with Riley, exchanging texts and emails over the years. While she'd extended her time in Boston, Riley graduated Tulane and returned home, eschewing her familial obligations to instead purchase the bookstore downtown from the elderly owners. Like everything in "downtown" Garden Hills, the bookstore was within walking distance of Leah's auto shop, so there was a good chance they'd gotten to know one another. Possibly far too well, judging by the way Riley dragged her eyes up and down Leah's body before biting her lip, Tori had to make the assumption Riley was more familiar with Leah than she'd let on. Something ugly rose inside Tori's chest, snarling and seething.

"I'll let you three catch up." Leah finished her drink, digging into her pants and slapping a few bills onto the bar top. "Thanks, Dan." Bartender Dan gave her a quick salute and Leah nodded toward Tori. "See you around, Lockwood."

Leah sauntered out the door, unknowingly watched by the three of them. Gabby turned back to Tori first. "Okay, Leah Vasquez got kinda hot."

Tori swallowed. "Uh, sure?"

"What were you two doing here?" Riley asked, crossing her arms.

"She fixed my fiancé Ben's car and I thought we'd get a drink. To catch up."

"You were always too nice to everyone," Gabby replied. "Still doing charity work."

"Leah's…cool, once you get to know her. She's really smart, funny." Leah didn't need Tori to sell her to Gabby and Riley, but Tori had to defend her. Maybe five years too late, but it mattered.

Gabby scoffed. "Okay, but she was also a massive bitch."

"She was probably only a bitch because you all bullied her for being a lesbian," Riley replied.

Tori narrowed her eyes at Riley. "I didn't bully her."

"That was mostly me." Gabby raised her hand sheepishly. "In my defense, she called me Blabby Friedman our freshman year and it took me years to shake off the nickname."

"I didn't bully her either, but we were both complicit." Riley put her hands on her hips. "So, not really much better than Blabby here."

"Hey!" Gabby huffed and stepped around Riley to order a drink at the bar.

Over the years, she and Riley discussed the horrible things they used to let Gabby say and do to kids in their class, but their discussions never involved Leah. Now, having seen Riley eat Leah up, maybe they avoided her on purpose.

"Well, we're adults now and high school crap is over. None of that matters anymore." Tori shrugged. "I don't think Leah holds it against us."

"I guess you're right," Gabby replied with a sigh, as if wistful for the days when she was an unrepentant bitch. "Oh! Do you think she'll come to the reunion? Her stoner friend what's-his-name is coming. And Jenna, obviously."

"There's no way Leah's going to the reunion," Riley derided quietly. "Even if Billy and Jenna are there."

"Ugh, annoying. You know, people think she's the one who messed with the prompter at graduation. I don't even remember how that rumor started. Somebody knew somebody who knew something. You should ask her about it, now that you're buddies."

"We're not buddies." Tori fidgeted in her seat, unable to stem the flow of anxiety flooding her veins. "It was just a drink."

"I'm gonna pop to the bathroom quick," Riley said in a rush, darting toward the back of the bar.

Gabby rolled her eyes. "Love her, but she's still so weird. Anyway, what's up with you?"

Once she'd satisfied Gabby with the CliffsNotes on her life, she left her in a booth to wait on Riley. Tori settled her tab, anxious to get back outside again. Being trapped in the bar with Gabby, who droned on and on about her idyllic life in Southern California, was hell. Hell is other people, but hell is mostly your former high school classmates.

A warm breeze blew debris down the street, tinkling cans against asphalt like a row of chimes. The sky ablaze with stars, Tori turned her eyes upward and inhaled a deep breath. Boston boasted many enviable qualities, but nothing beat the purity of the constellations at home. Like diamonds bursting from an unseen celestial fountain to be scattered among the heavens. The dazzling display caused Tori to wonder why Leah stayed in Garden Hills. MIT should've opened doors for her, all leading far away from their pretty, soulless hometown. Tori imagined Leah in Garden Hills like a firefly trapped in a glass jar, beautiful and doomed.

Rounding the corner toward the parking lot, Tori heard a noise before she could pinpoint its origin. A noise she recognized. A groan she used to know better than her own. To her left, Riley had Leah pinned against the back of the tavern, kissing her hungrily. Stunned in place, Tori watched as Riley shamelessly felt her up and kissed down her neck. Leah turned her head to give her access and caught Tori's eye. But Leah wasn't surprised to see her, nor did she stop.

She smirked.

"Come back to my place," Riley panted against Leah's skin. She grabbed Leah's tank top and tugged it. "C'mon, Leah. I'll ditch Gabby in like an hour."

Tori nearly threw up. She ducked around the other side of the building and slapped her hand over her mouth, willing herself not to be sick. What did she care if Leah was fucking Riley? Her best friend Riley, who spent most of high school so quiet she would often get perfect attendance records because teachers didn't mark her absent. How had she managed to seduce Leah? It was like a whisper going up against a gale force wind.

Whatever. Let them have their little affair.

Except. She peeked around the corner, and Leah gently stroked her hands through Riley's long, blond hair, placing a sweet, affectionate kiss against her lips. "Okay, *amante*. Your place in an hour."

The way Riley beamed at her. The soft look in Leah's eyes. Maybe she'd misjudged it as an affair. Maybe they were…dating.

CHAPTER THIRTEEN

At first, sleeping with Riley was vengeance.

Not that Riley had anything to do with the years of abuse Leah suffered at the hands of idiot teenagers, but she could represent them. She could be every person who whispered slurs in the hallway, or every teacher "surprised" by Leah's intellect. She could be every heartbreaker of Leah's youth. She could be one very specific heartbreaker.

For the first few months, their relationship existed only between sundown and sunrise. During daylight hours, they lived in their own spheres, rarely intersecting despite living in the same town and working blocks from one another. But at night, with one phone call or one text, they'd meet and fuck their feelings away. Over the course of a year, the nature of their relationship changed. Leah stayed over, sometimes. They talked after, sometimes. Nights turned into mornings, sometimes. Angry, cathartic sex evolved into a more palatable friends-with-benefits situation. Every so often, they unintentionally veered into lovemaking territory and Leah would pull back, unable to push their relationship to another level.

Tonight was different. Emotion roiled through Leah like a storm, dredging up past sentiments like sediment. A passion she'd left behind erupted and she poured it into Riley, who eagerly matched her energy. In the back of her mind, Leah knew transplanting her unresolved feelings for Tori onto Riley wasn't fair. Then again, had that not always been a benefit to their arrangement? What Riley got out of it Leah couldn't be sure. Far be it for her to ask and possibly ruin the only consistently decent thing in her life.

Leah stood at the sink afterward, nude and flushed, staring out of Riley's kitchen window. Her apartment looked out over a quiet street from the second story of a two-family home—a nice house in the nice part of town. Despite the performative town-wide event they held to officially stop using the terms "north" and "south" to refer to the town's neighborhoods, the railroad track remained nailed down in her mind. This was the nice part of town, she was from the poor side of town, and no amount of gentrification or ribbon-cutting would change how she perceived the communities.

"Can I ask you something?" Riley asked when she returned, gratefully taking an offered beer.

Leah slid back into the bed, sitting up against the tufted headboard. "Do I have to answer?"

Riley snorted. "Do you ever do anything you don't want to do?"

"Touché."

"Why were you really having a drink with Tori? She said you fixed her fiancé's car, but it rang a bit hollow."

Riley's gift for insight surprised Leah the first few times she witnessed it. She only remembered Riley as Tori's shy friend who wasn't an asshole. Turned out, her shyness obscured a staggering intellect and an off-the-charts emotional acumen. Her ability to read people, especially Leah, never failed to astound. "I did fix his car."

"But?"

What did she get in return for keeping Tori's secret shame from her friends? A burden she never wanted. She lifted it from her shoulders with an admission. "Tori and I dated after graduation. It lasted all summer, and it was a lot."

Riley's blue eyes went wide. Aside from her parents, Fatima, and Billy (and his now-wife Jenna by extension because Billy kept nothing from her—in an annoying but wholesome way), not a single soul knew about their relationship. Not for Tori, but because for a while, the thought of it hurt so acutely. Each memory like a death from a thousand cuts. Years later, it no longer left a burning pain. A sharp ache at best, and a profound grief for what could've been. "And I'm guessing it went badly?"

"It ended badly. Crashed and burned." Leah paused. "Otherwise, it was…maybe the happiest I've ever been."

Her partner fell silent, drinking alongside her in thoughtful quiet. They didn't have the TV on, or even music. What sort of playlist covered the opportunistic sheet-grabbing détente of two former classmates? Riley rested her drink on her leg. "You never got over her, did you?"

Not an accusation, but the dart-like accuracy pierced Leah like an insult. "Probably not. Isn't that pathetic? We didn't even date very long…and she's clearly moved on with the fiancé. Yet I see her and suddenly I'm eighteen again."

"It's not pathetic, and it does explain a few things."

Leah turned to her. "It does?"

Riley nodded, her curtain of blond hair falling around her face. Leah swiped it away from her cheeks, tucking it behind her ear. "There's a chasm in you. I've wondered what caused it as long as we've known each other. I thought maybe in time it might close, but whatever kept it open is clearly powerful."

"That…is a lot of analogy."

Rolling her eyes, Riley reached over and drew figure eights on Leah's leg. "This chasm, I assumed it was because of your dad, or because you were seeing someone. It never occurred to me it could be an old heartbreak."

Sometimes Leah did see someone. She'd seen a lot of someones. Her bedpost stood scarred with the amount of someones she sought to fill the chasm Riley spoke about. Certainly, her father's accident fractured her life, but she held on to her heartbreak like it was her only means of salvation. It eclipsed her ability to move on, even with someone as comfortable, stable, or as easy as Riley. But Leah didn't do easy. She didn't want easy. She wanted to be torn apart and smashed back together. And only one person she'd ever known had that ability.

"I can't say I'm shocked Tori is queer."

"Is she?" Leah asked with a rhetorical lilt. "She's engaged to a man. I don't think one summer stacks up against the person you agree to marry. And besides, when her mom found out about us, she said she wasn't a lesbian and let her mom think I was the fucking help."

"Honestly? That shocks me even less. Her mom sucks and Tori's always been afraid of her. You know, sophomore year, Tori ended up with a B in Chemistry as her final grade. Her mom took her driver's license, refused to let her go to any parties or events, and sent her to chemistry camp for the entire summer. She got a high B, too, like an eighty-nine or something. But Cassandra's insane, and since it wasn't an A, it wasn't good enough." They nursed their beers together as

Leah filed that story alongside the other bizarre tales of Tori's mother's horrible parenting. It painted a fuller picture of why Tori, someone who Leah thought of as extraordinary in almost every way, didn't value herself. A condition Leah didn't consider when storming off to college and leaving Tori without any support. "What happened after?"

"I went home, grabbed my shit, and drove to MIT with my dad."

"That's dramatic," Riley replied, and Leah took umbrage with the accurate but hurtful accusation. "You didn't stick around to talk to her?"

"Talk to her about what? She made her choice; it was pretty obvious."

Riley scoffed. "Leah, what sort of choice do you think she had in the moment? You or them? That's not a choice, that's an ultimatum. She was a kid in a corner with nowhere to go." Selfishly, she'd never fully considered Tori's feelings in that moment. Her eyes and heart only saw her girlfriend choosing to deny Leah and her love and refusing to stick up for her. "I'm not blaming past you for not understanding the situation better. I'm sure you were really hurt, and you had every right to be hurt. But you had your parents to fall back on, a place to go with your broken heart. Who could Tori turn to?"

A deep, uneven breath did nothing to calm the storm brewing inside Leah's chest. "I trusted her, Riley."

"And she trusted you." Leah wanted to lean into the storm, but the winds of her temper died down. "Again, not blaming anyone. Cassandra holds the most blame for what happened between you, in my opinion. I mean, you were kids. I guess the question is, where do you go from here?"

"Man, I don't know. She said she missed me, apologized about how things ended, but I didn't need an apology. I needed an apology four years ago. Now, I don't know what I need from her. Seeing her just… just…confuses the shit out of me."

"Because you're still into your ex like a sad lesbian?"

Leah winced. "Whoa, ouch, Myers."

"Truth hurts, babe." She turned over to face Leah in the bed and propped her head up on her elbow. "You never got closure. How can you get over someone you never had the chance to stop loving?"

"Damn, dude, you go for the throat, don't you?" Riley grinned. Exhaling sharply, Leah sank into the pillows. "I just don't want to get hurt again. She's engaged, you know what I mean? She must love him."

Riley considered that carefully. "I'm not going to venture to assume I know how she feels. I didn't even know she was queer. I must have, like, absolutely no gaydar."

"In fairness to you, you were both real deep in the closet. Well, up until Fatima's party when I thought maybe we were going to have a threesome in the billiard room. Then I thought maybe you both might be gay as hell."

Riley whacked her with a pillow and leveled a glare at her, her tanned cheeks turning pink. "God, that party. I was so drunk I nearly confessed my giant crush on you."

"Wait, really? I thought I caught some vibes from you at the party, but lots of straight girls get touchy and gay when they're drunk."

"I was all over you! I wanted you to make a move on me so bad."

"You could've made a move on me, princess."

"Needless to say," Riley continued, huffing, "that night played into the already elaborate fantasies I had about you."

"Thank God you didn't act on them. Tori would've murdered you. To this day, they still would not have found all the pieces of your body." The grin on Leah's face stretched. "Who knew little Riley Myers was a giant horn dog in high school?"

"I wasn't a horn dog! I just wanted to make out with the hot nerd who sat in the back of my AP classes."

Leah balked. "I wasn't a nerd."

"Oh, sweetie, yeah you are, but you wear it well." She exhaled hard through her nose at this unfair, but also possibly true, summation. "This explains Tori's weirdness those last few weeks at school. And the summer! I barely got in touch with her. She said she was interning with her dad. When I ran into you guys with baby Gremmy, I thought she'd combust from anxiety and I didn't understand why. Meanwhile, she's fucking my high school crush. Living my fantasy life."

They'd rehashed their high school lives before, but not within the context of their unexpected shared connection to Tori. "Not exactly. Unless your fantasy life included avoiding everyone we knew and hiding all the time. Which, for the record, I did not want to do."

"You did something you didn't want to do?" The outright shock on Riley's face prompted Leah to reach over and pinch her. "Okay, but for real, she must have meant a lot to you for you to make the sacrifice. And I guess it makes me feel better to know it wasn't exactly my high school fantasy. I would not have hid."

"Yeah, right."

"Nah, that's not me. I would've shouted it from the rooftops."

"No, not back then."

Riley's face suddenly sobered. "Yes, I would have. I wanted to be out. I wanted to have what other kids had—dates and heartbreaks and stupid slow dances. But I needed someone to help me be brave. If that had been you, Leah, I'd have never denied it to anyone."

"And lost all your friends, your reputation?" Leah inquired around the lump in her throat. "Come on. Everything changes when you're out. It becomes your whole life, even though it's only this one part of you. You want someone to spray-paint 'dyke' on your locker? You want your parents to be forced to change churches because the priest told them their daughter is going to hell? You want to never see your maternal grandparents again because they think you're a disgrace? Never hold the hand of the person you love because you're afraid of what someone will do to you? Being out is the only way I know how to be, but it doesn't make me brave. It makes me exhausted."

It got easier over the years, but Leah never shook the feeling everyone who liked her, did so with an asterisk. A good mechanic, for a lesbian. A hard worker, for a Mexican. Always "one of them" and never one of them.

"I'm sorry. I didn't mean to imply it was easy. I just meant..." She put their drinks on the side table and slid her leg over Leah's lap to look directly in her eyes. "I'm not Tori, and I wasn't Tori back then, either. I was scared, but I was scared because I felt like nobody in the world understood what I went through. So, no, it wouldn't have been easy, and I'm sure some days would've been hell. But I wouldn't have been alone, and neither would you."

Leah wondered where that version of her was now. The girl who gets asked out by the adorable best friend of her teenage crush. Dating a rich girl whose parents actually liked her. "If only, huh?"

"Yeah," she replied, smiling sadly. "If only."

They'd sailed into uncharted emotional waters Leah didn't know how to navigate. Their relationship thrived on its informality, and these emotions calcifying on their connection would only make it harder to break away. She leaned forward, kissing Riley firmly on the mouth and running her hands up her thighs.

"So, you fantasized about me in high school, huh?" Leah asked against her lips, smirking. "Do I measure up?"

"I knew telling you would be a mistake. I don't need to feed your huge ego."

"Oh, it isn't all bad. What if I agreed to entertain one of those fantasies?" Laughter cut short in Riley's throat and Leah raised both eyebrows. "They're already out of school, so the field behind the high school isn't being used. I could ask you to meet me under the bleachers at sunset. Wait for you in those huge flannels I used to wear."

"Would you—would you, um, put on dark eyeliner again, too?"

"Yeah." Leah used her thumb to force Riley's chin up and she grazed her teeth along her throat. "Dark eyeliner, the dark lipstick, the whole thing. Would you like that?"

"Oh my God, I would die."

In the middle of the night, with the little hand between little numbers on the clock, Leah woke up with a big gasp. Her heart bludgeoned her ribs. Cold sweat stuck her curls to her forehead and cheeks, and she swiped them away as she caught her breath. The watercolors of her surroundings sharpened into the familiar colors of Riley's bedroom. Soft blues of the curtains, a chartreuse plant in the corner, the charcoal smudge in the outline of a pile of clothes over a chair. Squeezing her eyes shut, she counted backward from eleven, breathing in deeply with each number.

"He's okay," Riley murmured against her skin. She skimmed kisses on the tops of her shoulders. "He's home, and he's okay."

Riley drew back and Leah laid flat on her back to stare up at the swinging ceiling fan. She envied its counterclockwise movement, spinning into the past, and she wished it would take her too. Fling her back two years ago and keep her dad on the phone for five more minutes. She nodded. "I know."

"You're safe, and he's safe." Bleary-eyed but awake, Riley calmly kept a grounding touch on Leah's arm, tracing her tattoos with the tip of her finger. "Do you want to call him?"

"No, no, it's okay. This wasn't…as bad as last time." Last time, when Riley frantically called Hector at two in the morning so Leah could hear his voice. Again, Leah needed comfort, but fortunately she didn't have to go far to seek it. She shuffled under the covers and tucked her head into Riley's chest.

"This is much better than when you used to leave." Riley's soothing, insistent circles on the nape of her neck relaxed her sprinting pulse. Her voice sailed over Leah's head, into the empty room. "I'd be worried sick you'd crash your car because you'd leave here so upset. I'm glad you stay."

In the morning, sober and well-rested, Leah lazily dripped pancake batter onto the sizzling pan in Riley's kitchen. The sun had yet to peek over the horizon, leaving the streets awash in a cold blue, like distressed denim. Riley padded across the tile and Leah handed her a plate of steaming pancakes with a nod toward the butter on the counter.

Riley took the plate in silence, fixing her pancakes and pouring herself a cup of coffee from the pot Leah brewed earlier. From her perch at the breakfast counter, Riley watched Leah cook with narrowed eyes. After many minutes of this unnerving stare, it became too much to bear. "What? Why are you staring at me?"

"Why are you making apology pancakes?" Riley stabbed a forkful and ate them slowly with a big smile on her lips. Leah turned to the pancakes, away from the scrutiny. "I know what these are. Last time you did this was because you shit on my favorite movie."

"Okay, but it is aggressively heterosexual."

"And again, I disagree. There's nothing overly hetero about a male dancer at an upscale resort." Riley took casual sips of her coffee, boundlessly patient. "Take your time, Vasquez. I know this isn't about your nightmares; I was clear about not apologizing for that."

With a sigh, Leah switched off the gas burner and faced Riley completely. She frowned at how much Riley clearly enjoyed her discomfort. "I…last night. When I came over and we had sex. And I…"

"Fucked me like I'm your ex you're not over?" Leah balked. From the girl who used to pale at Leah's mere presence, who now read her with annoying ease. "Oh, come on, Leah. I'm not an idiot."

"No, you're not. But I shouldn't have come here wrapped up in my feelings."

"Probably not, but hey. Nobody got hurt." She rose from the table and nabbed Leah by the hips to pull them flush. "Plus, I sort of asked for it."

"It was exceptionally horny of you to proposition me in the parking lot."

"Yeah, well, you looked really hot, sue me." Leah smirked. "Look, don't take this the wrong way, but I enjoyed last night. All of it. So, I appreciate the pancakes and the excellent sex, but I'm not confused about what this is."

Inwardly relieved, Leah attempted to pivot from the emotional heft. "So, you're not head over heels in love with me?"

"Babe, no offense, but what we have is about as much of you as I can handle."

"I'm glad you said no offense, it really softened the blow." Leah pouted, and a glint sparkled in Riley's eyes that immediately made Leah suspicious. "What? What is it? What are you planning, Myers?"

"Come to the reunion with me," she said, and Leah instinctively took a half step back. "Come on. Be my date."

The mere thought of seeing her high school classmates nauseated her. Riley and Billy were the only two she tolerated in any dosage—Fatima and Melissa via email, long distance. But in person? Where her past would be under scrutiny? Where the weight of who she was in high school could again bury her? "There is a long list of things I'd rather do than go to the reunion. Be gored by a bull, go golfing with Karl Rove, go golfing alone, go golfing at all."

"It might be fun."

"For who? Why would you want to parade your loser fuck buddy to the graduating class of 2000?"

The grin on Riley's face fell into a deep frown. "You're not a loser and you're not my fuck buddy. We're friends."

Leah tilted her head. "Who have sex."

"Obviously, yes." Riley rolled her eyes. "But we're also actually friends. And you're not a loser, Leah. You're a genius who single-handedly runs a business she took over at twenty-one years old and supports her family."

"I'm a college dropout who lives in her parents' attic." As Riley appeared to protest, Leah shook her head. "I don't see any benefit to hanging out with people I never liked to begin with, who never liked me."

"Some people you like will be there. Fatima flew in from California, Billy and Jenna will be there."

"I see Billy and Jenna, like, every other day."

"Leah, listen to me." Riley got suddenly serious, poking a stern finger into Leah's collarbone. "You should come because you deserve to be there. Maybe you don't find yourself impressive, but you are. I think all those dickheads who bullied you ought to know the intelligent, hardworking, honest, amazing woman you are. And, full disclosure, I cannot wait to see the look on Gabby's face when she realizes the 'hot dude' she thinks I've been sleeping with is actually you."

Thumbing through the portfolio of her life since graduation, Leah couldn't highlight anything to be proud of. Simply living in Garden Hills brought her embarrassment. She had done nothing, accomplished nothing, gone nowhere. Her life consisted of the drive between her childhood home and her father's business. And, of course, a tangent line to Riley's apartment. Where Riley stood now, entreating her with big blue eyes, silently hopeful. Riley, who never pushed or coddled, who expected little and often got less. Leah owed her, and perhaps in the grand scheme of things, one night was not such a great sacrifice.

"You want to come out to your friends?"

"Yeah, and I—I really want you there with me."

Leah nodded. "Then I'm there with you."

Riley lit up. "Wait, really? You'll go?"

"I'll go."

Chock-full of regret, Leah pulled up outside Riley's home. The noise of her engine roused the elderly downstairs neighbors, who peeked out of their drab living room curtains to spy on her as she stood on the sidewalk. While they'd never outright complained, Leah often caught their distrusting stares as she came and went from Riley's second-floor apartment. Leah waved and they quickly closed the curtains.

Riley emerged moments later, wearing a skintight black dress with the hem at her mid-thigh and a neckline plunging deep between her breasts. Her blond hair teased out, bouncing on her shoulders with each step. Leah whistled. "*Ay, no mames.* Holy shit, Myers."

Blushing, Riley swatted her with a purse once she got within striking distance. She reached behind Leah and placed her purse on top of the car roof. Hungry blue eyes devoured her, and Riley's fingers trailed up and down the length of Leah's suspenders. She'd gone simple but formal—a pair of black slacks, a crisp white button-down shirt, and a pair of black suspenders. Riley unbuttoned the buttons of her shirt to just above her breasts. Feeling generous, Leah had also applied her makeup near to how she used to in high school. Dark eyeshadow, a deeply crimson lipstick, and perfectly even lines of eyeliner on her lids. By the look on Riley's face, she'd chosen well.

Riley whined. "Fuck, now I don't even want to go to the stupid reunion."

"We could go to a swanky hotel bar somewhere, and you could let me pick you up like we're strangers." While she had no hope of her proposition landing, she did see the consideration cross Riley's mind.

"Hopefully you'd be slicker than you were the first time, when you didn't remember we went to school together," Riley replied.

"I don't know if I'd be any slicker, but you would be." Leah slid her hand up Riley's thigh, eyes widening as she encountered no fabric barrier beneath her dress. Riley had the audacity to wink at her and Leah let out something akin to a growl as she palmed the bare skin of her hip and leaned into Riley's ear. "But you were pretty slick the first time too."

With a laugh, Riley pushed her back against the car and nabbed her purse from the roof. "Real charming. Let's go."

They each took the opposite route around the car, Leah intentionally circumventing Riley's walk to the passenger side. She opened to the rear door to her back seat. "Want to be fashionably late?"

"In the back of your car? My bedroom is like twenty feet away."

Leah cocked an eyebrow and took a step closer. "What if I park us in the Garden Hills High parking lot, right in my old spot?"

Though her contemplation took a few moments, Leah knew she'd won. "Ah, damnit. All right, fashionably late it is. Stupid sexy suspenders. Stupid teenage crush."

Less than an hour late to the reunion, Leah and Riley entered a deserted hotel lobby. Signs guided them to the event room entrance where an abandoned check-in table had name tags spread across the top. Just to their right, the muted noise of throbbing pop music and loud conversation permeated the double doors. Leah already had regrets.

"Name tags? Really? It's been five years, not fifty."

Fixing Leah's name tag onto her shirt, Riley smoothed out the sticker and gave her a patient smile. "Says the girl who literally didn't remember my name a year ago."

"I was close."

"You called me Ryan Byers."

"And? That's close." Leah circled her arm around Riley's back and guided her into the event room. Balloons and streamers decorated the otherwise aggressively beige room, where dim soft white lights intersected red and blue spotlights. A vinyl "CLASS OF 2000" banner flapped in the breeze of the central air just after the entrance. In the far corner, a DJ stood in front of a modest setup of speakers, completing the "not quite a party, not quite a business conference" vibe. It didn't take Leah more than five seconds to spot Tori in the corner opposite to the DJ, standing in a circle with Gabby and two equally sized male classmates. Tori wore a halter dress with a thigh-length hemline, the deeply verdant color bringing out the subtle streaks of red in Tori's otherwise brunette hair. Green always looked amazing on her, like a scion of Scarlett O'Hara, devastating and alluring all at once.

Riley radiated nervous energy. Clearly not ready to make her debut, Leah nodded toward the bar. "C'mon, let me buy you a drink. If you'll remember, I do owe you a Coke."

Her lighthearted reference to their high school days appeared to lift a bit of Riley's apprehension and she smiled at Leah. "I'm gonna need something stronger than a Coke."

Leah led them toward the bar, hoping the alcohol quality would be better than the music. Thankfully, only two other people stood near them, neither of whom Leah recognized. The bartender, a pretty young woman who looked just old enough to be served herself, smiled and greeted her.

Leah gave her a nod of hello. "How's it going? Two shots of bourbon, please."

As the bartender fixed their shots, Leah watched with an amused grin as the bartender unabashedly checked Riley out. They were incidentally exclusive, but not out of any idea of possession. It was safer and required less effort. If this bartender wanted Riley, well, Leah couldn't blame her. Tall, gorgeous, and incredibly kind, any girl would be lucky to lock down Riley Myers.

They took their shots together and Riley coughed hard. "Christ, Vasquez, it's gonna be that kind of night, huh?"

"I agreed to be your date, I did not agree to be a sober date." She turned to the bartender. "Do you have mezcal?" Upon getting confirmation, Leah let out a long, relieved breath. "Good. I'll take an Old Fashioned with mezcal instead of whiskey, and my friend would love a dry martini with olives."

Apprehension again crept onto Riley's face as a sea of somewhat familiar faces floated around them. A faraway look gathered in her eyes, receding into a secret storm inside her psyche. Leah took her chin and forced their gazes even.

"You're going to be fine. I've got your back as long as you need it. Okay?" Focusing back in on Leah, Riley agreed and appeared to ready herself with a little shake. Leah smiled up at her. "You're gonna floor 'em, Myers."

Riley chased the sweet, nostalgic smile she gave Leah with the rest of her drink. "All right. Let's do it."

A drink in one hand and the other wrapped around Riley's waist, they stalked across the room toward the popular kid's corner. Each step closer increased the worthiness of getting dressed up and her attendance, as their expressions rode an emotional rollercoaster. Gabby's delight upon seeing Riley was tempered by the confusion of Leah by her side. Then, the eventual understanding when they saw her arm wrapped around Riley's waist.

"Riley! Wow! So glad you're here. And…Leah. What a surprise. We didn't think you were coming." Gabby desperately looked around for help. The men—whose name tags identified them as Jack and John—shrugged, and Tori's laser eyes focused on where Leah placed her hand. For good measure, she squeezed Riley's hip. "Did you guys…come together?"

"I'm a gentleman, Friedman. She usually comes first." Leah felt the shake of Riley holding in her laughter. "Oh, you mean here?"

"Leah is my date." Riley paused, letting the information sink into her friends. Jack and John shared looks of nonchalance, though they also appeared to share a brain cell. Gabby gaped like a fish and Tori stood still, emotionless. The satisfaction from their unspoken shock was nearly better than sex.

"Where are your dates, hmm? Where's Mr. Gabby Freidman?" Leah pivoted to Tori. "And what about Bernard?"

Tori clenched her jaw. "Ben."

"For your information, my husband didn't fly home with me." Gabby huffed, and it was so familiar to high school that the hotel lobby could've easily become a hallway full of lockers. Leah, however, felt no more vitriol for Gabby. Now, she mostly felt pity. "He's too busy with our business. We can't leave orders unfulfilled for a week."

"Doesn't mind leaving you unfulfilled for the week, though, huh?" Leah waited for Gabby to manufacture something resembling a comeback. Her ability to produce a decent comeback was the single thing Leah respected about her.

"Funny, Riley hasn't mentioned you once since I got here. You'd think, being her date and all, she'd have said something to me. It's almost like—" Gabby released a horrid cackle. "She's ashamed of you or something. But that can't be right, can it?"

Instinctively, Leah's gaze drifted to Tori, whose dark eyes reflected a sea of emotions kept hidden beneath an expression of mild shame. The familiar sensation of worthlessness crawled up the back of Leah's spine. Riley drew herself up in height. "I didn't tell you because I knew you'd be a judgmental bitch."

Gabby recoiled dramatically, as if Riley shot her. "Excuse me?"

"I didn't tell you because I didn't trust you with information precious to me," Riley continued, apparently unperturbed by Gabby's affront. "I'm a lesbian, and Leah is my date. I'm not ashamed of either of those things."

"Good for you, Ry," Tori said quietly from beside Gabby. "You seem happy."

"Yeah, it's amazing how freeing it can be to live out loud about who you are."

Tori's eyes widened only a touch at Riley's pointed comment.

Leah raised her glass. "Congrats, Myers. Who knew you'd become the coolest of your trio?"

"My sister's gay." Jack, the slightly taller twin, got nudged by the slightly shorter twin, John. "Uh, our sister. You want her number?"

"I'm not homophobic," Gabby blurted out. All eyes fell on her, and she appeared genuinely hurt as she moved toward Riley. "You could've told me."

Leah's drink nearly went down the wrong pipe. "You were mean to me for four years because I'm a lesbian, the fuck else was she supposed to think?"

"I was mean to you because you were mean to me!" Gabby stomped her foot. "You called me Blabby Friedman and then everyone called me that until junior year."

Leah snickered into her fist. "Oh, right. Forgot about that. Look, it didn't matter to me because, let's face it, I never liked you. But Riley likes you, and what you say matters to her."

Gabby sighed. "Well, I'm sorry. To both of you. I swear I'm not homophobic."

"No, you're just a bitch." Gabby had the audacity to gasp, then look shocked that no one else was shocked. "That's a compliment. That's always what I've liked about you most."

"Oh." Like stealing candy from a baby, Leah thought, as Gabby blushed. "Thank you."

Someone grabbed Leah's shoulder and forcibly turned her around. Prepared to be angry, she rolled her eyes when Billy came into full view. He stole her from Riley's side and lifted her into a bear hug.

"Ugh, Billy, put me down."

He carefully placed her back on her feet and grinned from ear to ear. Jenna, about seven months pregnant, observed with a fond but tired expression. "I'm so glad you came! I thought you said the reunion was for losers who peaked in high school."

"I stand by that," Leah replied, glancing behind her. "But Myers asked me to be her date, and it would be a disgrace to my ancestors to turn down a date with a beautiful woman."

"Oh, is that what you're doing over here?" Leah laughed at the tone of his voice, not laced with distaste for the crowd but confusion. He looked at Riley. "Can I borrow her?"

Riley smirked. "She'll be the first to tell you I don't control where she goes."

"Dope! Leah, come on, we gotta find our people." Extracting her from the popular crowd, Billy tossed her into the group of "their people," which ended up being chess team players and assorted stoners. The conversation ping-ponged between their current situations and their fond memories of school, and Leah quickly bored of the reminiscing. These kids got bullied too. Some of them more than she did, and still they maintained positive recollections of a time Leah knew as fraught with misery.

As the night wore on, she'd regretfully finished her drink, but a body sidled up behind her and handed another Old Fashioned from over her shoulder. She knew the feel of the body, and the scent of perfume. Taking the drink, she turned into Riley. "Plying me with liquor? Are you trying to get lucky again?"

"Actually, the bartender gave it to me for free. I think she's into me." Riley cast a glance across the room to the bartender, who, to be sure, stared back with a bashful grin. "I should go for it, right? When she's not working?"

"Hell yeah. Especially if it gets us free drinks down the line." Leah removed herself from the company of assorted misfits and walked with Riley to the table of hors d'oeuvres along the wall. Leah tilted her head at the person hunched over the table, inspecting the spinach rolls. "Fatima?"

Fatima abruptly stood up straight. "Leah!" She peered around her. "Riley, how's it going? Is this your doing?"

Leah smirked. "That's one way to put it."

"Yes, I did manage to get our lovable curmudgeon to attend, but it didn't take as much convincing as you'd think." Riley pivoted around to the other side of Fatima and nodded toward her crowd of former friends. "Turns out, she has one major weakness."

"Oh. So, you know about—" Fatima gestured between Leah and the group, clearly indicating Tori. Riley nodded. "And, wait—you too?"

"Guilty as charged."

Fatima looked at her. "Whew, Vasquez. Who's next, Gabby Friedman?"

"Blabby can only dream," Leah replied, holding out her fist for Riley to bump.

Riley, like a good friend, bumped her fist. "Fatima, you knew about Leah and Tori? Did everyone know but me?"

"I found out at my graduation party when they had some big, gay, dramatic fight."

"Sounds about right," Riley mumbled.

"And, Leah and I hung out at MIT, so eventually I got the full story out of her," Fatima explained. "Not after suffering through her being, like, ultra-grumpy for the entirety of our first year."

Leah glared between them. "First of all, this is bullying. Second of all, I'm not here because of Tori. I'm here for Riley."

"Aw, keep telling yourself that, babe." Riley and Fatima chuckled at her expense, and Leah frowned. "Oh, good, Carter is here."

And of course, the wider version of Carter Harcourt held court with his former cohorts, a circle of admirers ever widening. Tori stood a step away from everyone, warily eyeing Denny Douglas as he approached the group as well. "And No-Neck Douglas."

Fatima rolled her eyes, picking at the spinach roll on her plate. "Like anyone wants to listen to them relive their glory days of doing the absolute minimum and being praised for it."

Even as the room crowded with classmates and teachers, Leah looked right through them toward Tori. From this distance she spotted the telltale signs of Tori's growing anxiety—holding her elbow with her hand, or obsessively scratching behind her right ear. Riley followed her eyeline. "She's a big girl. She can handle herself."

"Hmm?" Leah only half listened, straining to hear Carter over the music, as he'd clearly singled Tori out. Anger burbled up inside her. "No, I know. I…"

"And there she goes," Fatima said from behind her as Leah followed the tug toward Tori. As she'd thought, Tori's anxiety was warranted—conversation had turned to prom. Tori looked about to either bolt or vomit.

Carter caught sight of Leah, and his friendly grin curved sinister. "Leah Vasquez, wow. Didn't think I'd see you here. Assumed you killed yourself or something."

"Didn't think I'd see you here, either. Wasn't sure you'd know how to read the invitation."

Carter's fake grin fell. "I'm surprised you even got an invitation. Figured everyone forgot about you. I know I did."

She stepped forward, sizing him up. "How could I forget about you, 'Small Dick'?"

Leah's eyes roamed Carter's neck and shoulders and she came to the conclusion he might still be on steroids. Veins protruded from his neck, his white skin flushing a deep pink. "That was a prank by some loser who was obsessed with me. It's a lie."

"Really? I heard it's the nickname all your exes call you."

Carter sniffed. "Yeah? Who'd you hear that from? Vicky? 'Cause she's just bitter because I dumped her loser ass at prom."

He jostled one of his friends and all the blood rushed into Leah's ears. "Oh, you dumped her? That's funny, because I heard you tried to holler at your own girlfriend and she turned you down because she'd rather get hit by a truck than get one-minute jackhammered by you and your tiny dick."

Gabby stepped up, shoulder to shoulder with Leah. "He fucked Amanda P at the lake after prom and she said it was like sitting on her lipstick."

Shocked, Leah barked out a laugh right into Carter's face. True or not, Leah gained a modicum of respect for Gabby in the moment. "What a loser."

Carter shoved Leah backward, and she stumbled but did not fall. His eyes quickly glanced to his friends, who stared on in interest and horror. "I'm not a loser. I was never a loser. I was captain of the football team and you're nothing but a worthless dyke nobody ever gave a shit about."

Someone tapped Carter on the shoulder and Carter turned. In a fraction of a second, the person sucker-punched him in the nose with enough force to send him flying backward into a waiter. They both crashed to the floor in an explosion of shrimp cocktails. Sprawled on the ground, Carter held his hands to his bloody nose.

"What the fuck? Who the fuck hit me?"

Tori shook her hand out. She stared down at him with narrowed eyes, her skin flushed in anger. "I did. Just shut the fuck up already, Carter. Nobody likes you. We've never liked you. Literally not a single person here cares about you as a person. Grow a personality, or if you can't, buy one. Maybe you were prom king, but now you're just a washed-up has-been who's done so many steroids he's got raisins for balls. Grow up."

Denny Douglas pushed through the crowd, helping Carter up from the floor. "What a psycho bitch."

"Yeah, why don't you go ahead and shut up before I fuck your girlfriend again, Douglas?" Leah wedged herself between Denny and Tori, peering over his shoulder at his date. "She's cute. You want me to go two for two?"

Tori barreled through their classmates and stalked to the exit. Without a second thought, Leah followed. Arid summer heat enveloped her as she left the cool comfort of the hotel. She found Tori near the valet, one hand on a marble column, the other on her stomach. Leah slowly approached until they stood side by side.

"Okay, now I believe you about the tae kwon do."

The delightful sound of Tori's laughter stirred a quiet song in Leah's heart. Not a tune she thought she'd ever hear again. "I should not have done that."

"What, hand Carter his ass? Hand to God, Tori, that was the best thing I've seen in a long time. You laid him out flat. You told him say hello to the ground. You asked him what the five fingers said to the face. You—"

"All right, I get it," Tori replied, laughing even harder. "You're ridiculous. What if he presses charges?"

"First of all, isn't that the whole point of having a family richer than God? Daddy Lockwood isn't going to let some short-dick townie give his daughter a rap sheet. Second of all, let him try and find one witness. You were right. None of those people like him. I think even Gabby was happy you flattened his ass out."

Tori rubbed her knuckles and looked away. "I should've punched him then too."

"Hah. Then they'd have definitely crowned you prom queen. But then you never would've left and we—" Leah shoved her hands in her pockets. Tori met her gaze and smiled sadly. "That's a nice dress, by the way. You've always looked beautiful in green."

Rosiness speckled the tips of Tori's cheeks. "Oh, thank you."

Leah smirked. "Now you tell me how smokin' hot I look in my suit. Geez, where are your manners? She spends a couple years in the big city and she's lost her gentility."

"Don't you have a date to do that for you?" Tori asked, and the green of those words was more beautiful than any shade of dress she could've worn.

"Sure, but it doesn't hurt to hear it twice." Tori rolled her eyes, but the tender smile on her face barely concealed an affection she kept below the surface. With one look back toward the door, Leah licked her lips and said the stupidest thing she could think of. "Do you want to get out of here?"

Glancing between Leah and the hotel, she narrowed her eyes in what appeared to be suspicion. "Like, together?"

If bad ideas were horses, this one would've been a full hitch of Clydesdales. Masochistically or not, Leah took the reins and nodded. "Yeah. Together."

CHAPTER FOURTEEN

Tori avoided most of her nostalgic triggers like potholes in the road. Swerving, careening from side to side to not get bumped by the memories. However, in a different car, with a different Leah, the same feelings of warmth and comfort and thrill thrummed through her senses. Music played from a CD player, a rosary dangled from the rearview mirror, a CD binder on the floor, and an air freshener noosed around the gear shift—if Tori closed her eyes, she could be seventeen again.

They climbed Freeman's Peak, twisting down the same roads they'd traveled dozens of times together. Tori lifted the binder from the floor and thumbed through the pockets. The schematic had not changed in five years. Each CD lovingly labeled with dates, all sitting in chronological order. Two were missing.

"Where's the one that's not in the player?" Tori asked, knowing full well how closely Leah had watched her out of her peripheral.

"Riley has it."

Just as she nearly closed the binder, something stuck out near the back caught her attention. Flipping all the pockets over she spotted a familiar date, chronologically far from the rest. JULY 2000, written in felt marker, smudged from use. A long, legal envelope sat in the back, the paper soft from years of rubbing against the material of the binder. Tori carefully untucked the envelope's closing flap and slid out a photo. A worn, dog-eared four-by-six of them at Not Prom, joyously kissing, clearly enamored with one another. Tori used her free hand to massage her neck, trying to soften the lump forming down her throat. The heft of the envelope caught her attention and she peered inside, uncovering several crisp hundred-dollar bills.

Immediately, the envelope fell from her hands onto her lap. She'd buried that moment and that day deep in the recesses of her mind. Sold that car without her parents' permission and used it to buy a vehicle where the cabin didn't have the scent of Leah's cologne in the air. A vehicle Leah's hands had not fixed, one where each seat didn't remind her of Leah pressed against them. And her mother, well, they barely spoke, and that suited them both just fine. But the money. Tori hadn't thought about the money in years.

"It's not like I was going to spend your mother's bribe," Leah said in a quiet voice as she turned into the parking lot atop Freeman's Peak. "I just never had an opportunity to give it back."

Tori slid the photo back into the envelope, closed the binder, and unbuckled her seat belt. Clad in their semi-formal garb, Leah led her over the dirt and brush to the lookout point in silence. Freeman's Peak was quieter than Tori remembered. Beyond the guardrail separating the cliff from the embankment, the street noise rose softly from the ground. Cars rushed over smooth asphalt, and the rustle of wind through the trees around them—a symphony of atmosphere sound as familiar as an old song. Other nighttime visitors walked the trails surrounding the peak, but nobody got close to the two of them.

"Why did you keep the photo of us? To remind yourself of how much you hate me?"

Leah chuckled humorlessly. "No. I didn't know how to get over you, you know? I thought maybe if I looked at the money it would help me be angry enough to burn the feeling away."

Nodding, Tori acted as if she understood. "Did it?"

"It did make me angry."

Tori let the unspoken lie. Gazing up at Leah, she found her thoughtfully staring out into the skyline. She'd always had an enviable profile. A gentle, squarish jaw with a chin perfectly proportioned to her face. Slanting cheekbones leading up to almond-shaped eyes. Stupidly, annoyingly, dead-droppingly gorgeous and had only grown more so in Tori's absence.

"So, you and Riley, huh?" Digging her nail into the wooden railing, Tori inquired, "How did that happen?"

"That's what you want to talk about?"

"What, you want to talk about the new pope? This shitty new war or garbage president? The finer points of being a 'Hollaback Girl'?" Tori rolled her eyes. "My ex is dating my best friend. Kill me for being curious."

After giving a disbelieving side-eye, Leah shrugged. "It happened the way it usually happens. I needed a book from the bookstore, saw a cute girl, hit on her."

"You didn't recognize her? She looks the same, Leah."

"And? I wasn't exactly checking out your cliquey group of sycophants. The only one I ever liked was you." Tori smiled, unable to hide it, and Leah laughed out loud. "Oh my God, get out of here with that smug grin, Lockwood."

"I'm not smug!" But she was, a little bit. "So, she certainly recognized you."

"She told me we went to school together and I put it together she was Myers. After that, we'd have a drink every once in a while. One thing led to another, and—"

"Now she's your girlfriend," Tori supplied. "Good, right. Yeah. I'm happy for you. Riley is the nicest of my friends, and evidently she got over her introversion, and she really likes you, so. Good."

Leah's intense scrutiny tumbled Tori's stomach, rattling her just as it had years ago. But Leah knew her better now, reading Tori out loud. "We're not dating."

"Oh. You're…not dating. But you are…"

"Fucking? Yeah." Refusing to give Leah the satisfaction of having shocked her, Tori absorbed this information with a neutral expression. As her ex five years removed, it shouldn't bother her, anyway. Leah deserved affection and Riley gave her that. Unabashed, unashamed, fully out-loud affection. "I don't love her."

Her quiet confession drew Tori's attention back to Leah's face, where the scrutiny faded and shades of guilt colored in. Tori ignored the cool breeze of relief swirling around her heart. "Does she love you?"

"Probably. I am fairly irresistible." Tori rolled her eyes at Leah's deflection. "Ah, I don't know. We're good friends, and she's been nothing but cool. I do get the feeling if we stopped seeing each other, she could find someone who loves her. She won't stop seeing me, though, because she's too fuckin' nice."

"She's a sweetheart," Tori agreed. "What she's doing with an asshole like you, well, that's one of the great mysteries of the universe."

Leah shared her laughter, kicking her gently with the foot she had swinging next to them. "Um, excuse you, I can be nice."

"You can?" Tori asked, placing her hand on her chest. Her dramatic fake shock made Leah laugh even harder. They let their laughter echo into the woods, and the vacating tension relaxed them in tandem.

Until Leah spoke again. "And your fiancé? That's…good, yeah?"

Nodding, Tori gripped the guardrail as to prevent her fingers from zipping herself back into her shell. No, with Leah she could be herself. With Leah, she could be honest. But not, you know, *too* honest. The full truth of her life was humiliating. "Yeah, it's good. He's smart. Disturbingly good at Pictionary? Always makes me laugh. So, yeah. It's…it's good."

For once, Leah didn't push her. She nodded, her turn inward interrupted by the buzz of her cell phone. A thin, black flip phone with a tiny cat charm on it. She smirked down at the message. "Riley says hi."

Tori blinked. "How…how does she know I'm with you?"

"Because apparently, I'm a—let me get the quote correct." Leah squinted at her phone. "'Useless, predictable lesbian.' But, uh, I think she might go home with the bartender, so good for her."

Understanding the dynamic between Leah and Riley used a lot of brainpower, but understanding Riley as a sexually confident lesbian took the entirety of her brain matter. Nothing at all in the years they'd been friends ever indicated to her Riley was even remotely homosexual. Little did they know they shared the exhaustion of masking who they really were every day.

"Damn, Myers."

"Right?" Leah slid the phone back into her pocket and stretched languidly. "Well, that means my night is free. Want to go for a walk?"

"Sure. I need to change shoes, though."

Leah swung her legs over the rail and peered down at Tori's heels. "Again? What a throwback."

One pit stop to the liquor store later, they wound up in a neighborhood with a lot of new construction, chock-full of half-built and fully furnished homes, none of them occupied. An uncanny model neighborhood with functioning streetlamps and manicured lawns, but no people. Imitating life in a way Tori found familiar and unsettling.

Walking alongside Leah in her borrowed sneakers, she tried to let go of her reservations. She wanted to reconnect. It was nice to be around someone who really knew her, whom she trusted with the unflattering and vulnerable parts of her personality. Additionally, this uninterrupted time with Leah brought her more joy than she'd had in a long time. The pleasant, mind-numbing buzz from whatever amber-colored tequila Leah insisted on buying raced through her bloodstream.

Leah passed her the bottle and started unbuttoning her dress shirt. "Fuck, it got really hot."

"Trying to attract some of those groupies you used to have?"

"Now why would I do that? My biggest fan is right here." Tori chuckled and handed back the bottle, wiping the sweat from her brow. The temperature had unexpectedly risen over the past hour of their aimless walking, making her fancy clothes cling to her and hang lifelessly from her body. Abruptly, Leah spun on her heel and stood in Tori's path. "How adventurous are you feeling tonight?"

"Are you going to suggest I do something more adventurous than punch my high school prom date and gallivant with my ex-girlfriend?"

"Yep." Leah left without her. Tori watched her jog across the front yard of a recently constructed home and easily hop the white fence around the backyard. Not willing to try to vault a fence in her dress, Tori opened the fence from the other side and let herself into the yard. Turf crunched under her feet—not quite grass, not quite plastic—as she neared the cement patio surrounding a huge in-ground pool.

Leah had already partially disrobed, her dress shirt now tossed over a bamboo patio chair. She yanked off her shoes and laid them on the ground, then started on her belt. The familiar motion triggered Tori and she stepped back. "What—what are you doing?"

Dressed in only her bra and an obscenely small pair of hipster undies, Tori nearly lost her breath at the reintroduction to a nearly nude Leah Vasquez. She'd been right about her muscle tone—every part of Leah flexed with muscle now, including but not limited to, all the skin she'd decorated with tattoos. The overwhelming attraction nearly drowned Tori without going near the pool.

"My eyes are up here, Lockwood." Leah placed her hands on her hips and fixed an infuriatingly cocky grin onto her face. "I'm going for a swim. You can join, or you can be a nerd. Your choice."

With that, Leah dove into the pool with a moderately noisy splash. Tori watched her undulate beneath the surface, popping up on the deeper side. Her curls were not yet tamed beneath the weight of the water, still bouncy and gorgeous and unfair. "I'm not a nerd because I don't want to trespass."

"You're already trespassing," Leah replied, doing lazy backstrokes in the water. "And, are we really? Nobody lives here yet. The owner is probably some jackass on the thirtieth floor of a high-rise in the city."

"That doesn't make it okay, Leah." As she spoke, she slipped out of her shoes and tiptoed to the edge of the pool in her bare feet. She submerged her legs up to her knees in the water, bunching her dress by her thighs to keep it from getting wet. Leah's nonchalance misled her on the frigid temperature of the water, and she gasped at the shock of cold. "Jesus. You're gonna catch a cold in there."

"You can't catch a cold from the cold, dingus."

"You're the dingus."

"Oh, okay, cool comeback." Leah splashed water at her, floating away toward the other side of the pool. Content to kick in the water, she leaned back and listened to the sound of Leah's slow swimming. Staring up at the star-filled sky, Tori didn't notice Leah's encroaching presence until she rose from the water, grabbed Tori by the hips, and pulled her in.

Sputtering and shaking, Tori shoved her away and glared at her heavy laughter. "Oh my God, it's freezing!"

"You'll get used to it. You were a varsity swimmer, I'm sure you've been in pools colder than this." True, of course, but still an obnoxious move on Leah's part. Tori dove beneath the surface in her clothes, coming up for air and slicking back her hair. Leah watched her, head bobbing just above the surface, her eyes glinting in the blue light from the pool's underwater light show. "I wasn't sure about the short hair, but it looks good."

"Oh, good. I love passing tests I never asked to take," Tori replied, rolling her eyes. "It's easier to manage, and according to my mother, looks more professional."

"I'm guessing Brett likes it too."

"Ben." Leah shrugged. "He doesn't comment on my hair. I wanted to go shorter, but I didn't have the nerve."

"Can't fly too close to the lesbian sun. It would suit you, though." With her hands dripping from the water, Leah reached up and pushed Tori's hair back, giving her the illusion of shorter hair. Gliding around her, she styled it from behind. Tori closed her eyes, biting back a moan at the sensation of Leah's hands in her hair. When she tugged it by accident, an embarrassingly sharp gasp exploded from her and Leah stilled. The water lapped against her back as Leah floated closer. Goose bumps rose along her shoulder and neck where Leah's warm breath hit her cold, soaked skin. Leah's voice dropped low. "Are you happy?"

One hand gripped her hair, the other around her upper arm, Tori couldn't move, even if she'd had the desire to. "I don't know what that means."

"Yes, you do. You know what happy is because you're afraid of it."

Tori peeked over her shoulder. She shouldn't have, because Leah's eyes shone in a dazzling display, like two Fourth of July sparklers. Gorgeous and warm. "Are you happy?"

"No." Tori blinked to clear the chlorine from her vision. Seeing Leah more clearly didn't help the beauty of her eyes, the tantalizing deep cranberry lipstick, which miraculously had not smudged in the water. Her mascara dripped from her eyelashes, giving her an ominous look, like an underworld goddess Tori could worship.

"Were you happy with me?"

"Yes. Were you?"

"Yes."

The unsaid swung between them like a rope, neither courageous or perhaps stupid enough to grasp it. Leah's face rested on the crook of her neck, and while the familiar contact aroused her, Leah didn't feel as charged. She felt world weary, as if Tori and the buoyancy of the pool held up Leah's entire existence. Tori reached for Leah's hands and found them pliable, so she brought them both around her neck and settled across her collarbone. Leah held on and she bore the weight of her as they floated in the pool. For all the intimate points of contact—Leah's lips on her neck, her breasts against her back, their arms entangled—it lacked sexuality. She provided a comfort Tori didn't know Leah needed. Or, didn't know why. All she knew for certain is how much she enjoyed being Leah's anchor. Maybe it was only a hug in a stranger's pool, but the seismic shift in Tori's heart could've swallowed the neighborhood whole.

Leah slipped from her grasp and Tori missed the weight of her. The shock of warm air when she climbed out the pool sent a shiver through her, and without towels they'd have to rely on the heat to dry them. Her clothes were done for, Leah saw to that, but she didn't have it in her to care. She'd felt something real for the first time in years, even if that something included wet cotton threatening to give her what Leah had aptly called swamp ass. Leah, of course, didn't have this issue. Her white dress shirt untucked and suspenders around her legs, Tori swallowed as she tried to ignore the places her dress shirt met wet skin and revealed the figure beneath.

They walked to Leah's car and drove home in silence, save for the music on low and the wind through the cracked windows. It barely took them two songs to reach Tori's block, where Leah ritually parked about four houses down from the Lockwoods' home.

Exhilaration spread shudders through her body, easily explained away by her soaked clothes. But Tori knew better. The heat, the intimacy, the attraction, everything echoed their relationship with pinpoint precision.

Her anxiousness forced her to speak first. "Thanks for...hanging out with me."

Leah smirked. "Thanks for punching Carter in the face."

Chuckling, Tori unbuckled her seat belt and exited the car, closing the door and leaning into the window. "If I text you now, will you answer?"

"Depends on what you text me. I don't respond to unsolicited naked pictures, so don't waste your time."

"Asshole. Good night, Leah."

"Good night, Tori."

Tori did not, in fact, send an unsolicited photo, naked or otherwise. She did, in fact, wonder how unsolicited it would really be. Instead, she sent a couple of texts over the weekend, most of which Leah responded to mildly. Much of their rapport fell flat, and Tori pouted about it over breakfast with her family. Thankfully, her father requested her presence at a short lunch meeting, which gave her a solid out on family time. Normally she avoided Lockwood Industries, but even that brick-and-mortar hell would be preferable than listening to her mother fawn over Vic and coddle Ben. Just before noon she slipped out, hoping to go unnoticed.

"Sneaking off again?"

Tori stopped, turning around with a guilty look on her face. "I have to attend a meeting with my dad."

"Take me with you," Ben begged, glancing at the front door. "Your mother is scary to be around for prolonged periods of time."

While she agreed, Tori declined with a shake of her head. For Ben's sake, she had to keep him away from Lockwood Industries. In fact, it might be the nicest thing she could do for him. "I know, I'm sorry. I don't know what this meeting is about, though I can't say I'm not glad to get away from Mother."

"All right." He took her hand and gave it a squeeze. His skin was baby soft, in direct contrast to Leah's rough, strong hands, and Tori shuddered to remember the feel of them against her skin in the pool. "And we still have Ward's party to look forward to. I can't believe we get to do laser tag. I'm so pumped."

"He wanted paintball and Mother thought it was 'too violent,' so they settled on laser tag."

"I think I would've wimped out on paintball, so I'm happy for her overbearing tendencies. In this particular instance." Her lips tightened into a smile. Ben reluctantly let go of her and shoved his hands in his pockets. "I won't keep you. Have a good time. Or, you know, don't burn the place down."

Tori threw her arms around him, hugging him tightly. "Thank you for putting up with them. I didn't expect to spend so much time away from home, but that's probably why I haven't lost my mind and become an axe murderer."

Ben smiled as he pulled away. "Not a problem. If sailing with my dad and three uncles didn't turn you into an axe murderer, nothing will."

The day she spent out in the Nantucket Sound with five men and Ben's sister stuck out in her mind as one of the most interesting and exhausting days she'd ever had in her life. Poor Ben was the only calm member of his family—the rest of them had giant personalities and even bigger egos. Her mother would've fit right in.

Ben watched her go from the front door, waving as she pulled her car out of the driveway and drove down their quiet street. Leah had driven this dozens of times in reverse, dropping Tori off at night several houses down. How had she thought her mother wouldn't notice her walking home from the same direction every night? Their flagrant disregard for prying eyes contributed to their downfall almost as much as Tori's own gutlessness. But, she remembered, they should not have had to hide. Tori had insisted they hide.

Clearing those thoughts from her head, Tori focused on her present. The auto shop conveniently sat on the road leading to the industrial park, so Tori pulled over for a quick detour to say hi to Leah. That's what friends did, right? Visit each other. Casual. Just two regular girls hanging out, shooting the breeze, avoiding the elephant in the room even as it rumbled the ground they trod.

The familiar horns and snare drums of ranchera music blared from the open shop door. "Leah?" Tori entered the shop proper, struck by how the scent of oil and rubber gripped her. She used to watch Leah work on occasion, but the smell really brought her to intimate moments together, and the leftover, faint whiff of metal or machine she'd inhale in Leah's hair. "Leah?"

"No beautiful ladies here today! Only old men!" Hector called from elsewhere in the shop. He came out of a back room, Gremlin on his lap in his wheelchair. "Tori! I take it back, there is a beautiful lady here today."

"Hi, Hector," she said breathlessly, remembering to smile. "Geez, you haven't aged a day."

"Did Leah tell you to say that? I've gotten very vain in my old age." Gremlin hopped down from his lap and sauntered to Tori, slinking between her legs. "*Mira*, she didn't forget her *amiga*."

Crouched to the ground, she stroked her nails through Gremlin's tortoiseshell fur. "I couldn't believe it either. She's gotten so big."

"That's because Leah spoils her, even though she won't admit it," Hector replied. "It is good to see you again. Leah said you're getting married?"

The slight wince in Hector's smile nearly tore her in half. She didn't know how much Leah's mom knew, but Hector certainly knew everything. Leah confided in him most of all. "Engaged, yes. We haven't...we haven't set a date." *Because I won't commit to one.*

"*Felicidades*. Leah told me she met the lucky man. Said he was very nice. Handsome too."

Tori could've laughed trying to imagine Leah choking out compliments about Ben. "Yeah, he's...he's great. Um, so, is Leah working today?"

"She is meeting a man to work out some paperwork for us. We'll have a big client soon, lots of cars to fix." Hector pointed to a post near the bay. "Leah designed this. The car goes up, right? But it can also go down, so I reach the hood. And these..." He moved to a worktable not far away, where two braces sat. "I put these on and I can control the pedals in the car. All Leah."

"That's incredible."

"She's a genius, *mi hija*." Hector's proud smile widened beneath his salt-and-pepper mustache. "But she works too hard. She's mad at me right now about the meeting."

"Mad at you?" Tori didn't even need one hand to count the number of times she'd known Leah to be angry with Hector.

"I did not tell her before I agreed. But I only took the deal so maybe we make more money and hire people. So, she can take time off. Maybe finish school."

Tori didn't know what an MIT graduate could need to learn, but she supposed a graduate degree wouldn't be out of the question for someone of Leah's intellect and ability.

"But you know the *torita* is not happy. She's focused on getting through each day and she forget to look to the future." He looked down. "That is my fault, but I believe it will get better."

"I'm sure it will. The two of you can do anything." Hector shot her a grateful smile. "I should be going. It's great to see you again. Please tell Mrs. Vasquez I said hello." Tori bent down, giving Gremlin scratches behind her ears. Gremlin purred and stood up on her hind legs to rub her face against Tori's chin.

Disappointed but now armed with more context, Tori stuffed away her thoughts about Leah as she rounded the pristine driveways leading into Lockwood Industries. Circling the fountain, driving past the man on the mower keeping the grass trim. Rather than give her car to a valet, Tori parked it herself in the guest lot and walked the short distance to the entrance. The brick building rose before her, built in a shallow semicircle, as if crowding in on her as she walked through the doors. Carpet cleaner and stale office air reminded her of her youth, of standing knee-high with one hand attached to her dad, the other on Vic, excited to spend the day at their often-absent dad's work. The receptionist, a young woman Tori didn't know, greeted her with a smile.

"Hi. I'm here to meet with my dad. Uh, Mr. Lockwood. We have a lunch meeting?"

The woman nodded and typed some unknown variables into her computer. "Right, Miss Lockwood. It's nice to see you. Your father talks about you a lot."

Tori pulled back from the counter. "He does?"

"Yes, he's very proud." Wonderful to hear her father spoke about her at all, but disheartening to hear it delivered from a stranger. "The meeting is on floor seven, room two. Big conference room with all glass windows, you won't miss it."

Tori leaned in. "Do you know what the meeting is for?"

"I don't, I'm sorry." Tori deflated and thanked her, and the woman glanced around before speaking again. "But, um, I can tell you only one other person has checked in for the meeting and the lunch order was small. If that helps."

"It does. Thank you." She crossed the unmarred tiles to the glass elevator and waited at the base. It took her up on the quick ride—the building only had seven stories—and she walked out onto the executive level. Thin, expensive carpeting rolled out over the tiles led her toward the conference room. So distracted by the carpet, Tori almost didn't notice the person standing outside the room.

Leah.

How?

For a split second Tori assumed she'd imagined her, but she never could've whipped up the image before her. Leah in tight gray houndstooth slacks and brown shoes with no socks, a tucked-in white shirt with a blue checkered tie, and the blue blazer she remembered Leah wearing to church quite often. Only now Leah's biceps barely fit in it and Tori scooped her jaw off the floor. The image of Leah in the pool hadn't left her, and knowing what lay beneath her incredible outfit made Tori's neurons misfire. In Leah's hands she clutched papers, and she appeared to be reading from them intently. Tori couldn't make out her words, only the anxiety in her posture.

She thought about the story Loretta told her, about Leah with her coming out papers, trembling in fright. Leah didn't look scared right now. Trepidatious, but not scared.

"You're the lunch meeting?" Tori flinched at the words her brain chose. "Why am I here?"

Leah looked up, her eyes wide in surprise. Tori hadn't dressed as nicely as Leah, just a skirt and heels and a scoop-neck blouse. Still, Leah's eyes lingered a second too long on the rather short hem of her skirt. Some habits were hard to break. "Are those questions for me?"

"No, I just—I didn't know you'd be here. My dad didn't say what the meeting was for, only that he wanted me there. Here."

"I almost didn't come," Leah admitted. "Some secretary called and said he couldn't come out to the shop and gave me this address. I, uh, really laid into my dad when I realized who it was."

Dumbstruck by Leah's presence, Tori had almost forgotten. "Right, your dad. I just saw him. How…Why didn't you tell me?"

"I didn't want to." Tori must've looked as hurt as she felt, and Leah softened. "I don't like to talk about it. And I definitely can't right now. Not when *Papi* wants me to sell myself to The Man and I'd rather eat a box of nails."

"Ouch. Look, my dad's a tough negotiator, but you're Leah Vasquez. You're ten times scarier than he'll ever be."

Leah smiled gently at her, and Tori did her best not to melt on the spot. "Fortunately, I don't think there's much negotiation going on. Just signing contracts or whatever."

"Oh, there's always room for a negotiation, Leah."

Tucking the papers in her back pocket, Leah nodded. "Right. After you."

They entered the conference room one after the other. Big windows stretched from nearly floor to ceiling on one side, looking straight out over the interstate and into densely green mountains. A long, glass conference table had her father at the head of it, reclined in a plush leather office chair, a corded phone to his ear. He waved them in and apologized with a gesture.

"Yeah. Yep. Okay, listen, I have an important lunch meeting right now, so I'll get back to you. But eleven o'clock tee time sounds good. Thanks. Okay. Okay. Bye." Mr. Lockwood hung up the phone, glancing left to right at the two women in the office. She and Leah had taken opposite routes around the table, and Tori had already sat down on her father's left. Leah stood at the corner, waiting to be introduced. "Sorry, that was the mayor. Love her work, but she is a talker." He stood up, towering over Leah with his broad, six-foot-seven frame and barrel chest. They shook hands. "Miss Vasquez, it's nice to meet you."

"Likewise, Mr. Lockwood."

"This is my daughter, Victoria—ah, Tori. She's going to be joining the business soon as well, and I wanted her in on the ground floor of this endeavor."

"We've met," Leah supplied. "Your daughter and I graduated together in 2000."

Her father appeared flabbergasted by this information. "Is that right? Gosh, I thought you were much older. The way your father spoke about you, he had me thinking you were a veteran mechanic."

"I am." Leah shrugged. "I've been fixing cars since I could hold a wrench, sir. I think it's safe to say I aged into it."

Tori had to hold back giggles at Leah's deferential use of "sir" but did so poorly. Leah shot her a dirty look. "Well, good! Now, I took the liberty of ordering us some sandwiches from the kitchen downstairs. My daughter is a vegetarian, Miss Vasquez, so I got us all veggie sandwiches, if that's okay."

Reflexively, Tori smiled at her father's conscientious decision.

"I'm a vegetarian, too, Mr. Lockwood, so that's fine with me."

"Oh, good! Please, please sit. The sandwiches are bánh mì, as I was told by our chef, made with something called tofu. She told me they're Vietnamese." Leah and her father sat down nearly in tandem, each of them plopping a sandwich onto their plate. Leah poured herself a glass of water from the carafe in the center of the table and offered it to Tori. As Leah filled their glasses, her father spoke up. "So, Miss Vasquez, the contract I spoke about with your father is fairly cut and dried. My previous mechanic, who oversaw all the transportation for the company, had been swindling me. My son Vic Junior brought this to my attention and I swiftly had the man fired. He took his company with him, and now I am left with a fleet of cars, SUVs, small trucks, and a few assorted limousines without anyone to fix them or keep up with the maintenance."

"My father explained that to me," Leah said between bites. "How many vehicles are there in total?"

Her father wiped his face with a big napkin and peered at the contract next to him. "I believe there are about fifty vehicles. I don't know the specific breakdown, but they're in the contract. As I explained to Mr. Vasquez, I will have a driver bring vehicles to your auto shop in Garden Hills to repair or perform maintenance. However, oftentimes this maintenance needs to be done on-site, in the event of a malfunction, within a radius of about fifty miles."

"Fifty miles is a wide net." Leah folded her hands on the table. Tori hadn't ever considered what Leah and her father's interactions might look like. So frightened of his disapproval, she hadn't given any thought to their chemistry as people. But, despite their obvious differences, they both shared an intense work ethic and a powerful set of principles. "On a good day in traffic, it might take me more than an hour to drive fifty miles anywhere. You'd be better off having the driver call a local tow truck."

"I don't trust a local tow truck," Victor replied immediately. "I trust the company I signed a contract with. Are you saying you won't drive fifty miles?"

"I'm not saying I won't, I'm saying it isn't the most efficient use of your time or mine, sir. If I've got clients at the shop and I'm taking, at minimum, two hours out of my day just to change a tire somewhere, it would cost you less to hire local help. Because now I'm losing time, and time costs me a lot of money, Mr. Lockwood."

Not that Leah could tell, but her father looked impressed. He hid it with a dab of his napkin, but the pause alone let Tori in on his inner monologue. "Did you always work in your father's shop?"

"Yes, sir. He opened it about a year after I was born. I basically grew up in the shop." The fondness playing at Leah's lips warmed Tori's heart.

"If I may be casual, I do envy you," her father replied. "Having such a close relationship with your father. It's very special, the bond between fathers and daughters, and I can only hope when Tori comes aboard permanently, I get to see a lot more of her."

Leah nodded, casting a quick glance Tori's way before returning her attention to him. "It's a balance. We're very close, but it also means we know each other too well. The overlap between home and work gets fuzzy. It didn't leave me with a lot of time to do anything else, to be honest."

"Did it interfere with your schoolwork at all?"

"No, sir. I had the highest grade point average in our class. I also worked as a delivery driver for Benny's Pizza, a restaurant just outside of town, from the day I got my license until I left for college. I've worked a lot, Mr. Lockwood, and the reason I could do that is because I know how to manage my time."

Intense pride spread through Tori's chest at Leah's words. She didn't often hype herself up this way—Leah always self-deprecated to the point of insult.

"Your father said you graduated from MIT, is that right?"

"Not exactly, sir. I did go to MIT, but I had to drop out the summer before my junior year." Her once fierce gaze lost a bit of its power as she looked down at her half-eaten sandwich. Tori gulped. "I had to come back to take over the shop while my father was in the hospital."

"Oh, Leah." Her soft exhalation came entirely unbidden. For a moment, her father's presence vanished. She just saw Leah, this brilliant comet streaking across the sky, snuffed out by an egregiously unfair intervention of fate. "I didn't know. I'm sorry."

"Ah, yes, we're both quite sorry about your father's accident."

"Sure, thank you. I thank God every day he's alive." Leah's eyes flicked upward to the ceiling, to the sky and God, then back down. "Eventually I—well, I hope to go back to school. I just don't have the time now with the shop and everything. I also won't get a scholarship and it's an expensive school, so." Leah attempted a smile. "Life's what happens while you're busy making other plans, right?"

A bell dinged in Tori's head, and she didn't even try to wipe off the giant smile on her face. She waited for her father to catch up. "Lennon! Do you like the Beatles, Miss Vasquez?"

"I don't know anyone who doesn't, but yeah. I actually started playing bass guitar because of Paul. I thought he looked like he was having the best time."

Sitting back in his chair, Victor Lockwood clasped his hands over his stomach and regarded Leah thoughtfully. It waned, though, and the tenderness Tori remembered on occasion from her childhood shone through. Two things were always true about Victor Lockwood, Senior: he'd golfed with two American presidents, and he loved the Beatles. "I used to sing 'Beautiful Boy' to my son Vic when he was a baby. In fact, I sang the Beatles to each of my kids. 'Yellow Submarine' was Ward's favorite. I don't know a single other child who could go to sleep to that."

"What did you sing to Tori?"

He smiled warmly at Tori. "'Till There Was You.' Bit more obscure, but very good."

"Oh, I know that one." Tori's eyes watered at the smooth, incredible tone of Leah's voice singing the refrain. It washed over her, and she found herself gripping the chair seat for dear life. If she let go, she might sail across the table to Leah and never let her go. "My dad and I used to listen to all his old records at the house, and he has a soft spot for the Beatles. Though I don't think anything tops Juan Gabriel for him."

They returned to their sandwiches as the conversation died down. Tori glanced between her father and Leah a few times, and a new, tingling sensation grew in her chest. Her dad liked Leah. Not only did that bode well for Leah's deal, but it also gave Tori a glimmer of hope. Hope for a situation that couldn't ever happen, but she couldn't suppress it. Then again, though Leah would ping a gaydar for several miles in any direction, she knew her father didn't know Leah was a lesbian.

"Well, Miss Vasquez, when you have a moment, look over the contract and see if there's anything else you'd like to change. I'd be amenable to bringing the radius of the service to forty miles."

Leah scanned the contract, plucked a pen from the cup near her father, and traced the printed text. She placed the contract flat on the table and slid it over to Tori. "What do you think?"

"Oh. Um, let me see." One pair of green-blue eyes and one pair of steel blue stared at her while she read through it. Most of it was standard legal crap, but the lawyers clearly outlined the logistics of the deal. Her father didn't do sneaky backdoor nonsense, but he got his way more often than not. "The only thing I don't see accounted for is fuel. Obviously to refuel our vehicles, we'd cover that cost via reimbursement or a company credit card. But there would also be a fuel cost to cover the Vasquezes using their personal vehicles or the tow truck in service for the company."

"I'm sure we can work out a standard fuel charge reimbursement," her father began.

"Which we'd then have to come back and adjust with the rising and lowering costs of fuel. Especially with this war going on in the Middle East, there's no telling how volatile the oil prices could get." Leah took the paper back from Tori and scribbled on it in the margins. "What I can do is disregard the fuel costs and absorb them myself, in exchange for a maximum twenty-five-mile radius of service. And I'll do twenty-five miles from either this location or mine, just to widen the circle. This way we don't need to come back and adjust the numbers."

Tori didn't want to find Leah's negotiation tactics attractive. But the cool, calm way she'd addressed her father…well, Tori squirmed in her seat while keeping her expression as aloof as possible. Her father nodded toward the paper. "I don't want to rely on the availability of random auto shops across the top half of the state."

"You don't have to. I'll supply you with a list of towing companies I trust who service the areas you'll need. I'll try to cover as much area as I can. They'll tow any problematic vehicles to me. And in the time it takes them to get to my shop, I can clear a space for them in the bay."

Her father rubbed his chin, which Tori knew to be the "closing in on the deal" signal. "I think that would be satisfactory. What do you think, Tori?"

"I agree. The less time she spends driving, the more time she spends doing the work you've hired her to do. Plus, even if the towing ends up eating into costs a little, we'd be saving money hand over fist by employing a trustworthy family company just like ours."

Her appealing to her father's pride in their family name worked like a charm, and he nodded along with her as she spoke. Leah shot her a secret, grateful smile. "Very well."

"I have one other request. It isn't in the contract, but I'd like your word."

"Of course."

"I won't do personal errands. I'm not going to come to your house to jump the car." Tori seized up in her seat. "I'm not gassing up the family cars on the side of the road or chauffeuring anyone around. If you need my services outside of a professional capacity, I'm more than willing to help you, but not under the umbrella of this contract. Those would be charged on a case-by-case basis."

Her father smirked. "Now I understand why Mr. Vasquez sent you. You're a savvy businessperson, Miss Vasquez. Savvy, confident, and protective of your interests. Smart. You know your business and you work hard. You've demonstrated a commitment to family that frankly, I find remarkable, especially for a person your age. Not to mention taking on a contract this large with a small business. Hugely risky, but you appear up to the task. You're exactly the kind of people I like to go into business with."

"Thank you, Mr. Lockwood. I appreciate that." Leah's voice didn't betray a single note of demureness, and the confidence struck Tori in the lowest part of her abdomen. "Putting your trust in a small business is admirable of you, sir. Not many business owners with the resources you have would take a chance on us."

"We're both risk-takers, I think, Miss Vasquez. And that's why we're good at what we do." Tori thought if her father puffed out his chest any farther, he'd be likely to explode like a confetti rocket. "And my daughter is right. The money I'll be saving using a company with reasonable rates and a spotless reputation, well, I can live with a couple of towing charges on the bills. Now, I will have my lawyers add the requested items and adjust the mileage radius, as well as inking it permanently that your services are only rendered for the vehicles owned and operated by the company for company purposes."

"Thank you, sir."

"Well, folks, it appears we have ourselves a deal. Thank you for your time, Miss Vasquez."

"Just Leah, please, sir." They stood and shook hands again over the conference table, while Tori sat and observed. Not that she'd doubted Leah's ability to go toe-to-toe with anyone, she became more impressed by the second at Leah's continued poise in the face of her father's subtle domineering.

"Leah it is." Tori stood, for lack of anything else better to do, and her father clapped her on the back. "I'll have Tori deliver the papers to you to sign, if that's all right? Since you two are old pals."

Leah snorted quietly and Tori forced a smile on her face. This new dimension to their relationship further complicated Tori's already labyrinthian feelings for Leah. "Sounds great. I look forward to our partnership."

"As do I. If you'll excuse me, I have to run to another meeting. Tori, do you mind escorting Leah out?"

"Sure. I'll see you later, Dad."

"See you at dinner, pumpkin." All three of them looked surprised at his term of address. Her father blushed. "That wasn't very professional. You'll have to excuse me, Leah, I'm excited to have my baby girl in my business with me. Having a proud dad moment and forgot myself."

"No need to apologize. You have a lot to be proud of in your daughter, Mr. Lockwood. I've always admired her." Leah's warm, earnest smile caught Tori off-guard, and she blushed deeply under the weight of her compliment. Thankfully, her father's secretary came to retrieve him, leaving her with just Leah. Finally, Leah's shoulders sagged and the more natural Leah Vasquez returned to her.

"Suck-up. 'Thank you, sir.'"

Leah laughed, smacking Tori with the stack of papers from the contract. "Shut up, pumpkin."

Walking Leah down the hallway toward the elevator, Tori shook her head in disbelief. "He hasn't called me that since I was a kid. I have no idea what came over him."

"He's proud of you," Leah said, pressing the elevator call button. She blinked hard and wiped tiny beads of sweat from her forehead. "It got him nostalgic, I bet. It was cute."

They stepped into the elevator together, and Tori looked over as Leah started loosening her tie and unbuttoning her shirt. "Whoa, little early for the celebrating, isn't it?"

"Sorry, I'm just…I feel really hot." Normally Tori might've taken advantage of a comment like that, but Leah's dark skin had an unnatural flush to it. "I thought I was just nervous, but I don't feel so good."

Once they were outside, Tori stopped Leah by grabbing her arm and placed the back of her hand on Leah's forehead. "Jesus, Leah, you're a million degrees. You need to go home."

"Can't. Clients at the shop."

"Let your dad take care of it. You're burning up."

"Stop telling me I'm hot, you're engaged." Leah shucked off her blazer and uncuffed her sleeves to roughly shove them up her arms. "I'll drink some water at the shop. I'll be fine."

The next step Leah took she nearly swooned, but Tori caught her and used her entire weight to keep Leah up. "No, you're fucking not. You can't drive like this. You can barely stand."

"Driving is done sitting down," Leah informed her, shoving her away. "Go, go home. Go back to Blaine and see if he wants you to play nursemaid."

With a wounded heart, Tori backed off, releasing Leah so she could stalk away toward her car. Tori watched from afar, ready to spring into action if Leah stumbled again, but she got to her car without incident. Leah paused at the car, pressing both her palms into the doorframe and hanging her head between her arms. But just as Tori moved to help, Leah got into her car and sped out of the Lockwood Industries lot.

Tori didn't hear from Leah for nearly two days. She filled those days playing video games with Ward or watching TV with Ben, but by midday on the second day and after several text messages went unreturned, Tori got fed up with being ghosted. In need of a distraction, she and Ben drove to the center of town to get a bite to eat and get away from her mother's hovering. Her drone-like presence in their lives could only be tolerated in small doses before Tori wanted to snatch the drone and smash it.

As Ben ordered them sandwiches over the deli, Tori caught the sound of a familiar voice at the other end of the counter. Two paper bags in his lap, Hector animatedly spoke to the owner of the shop, presumably the man they'd named the deli after—Harold. The owner walked away to tend to a growing line at the counter, so Tori sidled up beside Hector. "Hey, Mr. Vasquez."

Hector smiled brightly at her. "Tori! *¿Cómo estás?*"

"Good, good. Just grabbing lunch with Ben," she said, scooting to the right so Hector could see around her. "How's Leah? Is she still sick?"

"She is. Been up in her room since I sent her home yesterday." He lifted the bag in his hand. "Bringing her soup. Any time she is sick, ever since she was a little girl, she loves Señor Harold's matzo soup. It's the only thing she'll eat other than my lemon tea."

Tori frowned. "Oh. I'm sorry she isn't feeling well. Tell her I said hi and to call me if she needs anything."

"Well, actually, I do have a big favor to ask," Hector began with a strangely coy smile. "I have an appointment at the shop and won't be able to bring Leah her soup and get back in time. Could you bring it to her, please? I'm sure *tu novio* won't mind. He looks like a nice guy."

Tori cast a glance over her shoulder at Ben. "No, I'm sure he wouldn't mind. Ah, sure, I'll take the soup."

"Thank you. Okay, I see you later." Hector spun and hurried out the door, leaving Tori with the brown paper bag in her hand, staring after him. Pathetic as she was, she'd take any excuse to see Leah.

Ben walked up beside her, following her gaze to Hector's retreating form. "Who was that?"

"Mr. Vasquez, he owns the shop we got the car fixed in," Tori supplied without looking over.

"Oh. Leah's dad, then, right?" She nodded. "Cool. What did he want?"

"He asked me if I would bring Leah this soup." Tori lifted the bag into view for him and looked up into his quizzical face. "Do you mind? You can go home first if you want, you don't have to come with."

Ben shrugged it off and led them back outside into the temperate summer heat. "Nah, I don't mind. She lives in Garden Hills, right?"

"Yeah, on the other side of town."

"Okay, no problem. I mean, she did drive us back to the shop for free."

Tori carefully held the soup in her lap in the passenger seat as Ben turned the engine over. He went to reach for the GPS in the glove compartment and Tori placed her hand over his. "I know how to get there. Just turn left out of here and I'll tell you."

Tori knew these roads better than her own. They spent so much time on Leah's side of town, where nobody who Tori knew would see them, it was practically home. She called out the directions and her normally exuberant fiancé became quiet. As they slowly rolled up to the house, Ben placed the car in park and turned to her. "So, I'm guessing you guys were more than just people who graduated in the same class?"

Clutching the paper bag in her hands, Tori nodded and attempted indifference. "We were friends. I had a lot of friends in high school. I was the senior class vice president and everything."

"Right. And you and Leah, you…spent a lot of time together, or…?"

"Why? What does it matter?" Hackles raised, Tori's tone clipped so hard if Ben were any closer, he'd have lost the tip of his nose.

"It doesn't? I'm just curious. You guys acted like you barely knew each other at the garage and now we're bringing her soup. Just…feels like I'm missing something here."

"I'm doing a favor for a sick friend, Ben." Tori unbuckled her seat belt and let it slap the side of the car. She stepped out onto the curb and turned to shut the door. "I'll call you later when I need a ride home."

"What? Tori, are you mad at me?" Ben asked, visibly bewildered.

"No, I just…" Leaning in on her elbows, Tori softened at the hurt expression on Ben's face. "I'm sorry. Leah and I had…a falling out before we left for college. She meant a lot to me back then and I let stupid crap get in the way. So, I'm just trying to make up for being shitty in the past."

The look on his face morphed into sympathy, but Tori couldn't shake the vague suspicion she thought she saw in his eyes. "I get it. I wasn't trying to pry, you know that. I just feel like there's so much about you I don't know. I guess I'm a bit miffed about adding yet another mystery to the long list of pre-Boston Tori information."

"Well, I had to keep Leah away from my mom on account of her horrendous racism, so."

"True." Ben grimaced. "All right. Give me a call when you're done. Love you."

"I'll see you in a bit. Promise." Tori smiled and waved as Ben slowly drove away from the curb. Standing outside Leah's home for the first time in five years, Tori inhaled a long, deep breath to prepare herself.

The smells, sounds, sights of the Vasquezes' home could overwhelm her if she wasn't careful. However treacherous, she wanted to see Leah. If only to be smug about how splashing around in a cold pool probably did make her ill.

Tori's eyes followed the crisscrossed ramp in front of the house, only for her attention to be pulled away by someone coming around the side. The little alley between Leah's house and Billy's, where she'd often slip through to secretly see Leah. Riley walked over slowly, a grin on her face. "Tori. Good to see you."

"Hey, Ry."

She nodded toward the house. "Here to visit the patient, huh?"

"Yeah, yeah." Tori held up the bag between them. "I was told to bring soup?"

With an unnerving blue stare, Riley appeared to see through her. Like a gentle surgeon, Riley could carefully and respectfully pluck a truth from beneath many layers of defenses. In their suffocating friend group, often people confused her inclination toward introspection with shyness, so Tori ran interference so Riley could have space. The long stretch of years between then and now allowed Riley to emerge from her chrysalis and spread her wings, finding a soft place to land in Leah. "Good call. Is that the matzo from Harold's?"

Her eyes widened. "Ah, yeah, it is. Wow, she must famously love this soup, huh?"

"It's basically the only thing she'll eat when she's sick. She had the flu a couple months ago, and I was close to getting her a keg of it to keep in her room."

Tori laughed to hide the internal screaming at this casually intimate admission. Riley took care of a sick Leah? Clearly, the benefits in their supposed friends-with-benefits agreement included relationship-adjacent activities. "Right, well. I'll let you go. I've got to deliver soup and also hope her mom doesn't kick me out."

"Loretta? She's a sweetheart, she would never. But go on ahead, Leah will be happy to see you. Even if she is slightly out of her mind on cold meds." Riley stepped around her to pass but stopped and gently took Tori by the arm. "You know she's not tough, right?"

"Mrs. Vasquez?" Tori remembered her as very tough, but fair.

"No, Leah. She needs care. You can't…" Riley appeared frustrated, running her fingers through her hair roughly. "Leah's been through a lot."

Tori swallowed, nodding in agreement. "I've talked to her dad."

"Yeah, and that's only part of it," she replied. "Look, I don't even know what I'm trying to say here. Just…don't fuck with her. Whatever you're doing here, whatever this is, make sure you're doing it for her, and not just for you."

From someone else, Tori might've resented the chiseled-down version of a shovel talk. But whatever the true nature of their relationship, it was clear Riley deeply cared for Leah. Maybe the benefits were murky, but the friend part of their deal had diamond clarity.

"Honestly, I…I don't know what I'm doing here," Tori said softly. "But I can't stay away."

Riley gave her a look, sympathetic and knowing. "Yeah, I know the feeling. Good luck."

As Riley took her leave, Tori called to her back. "Hey…why didn't you tell me about you and Leah?"

"I could ask you the same thing, couldn't I? I might even get the same answer." One hand on her car door handle, Riley paused and sighed. "I didn't want to share her."

Whenever Tori drove to Leah's house, she'd always park on the street. Her coupe by the curb, a polite guest. Transient. Not like Riley, parked in their driveway, confidently inserting herself into Leah's life without trepidation. Tori imagined Riley squished into the Vasquez kitchen for family dinners, watching old movies with Hector, or even participating in Vasquez Karaoke Night. No fear, no complications. Their only missing ingredient was the one thing Tori had going for her. Rustling up her courage, Tori knocked on the door and held her breath as it opened.

"Victoria! What a lovely surprise," Loretta greeted with a surprised smile. Her scrutinizing eyes peered down at the paper bag in her hand. "You brought her soup."

Tori blushed at the slight insinuation in Loretta's tone. Leah's mother gestured for her to come in, and Tori removed her shoes by the door and padded into their living room. It was almost exactly how she remembered—shag carpeting that used to be plush, flattened by years of socked feet, a worn couch near the front window, and a slightly out-of-date television atop a small liquor cabinet. The smell of cleaner, spice, and perfume nearly brought her to tears.

"Hector asked me to bring it over."

Loretta crossed her arms, sitting on the arm of the couch. "He did, did he? I can't imagine he gave you much of a choice."

"He did not," Tori replied, chuckling fondly. "How have you been?"

"Just fine, fine. Gosh, it really has been a minute, hasn't it? You look wonderful." Loretta held her hands out to appraise Tori, almost like a proud mother. Tori wondered if this was what it looked like to have one. "I'm glad to see you again. I'm sure Leah is too. Go on upstairs."

As she jogged up the staircase toward Leah's room, the sound of music grew louder. She entered without knocking, as Leah would not have heard it over the volume of her music anyway. The pitiful creature she encountered on the bed resembled Leah only in broad strokes—a mess of hair, a tangle of limbs in blankets, and an unearthly groan as she looked up to see who had interrupted her slumber.

Leah slapped the play/pause button on her stereo. "Tori?"

"Certainly not the ghost of Christmas past." Tori stepped into the room, intentionally keeping her breath even. Much of her room had changed dramatically—the door to the outside being the most obvious, but also the wall bereft of posters, the larger bed, the tidiness, all of which spoke of the Leah she didn't yet know. Other parts were achingly familiar, to dizzying effect. "Hey. I ran into your dad at Harold's and he asked me to bring you soup since you still weren't feeling well."

"Is the soup a sham so you can gloat about the pool?" Leah asked, smirking. Her naturally dark skin flushed near crimson from the heat of her fever. "I'm too weak to defend myself. Be smug if you must, but only after you hand over the soup."

She arranged the soup and spoon for Leah, sitting on the edge of her bed near her hips. Leah shifted beneath her jersey cotton sheets, pulling herself up to sit upright and gleefully spooned the soup into her mouth. Tori gazed around the room at the lack of décor, the void where Leah's personality had been. Leah's eyes tracked along with her, sighing as she dug a matzo ball from the soup. Tori nodded toward the wall. "I miss the Selena poster."

Leah glanced at the space where it used to proudly hang. "I took it with me to college. It's still packed in a suitcase somewhere."

"What about your guitars?"

"I sold them," she said, blowing on the soup before downing another spoonful. "I wasn't going to use them, and we needed the money."

Tori placed her hand on the leg-shaped lump under Leah's blanket and gently inquired, "What happened to Hector?"

Leah rested her soup container in her lap. The fatigue Leah carried with her appeared to multiply tenfold, and not just due to her sickness. Something enormous and burdening sat not only on her shoulders, but also draped over her like a shroud. "You want the full sob story or the abridged version?"

"Full story."

"It was really early May, just after my finals. We were on the phone like we always were, since I called him every couple of days during the semesters. But, uh, he was in the car and saw someone on the side of the road who needed help. He hung up with me and…the next call I got was my mom from the hospital." Leah inhaled a painful breath. "Someone hit him while he was on the ground fixing the tire. We don't know who, they didn't stop. He was in a coma for a week. I left school, and about a week after I came back, he woke up. The doctors aren't sure he'll walk again, but he's just lucky to be alive."

"Leah." Tori breathed out her name, lungs constricted in grief. "I'm so sorry. I can't even imagine how painful that was for you guys. And you didn't go back to school?"

"I couldn't. My parents almost lost the house, and I couldn't let that happen. So, I took over at the shop until he was well enough to join me, and here we are. His hospital bills and therapy bills are nuts. My mom works now too. I've done as much as I can—updating the shop so we can get more people in, fixing the projects in the yard to sell, starting the towing—and it helps. The contract with your dad will get us out of debt but obviously it's a lot of work, and I won't be able to go back to school anytime soon."

Well, that explained a lot. The number of dreams deferred under this roof could make anyone explode. Tori squeezed Leah's knee in sympathy, but she couldn't quite find the words. All Leah had ever wanted was to go to college, to get her degree, to make something of herself. To stand on her parents' shoulders and do better. And yet, here she was, stuck in a town she hated, sinking.

"What's his prognosis?"

"It could go either way. He does physical therapy twice a week, but his paralysis hasn't improved much since the accident. He's got this idea that he'll 'be ready to dance at my wedding.' Luckily for him it'll probably never be legal, so he's got lots of time on his hands."

Tori snickered, rolling her eyes. "Ever the cynic."

"I like to stay in my lane." Leah returned to eating her soup, eyelids drooping as she shoved down another matzo ball. Tori leaned over and felt her forehead with the back of her hand, wincing at the heat. "I know, I'm hot. Literally, figuratively, metaphorically, existentially."

Gently, Tori took the soup from her hands and placed it on the table next to her. On instinct, she pushed Leah's hair sticking to her sweaty forehead and tucked it behind her ear. Her hand cradling beneath Leah's ear, she stroked her jaw with her thumb and smiled as Leah closed her eyes. She shouldn't be here. She shouldn't be in this room. She shouldn't be touching Leah Vasquez in her bed.

But where else could she possibly go?

"Stay with me?" Leah asked in a sleepy mumble, her eyes fluttering open to capture Tori in her magnetic gaze. "I was gonna put on a movie. Watch it with me. Stay."

Without much thought, Tori kicked off her shoes. As she'd done a million times that summer, Tori got comfortable on Leah's bed and waited for her to queue up the movie. She pressed play on her DVD remote and Tori heard the telltale whir of her DVD player coming to life. "What movie are we watching?"

"*Spice World*." Off Tori's droll stare, Leah pouted. "It's my comfort movie. I always watch it when I'm sick."

"I guess it can't make you feel any worse." Leah gave her the most pathetic, sulky expression she'd ever seen, and Tori softened instantly. "Oh, fine. Let's spice up our lives."

Leah snuggled into her side. "You could use more spice, *gringa*."

"Okay, Sporty Spice."

"I'm clearly Scary Spice." Leah bolted upright. "Oh my God. And you're Posh Spice! You're…Victoria!" Apparently, this was the funniest thing Leah had ever heard in her entire life, as she erupted into a long fit of giggles. Tori watched her laugh, totally enamored. And totally, completely fucked.

CHAPTER FIFTEEN

The abrupt growl of her air conditioner turning off woke Leah from her sleep. Drowsy, she blinked around at the room, trying to place the objects within it. The DVD icon bounced around on her TV screen, her window cracked open about an inch, her nightstand clock read 1:08 a.m., and Tori Lockwood slept next to her in bed with her arm curled around Leah's stomach.

An arm, attached to a hand, attached to a finger, adorned with a ring. A huge diamond set on a gold band, deceptively simple. A ring that simply said in no uncertain terms, no matter how desperately Tori reached out to her, Leah could not reach back.

"Tori." Leah jostled the slumbering brunette and received a disgruntled snore. "Tori, you gotta wake up."

"Why? M'sleepy. Come back." Tori patted around Leah's stomach until she bunched up a fistful of her cotton T-shirt and dragged her back into the cuddle from which she'd awoken. Leah wanted to kiss her. She wanted to wake her up with small touches like she used to. She wanted to scratch her blunt nails on Tori's scalp and bring that sleepy, adoring smile back to her lips.

But she couldn't do anything, could she? Touch nothing, do nothing, enjoy nothing. Yanking Tori's hand from her, she slid away from her and nudged her again. "Victoria. It's one in the morning. You need to go home."

Her stern tone finally drew Tori from her drowsiness, and she rubbed her eyes and instinctively looked toward Leah's clock. "Oh. Oh no. Shit." She grabbed her phone from her purse next to the bed and stared at it with bleary, wide eyes. "Fuck."

"Brian probably has a search party out for you by now." Leah kept her voice light, but she knew the distaste creeped in. Tori frantically pulled on her socks, then tried to smooth down her bed head with both hands.

"I can't believe you let me fall asleep," Tori accused, throwing her purse over her shoulder.

"Let you? I'm sick, I probably fell asleep before you did."

None of her words permeated as Tori spiraled into a panic. "How the fuck am I going to explain this to Ben?"

"You'll think of something. You're good at telling people what they want to hear." Leah snapped her fingers. "Oh, and lying! Really, this is in your wheelhouse, isn't it?"

The hurt in Tori's eyes came and went, but the anger persisted. Her fingers smashed against the cell phone buttons and she glared at Leah while waiting for someone to answer on the other end. "Hey, Ben. Yeah, I know, sorry. Are you awake enough to come get me? Yeah. Yeah, I'll text you the address. See you in a few." Tori slapped the flip phone closed and changed gears so abruptly that if she were a car, she'd have stalled. "Anything else you want to get off your chest while I'm here? Any other digs you need to make?"

"Why? Not coming back? Tired of trying to get validation from me?"

"Validation? I came here because you were sick. I was trying to help."

A pretense so thin a light breeze would've snapped it. "Great. You helped, all better."

"Fuck, you know what?" Tori said. Leah stood up and planted her hands on her hips. While her illness hadn't totally worn off, her patience for Tori's bullshit had. "It was a mistake to come here."

"That's all I've ever been to you anyway, isn't it? A mistake. A blotch on the otherwise unblemished reputation of Garden Hills's resident princess." Rubbing between her eyes, Leah pulled herself together. Or, tried to. "Sometimes I don't believe you loved me at all."

All at once Tori advanced on her with a swift, confident stride and got right in her face. "Don't you dare, Leah Vasquez. You don't get to deny my feelings for you. Don't you dare lie to me and say you don't know I love you."

"You're going to lecture me on denying feelings? You looked me in the fucking eyes and denied loving me at all." Anger fractured into pain, breaking her voice. "What should I have taken from that?"

"I was scared! We were just kids! What was I supposed to do? They could've unenrolled me from college, cut me off from my tuition money, from my own family. You wanted me to risk my future for a reckless summer romance that may not last?"

Leah flinched and took a step backward. Tori's mother's words recycled through her—reckless. Not reckless as in carefree. Reckless as in careless. As in intentionally rebellious. Meaningless. "Right. Who would ever choose me?"

"I didn't mean it like that."

"Do you ever mean anything? Or do you just talk to fill silence?"

"She knew." The desperate panic in Tori's face, not unlike the expression she had five years prior, gave Leah pause. "She fucking… she knew everything. She knew about us, she knew about me taking you to the beach house, she knew I was in love with you."

Slowly, painfully reconstructing the day in their garage, Leah fit together puzzle pieces she'd long stashed away. "Wait…it was all an act? All of it, the giving me money, acting like I was the help…she did it on purpose?"

"Yes, to scare me away from you. But it didn't work. I told her I loved you and she—she threatened you instead of me. Told me she'd ruin your future, try and get you arrested or something, and I couldn't let her do that to you. I agreed not to see you anymore. But, Leah, I wanted to." Tori huffed out a humorless laugh. "You know, I almost failed out of Harvard that first semester? I didn't care about anything. I hated myself. I barely showed up for class, I didn't turn in assignments, I bombed my exams."

"Tori."

"All I wanted was to see you again, but I lived in fear she'd find out. You know how many judges in this state have dined at my house? She'd have ruined you without even trying." Shuddering, Tori wiped the tears as they fell, and each one stung Leah's heart like drops of acid. "I'm sorry. I wish I'd been braver, like you always were. But I promise I was trying to protect you and what I did…I did it out of love." Perhaps one in the morning in Leah's childhood bedroom wasn't the place for them to have this discussion, but they needed it. Despite unburdening herself, Tori didn't appear lighter as a result. She looked pained. Repressed. "I'm not trying to seek absolution, but I need you to know the whole truth."

The whole truth provided a measure of relief to the angst-ridden teenager inside her. But it did nothing to stop the blossoming feelings she felt now. "Can I ask you something else, then?"

"Yeah, of course."

In anticipation of a deflection or a denial, Leah braced. "Why are you here now?"

Much to her surprise, she got neither a deflection or a denial. Finally, sifting through Tori's rose-colored words and pretty promises, she landed on a truth and stuck to it. "Something pulls me to you. It always has. I don't know what else to do with that feeling other than give in."

Every cell in her body responded to the idea of giving in. How badly she wanted to stop dancing around the inevitability building between them. "Don't play games with me, Lockwood. I didn't like it then and I like it less now."

"I still don't know how to play games, I promise." Gripping her purse like a lifeline, Tori inched into her space. "I didn't expect these feelings to resurface like this, Leah. It's like a door blew open. All at once it came back to me, as if I never left. God, I can't even tell you how hard it is for me to resist you. It exhausts me."

Leah had the rest of that conversation in her head. Because if she asked Tori what she wanted, she might ask for patience. Ask Leah to wait and she'd waited since she was thirteen. She grew tired of waiting. "Then you probably shouldn't be here."

"No, I shouldn't." Leah knew her sexuality wasn't a sin, but she wanted Tori in an unholy way. Her eyes roamed Tori's face, her lips, her body, and it screamed back at her to take, take, take. Until she landed on the conspicuous ring and cold water doused her feelings.

"You should get home. We don't want to worry Benji."

"So close." She smiled weakly. "I'll wait outside. He should be here soon. Feel better, Leah."

It took another two days, but Leah did feel better and returned to work. Other than casual texts from Tori, they didn't see one another. Leah didn't pursue her. She knew Ward's birthday party was this weekend and Tori tried to spend as much time as she could with him and her other brother. Plus, Leah wasn't in the business of ruining relationships, and their proximity affected Tori. After all this time, it was bittersweet to know she still had an effect on her. However, that

Tori was engaged and unreachable, Leah sucked on the bittersweet feeling like candy until only a sour taste remained.

"*Mija*, what's wrong?"

Of course her broodiness wouldn't go unnoticed by her dad. Even Gremlin circled her feet more often, attuned to some cosmic ripple in Leah's mood. She looked up from her work on the side door and fiddled with her screwdriver. "I don't know. Just thinking."

"*¿Sobre qué?*" They removed the panel from the door together and set it aside. Hector inspected the panel as Leah sat inside the passenger door, rooting around for the cause of the electrical failure in the door's mechanisms. "A girl? A special girl who brought you your favorite soup?"

"The regulator is busted," Leah said, reaching into the panel and pulling out the broken part. "You put her up to that on purpose, didn't you?"

"I am no *Cupido*."

"No, you're really not. But nothing happened. We fell asleep, woke up, and had a fight. Got some stuff off our chests, and now…well, I don't know where we go from here."

Listening intently, Hector nodded as he twisted the hex socket around the bolts. Leah had anticipated the issue and waited patiently with a new regulator on her lap. "Where do you want it to go?"

She shrugged and handed him the new part. "I don't know if I want it to go anywhere. I can't think about it because she's engaged. Nothing can happen between us."

"Doesn't mean it won't happen."

Leah's eyes widened. "*Papi*. She's engaged, *Papi*."

"*Mija, dime.*" Dutiful to a fault, Leah met his gaze and considered his incoming advice. "If she is still in your heart, you need to tell her. Engaged or no engaged."

"No, I absolutely do not. Maybe that's what they do on your *telenovelas*, but I'm not pursuing a woman in a relationship, regardless of how I feel." As her father held the part in place, Leah inserted the bolts and tightened them. After they placed the door's panel back on and slid the glass in, she stepped around his chair and wiped her hands with the rag from her pocket, sulking. "It just doesn't work like that. If she wants to pick me over the fiancé, then that's her choice."

"Okay, tell me this. How does she know she can pick you if she doesn't know how you feel?"

Leah didn't appreciate his self-satisfied smile. "Maybe I don't want her to pick me. Maybe I want her to leave me alone."

"Oh, okay, that makes sense," he replied, rolling his eyes. "You have always liked things very simple, you never like things difficult and complicated, no, no, no. Not *mi hija*, never."

Leah bit back the responses coming to her. Most of her life's complications at the moment were not her own doing, but she knew it was also not his fault. Regardless, she became proficient in ignoring what she wanted in favor of what she needed. She needed simple. She wanted…well, it didn't matter.

"Sure, whatever."

Before she could stomp out of the room in a mood, she heard the tires of his wheelchair crunching over the cement floor of their shop. He took her hand, patting the top of it as she turned to face him. "I want you happy, *mi vida*. I have not seen you happy in a long time. Like the light in your eyes has gone out, poof, like a candle. But when you talk about Tori, I see the tiny, tiny flames again. You deserve that light."

"Yeah, well." She shook his hand away and he frowned. "Who gets what they deserve?"

Perched on the edge of Riley's bed, Leah nabbed her underwear from the floor and stood up, pulling them back on. Topless, she searched for her shorts and found them shoved halfway under the bed frame. Riley watched her silently for a few moments, eyebrows raised.

Finally, she asked, "A dine and dash? Been a long time since you did one of those."

"Don't call us having sex 'dining.'" In a rare reversal of personalities, Leah glowered at Riley as she tightened her belt and searched for her bra. "And yeah, I know, I just have a lot to do at home."

"Yeah, for sure. Maybe some cleaning, bookkeeping, brood in a corner about Lockwood." Riley held her bra out and Leah snagged it with a droll look. "C'mon. Talk to me. You've been excessively dour recently."

"You want me to talk to you about Tori?"

"Sure, if that's why you're in a mood. Who else are you going to talk about your ex you never got over with? Your dad?"

"He tried. He thinks life works like a soap opera and his melodramatic suggestions were unhelpful." Sighing, Leah sat down on the edge of the bed near Riley and ran her fingers through her hair. "He just doesn't get it, you know? I don't have the extra time and energy to devote to whatever the fuck is going on with her. And I don't have the energy because of him."

"You and Hector have been overdue for a talk for a while now, and you know it," Riley replied, giving her a knowing look. Leah glanced away. "But that's beside the point. What is going on with Tori?"

"We had a talk. And I think she…" Leah groaned, massaging the furrow between her brows. "I think she still has feelings for me?"

"Whoa." Riley sat up, pulling the blanket over her chest when Leah's gaze dipped too low. "I'm not surprised she has feelings for you, but I am surprised she admitted it."

"Not in so many words. She told me she feels 'a pull' and that it is hard to resist me." Exasperated, Leah flopped back onto the bed and over Riley's legs. She stared up at the ceiling fan circulating the cool air in its usual rounds. "I don't know what to do with this. First, she tells me how she didn't want to break up with me but had to because her psycho mom threatened my life. Then she tells me she can't resist me…but goes home with the fiancé. I spent five years wondering why I wasn't good enough, and it feels like I'm still not. I'll never measure up against the life she could have without me."

Riley stared out her window in thought. "Have you considered she might not think she deserves you?"

"Deserves me? What do I have to offer?" Leah couldn't comprehend a world where Tori didn't deserve her. Tori had the face that could launch one thousand ships. Leah would be lucky to have been shoved into the big wooden horse.

"You, Leah. You're the offer. You were enough five years ago. You're enough now."

Leah slid her hands under her head. "You're just being nice because you're basking in the afterglow of my amazing sex."

"There's no room for my afterglow near the oppressive size of your ego," Riley replied. "But I'm not just being nice, and you know it."

"I know." They shared a small smile before Leah blinked back up at the ceiling. "I've been so angry about how she didn't fight for me, but I didn't fight for her either, did I?"

"I don't think you should start taking the blame, but it's very adult of you to acknowledge her side of things. Look at you, growing up so fast." Riley dabbed her eyes with the blanket. "Brings a tear to the eye."

Leah slapped Riley's leg through the blanket for her insolence before sitting up to inquire, "I can't do anything, right? She's engaged. That's…that's a commitment. That's your word before God, you know?"

"I'd agree with that." Leah silently thanked God for bringing sensible Riley into her life. She needed the dose of reality. Regardless of her past romantic overtures, Leah couldn't pull some Lord Byron move on a girl with a fiancé. A boyfriend, maybe, in an all's-fair-in-love-and-war kind of way. But when a ring gets exchanged, the rules change.

"Fuckin' morals." Leah flopped onto her back again. "Being a good person is boring, and it sucks."

Riley let the blanket drop and crawled over to her, then spooned her nakedness against Leah's half-dressed body. "You're a good person, Leah Vasquez, but you're still a little badass to me."

Leah pouted. "Thank you, that helps."

"You're welcome."

Experiencing the Benny's dinner rush as a patron and not an employee mesmerized Leah. Her instincts pulled her to help, to answer a phone or take a box to its destination, but she remained on the sidelines. In her place, teenagers did just that, bustling in and out as waiters swung through the kitchen doors. Jake handled the influx of phone calls, managing three phones at once with the inherent skill of someone brought up in a restaurant. Never losing his cool, he fielded calls and yelled out orders to the cooks, as well as ringing up walk-in patrons.

"How's your dad?" Jake asked between phone calls, stacking a box for the delivery driver to pick up. Leah resisted the urge to snatch it. "His tip for mixing hot sauce into the marinara? Huge hit. The spicy pie is flying out of here. I tried getting Dad to name it 'The Hector,' but that got shut down real quick."

"He's good. I'll let him know about the pie even though he's gonna be obnoxious about it."

Jake turned to consolidate a new batch of orders and Leah hung off the counter as she waited for her own. A well-dressed man, maybe in his late forties, walked inside hesitantly. His suit probably cost more than Leah's car, and his watch might've put her through a semester of college. He looked deeply uncomfortable as he waited at the counter for Jake's attention.

"Hey, gimme one second, sir." Jake picked up a ringing phone and started scribbling down an order. He placed another ringing phone in hold and slapped the notepad on the counter. "What can I get for you?"

"Actually, I wondered if I could borrow your phone, son," he said, his voice deep and authoritative, though friendly enough. "I need to call my mechanic. My cell phone died, and I think my car is overheating."

Jake grimaced. "I'm sorry, we're so busy I don't think I can lend you a line. Maybe someone in the dining room has a cell you can borrow?"

The man looked down at the phones, two ringing and one on hold, and nodded. "Oh, that's all right. Thank you, son. I can maybe find a pay phone."

As he turned and his full face came into view, his identity dawned on her: Mr. Lockwood. In Benny's Pizza, the literal last place on Earth she would've expected to see him. She followed him out and he heaved a big sigh, jingling change in his pocket. "Uh, Mr. Lockwood?"

He turned around and looked at Leah, then inside the restaurant, as if wondering how she got out there. "Yes? Oh, Miss Vasquez! I mean, Leah. Nice to see you."

"Listen, uh, there isn't a pay phone around here. They took them all out last year. But I could look at your car, if you want." Peering around the lot, she zeroed in on the car that cost nearly as much as a house in her neighborhood. Pristine white with shiny chrome rims, every window black as night. "Is it that one?"

Mr. Lockwood startled. "Ah, yes, yes, it is. Am I that out of place?"

"Little bit. I mean, I love Benny's, but if I could afford a nicer place, I'd eat there."

He smiled, chuckling softly. Mr. Lockwood was big, much bigger than her father, with a commanding presence. A thick, well-groomed pile of salt-and-pepper hair sat atop his head, styled with light hair spray. Blue eyes, good skin, and shiny white teeth, just like every other rich *gringo* in Garden Hills. But at least he was nice. "Well, I would love the help. My wife's always telling me to put the cell charger in the car, but I forget every dang time."

"Sure. Do you know where the hood release is?"

"I am ashamed to admit I do not."

"You're not the only one, trust me. I had a woman come in, car totally out of gas." Leah opened the driver's side door, feeling around for the hood release before hearing the telltale pop. "Turns out she'd never gotten gas in the car and didn't know how to fill it."

Leah lifted the hood and engaged the latch. Heat rose from the engine like a barbecue grill. The waning sun as her guide, she carefully poked around the sizzling engine system to find the culprit. Mr. Lockwood stood next to her with his arms crossed over his barrel chest. "That makes me feel a little better. A little worse about the state of the drivers on our roads, though."

Chuckling, Leah squinted underneath the hood. "Right? You wouldn't believe the number of tires I change. I knew how to change a tire at four years old."

"Trades are an underrated employment. Graduates with business degrees and liberal arts degrees, they have their place, but none of us know how to plumb our own toilets." A weariness overcame Victor, and he sat on the edge of his car with a sigh. "When the kids were small, I used to have time to build stuff for them. Treehouses or toys, even just Legos. I was good at that—building, doing things with my hands. But my father tanked our business and I had to commit all my time to Lockwood Industries. I miss it, though."

Tori spoke of her father's absence like a forgone thing, as if he were a soldier away at war. Her fond memories of him had spread across her childhood like meteor showers, but she never mentioned this burdensome part of his story. Maybe she didn't know. "Nobody helped you?"

"It's been all on me my whole life." He smiled warmly. "Kind of like you, huh?"

"Yeah, kinda like me," she replied, smiling back. When she peered into the car again, the issue presented itself in the form of a fissure in a hose. "Oh. I see what happened. I'll be right back, they should have the stuff I need to get you going again."

Leah jogged back into the restaurant and Jake smiled at her from across the counter. "LV, what's up? Your order's been ready for like five minutes."

"Can you put it under the warmers for a sec? I'm helping that rich dude with his car. And, while we're at it, can you get me some duct tape? And rubber gloves, if you have them?"

He raised his eyebrows. "Did you...murder the rich dude?"

"Would I be dumb enough to be seen on a camera if I murdered someone?" Leah pointed at the dusty security camera perilously hung from the drop ceiling.

"Probably not." Jake shrugged. "Just go back there yourself. I don't want to be involved in your crimes."

Exasperated, Leah pushed through the swinging door and scrounged the back of house for the items she needed. Ducking out of the way of the dishwasher, she nabbed a pair of dishwashing gloves and a roll of silver duct tape. She waved goodbye to the cooks and hustled outside, trying not to lose daylight to patch it up. Mr. Lockwood definitely didn't strike her as the kind of man to have a flashlight in his car.

"Okay. We'll give this another few minutes to cool off. The problem is one of your cooling hoses has a tear in it. You've probably been leaking coolant all over the roads and didn't know it. I can patch up the hose with the tape to get you going, but you'll need coolant and to have the hose replaced."

Mr. Lockwood took all of this information in with a nod, scrutinizing her as she sat down on the curb next to the car. He sat down next to her with a gruff grunt. Inwardly, she expressed surprise at his willingness to sit on the dingy curb in his expensive suit. "Will it last me until I get home, or should I bring it to the shop?"

"It'll last. You have mechanics working for you personally, yeah?"

"I do."

"Cool, then have them at least fill the coolant, but they need to replace the hose. I might have a hose at the shop, but this is a foreign car, so chances are I'd have to order the part. I'll text my dad and ask, he might know offhand. He's got a creepy photographic memory for our inventory."

Mr. Lockwood rubbed the stubble on his chin, appearing much deeper in thought than Leah's innocuous rambling about car parts warranted. "I'm close with my eldest son like you are with your father. Vic texts me, we chat, sometimes we take lunch together. My youngest, not so much. He's into a lot of activities and I don't see him enough. But Tori…I wish we were close like you are to your father."

"You could be. My dad and I aren't just close because we work together." Leah propped her elbows on her knees. "We're close because we make the effort to be close. At home, we don't talk about work. My dad has a strict rule about it: *pone el trabajo a la puerta*. Basically, leave work at the door. It helps, but sometimes…it's still hard."

"It's difficult to parent your parent. My father drank and gambled away a chunk of our company's fortunes, as well as his own. I had to put him in rehab, got him banned from casinos, and worked my ass off for years to dig us out at the expense of being in my kids' lives." Sitting on a dirty curb with his hands folded in his lap, Mr. Lockwood reduced from a powerful CEO to a run-of-the-mill, tired dad. "People like us, we work hard because our families count on us. But if you'll forgive me some overbearing and unsolicited advice: don't let work take you away from the people and things you love. You don't get time back."

Sound advice, even if it was hard to take in her current situation. Maybe he could afford to slow down, but she couldn't. "At least your kids are coming to work with you, right? So, you'll see them more often."

"That's right, yeah. Plus, with Vic and Tori in my business, I can do less. I trust them. Then maybe I can take my daughter out to more lunches. Go on a trip or something. Get her away from this boring fiancé before he talks me into a coma."

"Ah, so you don't like the fiancé, huh? I met him when they got to Garden Hills, actually. They had some car trouble. He seemed…nice."

Mr. Lockwood groaned, as if he'd been holding his opinion in his entire life. "He's too nice. My daughter is a smart woman. Always been smart as a whip and very independent. But this boy she's with, he…he's boring. I always thought she'd end up with someone with more fire. With ambition, with drive. And this isn't a sexist thing, but his hands are too damn soft. He's never done a day of hard work in his life, and it shows."

Leah laughed, stretching her legs out in front of her. It didn't look like Mr. Lockwood did much hard labor, either. "As long as she's happy, though, I guess? And he treats her right?"

"She'd kick his ass if he didn't treat her right, of that I have no doubt. But there's no spark when she talks about him. No spark when she looks at him. I can tell she's fond of him, but fondness is for pets. Not your future husband." He laughed abruptly. "The pathetic thing is…I don't know her well enough to know if she's happy. Does your father know when you're happy?"

He used to read me like a book, Leah thought. A wave of dejection came over her and Leah rose to check if the parts were cool enough to touch. Warm, but not scalding. Leah pulled on her gloves and started the fix. "Sometimes. It's been tough recently. I have to hold back a lot. He's the one in the wheelchair, you know? I can't be as honest with him as I used to be."

"I'd want my kids to tell me," he replied. "If I were making them unhappy, I'd want them to tell me. He can't make it better if he doesn't know he's making it worse."

"You're probably right." That talk she had to have, the one Riley mentioned, ate her up inside. Being honest with her feelings used to come easily, but the accident all but shut down her ability to communicate. Every message could be your last. "And, by the way, if you want the unsolicited advice of a daughter: don't tell her you don't like the boy. Ask her how she feels about him. Ask her what she likes about him. Maybe there's something you're not seeing. Or maybe you're right and he just sucks."

He watched her tape up the cooling hose and secure it tightly. "I don't want her to marry anyone she's not crazy about."

"Tell her that. It's good advice."

She closed the hood and pushed it shut. Pulling off her gloves, she froze when he asked, "Are you married?"

Wearing her Tracy Chapman concert T-shirt over ripped shorts and a pair of combat boots, Leah looked gayer than a clear summer's day. "Oh, no, sir. It's not legal for me to marry the woman I'm crazy about."

He stared back blankly at her. Leah braced; she knew one hundred thousand different ways to respond to homophobia, depending on the level of acrimony. Every queer person understands the rules, as the coming out process never ends. Unwitting acts of otherness outed her to doctors, friends, teachers, and priests in a never-ending loop of bracing for rejection. After a few beats, he relaxed and laughed. "Oh! Oh, okay. Well, I hope it becomes legal for you soon. Eventually these boneheads have to give up on their spurious moral crusade."

Leah fought to keep her face neutral. Tori's anguish about not meeting her father's standards for a daughter, had that all been for naught? If this man had only spoken to his daughter, done the bare minimum as a father, they could've avoided a lot of pain. Leah pushed aside her anger and mumbled, "We'll see, I guess."

He fished his wallet from his back pocket and Leah stopped him with a hand up. "Please, consider it a favor. First one on the house, or whatever."

Instead of money, he offered his hand and she shook it. "Thanks, Leah. I'll text you if I need to bring the car to the shop. And you'll let me pay then, won't you?"

Leah understood it wasn't a question. "Sure thing. Good luck with the car, Mr. Lockwood. And with Tori."

"Good luck with your dad."

Leah nodded. They both needed as much luck as they could get.

After dinner, Leah sought refuge on the warm hood of her car. She stared down her street, trying to make her mind as clear as the road. It didn't work, and the traffic of stressors choked her thoughts until she squeezed her eyes shut to clear them out. She heard footsteps coming and braced herself for the inevitable intervention of her mother. There'd been an obvious coolness to her dinner with her parents, and while Hector allowed her breezy standoffishness, it bothered her mother.

But, as she turned her head, she was surprised to see Billy instead, plodding up her driveway from his backyard. While Billy had grown into his manhood—filling out physically, cutting his shaggy hair, growing a short beard—he still walked with the same leisurely gait of a carefree teenager. In his beat-up skate shoes, he hopped up onto the hood with her and forced her to slide over to accommodate him.

"Hey. How's Jenna doing?"

"Large and miserable," Billy replied. "Her parents came by today, so more miserable than normal."

Leah grimaced. "Are they still on their crusade to get her to move back home?"

"Yeah. And look, I get it. Who doesn't want their kid to grow up in a big house up in the hills? Have a baby butler or whatever. But they weren't good parents to Jenna and I'm not gonna let them ruin our kid. Maybe we won't have as much money here, but the kid will be loved. My dad even quit drinking when he found out Jenna was pregnant."

"No kidding? That's awesome. Your dad is cool when he's not wasted."

"Right? He was my best friend before he got into the sauce," Billy replied with a wistful smile. "I'm hoping eventually we can be like you and Hector. Real close, you know?"

"Don't get too close." Billy raised an eyebrow as he reclined against her windshield with his arms across his stomach. "I've been so stressed out about my dad and the shop, trying not to lose the house, upset about college…and I can't talk to him about it because I don't want him to think it's his fault or anything."

"He's not gonna be mad at you, man. He loves you. Just talk to him."

"What would I say?" Leah grunted in frustration. "That I wish I didn't live here? That I'm mad about leaving college? I was doing so well, Billy. I had friends and my classes were so sick, and now I'm back where I started. Doing all the same shit. And it isn't his fault! I know it isn't his fault. But my mom's exhausted all the time from working and I'm running myself ragged, and for what? A shop that's nobody's dream."

"Leah…"

She barreled forward. "And what's the solution? I can't leave. I can't quit. I can't close the shop or sell it. I'm stuck in this stupid town because I love my dad and I'm terrified of losing him."

"¿Mija?"

Leah froze. To her right, Billy grimaced and slid off the hood. To her left, her father had somehow approached without making a noise. Stupid fancy wheelchair. She should've put a bell on him.

"Hey, Hector." Billy waved. "I'm gonna go…check on Jenna. Don't want to find her overturned like a turtle. It's hard for her to get up, you know, on account of the…" He gestured in a backward C over his stomach. "Uh, anyway. Have a good night?"

Billy scampered away and Leah spun on the hood to face her father. On his face she saw her face, just sterner. More slants and angles, more wrinkles, but not from age, from experience. The map of his life from a village in Mexico to a suburban town in the United States, and each fine line represented each tangential path he'd taken to get where they were. The opportunities he missed and took, the family he missed back home, the brutal reality of the immigrant experience in America, and the hope and ferocity in his DNA. The same hope and ferocity in hers, passed down from ancestors who toiled in soil and fought as warriors in the greatest empire of their time.

Her father moved toward the front quarter panel, between Leah and the street, and stared down the road. "Your mama and I chose Garden Hills because it was the nicest town we could afford without her parents' money. Not a perfect town, but the schools are good and we wanted our *niña* to go to a good school. The garage was empty when we moved in, so I bought it really cheap with money we saved up and help from the bank. And I like it, I do. I like to fix, to mend. I made enough so your mama didn't have to work and could stay home and make sure you had a good life."

"I know, *Papi*. I'm sorry, I didn't mean—"

"Let me finish." He turned a few degrees to his right to look at her. "Our dream is not Garden Hills. Our dream is not this house, or the shop. Our dream is you, *mija*. You make us so, so proud. We could not have dreamed of a daughter more smart, more kind, more beautiful, more talented than you, Leah. And I am not saying this to make you feel guilty. I see it in your eyes, the guilt. I see it every day and I don't say nothing because I thought if you wanted to talk to me, you would. I didn't think about how hard it would be. I never think talking to me is hard, you know? I'm your *papi*, you can tell me anything. I should know better, *porque* your whole life you watched me and your mama sacrifice and you think you have to do that too. You think work is love, but it isn't, *mi vida*. Love is love. And love means talking to your *papi* to tell him he's being a selfish...how do you say it?"

Leah rubbed her face to keep her tears from falling. "You're not selfish, *Papi*."

"A butthead!" He clapped his hands in triumph for remembering the word. "A selfish butthead. Because I don't say anything either, do I? No, because I like that you are here. I like you living in our house, at the shop working with me. But it is selfish of me."

"It's my choice to stay."

"You stay because you are afraid, you just said," he replied, giving her a disapproving look as if he'd caught her in a lie. "The deer in the headlights, he chooses to stand still out of fear. That's what you are doing and that is what is causing you pain, because you are not a deer. You are a lion. A great, big lion with *una melena grande*."

Leah laughed through her tears. Her father, his nearly black-colored eyes shiny with unshed tears, smiled at her. She didn't feel very much like a lion with a great big mane, but her father's earnest face made her believe it, if just for a second. "I am afraid. I'm afraid if I leave again, something will happen to you or to Mom, and I don't think I could deal."

"*Mira*, it was an accident. We cannot live our lives afraid of losing them. That is half-living." Her father reached up and took her hand in his. "We want you to be happy, Leah. If that means go back to school, then we will make that happen. If that means we chase the *novia de* Tori out of town, we do that too. I don't care. I'm very fast in this chair, you know."

Of course, everything led back to Tori. Even this long and winding road she'd taken with her dad, ultimately, she knew her happiness lived in the heart of a woman engaged to someone else. "It's not realistic. We don't have the money for school."

"So? We will get the money. We didn't have the money for this house or the shop, but we got it. We are Vasquezes and we are makers. We are fixers." She jumped down and embraced her father tightly. Of all the DNA they shared, his optimism missed her. It was, however, the glue holding their family together, and Leah cherished it. "And I could run over the *gringo* with my chair. You say the word."

Leah chuckled and wiped her tears as she pulled back from him. "It's not that easy, *Papi*. She might love him."

"Ah, no." Hector adamantly shook his head. "Nobody who looks at my *mija* like she does could possibly love anyone else. I am one hundred percent sure."

Gazing up to say a silent prayer, dark clouds impeded Leah's view of the stars, and tiny droplets fell around them in anticipation of the payloads about to be dropped from above. "I'm sorry I didn't talk to you about this. I didn't want you to feel bad."

"So, you feel bad instead? Oh, *mi vida*, you put too much on those shoulders. Let your *papi* bear some of the burden, okay? Maybe my legs don't work so good anymore, but my arms are still very strong." To prove his point, he did an exaggerated flex of both of his arms. "I could throw *el novio* right across the highway. Whoosh! Like a *jabalina*."

"No *jabalina*." She took control of the chair and navigated them back toward the house. "Love is patient, love is kind. It always protects, always trusts, always perseveres. It does not, however, throw their romantic competition like a javelin."

Hector shrugged. "Maybe it should."

CHAPTER SIXTEEN

Amidst her personal drama, Tori enjoyed bonding with her brothers. With Ward finally closer to adulthood, hanging with him was less like babysitting and more like talking with a young friend. In the short time between her arrival and his birthday, they'd slid back into sibling harmony as if she hadn't abandoned them for five years.

For his party, she and Vic took a team each of Ward's friends—a surprisingly diverse mix of kids—and split up for laser tag. The arena itself resided inside the husk of a department store, converted into a post-apocalyptic arcade full of obstacles and places to hide. Lit only by random spotlights and atmospheric green strobes, they snuck under pretend broken-down buses and hid behind blown-apart brick corners. Dry ice coated the ground in thin stripes like cirrus clouds, enhancing the inherently creepy vibe of an abandoned retail space. While Tori initially felt she, Vic, and Ben had an unfair advantage due to age, it became rapidly apparent they were out-skilled. The competitive streak in her had to be circumvented in the spirit of Ward's birthday, though Tori itched to try to win. She compromised with herself and only eliminated two of his friends before taking residence in a deserted corner to pick off a few more when the urge struck.

Ben got eliminated midway through, and Tori watched from her hiding spot in a corner as he sadly trudged away. Once she was finally put out of her misery by Ward's friend Oliver, Tori jogged over to the lobby area to remove her equipment and head toward the cafeteria. She and Ben sat across from each other in the makeshift lunchroom, snacking on large slices of floppy pizza and sipping soda from a waxed cup.

"These kids are ruthless." Ben bit the end of his pizza slice, chewing glumly. "Really felt like my height was going to help. Instead, it made me a target. I looked like Gulliver out there."

Tori shrugged. "I hid."

"Camper!" Ben looked aghast. "I'm marrying a camper?"

Together they watched a big dollop of oil-ridden cheese slide off her pizza and hit the paper plate with a squishy thump. "I don't know what that means."

"In video games, if you hide during a match and kill from one location without moving, they call it camping."

She raised her eyebrow at him. "Isn't that tactically more efficient?"

"Yes," he admitted reluctantly, huffing into his soda. "But there's no honor in it."

Eventually the kids tired of laser tag and they retired to the lunchroom to eat pizza. Way better than Tori's own Sweet Sixteen, where her mother put her in a giant dress, rented out a gaudy hotel bar, and coerced her into slow dancing with the son of a business associate of her father. Ward's friends were nice, playfully arrogant with each other but none of the toxic masculinity or passive-aggressive bullying she remembered from kids her age back then. More importantly, they appeared to be having a good time. Her party had rightfully bored her friends to tears.

The bench trembled with the weight of her older brother plunking next to her. He gulped down an unsightly lime-green soda. "Got my ass kicked."

"You did okay," Ward said as he walked by, patting Vic on the back. "Better than Tori, who camped the whole time."

Ben sniffed. "Told ya."

"It's a viable strategy," Tori replied.

"For noobs," one of Ward's friends said, and all three men in her life pointed at that kid like he was the smartest person in the room.

Once they'd served the cake and sung happy birthday, Tori departed their company in favor of waiting outside the desolate strip mall. Kids trickled out one by one, scooped up by anxious parents in high-end minivans. Eventually, Ben and her brothers brought up the rear of the party, accompanied by the gangly kid who shot Tori in tag standing next to Ward, hand in hand.

"Can Oliver sleep over?" Ward peered up at their mother, who looked down at their joined hands with alarm.

"No, honey. Not tonight. I think it's time for your friend to go home." Her mother directed her attention to Oliver. "Go call your parents, young man."

Oliver turned to do just that, but Ward spoke first. "No. Don't go anywhere. You don't have to do what she says."

Her mother balked. "Excuse me? It may be your birthday, but you are not king of the castle. There will be no sleepovers, okay? You boys are too old for that now."

"It's not because we're too old, it's because we're both boys." Tori's eyes bulged. She glanced at Vic, who shrugged and watched the carnage alongside her. "And because Oliver is gay."

Oliver looked like he wanted to melt into the floor. Visibly torn between staying near his friend and getting the hell away from their dragon mother, he trembled. Cassandra shook her head. "Ward, do not start this here. Let's get home and we can talk about this."

"What is there to talk about? Go ahead, tell me." Arms crossed, he openly defied their mother and Tori felt panic by proxy. "Tell me why you don't want my friend to stay over."

Cassandra scoffed. "I don't have to give you a reason."

"That's bullshit. You're bullshit. This whole family is bullshit!"

Tori reached out and gripped Vic's wrist. In response, he took a side step closer to her. Her brave, brave younger brother. She would include this act of bravery in his eulogy after their mother killed him.

"Excuse me?" Their mother's indignance turned to cold rage, one Tori remembered vividly. "You do not use that language with me, young man."

Unlike Tori five years earlier, Ward didn't budge. "Tell me why he can't stay over."

"Durward, I am giving you one minute to say goodbye to your friend—"

"He's not my friend! He's my boyfriend, okay? You don't like him because he's gay? Well, fine. Then you don't like me either, because I'm gay too."

Tori could've been knocked over with a feather. She nudged Vic. "Is he really?"

"I think so," he whispered back. "He's not the dramatic one in the family, so I doubt he's lying."

"Are you implying I'm the dramatic one?"

"No, our other sibling who's engaged to a guy and in love with her ex."

Tori glared at him, thoroughly regretting her decision to confide in him about what was going on—or, not going on—with Leah.

"Don't be ridiculous, you're not gay," Cassandra insisted dismissively. "You're sixteen. You don't know what you want."

"Yes, I do. I'm gay, Mom. Deal with it. You have a gay son, and I'm not changing."

"Good for you, bud," Vic called to him. "Proud of you."

Their mother shot daggers at Vic, then attempted to soften as she looked at Ward. "Ward, listen to me. I know it's been a long day. But you're not gay, honey. Maybe your…friend here has given you ideas, but this isn't who you are. You're not like that."

"Why are you like this? Why do you have so much hate in your heart?" Cassandra gasped. "You're the reason Tori doesn't come home. I only got to spend one Christmas with her in the past five years because you drove her away. And for what? Because she liked some girl? Big deal."

Tori's stomach clenched in nausea. She tightened her vise grip on Vic's wrist. "He knows?"

"I told him. He wanted to know why you never came home," Vic whispered, meeting her gaze with his soft brown eyes. "I told him the truth."

Cassandra reached out and Ward recoiled like she might poison him. "Don't touch me! You pushed away Tori, and now you're pushing me away too. So have fun with Vic, I guess. The only normal kid."

"Eh, maybe the only hetero kid but definitely not normal," Vic replied.

"That's not helpful, Victor," Cassandra warned. "Ward, I love you. I love all my children. I don't love the choices they make, but I love them."

"No, you don't. You can't love us because you don't know who we are. And that's not even the worst part. The worst part is you don't want to know who we are."

"That's not true," Cassandra replied. "I love you."

"You don't know how to love anyone. You're cold and heartless and one day you're gonna be a lonely old lady because your kids hate you."

Cassandra stared, open-mouthed, holding her heart as if she'd been stabbed. Ward's courage filled Tori with so much pride and love for her little brother it completely eclipsed any leftover sympathy for their mother. He was right; she made her choice, and it could cost her the children she claimed to love. Tori didn't think she'd mourn losing her very much, but she would be devastated if Ward and Vic abandoned her too. "You don't mean that."

"I do." Ward stuck out his chin proudly, looking more like their father than ever before. "I'm not going home with you. I'll get a ride with Vic and Tori."

"Ward..." Cassandra took a step forward and Vic met her step.

"Let him go, Mom. I think we all need to cool off. We'll drive him home." Cassandra looked between all of them, embarrassed and upset, but said nothing as she turned on her heel and swiftly made for her car in the lot.

"Why don't I bring Oliver home?" Ben offered. "Not in a homophobic way. Just to let you guys have a chance to talk."

Oliver shyly stepped to Ward. "I didn't mean for you to have to come out to your crazy mom."

"I don't care," Ward said, shrugging. "I like you. Why should I hide it just 'cause my mom's a bigot? That's her problem."

He leaned in and kissed Oliver softly, and the boys smiled as they broke apart. Tears welled in Tori's eyes at their unabashed affection and the sweet hopefulness on their faces. "Okay. See you, Ward. Happy birthday."

"Thanks, Ollie. I'll call you later." Oliver nodded as he walked away with Ben, whom Tori shot a grateful smile at as he looked over his shoulder at them. "Can we go home?"

"Yeah, bud." Vic led them to his car, and they piled in back toward Garden Hills. They rode in contemplative quiet, save for the rock station playing on low.

Tori watched Ward in the rearview mirror as he wiped the tears silently falling from his eyes. "Hey. I'm proud of you too."

Meeting her eyes in the mirror, he asked, "Is Dad gonna be mad at me?"

"Maybe for telling off Mom." Vic rested his wrist on the steering wheel and shrugged. "But not for being yourself. Not for being honest about who you are. It's your life and nobody gets to tell you how to live it."

Not strictly true, but Ward needed encouragement more than truth at the moment. "Trust me, you won't regret defending yourself and Oliver to Mom. If you'd let her say those things and get away with it, it's really hard to live with."

"Is that what happened with the girl Vic told me about?" Ward ventured quietly.

"Sort of, but I didn't have your courage. What you did today was really brave. I hope someday I can be as brave as you." She and Vic shared a smile. "And if Dad gives you a hard time, Vic and I have your back."

"Tori knows tae kwon do," Vic supplied. "I'm mostly there as a hype man."

"Both true! However, we do need to talk about something first." A sly grin on her face, Tori turned in her seat to face Ward. "So, how long have you and Oliver been dating? He's a cutie."

Ward groaned and slapped his hands over his face. "Oh my God, stop."

Their mother had spun away somewhere in a tizzy and their father wasn't home yet, so each Lockwood child retreated into their bedrooms separately. Music seeped out from Vic's door, the sound of video games blared from Ward's room, and Ben sat quietly on Tori's bed, looking up at her with a gentle smile when she entered.

"Hey."

"Hey." Tori closed the door behind her. Leaning against it, she tried to summon Ward's confidence for the conversation she was about to have. "So, I think we need to talk."

"Seems like it. I mean, I'm here for whatever you want to tell me. Clearly there is a story I'm missing." Ben ruffled his hair, a nervous habit he rarely exhibited. "I'm all ears."

"Okay. When I was seventeen, I fell in love with a girl in my class. It got intense very quickly, and basically took over my life for the summer between high school and college. I loved her with a passion I didn't know existed inside me. Just before I left for college, my mother caught us kissing and blackmailed me into never seeing her again. It devastated me. I couldn't forgive her for it and that's why I never came back to Garden Hills." She inhaled sharply. "I'm sorry I didn't tell you. It's not easy for me to talk about. And you never know how someone is going to react when you tell them you're...queer."

She didn't know how anyone would react because she'd only ever told Leah and Vic. Two people who loved her dearly and would never judge her. Saying it aloud, even to Ben, choked her. Ben absorbed her story with a few sympathetic nods. "I accept you as you are, Tori. I don't care if you're bisexual. I mean, I care, like it's a part of you and I love every part of you, but it doesn't bother me. Not that it should bother me, or that it's your problem if it bothers me, but...uh, I feel like I'm trying to be supportive and I'm doing it wrong."

"I'm not bisexual," Tori replied.

He blinked. "You're...not? Okay. Not that you need me to tell you it's okay. But, you know, lots of people have gay experiences and aren't gay. Who hasn't had gay thoughts? We've all been in a locker room."

"Ben." Stepping forward, she reached down and took his hands in hers. "Ben, I'm not bisexual. I'm a lesbian."

Blue eyes wide, he slowly drew his gaze from her hands to her face. She'd begun crying at some point during Ben's supportive spiral, and he reached up to wipe away the tears on her cheeks. "You're a lesbian. But I'm not a lesbian. I'm a man."

"That is correct."

"So..." Visibly distressed, Ben abruptly stood up and paced the room. "All this time, Tori, you...I've...We've slept together! How could you let me..."

It took Tori a couple of seconds to catch up to him. "Oh, God, Ben. Everything we did, you had my consent."

"Why did you sleep with me if you didn't even want me?" Pain stretched his voice to higher registers and Tori winced. "Why did you agree to marry me? Out of pity?"

"I thought it would help me find deeper feelings for you, but it didn't."

Sniffling, Ben attempted to gather himself with a long, deep inhale. Part of Tori empathized with him, and it hurt to see him so upset. But the other part of her, a much larger part, felt such a wave of relief she wanted to sob.

"I can't believe you were willing to spend your life with me and you don't even love me. That's...that's insane, Tori."

"I do love you, Ben. Not in the way you need, want, or deserve, but I do." In her heart, a blossom of platonic love bloomed for Ben over the past year or so. No matter how often he tended to it, it never grew into anything more. "I'm not asking you to understand me or forgive me. I did what I thought I had to do because I'm afraid of what I am. My fear drove me to you because I knew you'd protect me."

Ben balked. "Protect you by what, being your beard?"

"Being my what? What's a beard?"

"What gay person doesn't know what a beard is?" Ben asked, flabbergasted.

"Sorry, I've been too busy hiding my sexuality from literally everyone, I didn't have time to look up all the cool queer terms."

"I've always said you don't watch enough TV," Ben replied flatly. "Obviously, I don't want you to be hurt or to live a lie, and I definitely don't want to be in a relationship with someone who isn't attracted to me. I mean, how long did you plan on keeping this up? Until the wedding? Until our fiftieth anniversary when my dentures dropped out of my mouth into our cake?"

Shamefully, she might've hid forever if she hadn't seen Leah again and had her pretenses blown away like the seeds of a dandelion. "No, I—I…I don't know. My whole life, literally my whole life, I've done what's asked of me. I didn't know there was another way to be. I figured everybody's parents chose their college and their major for them. That their mothers picked out their holiday outfits well into their teens, or scrutinized each grade on their report cards. Every single school photo of me my mother would show up, plant herself behind the photographer, and command me to smile."

Tori strode to her desk and opened one of the drawers to pull out a folder of photos. She selected one for Ben and handed it to him. Her fourth-grade photo, where her mother put her in a puffy blouse and did her makeup as she sat in front of the black background with two shooting lasers behind her. "Jesus Christ, Tori, you look like a hostage."

She slipped the photo back into the folder and tossed it onto the bed. "I've been controlled my entire life. And then I met someone who helped me seek my own wants for the first time. She loved me for who I really am and encouraged me to be myself and I…lost her. I figured I deserved it, you know? What did I have to offer her but a life of hiding, or worse, a life of being under the constant threat of my mother?"

Ben roughly wiped the tears from his face, drawing the back of his hand over his mouth. "A life with you is a pretty good reward too."

"That remains to be seen, but thanks."

"No, it will be. Our life in Boston was pretty good," Ben said, wiping another tear with the heel of his thumb. "I…I always had a feeling something was missing, and I was naïve in hoping we could find it. I guess unless I found myself another X chromosome, we were always doomed."

Tori chuckled through her tears and wrapped him in a tight hug. "No, you're the perfect man. If you were a woman, you'd be insufferable."

Ben laughed in surprise. Her anxious fidgeting drew both their attention to her ring, which she gazed down at with a small smile. With a few quick twists it came off her finger, and she placed it in his palm.

"Ouch. That makes it…very real." He closed his hand and jammed the ring into his pocket. Two bloodshot blue eyes gazed at her. "Can I ask…is there someone else?"

"Um." Anxiety quickened Tori's pulse and she felt her skin grow hot. "Not…exactly."

"It's Leah, isn't it?" Ben snickered in bemusement at her alarm and grabbed his jacket from her chair. "Tori, I am not a jealous man. But when I saw the way she looked at you at the garage? I almost puffed out my chest a bit." With a weak smile on thin lips, he relented, "Then I saw the way you looked at her. I realized...you've never looked at me that way before. I don't think I've ever seen two people convey such intense longing. Whatever you two have, we've never had that."

She didn't know what to say. Had she projected her long-buried feelings so strongly when they first encountered her? "For what it's worth, nothing between Leah and me happened since I've been back."

"Really? Nothing?" He looked right through her. Not an accusation of cheating, but the knowledge that she didn't have to cheat to have strayed. "When you spent the night at her house..."

"We fell asleep. Nothing physical happened."

"Maybe it would've been easier if it did. Sex is a betrayal and a betrayal you can forgive. You can't forgive someone for falling in love with someone else. You just have to let them go." Ben stifled a short sob and Tori drew toward him, but he backed away. "I need to go. Try to sneak out before your parents come home."

"That's a good idea. If you do see them, don't—let me tell them." She hugged him again and felt his arms wrap around her, possibly for the final time. "Have a safe drive home. Text me so I know you got back okay."

"Yeah. Will do. Bye, Tori. And...good luck."

In one swift step, he exited her bedroom and closed the door behind him. Relief and grief tangled like snakes in her heart, twisting inside her chest. Only a minute later, Tori heard footsteps and looked up as Ben burst back into her room like he'd made a groundbreaking scientific discovery. "It's your initials!"

"I'm sorry?"

"At the café when we got here. I can't believe I didn't get it. What a dummy." He smacked himself on the head. "I thought it was roman numerals. It's your initials. And Leah's. LV and VL."

Tori chuckled hysterically through her tears. "Oh my God, right, the diner. Leah carved them years ago."

"Ugh, I'm so mad. I'm so mad because of course I never stood a chance against this long-lost love. And I'm mad because it's extremely romantic and I'm interested in how it turns out despite being totally devastated right now. So, I will call you when I'm less sad and I want to hear the whole story, okay? Not like, the whole-whole, but most of it."

"Okay, I promise."

"Good. Okay, bye."

As evidenced by her mother's voice downstairs, Ben's intent on circumventing her parents had been thwarted. After a short conversation Tori couldn't hear from her room, the front door opened and closed, and no sooner did the lock engage, her mother called for her. Reluctantly she ventured toward the interrogation, padding down the stairs toward the foyer.

Her mother, clearly still frazzled from Ward's coming out, glanced back and forth between the door and Tori several times. "Why is Benjamin going back to Boston?"

"An emergency meeting at his firm," Tori lied easily, clasping her hands behind her back. "His dad called."

"Oh. When is he returning?"

"He's not."

"I see. I was looking forward to introducing him to your father's colleagues at the award ceremony." Her mother frowned. "Victoria, there isn't anything wrong between you and Benjamin, is there? He appeared to be less than his gregarious self when he left."

"Not that I know of," she replied, feeling the anxiety creep up the back of her neck.

"Mm, okay." Her mother took two steps toward her, heels clacking against the marble like the cocking of a gun. "I know your father is doing business with Leah Vasquez. He appears to be very fond of her, and we wouldn't want to upset their business arrangement, would we? No, I imagine she can't afford to lose the contract after her father's tragic accident. All those hospital bills are surely piling up."

Tori crossed her arms and attempted to be as brave as her little brother. "Say what you want to say, Mother."

She leaned in. "Do not jeopardize your engagement for some delusional fantasy life you think you could have with Miss Vasquez. There is no place for her in your life, do you understand that? Doors will be shut in your face. The Lockwoods will cut you out of the family forever. Your father will be filled with disappointment. Everything in your life falls away if you choose her."

She bit her bottom lip to keep it from trembling. "I don't understand why you hate her so much. Or why you hate me." Her mother pulled back, blinking in surprise. "You've controlled me my entire life and I have always listened to you. I've done exactly as you wanted. I stayed out of trouble, got stellar grades. I dated the boys you liked. I joined the clubs you thought looked good on college applications. I went to the college you chose, majored in the major you and Dad picked for me. I've always fallen in line. Why can't I have this one thing? The only thing that's made me happy…possibly ever."

"Victoria, I don't hate you. I could never hate any of my children. I am trying to protect you, and perhaps I've come off as abrasive at times. Demanding, even. But that's only because I want you to succeed and not be taken advantage of."

"Well, I'm sorry, but that sounds like bullshit. I don't need to be protected from Leah. She's never hurt me."

"Not yet," her mother replied lowly. "Even now, Victoria, don't you see? You're here pining for her, letting your perfect fiancé walk out the door, and where is she? Shacked up with your best friend."

Tori barely held back a scowl, because of course her mother would exploit her jealous weakness. "That's none of my business, and it certainly isn't yours."

"People like her are opportunists. Desperate to climb up the ladder of society in any way possible. You're naïve, you always have been, and I have tried to protect you from people like her."

"Leah isn't like that," Tori gritted out. "She's a good person."

"I'm sure she's shown you every kindness she's capable of. That's what opportunists do. Let me put it this way, and I'll stop belaboring my point." The smirk on her mother's face chilled Tori's blood instantly. "If she had the choice between being wealthy, financially stable and possibly flourishing, and having all the resources and privileges you've enjoyed in your life…or being with you, which do you think she'd choose?" Tori paused, and it was long enough for her mother to nod once and assume she'd made her point. "Stay away from Leah Vasquez."

Tori could not stay away from Leah Vasquez, but Leah Vasquez stayed away from her. Over the course of two weeks, Tori unofficially moved back into her childhood home, and her calls to Leah went unanswered. Her texts received bland, mild responses, and her attempts at arranging for them to talk were routinely thwarted. Undeterred, Tori gave Leah the space she was clearly requesting and focused on what the architecture of her future might be. She and Ben planned to discuss where they'd live after they got married—in fact, Tori thought he might be her Get Out of Garden Hills Free card—but now she had no tethers to Boston other than an undecorated condo her father bought.

Without much else to do, Tori accompanied her father to work and started digging into the programming and software development.

The systems used by Lockwood Industries badly needed an upgrade, and Tori would spearhead the application of these upgrades once she came on full time. They hadn't spoken about it outright, but Tori felt less suffocated by the idea of joining her dad and her brother now. Her father took her to lunch, just the two of them, almost every other day since she moved back home. The layers of her father peeled away, and Tori began to recognize the man she remembered from her childhood. Funny, smart, intensely proud, and an unrelenting perfectionist with an impeccable work ethic. Doting over computer systems at Lockwood Industries wasn't quite the dream she had for herself, but it wasn't the worst future she could imagine. The threads of her life started to weave together. She had a job she'd all but officially accepted, she started apartment-hunting to get out from under her mother's roof, she'd written poetry again…but still, there was no Leah.

Finally, after days of badgering her with texts escalating in desperation, she convinced Leah to visit her new office. Her office boasted naught but three chairs, a desk, and a computer, however, the pretense was enough to get Leah to drive across town. Leah agreed to a lunch on a sunny Thursday afternoon, and Tori couldn't hide her anxiousness as she sat behind her desk and waited for noon to arrive. Tori thought about meeting her downstairs at reception, but she didn't want to look as baldly desperate as she felt. She was still a Lockwood, and there was at least the pretense of decorum to protect.

After what felt like eighty-four years, her father's secretary peeked around the doorframe to put her out of her misery. "Miss Lockwood? Miss Vasquez is here to see you."

"Send her in. Thank you, Vivian." The woman nodded and stepped aside, making room for Leah to enter. With a brown paper bag in one hand and flowers in the other, Leah also thanked the woman and entered the office, taking a slow look around. Tori sat up straight in her chair and allowed Leah to commence her inspection. The empty bookshelves lining the wall led her to the floor-to-ceiling windows and Leah took in the view. Outside Tori's window lay most of the downtown and up into the hills of their hometown. The sunlight cast a glow over Leah, especially the peeks of exposed skin. Dressed in her sleeveless mechanic's jumpsuit and boots, Tori could only glimpse her toned, tatted-up arms, but it didn't take more than that to make her stomach tumble.

Finally, Leah turned and offered a vase overflowing with beautiful round flowers in yellows, pinks, and oranges. "I feel dorky about it, but I thought…" Much to Tori's surprise and delight, Leah blushed. "They're dahlias. It's the national flower of Mexico. I know a woman who grows them in a greenhouse a few towns over. She brought the original seeds from Mexico. It's…it's stupid. I should've brought something practical, like a lamp."

Tori took the vase and set it on her desk, smiling at the gorgeous flowers. "It's not stupid at all. They're beautiful, Leah, thank you. You didn't have to bring me anything."

"It's your first office. I didn't want to come empty-handed, even if you are a corporate sellout." Leah grinned at her and dug into the paper bag to withdraw a paper-wrapped sandwich. "I got us lunch too. Hope you don't mind."

"Not at all. The corporate sellout lunches here are good, but they're not Harold's Deli good." Her eyes never left Leah as she got comfortable in the seat across the desk and pulled it close. "So, I guess you've been really busy, hmm?"

"I have. Your dad's previous mechanic was shit and a lot of the cars need maintenance. I've been in the shop from dawn to dusk almost every day."

"He's lucky to have you," Tori murmured. She ate her lunch quietly—a rather exceptionally delicious sandwich stuffed with vegetables and hummus—and avoided the impulse to make small talk. Across the desk, Leah still hadn't touched her sandwich. Instead, she stared down at it, the lines between her forehead deepening with every passing moment. "Leah?"

"We need to talk," Leah said hoarsely.

Tori put her sandwich down. "I agree."

Leah stood and jammed her hands into her pockets. "Um, I guess there's no good way to say it, so I'm just gonna say it, okay? We can't be friends. Or, really, I can't be friends with you. You're a good, kind person and I should want to be friends with a good, kind person, but I can't because when I look at you, I'm in love all over again. My heart never learned any other way to feel about you. I don't think it ever will."

Every syllable of her words was punctuated with the stomp of her boots as she paced the room. Tori rose from her chair, following Leah back and forth with her eyes, and rounded the desk to lean against the edge. "Come here." Her tone, softened like a ripe peach, had the desired effect of halting Leah midstep. Her senses rejoiced in the nearness of Leah as she drew closer, but her heart enjoyed it most of all. Leah's eyes raked up her body and she saw the barely perceptible bob of Leah's throat. Their proximity appeared to have the same effect on Leah. "Don't play games with me, Vasquez."

"You know I don't." Tori reached up and slid her fingers under Leah's hair, tracing her thumb behind her ear. Leah appeared pained at the contact. "Tori, you have to stop. You're engaged. He got on his knee and looked in your eyes and asked you to marry him and you said yes. You said yes."

"Leah, I—"

"No." Leah grabbed her hand and forcibly shoved it away. "That covenant means something to me. It means you can't touch me like this, or look at me like that."

"Leah."

"Just wait, okay? I have one more thing to say. I'll only say it once, and I'll never say it again." Tori's heart leapt as Leah dropped to one knee and took her hand. "Don't marry him. Please, please don't marry him. Now, I know I can't offer the same life. He's got money and pedigree and probably a summer home on a cape. I'm sure he's a good guy and he treats you with respect. And—and I know being with me is hard. I'm a mess. I'm…work. But I love you, Victoria. I love you, and I'll give you everything I have. Every inch of my heart, of my life, is yours if you want it. Just please, I'm begging you, don't lie to God and vow to love someone else. Love me. Love…only me."

Tori gazed at Leah in wonder, tears welling in her eyes. She pulled her up from the ground and clasped her hands around the back of Leah's neck. Searching Leah's eyes, she found deep, profound love and a chasm of anguish wide enough to swallow star systems. "Leah. I left Ben."

And, bless her, Leah's eyes glanced to each side of them, as if Ben had been stuffed in a storage closet. "Left him where?"

Tori let out a fond, exasperated sigh. "I broke off the engagement. It's a long story, but the important part is I'm not going to marry him."

"Oh." A fascinating array of emotions changed on Leah's face, like the slides of a magic lantern. "Thank God."

Leah sank into her and kissed her with the urgency of a house fire. Tori could've wept if she hadn't been preoccupied by the glorious sensation of kissing Leah Vasquez. She surrendered to the authority of Leah's tongue sweeping inside her mouth, of Leah pressing her into the desk hard, of the possessive feeling of Leah's hands splaying on her back. Tori groaned when she got a moment to take a breath and wound her fingers into Leah's wonderful, thick curls. One of Leah's hands came down and gripped beneath her thigh, wrapping Tori's leg against her waist as she brought them as flush as possible. Tori wanted to be consumed by her, but not all at once. She wanted a slow heat death, like the flaming out of a star.

Leah suddenly broke their kiss, and the loss of heat made Tori shiver. "Wait a second. You let me say all that shit and you already left him? I did a big speech and everything."

"It was very romantic," Tori replied, placing a kiss on the disapproving crease between Leah's eyebrows.

"You broke your engagement and you let me come in here and talk about dahlias." Leah frowned at her. "Feels like maybe you could've led with that."

"Noted. Next time you want to tell me not to marry someone, I'll make sure you have the pertinent information beforehand." With eyes narrowed in irritation, Leah tugged them back in flush. "However, I can wholeheartedly assure you there won't be a next time. You're the only one I want. The offer for your life, your heart? I'd like that very much, please."

Visibly overwhelmed, Leah leaned up and kissed her again, a more thorough and more Leah Vasquez kiss than before, hot and slick and urgent. Leah peppered kisses down the side of her neck, resting her forehead on the top of Tori's shoulder. Leah's body convulsed once and Tori tried to pull back to see what was wrong, but Leah held her close. "No, don't let go. I just...I really thought you were going to marry someone else and it was killing me."

Slowly, Leah kissed Tori's shoulder over and over, her tears soaking into the fabric of her shirt. Tori put one hand into Leah's hair while the other soothingly rubbed her back. "I'm sorry. I'm sorry I've never been brave enough."

"Stop, stop." Leah lifted her head from Tori's shoulder and gazed at her with prismatic eyes, the whites rimmed red. "You want to know how I've been able to live and be out? Not because I'm somehow braver than anyone else. It's because I've never done it alone. You've borne all your burdens by yourself and you want to tell me you're not brave enough? Tori, you're one of the bravest people I know. You're so much stronger and braver than you realize."

Leah's levitating words lifted the anvil that had sat on Tori's chest for five years. She inhaled deeply—the mix of rubber tires and vanilla musk unmistakably Leah—and her lungs expanded like great helium balloons. For years she'd assumed everyone had access to some fathomless fountain of fortitude she was prohibited to drink from. But Ward proved Leah right. With his siblings and his boyfriend by his side, Ward conjured the courage to live a truth so blindingly wonderful it could be seen for miles. "I…I don't know what to say."

Leah stroked her hair, reversing their position as the one giving comfort. "When I came out to my parents, I was so scared. All you hear are horror stories of kids becoming homeless because their parents kick them out, or worse. I even asked Billy if I could stay with him if things went bad. Thankfully they didn't, especially because Billy's room always smelled like a gym sock."

With tears in her eyes Tori chuckled, holding tight to Leah as she spoke. "Poor Jenna."

"Right? Anyway, a couple days later my dad and I are at the shop. He'd been really quiet since I came out, just not his normal self. I figured he was bracing to tell me he didn't approve or something. Instead, while we're doing a routine oil change, he starts quoting a passage from Numbers. At first, I'm like, that's really weird. He's quoting the part where God asks Moses to go into Israel, grab some elders, and he'll sprinkle the magic God dust on them."

"I get the feeling that's not the exact passage."

"It's an accurate paraphrase." Leah sniffed. "But the point was the end: 'They will share the burden of the people with you so that you will not have to carry it alone.' It was my dad reassuring me he would always be there for me and with me. You don't have to shoulder all your worries. I know you're afraid of your parents, of your family legacy or whatever. Of the backlash of coming out. But me? Riley? Your brothers? We can share your burden with you. You've always been brave enough, but you've always been brave alone. You don't have to be. Let me be brave with you. Let me be brave for you, when you can't."

Again, Leah left Tori dumbstruck. Quietly she wept, falling into Leah's arms. When she'd invited Leah to lunch, she hadn't expected to spend so much of it crying. But she didn't feel foolish; she felt relief. Each tear shed represented a droplet of her past swiped away. "I want to be out. I want to be myself. I want to be happy. And more than anything else in the world, I very, very badly want to be yours."

Her words sparked a change within Leah, as the pensive look in her eyes flashed to desire. After a few tentative pecks against her salty lips, Leah resuming kissing her in earnest. Passionate tongues dueling, articulating the words their hearts tried to say. Leah nipped the skin of her neck with her front teeth and Tori reflexively tugged her hair in sharp arousal. Leah's chuckle ghosted across her skin and she lifted her head to meet their gazes again before devouring her in another kiss.

Leah's thumb traced down the ridges in the center of her throat as her other hand drifted up Tori's skirt. "You've always been mine," Leah insisted between furious kisses. "And I've always been yours."

Stopping Leah's hand just before it could reach her intended destination, Tori disengaged from Leah's captivating kiss and whispered a short demand. "Take me home."

CHAPTER SEVENTEEN

They drove from the Lockwood office to Tori's home in silence. No music, no conversation, just the two of them side by side, with Leah's one hand on the wheel and the other clasped with Tori's. She drove through Garden Hills, over the tracks, into the north side, and up the winding roads to the Lockwoods' enormous residence. Her imagination took her here often, her memory cruelly constructing every detail of the garage with pitiless accuracy. Austere walls painted fancy white-people shades of off-white. Expensive tool chests, glistening red and barely used. The clearest details of course were Tori, Mrs. Lockwood, and the shattered remains of Leah's heart scattered across the cold cement floor.

"Is this a trap? Like the opposite of an intervention?" Though Leah voiced her apprehension, she didn't resist. Truth be told, she was tired of resisting.

"Come."

Tori held out her hand and Leah took it, crossing the threshold of the front door together. Leah immediately removed her boots and Tori gave her a strange look. "Are you kidding? I'm gonna wear my boots in this house? Never mind your mom, Carmen would kill me."

Evidently Tori found this reasonable, and she left her shoes near the door as well. Leah didn't remember the interior of the Lockwood home, having only seen glimpses the one time they snuck in together. It looked to Leah like the interior of most rich homes, the ones she got glances into when she delivered pizza. Too much money packed in one place, with elaborate decorations Leah had only seen in movies. Oil paintings of the three children, because these were the kind of people to make their children sit still for hours in formal wear. Sculptures crafted by non-American artists, lifted from their rightful culture to make Mrs. Lockwood feel exotic. Money blared at Leah from every wall and floor, like walking through Times Square at night, a relentless onslaught of wealth and ostentatious capitalism.

With her hand in Tori's, she followed her up the staircase and down the hallway to her room. No sooner had Tori closed the door behind them did Leah press her against it, kissing her with hard, burning purpose. Every time their lips met her stomach flipped; the migrating butterflies fluttered back after a five-year absence. The instinct to take, to devour, overwhelmed her and she slid to her knees, pushing Tori's skirt up with both hands.

"Wait." Leah stilled and peered up at Tori's disheveled face panting above her. With a fist full of her jumpsuit Tori yanked her to her feet again. She resumed kissing and nipping Tori's jaw and neck as she waited for her direction. "The bed. I want…I want my sheets to smell like you."

Her pulse quickened at the request and Leah wasted no time in lifting Tori from the ground. Tori giggled into their kiss as Leah guided them to the bed, laying Tori on the expensive white sheets and gently climbing on top of her. "I need this to be real."

Tori tore open the snap buttons of her jumpsuit and pushed her sleeves down her arms, freeing her upper body. She slid her hands beneath the tank top Leah had worn underneath, dragging her nails up her back until she was clutching her shoulder blades as Leah groaned into her skin. "It's real. You're the only real love I've ever had."

Allowing Tori to yank the tank top over her head and toss it, she ground down and lavished kisses up the side of her neck. She remembered every curve, every freckle and mole, like a mariner navigating home via burning constellations. "All this time, every woman I've been with, they never came close to being you."

Tori growled under her breath and dug her nails in harder. Leah gasped, followed by a short chuckle. "Are you trying to make me jealous?"

"Trying?" Leah replied, running her free hand up and down Tori's side, gripping her hip and holding her down with enough force to keep her immobile and arouse her. Palm flat, she inched up Tori's twitching stomach and cupped her breast roughly, swiping her thumb over her nipple. Apparently aggravated at the teasing, Tori swatted her away and aggressively removed her shirt and bra, nabbing Leah's wrist and forcing it back on her bare chest. "I know you're jealous."

"Fuck you. Like you're not."

"Oh, I don't deny it." Leah detoured from Tori's chest to lift her head and kiss her. "I hate everyone who has ever touched you like this. Anyone who isn't me."

This statement apparently hit the right note for Tori, who rolled her hips up in a desperate bid for relief. She whined and gasped at Leah's mouth and hands on her, and Leah became nearly dizzy from desire. "Nobody has ever made me feel like you do."

And whatever stupid, primitive instinct that statement awakened, Leah did not try to stop it. "Did you try? Did you try to fuck me out of your system?"

"Yes."

"With other girls?"

"Yes." A hot iron of jealousy branded Leah's insides. To think of Tori, less than two miles away in college, touching some other girl to conjure Leah in her bed, filled her with envy and anger and grief. "It didn't work."

"No kidding." Leah kissed her deeply but sweetly, and pulled back to gaze into her eyes. She returned to the task at hand, nosing a line between Tori's breasts, then across her ribs. The tip of her tongue darted out periodically to taste the clean, slightly salty skin as she took deep inhales of Tori's scent. God, how she missed it. Nothing smelled quite like home as Tori's soft, warm skin. "They never feel like you. They don't smell like you."

Tori yanked her up for another long, hot kiss that burned her lungs from the inside out. "No?"

"No. They don't taste like you." She slid her tongue into Tori's mouth to steal her breath once more. Obliging Tori's attempts at friction, she slid her leg between them and pressed into her. Tori's head fell back, and she let out a high-pitched whine. "They don't sound like you."

"Leah." Tori breathed out her name between kisses, urging her on with a hand around Leah's back. "Touch me."

And she would, in time, but for the moment Leah needed to savor the heat of their kiss. "When they kiss me, they don't make me feel like you do."

"How do I make you feel?"

"Like I'm falling off the edge of the world." In fact, every kiss tasted like agony, like years of pent-up aggression and sadness. Belated hunger and regret. Passion, and maybe a bit of hope. "I've missed you so much," she whispered, so low she wasn't sure Tori heard her.

But when she opened her eyes, tears had accumulated in the corner of Tori's eyes. She moved her hands to either side of Leah's face, cradling it softly. "I missed you too."

Her eyes locked to Tori's, she slid her hand beneath her skirt, pushing aside the remaining fabric barrier and running her fingers along the wetness between her legs. "When I'm with them, touching them, tasting them, it didn't feel like this." She pressed two fingers inside and Tori keened, arching her back as Leah watched her reaction with wide, dark eyes. "But when I'm inside you, it wrecks me."

Every thrust felt like a wave smashing against rock. Destructive and inevitable, constant, breaking Leah into pieces. Each sweet exhale from Tori's lips infused her with life, every kiss resuscitated her with lungful breaths. They eased into lovemaking as if no time had passed, as if Leah hadn't spent five years aching to touch her again. She remembered when to be rough and when to go slow, unraveling Tori like a conductor leading an orchestra in the sweetest symphony ever heard.

"Fuck. Please, don't stop." Tori begged her between pants of breath and short, sharp whines of pleasure. "Please, Leah."

Her name cried like a broken prayer spurred Leah on, and her eyes rolled back in pleasure. She curled her fingers and sped up the rhythm until Tori opened her mouth in a silent scream. A noise choked out and she whipped her head to the side and bit down on Leah's forearm to muffle her cry as she came. Tori kept her teeth clamped on her skin, panting as her heart rate slowed. All of Leah's senses came alive at once. The sight of Tori flushed beneath her, the smell of her conditioner, the taste of her skin, the sound of their shared breaths, the rapidly drying wetness on her fingers.

"I'm glad you came back," Leah said, finally giving herself permission to say aloud the feeling she'd bottled and buried since the moment their eyes met weeks ago. "I never stopped loving you, you know. Not for any single minute of any single day."

Tori kissed her, furious and aching, gripping Leah's upper arm so tight it was like being tethered to the ground, as if Tori thought if she let go Leah might slip through her fingers like sand. "Really? Do you mean that?"

"I do. It's mostly been hell, to be honest."

"Gee, thanks."

"You know what I mean. Without you, I felt like I was living cleaved in half. On my best days, any real joy stayed locked behind a door I couldn't open. No matter how I tried to unlock it—with girls, school, liquor, drugs—I couldn't do it. And on my bad days…" Leah let out a sad, humorless laugh. "When my dad got in the accident, the first person I wanted to call was you."

"I wish you had. I wish I could've helped." Tori kissed the tip of her nose, conciliatory and sweet. "It was the same for me. I started failing classes and I thought, Leah would know what to do. She'd make all of this better. Even little things—like I'd go to a record store and they'd have a vinyl of a band you like that I'd never heard of. And I wanted to…call and tell you. If only to hear you call me a preppie for not knowing your obscure punk bands."

Leah smiled. "I would've hated that…but I also would've loved that. And I would've hated that I loved that."

"That's my Leah." The instant warmth upon hearing Tori take possession of her should've embarrassed Leah, but it didn't. She'd been a lost cause for years where Victoria Lockwood was concerned. "Thank you for giving me another chance."

Another short, mirthless laugh left her chest. "What other option was there?"

"Well, you could've said no."

"Could I? Tori, I was in love with you in an instant in eighth grade when you looked at me. I loved you freshman year when you gave your class president speech and stumbled over a word and people laughed, but you pressed on with a big smile, totally undeterred. I loved you junior year when we went on the field trip to the natural history museum and you were the only one listening to the curator talk about some weird fossil. I loved you when you told me why you left prom and I started to understand how strong you are. I loved you when you picked up a dirty kitten in an alley and forced me to keep it. And I loved you when you broke my heart."

Tori looked as if the breath had been knocked from her lungs. "God, I don't deserve you. You're so good at love, Leah. I'm not. I just…break things."

We are Vasquezes and we are makers. We are fixers. Her father's voice echoed in her mind as she cupped Tori's jaw in her hand. "You know how to love just fine. You didn't break anything, you understand that, right? Your mother broke us up, not you. We were just kids." Leah gazed into her eyes. "I forgive you, okay? Whatever you think you need my forgiveness for, I forgive you."

Tori kissed her again and she tasted the salt of her tears in their embrace. When their lips parted, Tori carded her fingers through Leah's hair, tucking it behind her ear. "I'll do the work. I'll be better. I'll be anything you need."

"Stop promising me the moon." Leah made her demand gentle but full-throated. Tori's weakness lay inside her greatest strength: her words. The palaces she could build with her poetry turned to sandcastles when she spoke. Leah didn't need words. She needed deeds, heat, and flesh. "I've only ever needed you."

Tori urged Leah onto her back and snuggled into her hair. She inhaled Leah's scent so deeply, Leah thought her whole soul might get sucked up. "So, you won't let me spoil you?"

Wet, hot kisses against her ear and her neck sent shivers down Leah's spine. "You want me to be a kept woman?"

"Mm-hmm." Tori kissed down the middle of her chest, tracing her tongue around the rim of Leah's navel. "I'll give you anything you want."

"And if I want…a biplane with a big banner to fly over the town that reads: 'Tori Lockwood Loves Leah Vasquez' or 'Leah Vasquez Has A Huge Ween,' you'd put that together for me?"

Tori's rebuttal came in the form of her teeth sinking into the tender flesh between her stomach and her pubic bone. Her hips jerked involuntarily, and Tori's strong hands held her down as she finished creating an angry red spot adjacent to her tattoo. Leah thought she might've forgotten how, but Tori expertly removed her jumpsuit and briefs just as she'd done a dozen times in their fervid youth. "Anything you want."

"I want you to not be wearing any clothes, for starters." With a smirk, Tori went about undressing rather quickly, and Leah's extremely gay heart palpitated as all of Tori revealed herself. "Fuck, you are so gorgeous."

Tori blushed and crouched near her feet. She flattened her hands on either of Leah's shins and stretched forward, curving her back as she lay between her legs. Tori snaked her arms under Leah's legs and dug her fingertips into the soft flesh of Leah's inner thighs. Leah's head nearly hit the headboard when she came in contact with Tori's tongue. Something guttural came out of her mouth as she wrapped one hand around a bar of the headboard and the other tugged Tori's hair. Heat coiled in her stomach and Leah rode the waves of warmth as they spread from her core. She rolled her hips against Tori's mouth with increasing frequency, swearing under her breath in Spanish as she neared her climax. Spurred on by her desire, Tori's stupidly talented mouth, and the bruising grip of her fingers on Leah's thighs, she tumbled over her peak with a long groan and shudder, flopping back onto the mattress, nearly boneless. Tori lapped at her until Leah could no longer handle the sensation, then wiped her mouth across the back of her hand and lay beside Leah on her plush pillows.

She snuggled into Leah's side, draping an arm and a leg over Leah's torso. Again, Leah felt like she was being purposefully weighted down. Stroking her fingers through Tori's hair, Leah tried not to stumble into more prickly emotions again. Life between this moment and the last time they were like this had been a series of cruelties punctuated by brief moments of joy. Even the joy—going to college, her dad surviving the accident, Riley's friendship—were muted. They took on the shape of joy, like handblown glass vases, but Leah could not fill them.

But she didn't want to say any of that. So, instead she said, "You're still really good at that."

Tori laughed, and how unfair of Leah's heart to soar at the sound. "I've always been pretty good at oral exams."

Leah joined her in laughter, giggling like children poorly suppressing a secret. They kissed again, but it didn't ache or yearn. It was a kiss like fireworks, like the cheer of a home crowd. For the first time in a long time their connection didn't feel fraught or temporary. Kissing Tori felt like sliding on a favorite T-shirt, or spinning a favorite album. Kissing Tori felt like falling asleep in the back seat of the car driving down the road home in the sunset. It made her believe, if only for the moment, that Tori could be the road home.

Of course, Leah spent her entire life in cars and knew the roads like the back of her hand. She knew the road with Tori would not be a straight one, nor would it be an easy one. As Tori showered, Leah re-dressed from her clothing strewn around the bed. Not wanting to leave without saying goodbye, Leah sat on the edge of the bed to wait.

She snagged a slim navy notebook from the nightstand next to the bed and flipped it open. In Tori's neat script, lines and verses of poetry graced each page. Not strictly in any one form, Leah noted as she flipped through, but beautiful prose. The masterful imagery and metaphor revealed a keyhole into Tori's inner mind. It tracked perfectly that Tori and her beautiful, bedeviled soul produced incredibly moving poetry.

A creep of steam heat crawled into the room, and Leah looked toward the bathroom door with a smile. Wrapped in a robe and grinning from ear to ear, Tori padded toward her, her exposed skin turned pink from the heat of her bath. As her eyes traveled down from Leah's face to the book in her hands, her smile fell with it.

"No, don't read that. It's just scribbles. Nonsense." Tori snatched the book and snapped it closed like the jaws of an alligator. She winced at Leah. "How much did you read?"

"I already know you're a brilliant poet." Leah swung her legs over the bed and stood, taking the book and placing it back where she found it. Running her hands along the incredibly soft robe, she attempted to soothe Tori's immediately frazzled nerves. "But this proved it. You're good, Tori. I mean it. I wouldn't say it if I didn't. In fact, I'd probably just have lied and said I didn't read it at all."

Tori poked her in response, but the hardness on her face melted into appreciation. "Thank you. I...took as many writing courses in college as I could fit into my schedule alongside what I needed to graduate. I won a couple of contests too. Locally."

"That's amazing." Tori's pearlescent personality glittered when exposed to the sun, and this was yet another colorful, incredible part of her. Leah could spend the rest of her life parting dark clouds just to watch her shine. "You've always been annoyingly good at everything."

"Flattery will get you everywhere." She pushed the robe over Tori's shoulder to lean down and give the exposed skin a kiss, pecking the freckles scattered across the top. Suddenly, Tori apparently realized Leah was fully dressed and snapped back. "You're not leaving, are you?"

"I think my luck here is bound to run out soon, isn't it? I'd rather your father not walk in on me boning the prodigal daughter."

"Okay, let's not say 'boning' ever again. And everyone went golfing."

"I see. Still, I was supposed to only be gone for lunch and now I've been gone..." She lifted her watch from the bedside table. "Two and a half hours. I have to get back to the shop."

Tori pouted. She had an absolutely devastating pout and knew how to wield it like a knight with a broadsword. Adding insult to injury, she gently pulled at the knot keeping her robe together and gave Leah an entirely insincere coquettish look. "There's nothing I can do to convince you to stay a little longer?"

On the precipice of abandoning her principles, Tori's bedroom door opened and Carmen strolled in. Tori shrieked, Carmen shrieked, and Leah did not shriek but winced at the sudden increase in decibels. Tori skittered around behind her, frantically tugging her robe closed.

"Why you hiding? I bathed since you were born. I see everything."

"Why are you in my room?"

Carmen showed her hands clad in rubber gloves with an unimpressed look. "For to clean, Miss Tori. I thought everybody be golfing."

"Right. Well, uh, you remember Leah Vasquez."

"*La hija de* Hector," Carmen replied. "She work for your father. Your father know she also do this?"

"No, he doesn't. We…it's new. I mean, it's old? But it's new to us now."

"Uh-huh." Unimpressed and understandably confused, Carmen put her hands on her hips and glared at Leah. "Explain. *En Español.*"

Leah sighed and launched into a somewhat detailed, PG-13 explanation of their situation. Omitting some of the less favorable parts, she got Carmen caught up on the last few years. Tori stood by her side, entwining their fingers and giving them a quick squeeze. Unbeknownst to Tori, Carmen started grilling Leah on her life and her intentions for Tori. The Spanish Inquisition had nothing on the Spanish inquisition of an overprotective Mexican *madre*.

Carmen's dark, suspicious eyes clocked each of them separately with long stares before she gave Leah one final nod. "*Dios mío. No mas gringo grande?*"

"*Gringo*…oh, Ben?" Tori asked and Carmen affirmed with a curt nod. "No, he left. I love Leah. I've…always loved Leah."

Though she tried to stay cool under the scrutiny of Carmen, Leah melted due to the adoring, amorous look in Tori's eyes. Carmen didn't appear overly impressed with any of this information, but she sighed and asked, "You stay for dinner?"

Leah glanced between her and Tori. "I should go."

"No, stay," Tori pleaded softly.

Leah politely requested in Spanish that they be excused, and Carmen reluctantly took her leave. Once they were alone again, Leah turned back to face Tori. "I don't think you're ready for me to meet your family. Not like this."

Tori squinted at her. "Because of the…boning?"

"Because in the span of a few weeks you went from engaged to a man to sitting on my face, and I think maybe we need to slow down." Tori blushed a deep crimson and her eyes glazed over a bit as they dropped to Leah's mouth, perhaps imagining the events of the past couple hours. Leah placed her hands on either of Tori's shoulders, squeezing them once. "I'm happy you want to be out, and I'm happy you want to be with me. But I think maybe you'll forgive me for…not taking your word for it."

"You don't trust me," Tori stated. Not in surprise, but in resignation.

She took Tori's soft, warm hands in her own. Years of using an expensive hand lotion kept them from falling victim to the drying effects of the chlorine Leah knew she spent most of her teen-hood in. Still incredibly strong hands, and Leah's insides clenched to remember the way they filled her. "No, not yet."

"That's fair, I guess." Tori's mouth moved into a glum frown and Leah sighed, pressing a kiss against her temple. "Can I see you again soon?"

"It depends—are you even staying in Garden Hills?" Leah dared not hope.

"I don't know. The idea was for Ben and me to start house-hunting but obviously we will not be house-hunting anytime soon." Leah couldn't suppress the angry twitch on her face. She could never provide Tori that life—the big house, picket fence, a brood of blond-haired, blue-eyed legacy children—and she couldn't help but wonder if Tori, deep down, would've been happy in that life. An easy, unexamined life. "Nobody knows I broke the engagement. Well, my mom knows something is up because she saw Ben leave."

"What did you tell her?"

"That he went back to Boston. Which is technically true, I just didn't tell her the truth as to why." Tori peered down at her feet. "Because I don't want to go down the same road, I need to be honest with you. She suspects something is going on between you and me."

"How does she have such incredible intuition and still be a piece of shit? I mean, sorry, I shouldn't call her that. But it's amazing how she can sniff out a lesbian from a mile away. She's like a homophobic bloodhound."

"She warned me to stay away from you. Obviously, that's not something I'm willing to do anymore. But I don't want anything to happen to you."

"Tori, listen. What is she going to do, really? Deport my dad? He's a citizen. Have me arrested? For what? I know every cop and sheriff in this county from delivering pizzas, and they use my shop to fix their cruisers. Cut me off from my contract with your dad? Good luck. That shit is ironclad because your dad doesn't fuck around." Leah placed her hands on Tori's shoulders and rubbed them soothingly in a mini-massage. "You don't have to protect me. I can protect myself."

Tori didn't appear convinced, but Leah could feel the clock ticking before Tori's family returned from their outing. They could assuage her anxieties later. "She's awful, Leah."

"She's a bitch, so what? I'm a bitch too."

"Maybe, but you're a soft marshmallow underneath and she's a matryoshka of rancid personalities."

A laugh erupted from her chest and Leah distanced herself from Tori. "We'll figure it out, okay? I'll call you later, promise."

Two steps toward the door Tori caught up, pulling her close for another long, passionate kiss tingling her body from head to toe. A gorgeous pair of blinking, wet, maple-colored eyes regarded her with such affection, Leah's heart battered her chest. "See you soon?"

"Soon."

Reluctantly parting from Tori's company, Leah headed downstairs and detoured to the kitchen to say goodbye to Carmen. The sound of the front door opening and closing startled her, and she nearly leapt behind the breakfast counter to hide. Before she hit the marble floor, Leah remembered she was a full-grown woman and stopped.

Victor Lockwood stepped into the kitchen, dressed less formally than Leah had ever seen him. Khaki shorts, a baby-blue polo, and a white visor he quickly removed. Beside and just behind him, Tori's mother, Cassandra, stood in equally casual clothing, her expression unreadable. Leah had never felt so much like prey before that moment, as if she might be shot and mounted on their wall alongside the deer. "Leah? What are you doing here?"

"Oh, I was um…I was…" *Don't say boning your daughter. Don't say boning your daughter. For the love of baby Jesus and teenage Jesus and adult Jesus, don't say boning your daughter.*

Carmen scurried behind her. "Miss Leah helped me with my car. I told Miss Tori my car was very loud and she said she fix. I know the *padre de* Miss Leah, Señor Hector. We go to the same church."

"Oh." Victor reached for his wallet. "What do we owe you?"

"Nothing, nothing. Señora García is practically family. My father would have my head if I charged her a cent." Leah plastered on a smile and tried not to let the fear freeze her to the spot. Thank God for Carmen and her quick thinking. Whatever she owed her for this, Leah would pay it tenfold. "It's nice to see you again, Mr. Lockwood. And nice to meet you, Mrs. Lockwood."

Cassandra stepped forward, all grace and poise like an upright cobra, and held out her hand. "Likewise, Miss Vasquez. It's a good thing my daughter knew exactly who to call, isn't it?"

Leah shook her hand as calmly as she could manage with her heart pounding in her ears. "She's a smart woman, your daughter, and she knows I do good work."

"Does she now?" Cassandra's eyebrows lifted on her uncreased brow.

"Of course. You know, I fixed her fiancé's car when they arrived in Garden Hills? So, she's seen how efficiently I work." Leah lowered her tone, lacing every syllable with innuendo. "She knows I take my time, looking at every part, top to bottom. She's seen firsthand how thorough I am. I don't stop until the job is done. You might say she's familiar with my special Vasquez Touch."

Certain she'd laid it on thick enough to choke, Leah preened and stood up straight. The challenge in Cassandra's eyes reminded her of Tori's competitive streak, but riddled with venom. Leah did not back down. Bigots came a dime a dozen and the only special thing about Cassandra was her proximity to Tori, and that only decreased her sufferability in Leah's eyes.

"Yes, you've made quite an impression in a short amount of time."

"I like to work, and I'm very good at what I do."

"Oh, speaking of!" Victor took a step into Leah's space and clapped a hand on her shoulder. "I got news for you, Miss Vasquez. Now, normally there's a formal letter and whatnot, but I decided to do things differently this year."

Even with a low probability of being fired, Leah tensed. "Okay."

"I don't know if you're aware, but Lockwood Industries is the largest employer in Garden Hills, and in Lambert County overall."

"Yeah? Cool."

"It is cool! As such, we like to give back to the community as often as we can. One of the ways we do that is through our Hometown Heroes program. Every year residents nominate someone who has positively impacted the community and our board chooses one winner." Leah grew increasingly anxious as Victor's smile widened. "And I'm choosing you, Miss Vasquez. So, congratulations. You are the 2005 Garden Hills Hometown Hero."

Leah didn't know how to react. She stood stock-still, barely breathing as Tori's brothers came through the door. "But I...Who nominated me?"

"I did," he answered simply. "I want to acknowledge the work you've done with your business, your commitment to helping the less fortunate with the cars you fix and give to low-income families. To your bravery for steering a business through an incredibly tough personal event. I think you're very deserving, Leah, and I hope you'll accept."

"Accept what?" Vic asked, nabbing an apple from the bowl on their counter and taking a large bite. "Good to see you, Leah."

"Hey, Vic," Leah replied without looking over. "I don't know what to say, Mr. Lockwood. What...what do I have to do?"

"Do? Nothing! Just show up to the award dinner and accept the award. It comes with a check and a trophy or something, it's cute. But the company will take care of everything. Just let me know how many seats to reserve for you."

"Oh, my big, strong, Hometown Hero!" Vic exclaimed, opening his arms wide. He slung one arm over Leah's shoulder and jostled her like they were teammates. "You know what would be perfect? We should have Tori give you the award. Since you two are gal pals from the same graduating class. Bosom buddies, one might say."

Tori often talked about wanting to punch her brother and Leah finally understood, instantly appreciating her lack of siblings. "I'm not sure she would want to."

"Nonsense, it's a great idea," Victor insisted. "She believed in you at our meeting, and she was right."

Smoke practically billowed from Cassandra. Leah smirked and aimed her gaze at Victor. "That's great. Thank you, Mr. Lockwood, I'm flattered. I...I would only need two seats, I think, for my parents."

Leah only realized she'd opened a window for Cassandra to strike after she saw the flash of fangs. "Aren't you seeing Kelly Myers's daughter, Riley? I'm sure she'd love to come and support you."

The thing about venom is, once it's sunk into your skin, you can suck it up and spit it back out. "Riley and I are just friends. Mrs. Myers has tried to set us up for a while now. She is just crazy about me and is dying for me to be her new daughter." Leah smiled as brightly as she could. "But you're right, Riley would love to come to support me. No date for me, though. I'm single, if you happen to know any single, twenty-something lesbians."

"Tori!" Victor boomed.

"I don't think she's single," Vic muttered. In Tori's place, Leah nudged him with her elbow.

To their left, Tori froze on the staircase. Shaking off the ice, she came down the last couple steps and approached the wary circle of acquaintances. "Sorry, I didn't hear all the talking until I got out of the shower. I didn't think Leah was still here."

"Right, I fixed Carmen's car but I have to get back to the shop." Tori's eyes glanced back and forth between Leah and Cassandra like she was choosing which bomb wire to cut. "Thank you for the award,

Mr. Lockwood. I suppose you can just give me a table and I'll see if I can scrounge up any more friends to invite."

"You got it, Miss Vasquez. And Tori, would you mind presenting Leah the Hometown Hero award? It does require a little speech, but you've done some writing, haven't you?"

Obviously blindsided, Tori sputtered before replying, "Of course. I'd love to. I can't think of anyone more deserving than Leah."

Victor beamed at them. "Great! And we'll all be there to support you. I'll get a table for the family right in front."

"Don't forget a seat for Tori's fiancé." Cassandra blinked innocently. "I'm sure he would love to attend."

He probably wouldn't, Leah ventured silently, if he knew Leah could lick the salty flavor of Tori on her lips. The proud smile fell on Victor's face and he acquiesced to his wife. "Right, of course. A seat for Barry as well."

"Benjamin," Cassandra replied with a stern look. Victor shrugged.

"Right, uh, listen, I really need to go. Thank you again." Leah bowed out of the conversation, waving to Carmen as she walked out the door. Just outside the threshold, Leah breathed out a long sigh. A deeply yellow sun shone brightly on her scandalous exit—no shadowy walk of shame for her today—and she strolled toward her car parked near the curb. In her driver's seat, Leah sat and stared out the windshield without moving for a few minutes. She'd successfully dodged Tori for almost two weeks before finally succumbing to the suspicious invite to "see her new office." But she knew eventually she'd give in. Eventually, she always gave in. They were like grass and dew—one begot the other in a cycle. But unlike dew, Leah hoped they could last beyond the late afternoon sun.

CHAPTER EIGHTEEN

Tori theorized not everyone could make bold strokes. Some painted their lives in bright yellows and verdant greens, or could reach the depths of sapphire blues and indigo purples, but Tori never felt comfortable in those colors. She lived in a world of neutrals, of pale turquoise and washed-out pinks. Pastels and watercolors. Leah was a tenacious swath of fire-engine red, the tips of the bristles dipped in blood orange. The dahlias—the ones Tori stared at instead of working—reflected Leah better than a mirror. Bright, bold, beautiful.

Her own colors blended in. Even as her exemplary academics and prolific extracurriculars kept her in a popular caste, Tori did her best not to stand out. From birth, she'd been taught to fall in line, do her part, be ordinary and predictable. Leah stood out by default as a stunningly gorgeous dark-skinned girl in a town full of white European descendants, but her fearlessness dazzled. Tori wished the more they suffused, the more Leah's valiant colors might rub off.

Having not seen Leah in two days, Tori's imagination worked overtime to relive their last encounter. She squirmed in her seat, feeling the phantom sensation of Leah inside her. Her fingers brushed the purple bruise on her chest where Leah's teeth had dug in and marked her as taken, however the faint throb of pain couldn't quite compare to the thrilling sting of her original injury. Her phone vibrated on her desk, startling Tori from her daydream.

Leah. Giddiness tingled through her like a shudder. Instead of replying, Tori immediately called and waited for her to pick up. It only took one ring before a throaty voice came through. "A text is usually replied to with a text."

"I wanted to hear your voice," Tori replied softly. She heard the sigh on the other line and smiled. "So, you asked me if I wanted to come over tonight."

"I did."

"And I want to do that. But, um, I'm calling because I want to take you out to dinner tonight."

If not for the ambient noise of the auto shop, Tori might've thought Leah hung up from the long stretch of silence. "Oh. You—you want to take me on a date?"

The timbre of Leah's voice rose, going small and hopeful, and Tori's heart fluttered. "I'd love to, if you'd let me."

"Um, sure. Where did you want to go?"

Tori reclined in her chair, spinning it around to look out her window as if she could take stock of the county's restaurants from her seat. "Let me surprise you. You don't have to dress up or anything."

"Aw, man. You're not going to throw me my own prom?" Leah's raspy chuckle warmed her. "I guess it's only romantic once. Twice is sort of uninspired."

"Leah," she admonished fondly. "How's eight? Is that enough time after the shop closes?"

"Plenty. Do you want me to pick you up?"

"For the date I'm planning? No, dummy, I'll pick you up."

"Fine, fine." Leah paused. "If you're borrowing one of your dad's cars, make it the Spyder. I've never ridden in a Maserati before, and I just replaced the sound system for him."

"How adorably high maintenance of you," Tori replied, and in return she received a tiny huff. "But you got it. I'll pick you up around eight, okay?"

"Okay." Muted noise came through the line and Leah laughed. "*Papi* says hi but I also need to go before he gets stuck under this Chevy. I'll see you tonight."

"Tell Hector I said hi. And Gremmy. Bye, Leah." Tori flipped her cell phone closed and clapped excitedly to herself in her seat. Second chances only happen once, despite the name, and Tori needed to dip into the palette of her heart and draw in the boldest colors in her capabilities. Nothing less would do for someone as vibrant as Leah Vasquez, and Tori would not let her down again.

She pressed the button on her phone, and within thirty seconds the secretary appeared in her doorframe. "Yes, Miss Lockwood?"

"Hey, Vivian. Do we have any blank CD-Rs lying around?"

Anxious energy coursed through Tori as she waited at the curb for Leah. The sky flamed out above her, streaks of red and pink clouds catching the fiery sunset stretched across the ever-deepening blue of the hot summer night. She'd gone out and bought a new outfit for the date—a green vest over a white button-down and with a matching green skirt. Overall, she preferred shorts, but Leah always had a weakness for Tori in skirts, so sue her if she wanted to exploit that weakness. The double layer proved a bit warm for the night, but Tori hoped, wished, prayed she wouldn't be wearing both layers all night.

Loretta approached, hefting a blue recycling can, and crossed the freshly cut grass toward where Tori stood next to her father's ostentatious car. "Hi, Mrs. Vasquez. How are you?"

"Oh, Tori, we're both adults now, you may call me Loretta." She plunked the blue can away from the car and dusted off her hands. "I'm well, dear, how are you?"

"Good, yeah. Great. How are you?"

Loretta lifted her lips in a tired smile. "You already asked that."

"Right, of course I did. How embarrassing," Tori replied, blushing. "I'm a little nervous, to be honest. I—I don't know how much Leah's told you about what's gone on since I came home."

"I got the gist." Correctly reading the extra-large print insecurity on Tori's face, Loretta huffed out a short laugh. "I don't have any opinions on what Leah does with her heart, or with who. She's a big girl now."

"But you're her mom. I don't want you to hate me."

Loretta crossed her arms. "You're both adults now. Young adults, but adults. Even if I didn't approve, it wouldn't matter. Leah's stubborn. And where you're concerned, she's practically immovable."

Tori tried to hide her smile but failed. It helped ease her anxiety to know behind the scenes, Leah felt as strongly about her as she claimed. "Can I ask you…why didn't you tell Leah I came to find her the day we broke up? She says she didn't know. I'm sure it wouldn't have made any difference, but…"

"It wasn't out of malice, if that's what you're thinking. I didn't think it would benefit Leah to know, considering the state she was in." Loretta shrugged, not dismissively, but almost haplessly. "I kept your mother's threats in the back of my mind, but I did not share them with Leah. She didn't want to talk about you with me or with Hector anyway, so I respected her wishes. I didn't know what to do. I felt badly for you both, but I gave Leah space in regard to her breakup. There's no guidebook on dealing with teenage heartbreak, so I did my best."

"I can safely say you did better than my mother, so..." Tori chewed on her lower lip, staring into the relentless eyes of Leah's mother. Maybe Riley could sweet-talk Loretta, but Tori still felt a chill from her. "I'll never hurt her again."

"Never is a long time, Victoria." Leah loudly bounded out of the doorway and Tori immediately brightened, sending Loretta's gaze to her right. She smiled again. "Have fun. Don't get into any trouble. No dress burnings."

Tori chuckled, inwardly relieved to be free of Loretta's analysis. "No dress burning, I promise."

Upon reaching the end of the walk, Leah detoured around them to admire the car, whistling at it. "You're at least going to let me drive us home, right? Like...I only got to sit in the driver's seat while I did the install."

"Leah insisted on the garish car," Tori explained to Loretta.

"Oh, I believe you." She waved to them and started back up toward the ramp. "Enjoy yourselves."

"Damn right I'll enjoy myself in this beauty," Leah replied absently. Tori's eyes went so wide she knew Loretta could see the whites of them from several yards away. Blinking innocently at her, Leah's brows furrowed. "Hah. Oh. I meant the car. G'night, Mom."

They got into the car together and Leah's face lit up in glee as the engine turned over. Not much of Leah's knowledge or love of cars had rubbed off on her in their time together, so the sound of this engine was like any other engine Tori had ever heard. But to see Leah's face was like a symphony only she could hear filling her ears. She did her best to control the ridiculous speed of the car as they drove away from Leah's block and toward the highway.

Leah reached for the radio, and Tori caught her wrist and raised her eyebrow. "I have one rule for passengers."

"You do, huh?"

"Reach under your seat."

Casting a wary glance, Leah reached between her legs and pulled out a much smaller version of the CD binder Leah kept in her vehicle. It didn't have any CDs in it but one: a blank CD with the words "FOR

LEAH" scribbled in a felt marker. The smirk on Leah's lips softened into a genuine half-smile, and she slid the CD out and regarded it with affection. Every so often Leah would allow Tori to see the young girl she hid beneath several coats of armor, and each time she did it, Tori fell further in love with her. As much as she adored Leah's prickly nature, Tori couldn't help but want to scoop up the tender child inside Leah and protect her from the elements that hardened her.

"You made me a mix," Leah said softly.

"Pop it in." Leah did as told, and Tori smiled as the CD player silently gobbled the disc and the stereo system—which did sound good, a testament to Leah's knowledge and skill—played the first track. No sooner did they get through the first couple measures did Leah slide her hand over and entwine their fingers. She raised their joined hands to her lips and kissed the top of Tori's knuckles. "You look gorgeous, by the way."

A pair of skintight blue jeans flared out over her boots—not her usual, beat-up pair but a shiny, trendy brown pair. Her dark pink tank top gave Tori a front row seat to her incredible arm muscles, and the hemline dipped between her breasts low enough for her to catch a glimpse of a black satin bra. She'd pulled her thick curls back into a high ponytail atop her head, the curls spilling around her forehead and ears but exposing the graceful curve of her neck. Leah blushed, coloring her face she left otherwise bereft of makeup aside from mascara and a deep mulberry lipstick that probably had some ridiculous name like "Lust" or "Burgundy Skyline" but on Leah looked sultry and inviting. Tori wanted that color smeared across her skin like smashed raspberries.

"Thanks. You said not to dress up, but I didn't want to look like a scrub." Leah's free hand rubbed the thigh of her jeans in what registered to Tori as anxiety, and her outward nervousness made Tori smile to herself. Over the short journey only four of the tracks played, but Tori knew Leah listened intently to every lyric. The same way she had done five years ago, playing Leah's mix over and over until those twenty-some-odd songs became the soundtrack of the first few years of her twenties. "This is a good mix so far. I'm impressed."

"Glad it passes muster," Tori replied, turning into the lot of the low-key Japanese restaurant she'd found online. After parking, Tori met Leah at the front of the car and took her hand. Leah looked down at their joined hands in a silent *Are you sure?* Tori squeezed her fingers and confidently walked them into the restaurant toward the host.

Aside from a glance at their joined hands, the host's pleasant demeanor didn't change and he escorted them to their table. The interior was cozy, warm exposed woods with dim, inset lighting. A faux bonsai tree grew in the center out of a stone structure. Their bamboo table was quickly filled with the few vegetarian dishes they sold and a cold bottle of shochu. "So," Leah began, plucking a cube of tofu from her soup. "Hometown Hero, huh?"

Tori beamed at her, unable to keep the pride from stretching her smile from cheek to cheek. "I had nothing to do with it, I swear, but you're the most deserving. I had no idea how much you've done for the town since you came back. The bus program for seniors, the free driving lessons, the discounted work on people's cars. And that's separate from everything you've done for Hector. I spoke to Riley last night and she gave me the rundown on all your philanthropy. It's incredible. You're incredible."

Leah put a roll of cucumber sushi in her mouth and chewed it deliberately. Eyebrow firmly raised, she asked, "You spoke to Riley about me?"

Laughing, Tori sat back in the wooden chair and crossed her arms. "You think you're a taboo topic because we've both slept with you? Worried we'll compare notes?"

"Compare notes," Leah scoffed. "I've always gotten better grades than both of you. This area is no different."

Truthfully, she and Riley didn't talk about Leah in an intimate way. Tori understood, at least on the surface, they had a palatable, easy, friends-with-benefits situation neither wanted to change. The only part she didn't understand was how Riley hadn't fallen in love with Leah. She didn't know how it was possible to look into her marvelous eyes and not get lost in them forever. Plus, part of Tori thought Riley did have feelings for Leah and it made her jealous, so she didn't want to bring it up and potentially drive a wedge between them over what appeared to be a nonissue. "You're not…are you two still?"

Leah took visible delight in her plain jealousy. "That wasn't part of your chat about me?"

Tori frowned. "We didn't get into the finer details, no."

"Would that bother you?" Leah asked over the top of her glass.

"You know it would."

Curse the damnable smirk on Leah's face and the thrill it sent through Tori's stomach. "I just wanted to hear you say it. No, we haven't slept together in the two days since I saw you last. I haven't had a chance to tell her anything because I've been so busy. But she's known about my feelings for you since you and I went out for a drink, so I'm sure she isn't surprised. Did you tell her about us?"

"A little," Tori admitted with a sheepish smile. "I told her we'd, you know—"

"Fucked? Had two not-so-straight hours of mind-blowing sex?"

"Leah." Her embarrassment only served to deepen Leah's smirk. Tori wanted to leap across the table and dive into the dimple in her cheek. "Yes, that. She was happy for me. For us, really."

"She's always been too nice for either of us," Leah replied. "She needs a good girlfriend. We should find her one."

"Sounds like a job for the Hometown Hero." Leah gently kicked her under the table and turned away, embarrassed. "My big, strong hero."

Her girlfriend—ex-girlfriend? Lover? Leah, whoever she was, turned introspective for a moment. The high alcohol content of the shochu surely didn't help Leah's tendency to brood. "I really don't want to make a speech. What am I supposed to say? 'Hey guys, I'd rather be dead than live in this town, but since someone decided to sideswipe my dad, I figured I might as well make the best of it.'"

"I probably would not say those exact words? But no, not really. It's usually a couple thank-yous and that's it. I have to make the speech. Usually, my mom does the speech."

"Okay, word," Leah replied, visibly relieved. "I'm glad you're the one doing it. Your mom would probably cast a spell on everyone like the Sanderson sisters in *Hocus Pocus*. Turn the town on me or something."

"Is that why you think my mom's hot? Because you think she's a witch like your girlfriend Vanessa from *The Little Mermaid*?"

Leah refilled Tori's glass with the last of the liquor and grinned at her over the table. "I think your mom's hot because she looks like an older version of you, and you're hot. Not the other way around."

Tori smiled. She missed their playful banter. Being Leah's girlfriend had a lot of perks, but their underlying understanding of one another pushed them to another level. The antagonism, the challenge, the love, the friendship—Tori knew nobody else in the world matched with her like Leah. Even Ben, by standard metrics a great guy, couldn't connect with her. Not only because of the whole being-a-lesbian thing, but also because nobody knew how to root inside her heart like Leah did. Nobody made her feel as safe, as worthy, or as loved.

After sharing a delicious dessert and settling the check, Tori and Leah left the restaurant arm in arm, using each other for support. The alcohol raced through Tori's bloodstream, while Leah looked frustratingly sober. Leah inhaled a deep breath of warm night air. "So. This is what it's like to be a kept woman, hmm? Get picked up in a nice car, taken out to dinner, wined and dined."

Tori giggled, stumbling a bit into Leah's side. "Could you get used to this?"

"That depends," she said, lowering her voice, "on where the night leads."

"Oh, really?" Tori placed a hand on her chest, backing her against the exterior of the restaurant. She put one hand on the façade next to Leah's head and the other on her hip, effectively trapping her. "Where do you think it leads?"

"Hmm. My doorstep, isn't it? You lay a chaste kiss on my cheek, we part ways filled with longing."

"Do you think being a kept woman is like a Jane Austen novel or something?" Leah shrugged and Tori leaned into her space, skimming her lips along the line of Leah's jaw. "It isn't. I want to spoil you, but I also want to debauch you."

"You do, huh?" The confidence in Leah's voice wavered as Tori reached around to grope Leah's butt through her jeans. Tori stayed intentionally out of kissing distance, dodging Leah's attempts to make contact.

"I do. I want to make love to you, over and over, until you can't remember anyone's touch but mine," Tori said, gazing into her eyes.

"And what do you get in return?" Leah whispered.

"You. Your humor, your kindness, your boldness. Your body, your incredible sex, your brilliant mind, your generous heart." Tori slid her hand under Leah's ear and rubbed her temple with her thumb. "I get the love of my life back."

She teasingly dodged Leah's attempts to kiss her three more times before Leah wrapped an arm around her neck and captured her in a bruising kiss. The warm slide of Leah's tongue against her own sent a shudder down her spine, and she arched into Leah's torso. Though recently sated from a good meal, hunger consumed her. She wanted to devour Leah on the spot, and be devoured in return.

Before they surrendered to their baser instincts and got arrested for public indecency, Tori pulled back and fished the car keys from her pocket. She jingled them near Leah's flushed, panting face. "Want to drive me to your place?"

Leah whistled. "Damn, Lockwood. You put out on the first date?"

"Why don't you take me home and find out?"

Leah's attention shifted from the keys to Tori's face as she visibly fought an internal battle between her desire to drive the car and her desire for Tori. She snatched the keys and smirked. "After you."

When she'd arrived in Garden Hills with Ben, Tori felt like she'd gotten there via DeLorean. Rocketed into the past, forced to crawl into a hermit shell that no longer fit her. That feeling, of fitting in but not quite fitting in, persisted her entire life except for one time. In one place. With one person. In Leah's room, her tiny attic sanctuary, with Leah in her arms. Here, her life slotted into place.

Her back to Leah, she stared out the familiar rectangular window on the other side of the room. Leah spooned her from behind, their naked bodies contiguous and warm. A pleasant soreness throbbed between her legs, slow like her heartbeat. Leah's lips kissed the nape of her neck lazily while she held one arm over Tori's chest.

"Leah," she called softly. A short *hmm* reverberated against the top of her spine. "Do you think we'd have stayed together if we hadn't broken up then?"

For a little while Leah didn't answer but pecked kisses on her back and shoulders. Eventually, the kisses stopped. "Maybe? I don't know. Some other bullshit could've come up. Nothing is ever in a straight line, and we're no different."

"Right." Tori turned over into Leah's arms and regarded her face with an affectionate smile. Her nice lipstick was nearly entirely kissed off, and Tori's pink gloss streaked across her skin. Her curly hair frizzed out from all the movement, friction, and Tori's hands gripping the tresses for dear life. "Without an outside factor, though?"

"Probably not." Unable to stop touching, Leah wrapped her arm around Tori and stroked her back in a soothing figure eight. "For years, you've been this unreachable crossbar for other women to vault. But even if someone did, even if they came close…" Leah's eyes glazed over a bit, as if picturing someone else. She focused back on Tori and smiled. "At the end the day, they couldn't be you. So, no, I would not have left because there's no one else I could love the way I love you."

As someone who enjoyed poetry and the gymnastics of the spoken word, Tori had consumed a lot of prose. It had the power to move her, and sometimes she felt it touch the deep well of her soul, where Mary Oliver or Anne Sexton frolicked in the puddles of her heart. However, none of the great poets cut directly to the marrow of her being like Leah. Not with poetry or charming phrases, but with honesty. Leah didn't have to seduce her, or find the perfect rhyming couplet, she just spoke from her heart. Maybe that's how you know you've found your soulmate—because their words beat like music to the rhythm of your heart.

"I love you," Tori said quietly. "You know, the other day when you called yourself 'work,' I didn't get the chance to tell you how wrong that is. You're not work, Leah, no matter how much you've changed since we were eighteen. Loving you is the easiest thing I've ever done in my life."

The short exhale through Leah's nose washed over her forehead and she looked up into the skeptical expression on her face. "I've been a mess since my dad's accident. I forget to eat. I don't sleep well. I get…I get these bad nightmares. I wake up panicked until I remember he's alive and he's okay."

Tori coaxed Leah onto her other side so she could spoon her from behind. She knew no amount of neck kisses or gentle strokes could undo the hurt, but she had to try. "That's not work, Leah. You need support, but that's not work. It's part of loving someone. I'm sorry you're dealing with that, and I'll do whatever I can to help you, if you want it."

"Thank you, *mi amor*." On reflex, Tori gave Leah a squeeze and Leah's chest rumbled in low chuckles. "I forgot about your thing for me speaking Spanish."

"It's not that. Well, not entirely." Leah hummed in question and Tori buried her face in Leah's soft hair. "I've just missed hearing you call me that."

Leah shuffled over to face her, and it struck Tori how different it felt from the first time they had lain like this. When they were not friends, not enemies, but Tori had stared down a feeling she didn't understand. They'd crossed a distance in that time, from two people on different paths to the inevitable smashing of their destinies.

"Don't leave again," Leah whispered. "Stay. Stay and be mine."

"I will. I'll always be yours."

She held back the promise on her tongue.

Their relationship warmed as the weather cooled. Strikingly similar to their first time around, Tori saw Leah as often as their schedules allowed. She frequently took Leah out on dates—the movies, a show, dinner, lunch—and spent her other hours unofficially working for her father. Part of her felt like a teenager again, aching to see Leah in the hours between. But part of her knew this time it was different. It wasn't a summer fling. In fact, they'd been dating steadily right through autumn and into late November. On a particularly busy day for Leah prior to the award dinner, Tori accepted an invitation to hang out with Riley.

She sat at the counter in the bookshop, scribbling away in her notebook as she did drafts of her speech for Leah. After sending a customer away with a new book, Riley joined her on another stool and tried to peek at the notebook. "Aw, come on. Let me at least hear a little of it."

"It's not done yet," Tori replied, sticking out her chin. "It's just a draft."

Riley lifted an eyebrow. "Tor, the dinner is this weekend. How much else could you need to write?"

Tori peered down at the paper. In between the ruled lines, in the negative space, Tori had laid out her feelings for Leah. Of course, she spent time deftly weaving it in and out of remarks upon Leah's accomplishments, but she'd laid bare her heart and her life on the page. "I'm…going to come out in this speech," Tori said slowly. "I'm telling my family I'm in love with Leah. And, well, the town and the board of Lockwood Industries."

"Whoa." Her friend's eyes widened. She came down from the shock and a warm smile spread across her face. "You're really right back in it, aren't you?"

"Almost more than I was the first time." Tori sighed wistfully. "I need this speech to be perfect because if I don't prove to Leah I'm real about being out, she won't stay. Regardless of how much she loves me."

Riley offered nothing in the way of an expressive response, keeping her face frustratingly neutral. Tori tried not to resent how well Riley knew Leah now and attempted to graciously pivot to appreciating her best friend's good relationship with her girlfriend. However, she could not completely stifle her jealous nature.

"I like you two together. It somehow makes perfect sense without actually making any sense at all. If that makes sense."

"It did not, but thanks." Peering up from her notebook, Tori inquired, "You're not…upset?"

Riley laughed, easy and carefree. "I already told you, Leah and I weren't serious. I'm more than happy to keep her as a friend. The sex was just a fun bonus. It's not as if there's a lot of queer women in this town."

"Fair enough."

"Besides, Leah's never been available in that way. I didn't always understand why, but I knew something was missing. I knew I was borrowing her, so to speak. I told her as much the other day." Tori narrowed her eyes. She'd have to get used to the idea that her best friend and her girlfriend would talk without her. Possibly even hang out without her. "Our relationship aside, you're wrong about the speech."

"I am?" Tori had hoped for more optimism from her friend.

"Yeah. There's no doubt in my mind you love Leah and she loves you. But for her to trust you, for her to invest her heart with you? You need to be steady. Not a one-off speech—that's the first step, and an important one. But it's the steps afterward that matter most."

Tori pouted down at her notebook. Apparently, Riley understood that her anxiety about what happens after coming out had been funneled into this extravagant speech. "My mom's going to throw a fit. And my dad...I don't even know how he'll react. He might fire me."

"There are worse things in the world," Riley replied. "Like living a lie or breaking the heart of the woman who loves you unconditionally."

"Okay, okay, geez. Need I remind you we were friends first? I saw you lose your first tooth," Tori grumbled in her seat. "Just saying. Keep taking her side like we don't have a lifetime of friendship under our belt."

The bell in the shop rang as someone walked in the door and Riley hopped off the stool, then slung one arm around Tori and side-hugged her. "Now I'm not sure which one of us you're more jealous of."

"It's still you," Tori replied glumly. "I'm still trying to unlearn the knowledge Leah took both our virginities."

Riley smirked. "Could be worse. I sometimes think we could've been convinced into a threesome at Fatima's party. Then we would've lost our virginities to Leah and to each other."

Tori slapped her notebook over her face. "What a cursed proposition. Never say those again, in that order or in any other order."

"I won't," Riley called as she rounded the counter. "But Leah probably will."

On cue, Tori's phone vibrated with a message from Leah, sparking a thrill in her chest. The message consisted of a racy suggestion causing Tori to blush considerably, but she immediately fired back a positive response. Her varsity jacket lay deep in her closet, but for Leah, she'd wear it again. Apparently only the jacket, if Tori understood the text correctly.

As the customers perused the shelves, Riley leaned on the counter from the other side. "But serious talk, it's going to be fine. No matter what happens when you come out, I've got your back. Me, Leah, Vic, even little Durward. Worst-case scenario, you come live with me for a bit. Whatever happens, we'll get you through it. You won't do it alone. Not again."

Tori couldn't hold on to her jealousy for long. Not when Riley was so consistently magnanimous, so giving and open. She and Leah were lucky to have Riley in their lives, regardless of how those relationships came about. "Thanks, Ry."

"Anytime." Riley pulled her phone from her pocket and laughed, turning it around to show Tori the text. It was also from Leah, but it read: *So that's a no on the threesome, then?* Tori snapped the phone closed and Riley threw her head back in laughter. "Don't look at me, you're the one who's in love with her."

"I love and hate you both."

Assembling the Lockwoods for a family event entailed a lot of last-minute adjustments from their mother. Inevitably Ward or Vic would choose the wrong color tie or Tori's outfit wouldn't be "flattering," and they'd be scrambling at the last minute to appease her. But two of the three of them were adults now, and Ward dressed better than all of them combined. Vic and Ward waited in the living room with their father, all three dressed in suits. Tori, with her speech tucked into her purse, came downstairs to join them in a pale green satin dress hugging her figure and a pair of matching heels. Carmen, whom Leah had also invited, stood beside them in a lovely purple dress.

"Carmen, you look amazing," Tori said, grinning. "What does Leah always say…*hermosa*?"

"Thank you, Miss Tori."

"Your mother is at the venue waiting for us," her father informed them. "She likes to get ahead and make sure everything is just so."

"Harass waiters," Vic tacked on. "Make someone cry. All in a day's work."

Victor laughed, leading the group of them out the front door and to the bloated SUV waiting for them. "She's a perfectionist. Though she could use softening around the edges, I will admit."

Beside her, Ward emitted unhappy grumbling noises and Tori slowed her walk, leaning to him. "Have you talked to Dad about what Mom did at your party?"

"No," he admitted softly. "She forbade me from telling him. She said it would devastate him. Disappoint him, or whatever. I don't...I don't know what to do. I don't want her to do something mean to Ollie, but I don't want Dad to hate me."

"It's all right. We'll figure it out, okay? When the time is right, we'll tell Dad, and however he reacts, he reacts. Vic and I got you. And we'll have Ollie's back too."

He remained skeptical, even in the face of her most convincing smile. "How do you know?"

Tori stopped walking and turned to him, placing a hand on either of his shoulders. His boyish features had nearly receded, with cheekbones and a jaw much like her own appearing where baby fat had been, the tiniest whisper of whiskers growing near the corners of his mouth. "Can you keep a secret?"

"Yeah?"

"I'm gay too." Ward blinked a few times, visibly processing her secret. "I wasn't ever brave enough to say it out loud, or tell Mom and Dad, but after I saw you stand up for yourself—and for Ollie—I thought maybe I could."

"What about Beck?"

"Ben. He knows. I broke up with him because I'm in love with someone else. A girl. A woman. And tonight..." She opened her purse and let Ward peek at the papers. "I'm going to tell Mom and Dad in my speech. You made me realize that it's possible, and Leah—that's the person I love—gave me the courage to do it."

"Leah..." Ward sounded the name out slowly. "The one getting the award? The one who works with Dad?"

"Yes."

"Oh." Ward smiled at her, his eyes that matched her own gazing at her with affection. "So, that's why she's been hanging around a lot when Mom isn't around. I like her. She likes *X-Files*."

Tori smirked. She didn't know if Leah liked *X-Files* or if Leah liked Agent Scully, but if it endeared her to Ward, she wouldn't question it.

They ritualistically held the dinner in Garden Hills, despite the severe dearth of nice event spaces. In place of a grand hotel or lodge of some sort, they decked out the largest conference hall in the Lockwood Industries office. Their mother did, in fact, have it glittering with fancy décor. Fresh white linens lay draped across circular tables, each of them populated by business owners in the town, members of the board of Lockwood Industries, and public servants. Tuxedo-clad waiters buzzed around the room offering bite-sized appetizers and flutes of champagne. Tori took a glass, as did Ward, and she snatched his and drank them both.

Near a table at the front of the room, Leah stood in a semicircle with her mother, father, Riley, and a woman Tori didn't recognize. The warmth upon seeing Leah rivaled the warmth from the champagne, and Tori beelined toward their table.

Cassandra, jingling in her fine pearls and golden jewelry like a Victorian debutante, slinked into Tori's path. The air in the room dipped several degrees. "Victoria."

"Mother."

Cassandra's eyes peered down at Tori's hands clutching her purse, then back up to her with a raised eyebrow. "Where is your engagement ring?"

Behind her mother's back, Leah caught her eye and appeared concerned. Tori looked away from her. "Why?"

"We don't want to present a conflicting image to the board members, do we? We can hardly expect them to take you seriously as a director of operations if you're unmarried." Tori gripped her purse harder. She had a mission tonight, and none of her mother's deflections could divert her from that path.

"Too bad. I don't have it. Ben does."

"Well," her mother began, waving to someone behind Tori. "What fine luck that he was able to get away from his duties in Boston and be here tonight."

The chill her mother brought with her like a billowing blizzard froze Tori to the bone. "What?"

Cassandra leaned in close. "Listen to me very carefully, Victoria. You will not tarnish our family's reputation tonight, understand? Your mistress may have convinced your bleeding-heart father she's worthy of this excessive award, but the caliber of guests in attendance will not be so easily swayed. They'll see right through her to what she really is—glorified trash."

The champagne erupted back into her esophagus and Tori swallowed down the bile as she slowly turned around. Dressed in a tuxedo and a sheepish expression, Ben approached them from behind and plastered a smile on his face. "Hey."

"Now, where is your speech?" Cassandra asked.

Tori wished for the floor to open up like the Hellmouth and swallow her. "What? Why?"

"Because you're not using it. You will recite this speech." From within her own purse, Cassandra withdrew a short stack of index cards and handed them to Tori. "This is your speech. Do not deviate from this script. If you so much as mutter a consonant that isn't on these cards, I will make it so difficult for her to receive her precious award money, she won't see a cent before retirement."

"Award money?" Tori lagged ten steps behind the conversation. "What are you talking about?"

With an eye roll, Cassandra elaborated, "Your father funded an endowment for Miss Vasquez to put her through college. In addition to the award money—a check for ten thousand dollars—she will receive this collegiate endowment and a twenty-thousand-dollar investment into her business."

Tori gasped. "Oh my God. That's amazing."

"Super rad," Ben interjected, and Cassandra glared at him.

"So, you understand what is at stake here, don't you, dear? Put on your engagement ring, smile for the cameras, and give the speech I wrote." She looked up at Ben. "Oh, don't look at me like that, like I'm a puppy-snatcher. The men on the board at this company are bigots and morons. They'll not only never allow a deviant to be the face of the company, but they'll make us suffer for it. Not to mention what it will do to our reputation in this county, in this state? Your father has worked too hard to make our company successful for you to flush it down the drain."

Ben grimaced as Cassandra stalked off in another direction. Tori slowly looked to her left again, catching Leah's eyes through an ever-growing crowd. She watched Leah's face fall at the sight of she and Ben, and Tori's heart squeezed. Ben handed her the ring. "I'm sorry. Your mom called and said you wanted to see me. I—I should've been more suspicious."

Swallowing the lump in her throat, Tori slowly put the ring on her finger. Members of the board—stuffy white guys with more money than brain cells—milled around, shoveling food into their faces. These were the men her mother wanted to appease with this fake ring and fake fiancé. The amount of farce might bury their whole family alive. "I'm sorry she swindled you into this."

"Yeah, you weren't kidding about her." Over her head, Ben saw something that made him grimace again and stare down at her with wincing, sympathetic eyes. "I think you need to talk to Leah. I'll go schmooze."

When she turned, Leah and Riley were escaping through a side door. Tori brushed through the guests to follow them into a darkened hallway, finding Leah leaning against the wall and Riley close by, arms crossed. They both looked in her direction at the sound of the door. Riley took the unspoken cue and headed back toward the room. "I'll let you guys talk. It starts soon, though."

"Thanks." Tori let the door close before taking a step toward Leah. "I know how it looks."

"You do, huh? Great."

"I'm sorry. My mother invited him under a false pretense and now he has to stick around for optics or whatever. You have to believe me, I don't want this."

She reached for Leah's hand, only for her to snap it away. "Don't fucking touch me when you're wearing his ring, Tori. I'm so, so tired of this shit."

"I know, but listen to me. There's more at stake here than my reputation. There's, like, life-changing money coming with this award for you, and she said she would make sure you never saw it."

"I don't give a fuck about the money," Leah shouted back at her. "Don't you get it? I don't care about the award or the money. If I haven't been clear before, let me be clear now. All I want is to be with you. Rich, poor, here, there, anywhere. All I want is you. Do you understand what I'm saying? More than money, more than going back to college, more than whatever other dreams of mine your mother wants to dash, I want you. Years ago, I told you that you were going to need to make a choice. Now seems like a pretty good time."

Behind Tori's back, the door opened and Riley peeked out. "It's starting."

Leah's eyes searched her own and surely all she saw was the sheer panic Tori felt in her heart. Scoffing, Leah walked around her and through the open door Riley held. Tori's breath came shallow as she did the same, only to be stopped by Riley's hand on her chest. "I saw Ben. I told Leah it was probably your mother's doing."

"Doesn't matter whose fault it is, does it? It still hurts her all the same."

Riley nodded. "Right, but only you can make it better. Do not fuck this up."

The lights inside the room dimmed and guests shuffled toward their assigned seats. At her table sat her mother, Vic, Ward, and Ben, who shifted in his seat uncomfortably under the stares of her brothers.

"Welcome, welcome." Her father placed a hand on either side of the podium and looked out into the crowd. "As most of you know, every year Lockwood Industries bestows the honor of Hometown

Hero to a deserving citizen of Garden Hills. Eagle Scouts and Girl Scouts, firefighters, veterinarians; our board has voted fifteen times in fifteen years to give this award to a deserving resident of our beloved hometown. This year, I had the privilege of working side by side with the young woman we're here to honor tonight. I've seen firsthand the honorable, diligent, incredible work she's done, not only for her business and mine, but for our shared community. As such, since I knew she would be too humble to accept a nomination, I made the decision to forgo our board vote and give the award to her directly. Here to present the Hometown Hero award is my daughter and future business partner, Tori Lockwood."

Polite applause sounded throughout the room and Tori shakily got to her feet. To her right sat Hector, Loretta, Billy, Jenna, Carmen, and two empty chairs. Wherever Leah and Riley had gone, they still hadn't returned. Tori left her purse on the table and took only the index cards, then climbed the few steps on the side of the stage and slowly walked toward the podium. Not a single face in the audience was recognizable—a sea of grumpy white men with white hair, with the occasional Garden Hills business owner at a table with their family—but it didn't help unnerve her.

"Thank you," Tori said into the microphone, wincing at the sound of her own voice. She looked down at the cards in her shaking hands and began to read. "Thank you for being here tonight. Lockwood Industries is proud to be a loyal friend of the small business owner. For decades, Lockwood Industries has paved the way for small businesses to grow and thrive in Garden Hills with endowments and investments, as well as generous donations to local charities. Tonight, we celebrate my friend—"

Light poured in from the side of the room. An open door, with Leah and Riley walking through it. Tori cleared her throat. "My friend—" Tori stared at the cards. She moved her gaze across the room from her expectant mother to her disappointed brothers, and finally over to Leah. Slowly, she turned the cards over and took a deep breath. "Tonight, we honor our Hometown Hero, Leah Vasquez. I've known Leah since middle school, but some of you may be meeting her tonight for the first time, so let me help you understand why, out of all the wonderful residents of our town, my father chose Leah to receive this award.

"She grew up on the south side of Garden Hills, in a modest home with two hardworking parents. Every opportunity, every cent in her pocket, every road laid before her, she created with her own two hands.

Leah came out as a lesbian at the tender age of eleven and stared down a world telling her she was wrong and trying to squeeze her into the margins of society. Believe me when I tell you, there is no margin big enough to hold Leah Vasquez." Tori paused for light clapping. "Her generosity knows no bounds, and her capacity to love is unrivaled. We've all heard the phrase, 'So-and-so would give you the shirt off their back,' but I know for a fact Leah will give you the shirt off her back because I've worn it."

Leah, standing near the edge of the stage with her arms crossed, smiled at her. It gave Tori strength to soldier on. "When her family needed her, Leah did not falter. She placed her dreams on hold and stepped up to take care of her family without hesitation. At twenty-one, she took over her father's successful auto shop and kept her family from sliding underwater. Leah poured her heart and soul into the business. With burdens and bills piling up, Leah never ceased in her philanthropy and her commitment to help those in need. She volunteers her precious free time and exceptional mechanical skills to fix our public school buses and local police cruisers. Leah fixes and donates cars to low-income families across the county. At their shop, the Vasquez family offers heavily discounted rates of service to those for whom having reliable transportation is the difference between putting food on the table and starving.

"I'm unbelievably honored to present this award to Leah tonight. Not only because she's so deserving…" Tori inhaled another deep breath and slid off her ring. Time for bold strokes. "But because it's the great privilege of my life to be her girlfriend."

Scattered gasps percolated up from the audience. Tori didn't look away from Leah. "To you all, I'm sure this doesn't seem like the time or the place, but there is no time or place better than right now to tell someone you love them. Leah is the most incredible person I've ever known, and being with her makes me a better human." The quiet of the room broke with the screeching of chairs and scattered applause. Tori ignored the clack of dress shoes leaving the room and continued, "I'm the luckiest person in the room, as I've only loved one person in my life, and she's extraordinary."

An employee of Lockwood Industries timidly handed Tori the plaque and scurried off stage to escort Leah up to the lectern. As Leah walked closer, the lights on the stage caught the tears in her eyes. Happy tears, Tori hoped, as she reached up and swiped one of the rogue tears running down her cheek. Her hand lingered near Leah's face, and she pulled her close to a deep but brief kiss. Away from the microphone, Tori said in low tones, "I choose you."

Leah grinned at her, so wide and adoring that in an instant Tori knew she'd made the correct decision, no matter the fallout. From the corner of the stage, she watched Leah gather herself and lean into the microphone. Tori didn't dare to look into the crowd. "Uh, well, thank you. I—I don't know what to say. Not big on speeches, so, I'll leave you with a thank-you to Lockwood Industries for the award and the generous gifts. And a thank-you to my parents, who work harder than anyone I know. *Gracias.* Thank you."

Polite applause filled the room, punctuated by Hector's loud whistling and Vic's whooping. Tori walked off the stage and right into Riley's outstretched arms. Her friend rubbed her back, allowing Tori to soak her shoulder—and the top of her nice blouse—in tears. "That was really brave, Tor. I'm proud of you."

"Thanks," Tori replied, muffled in her shirt. Footsteps from behind her prompted Tori to pull away from Riley and turn halfway, meeting Leah's wide eyes. Words were not necessary, and they would not suffice. Leah handed her award to Riley, took Tori by both of her cheeks, and kissed her. Tori melted into their kiss, an arm wrapping around Leah's back and the other resting on the top of her chest. "I'm sorry."

"No more apologies, okay? It's us against them now, and we have nothing to be sorry for." Leah turned her around just in time to see her fuming mother and perplexed father approaching them from the table. Tori steeled herself, but she needn't grow too hard, as Leah was a woman forged of steel and fire.

"Do you have any idea what you just did?" Cassandra spat at Tori through clenched teeth. "Why did you tell the entire town you're a lesbian?"

"Because I am a lesbian, Mom."

"Oh my God," Cassandra replied. "What is with the dramatics in this family?"

"As much as you wish it isn't true and tried to blackmail me into heterosexuality, it's always been true. That's always been who I am. I'm gay."

"I'm still gay too," Ward interjected.

Vic raised his hand. "I'm not gay, but I do love mess."

"You will all stop this nonsense at once!" The three Lockwood kids clamped their mouths shut. Their mother never yelled. She didn't normally care enough about them to raise her voice. If they were ever poorly behaved, a nanny or an au pair on staff reprimanded them. "You are not gay, any of you. You are normal children."

"Oh, we've never been normal, Mother," Vic deadpanned.

Loretta, arriving at Leah's side with Hector, bristled in affront. An angry Loretta was a sight to behold. Tori did not envy her mother on the receiving end of her ire. "Are you implying my child is not normal?"

"Hold on a moment," Victor interrupted. "Tori, did you say blackmail?"

Lip quivering, Tori nodded. "Mom saw Leah and I together just before college. She told me if I continued to be a lesbian, and especially to consort with someone so, and I quote, 'below my station,' she could effectively cut me off. No college, no inheritance, no job. Seal me off from the family for good, like a gangrenous limb."

Her father's grave expression gave way to shock. "What? Cassandra, what is she talking about?"

At this, the ferocity in her mother's features waned. Tori snorted. "Of course. You didn't even tell him."

"Below her station?" Loretta inquired, casting an unimpressed glare at Cassandra.

Their father huffed. "Explain the blackmail, Cassandra."

Fearful—a strange look on her mother—Cassandra faltered. "Well, I explained to Victoria that we would not tolerate aberrations in this family. We have a reputation to protect. A company to protect. She can't go around sticking her fingers into the hoi polloi. You should've seen your daughter, letting some guttersnipe smear car oil all over her."

"Call her that again and I will drown you in car oil," Tori snarled.

"Hold on." Her father rubbed his forehead, not unlike Leah did when upset, and sighed. "You're telling me you told my daughter we would cut her out of the family for being a lesbian?"

"Well, yes, but not just being a lesbian. A lesbian who dips into the population to get her jollies with some mechanic's untoward daughter."

"Untoward?" Loretta bristled, her eyes flaming in anger. "That's my baby girl you're talking about, you malignant shrew."

"Are you kidding me right now, Cassandra?" Victor's voice rumbled like a nearing storm, and Tori took shelter closer to Leah, who squeezed her hand in support. "Where the hell would you get an idea like that?"

"Victor, how will the company look when their newest executive shows up in men's suit and a butch haircut with a spicy number on her arm?"

"Spicy number?" Loretta began taking off her hoops, handing one to Hector. "I hope you have good insurance, lady, because I'm gonna kick your a—"

"It will look like none of their fucking business!" Victor's shouting caught the attention of several tables nearby, gossipy onlookers sipping cocktails and listening intently. "It's none of their business who any of my children choose to love, or sleep with, or do whatever they want with. I don't care if they're with a man, or a woman, or the flying purple people eater. All I ask is that they work hard, and they're proud of whoever is on their arm, and whoever is on their arm is proud of them."

"If I could interject one second," Vic began, clearing his throat. "I think Mother thought you shared this grotesque opinion based on the fact that lots of the men at the company are loudly homophobic, and you frequently donate to the campaigns of anti-gay politicians."

Her father's eyes widened. "What? What are you talking about?"

"Senator Troy? Senator Greene? Those guys are major homophobes. They support conversion therapy and all sorts of crazy bullshit. They oppose gay marriage, gay adoption. I mean, the list is extensive, and I only know the half of it."

"I don't...I don't donate to them because of that. I like their fiscal policies. They...I had no idea they had any opinions on gay people. What kinda donkey's ass campaign platform is that?" Her father appeared genuinely bewildered. "Well, I...I'll put a stop to it immediately. I won't donate money to a bunch of bigoted idiots." Resolute, her father turned his attention fully to his children, taking one step away from their mother. "I'm sorry, guys. I won't let you down again. And I hope all three of you know you're welcome to bring anyone to our dinner table."

"And the bigots on the board?" Vic ventured, raising his eyebrow. "I heard at least one of them call Tori a slur during her speech."

"Who?" Victor demanded, glancing around wildly.

"Don't sweat it. I know who it was, and I'll beat his ass when we're done here. I don't care how old he is, I'll windmill all of those geezers." Leah looked at Vic and nodded in approval. "You've got a lot of white-haired dickheads who talk a lot of sexist, racist, homophobic shit."

"When the hell do they have time to say that? They've got time to spout nonsense instead of running the company? Jesus. I'll look into it. Get me some names, all right, son?"

Half laughing and half sobbing, Tori shook her head at her father's slow realization that his laser focus on the financial side of the company meant he somehow missed the culture and how toxic it had become. Ward crossed his arms. "Mom won't let me see my boyfriend."

"Why not?" Victor turned to Cassandra. "What have you been telling our children?"

Desperate, Cassandra implored him, "Victor, think about this. Did you see how many people walked out when your daughter outed herself in front of the town? What do you think the papers will write in the morning?"

"Who gives a shit?" Leah asked.

Cassandra glared at her. "Keep out of it. This is all your fault, anyway. If you hadn't seduced my daughter and kept your dirty hands off her, we wouldn't be having this conversation right now."

"Don't tell my *mija* what to do, *bruja sucia*," Hector growled at her, his fingers clenched around the armrests of his wheelchair. Now that she'd given rise to the anger of all three Vasquez family members, Tori worried for her mother's well-being for the first time. "You have caused enough pain, don't you think?"

"Pain? If protecting my family means causing a little pain, so be it," Cassandra replied stiffly.

"Cassie." Her father's tone softened and his eyes winced in anguish. Tori hadn't been much taller than her father's hips the last time he used that nickname for their mother. "Go home. I need to talk to our kids. Please."

"Victor, listen to me."

"No." Second-guessing his sternness could prove disastrous, and Cassandra stopped short of arguing. "Take the car service and go home. We will speak later."

Cassandra huffed. Realizing their father would no longer banter with her, she turned sharply to Leah. "This is not over."

"Oh, okay, great," Leah replied. She put her arm around Tori's waist and bolstered them together as a blockade against any further argument. "If you need me, I'll be in my bedroom with your daughter."

"Leah," Loretta admonished her daughter, but Hector chuckled and received a smack in the shoulder. "Hector, don't encourage her."

Leah attempted to rearrange the snark on her face into the picture of innocence, but instead it mirrored a fox peering through a bush at prey. "What? I didn't say in her or on her. I said with her."

Vic cackled. "Amazing. What a night."

"Oh! And." Leah reached into her tuxedo jacket and withdrew a worn, folded envelope. She tossed it at Cassandra, who caught it with a look of shock on her face. "Looks like you can take your money back."

Cassandra barreled her way through the moderately scandalized guests. Tori sniffled and broke from Leah to hug her dad around his waist. How long had it been since she really hugged him, or vice versa? Since she was single digits, at least. His constant smell of

Creed cologne and the soft cotton of his shirt, slightly nostalgic and somewhat unfamiliar, gave her the kind of comfort she'd only found in her brothers, or Leah. "Thanks, Dad."

"Group hug!" Vic announced, and before Tori or her father could protest, he enveloped them both in his weirdly long giraffe arms. Ward came up from behind and squished them together, snuggling into Tori's side.

"Victor, can I be released from this hug, son?"

"No, Father. We have, like, twenty years of hugs to make up for. Keep bringing it in, big guy."

Once Vic did allow them to leave the hug, Tori found Leah and her family on the side of the room chatting with Riley. She searched for Ben but could not find him in the sea of unfamiliar faces. He'd probably wisely decided to leave when Cassandra started shouting. She'd have to give him the ring back another time. For now, she tucked it into her pocket.

Her father pulled her away and gestured toward a chair. "Have a seat, Victoria." Tori sat knee to knee with her father, whose entire body sagged with emotional fatigue. They'd never had a heart-to-heart as father and daughter before. Her father stayed in his head a lot, doing calculations and working on imaginary spreadsheets while Victoria navigated her teenage years. "I'm sorry about your mother's behavior tonight. It appears she has some soul-searching to do."

"And if she can't find a soul, she can always steal one from someone who ventures near her gingerbread house."

Her father did not look amused. "I know this has been very difficult for all of you, especially for you, Tori. Let's give her grace while she figures things out, okay?"

"She threatened to have my ex-girlfriend arrested, Dad. For crimes that didn't exist, for the sole purpose of ruining her future. Excuse me if I'm a little short on grace."

"I'm sorry. I swear, I don't know what's happened to her."

"Well, she hates me, for starters."

Her comment didn't provoke her father's anger, but a strange sadness settled over him. Tori didn't know anything about the intricacies or intimacies of their marriage. She didn't know if they loved each other, or they tolerated their union for the sake of appearance. Tori never witnessed any displays of affection, but affection didn't run thick in the Lockwood blood. Not like at Leah's house, where love oozed from every nook and cranny.

"Your mother wanted a baby girl so badly. When we had Vic, she was ecstatic, like any new parent. But I could tell, immediately, we were going to have to have another child." Victor chuckled, smiling briefly at the memory. "That's why you two are so close in age. And when you were born, Tori, I wish you could've seen the joy on her face."

"Me too," she replied quietly.

"'The world is hard for girls,' she would say to me. We'd be sitting on the couch, Vic in a rocker and you in her arms, and she'd talk about all the challenges you were going to face. All the cruelties."

For most of her life, Tori assumed she and her mother missed out on maternal bonding. None of her earliest memories were loving at all. "The world was never as cruel to me as she was."

"She was tougher on you. In her mind, I think, she wanted to prepare you for the road ahead. She forgot to stop and just enjoy you as a daughter, as a person. As the wonderful young woman you've become. But, Tori, as much as she's lost her way, your mother loves you so much."

"I want to believe you," Tori replied, sniffling. "I want to believe she loves me. But everything she's ever done and said to me says otherwise."

Reaching over, he placed his hand on top of hers. She'd never seen that kind of pain in her father's eyes. It seemed like a pain only parents were capable of, like he was trying to seep the sadness from her and take it on himself. "If you want to repair your relationship with her, I'm here for you. If you choose not to, I would understand. I'm sorry for the unkind and untrue things she's said to you. I thought…she knew better than me. She's a woman, you're a woman, surely, she's doing something right. But I failed. I failed her as a husband, and I failed you as a father. If I'd been around more, maybe I could've set things right for you two. I was always away, always gone. I thought if I kept the family in money, you'd all find your way to happiness. But how would you know what to look for if you never saw it at home?"

She peered down at their joined hands. "I was happy. With Leah, I was happy. A little while ago, she asked me if I was happy, and I told her I didn't know. And she said I did know, but that I'm afraid of being happy. Because she knew the only way for me to be happy is being honest about who I am."

Victor smiled. "Sounds like she knows you pretty well."

"Better than anyone I've ever met." Tori couldn't stop. Like a faucet stuck open, she kept pouring out her truths. "We started hanging out again when I came back and I…I'm happiest when I'm with her.

Which is amazing because she's frustrating and moody, she doesn't let me get away with anything. But I love her. I always have. I've never loved anyone else."

She could tell her father's gears were churning inside his head. His brilliant mind he used for keeping a multimillion-dollar company afloat, now rendered almost useless by the introduction of his daughter's romantic life. But he did catch up. "All this time...You two sat in that meeting with me and pretended to barely know one another."

"I was afraid you'd be mad at me for being gay and I didn't want to jeopardize Leah's negotiations."

"I talk to her nearly every day and she's never once mentioned being in love with my daughter." Her father filed through his indignities. "I told her how much I didn't like Barney and she didn't even say anything!"

"Wait—you don't like Ben?"

"Oh, I liked him just fine, but he bored me to death. Not interesting enough for you, anyway." He dismissed the entire idea of Ben with a flick of his hand. "I told Leah I wanted you to marry someone you're crazy about. Someone who made your face light up when you talked about them. And there she was, right under my nose, giving away nothing."

"When did you tell her that?"

"A few weeks ago. My engine overheated or something and I was near that pizza place she used to work at. She happened to be there and offered to fix my car."

"That's Leah." A warm smile spread across her face on reflex. "She must like you. She doesn't like most people."

"Well, I certainly like her. We talked for a good while, and she didn't even mention you two had been..." Her father made some bizarre gestures before giving up and returning his hands to the table. "She's a good kid, that one. You have much better taste in women than men."

"Gee, thanks. You sound like Vic."

"It's not as if he got his sense of humor from your mother," he replied with a chuckle that devolved into a sad sigh.

Tori paused. While she'd always wanted to have this kind of rapport with her father, part of her still didn't believe the topic wouldn't somehow get disowned. "You're really okay with this? All my life I thought you were homophobic, and now you're like the president of PFLAG."

"Pee flag? Like, urine?"

"P-F-L-A-G. It's an ally group for families and friends of the LGBT community. It's—that's not the point."

"I've never had a problem with gays," her father said, sitting back in his chair. "It's because I voted for Bush, isn't it?"

"It doesn't help."

Her father sighed, his shoulders sagging. "But yes, I'm really okay with it. I'm okay with any gay. My daughter's a lesbian, my son's a young gay man, and my other son is a chaotic heterosexual. Not many fathers can say they have kids in all the flavors."

Tori laughed, kicking her dad under the table with the tip of her heel. "Very funny."

Victor peered over her shoulder and smiled, giving her a pat on the back. "Go talk to Leah, she's looking for you. And maybe when you get home, we can talk about her a bit. I've heard the tough spots you've had together, but none of the good parts."

"There's a lot of good parts," Tori replied.

"I imagine so. She's a great kid. Way better suited for you than Bennett." Victor blinked and looked at their empty table. "Oh, did he leave? Where did he go?"

"Probably somewhere people actually know his name." Tori got up, placed a kiss on her father's forehead, and hugged him around the neck. "I'll see you at home. I may stay at Leah's tonight."

"By all means, celebrate. You both deserve it. I need to go home and sort things out with your mother. But enjoy the night, please."

"We will. Thanks, Dad." Tori found the Vasquez family near the exit, and she scurried around the linen-draped tables to grab Leah from behind and give her a hug. Leah startled in her arms but immediately relaxed, glancing over her shoulder and smiling. Tori smiled back and murmured a quiet, "Hey."

Loretta, busy putting her earrings back in, gave her a wary glance. "Are you okay, Victoria?"

Hector handed her a handkerchief and she took it with a grateful smile. While her family lay fractured, this family remained whole, perhaps strengthened. Tori didn't think Leah understood how lucky she was. Money could not replace having parents like Hector and Loretta. "No, but I'll be fine. Sorry I overshadowed Leah's night. I didn't mean to."

"Totally worth it to watch your mother nearly combust in her seat," Leah replied. "And, you know, hearing you tell everyone at your job and basically the entire town that you're super into me."

"What my daughter means is she's very proud of you for standing up for yourself tonight." Loretta gave Leah a look, at which Leah rolled her eyes. "If you need to stay with us, you're always welcome in our home."

"Thank you. I need to talk to my parents, but I think it can wait until morning." They had almost two decades to talk about, in fact, but the conversation didn't feel like an albatross any longer. In fact, a lightness came over her, one she'd never before experienced. Finally, the two melodies in her life merged into one grand duet. Leah's gaze settled on her, and she took Leah's free hand in her own. "And we have a lot to talk about too."

Leah nodded. "For sure. But first, I think we need to get very, very drunk on some of *Papi's* secret expensive tequila he keeps in the Saltine box under the sink."

"They call it a secret, *torita*, because you are not supposed to tell people," Hector whined. "*Pero*, I agree. It is the only liquor worthy of celebrating my *mija* being the town hero."

"I guess we should ask Riley if she wants to come," Tori said, craning her neck to try and spot her friend among the guests milling around the room.

"Ah, Riley snuck off into the bathroom with the mayor's daughter." Leah grinned ear to ear. "She's got impeccable game."

"It can't be that good," Tori said, taking Leah's arm as they walked toward the exit. "'Cause I'm the one going home with the Hometown Hero."

"We could ask her to join…" Tori slapped Leah's butt hard. "Okay, okay, just kidding. Unless you wanna…"

"Leah Vasquez. I'm not sharing you with anyone else on the planet. Or on any other planet. Is that clear?"

"Loud and clear," Leah replied, smiling fondly at her. "Might be clearer as a message on a biplane, though."

CHAPTER NINETEEN

Outside her window, waves crashed against rocks and the scent of sea salt wafted in through the screen. It took some getting used to—the spacious condo, the ocean view, the fancy amenities—and Leah loathed to admit how quickly she'd come to enjoy it. Putting pen to paper, she let the sea breeze waft through the window as she barreled through her project. Graduation loomed around the corner, and she desperately sought the finish line to her years of work. You don't get two second chances at your first college degree.

The waves lapped in rhythm with short nails tapping against a keyboard on the other side of the room. A sigh, followed by the snapping of the lid as the computer closed, indicated to Leah the countdown to a hug from behind had begun. And, on cue, within fifteen seconds Tori had wrapped her arms around Leah's neck and kissed her earlobe.

"How's it coming, babe?"

Leah smiled, turning her head to catch Tori's lips in a brief kiss. Joy filled Leah's lungs like breath at their touch. The serenity of their relationship overwhelmed her at times. Two people shouldn't be allowed to be this happy. The catch had to be coming. Two years into the rebooted version of their relationship, Leah still fought the voice telling her how girls like Victoria Lockwood didn't go for girls like Leah Vasquez. Every day they proved that voice wrong, and every day the voice grew softer. "Good, good, just the last touches on this project and then I'll be good for the semester."

"You've worked so hard." Leah rolled the office chair back and Tori sat on her lap. "I can't believe you're gonna graduate soon. It feels like time flew by so fast."

Leah agreed. Not long after the award dinner, Leah took the college money and reenrolled in MIT. They moved into a condo on the waterfront in Boston, and Leah studied as Tori worked remotely for Lockwood Industries. Using some of the money from the award, Leah and Hector hired three mechanics at the shop—one woman and two men, all immigrants—to work with Hector in Leah's absence. Leah got one of the Lockwood's many lawyers to invest in a retirement fund for her parents with whatever money remained.

Pieces of their lives fell into place like stones settling at the river bottom. Piling up, one by one, creating the foundation for their future.

Gremmy leapt onto the desk to get in on the free affection and butted Leah's arm with her head. She scratched the base of Gremmy's neck, wistfully staring out the window. "It's been a ride, I'll tell you what. I'm gonna miss this place when we move back."

"I'm keeping the condo," Tori replied easily. "It's paid for, and I think it'll be nice for us to have a place to get away."

Money came so easily to Tori, and Leah didn't think she'd ever adjust to how freely Tori spent it and how little she thought about it. "I forget you can just, like, afford stuff. It's hard getting used to being a kept woman. I keep thinking someone is going to chase me out of the lobby when they realize I don't have enough class to be in a nice place like this."

"I find it hard to believe you'd let anyone chase you out of anywhere," Tori replied, kissing her temple. "And I think you know money doesn't make any of these people classy. The teacup dogs make them classy."

"Right, right, how could I forget?"

"But I'm happy you like it. I loved living in Boston during college and I couldn't stop thinking about how much better it would've been with you." The same thought had crossed Leah's mind several times at MIT. It led her to taking home anyone who even slightly resembled Tori and widening the void she left behind. "Listen, I know we've talked about it a bunch, but we don't have to move back to Garden Hills. We can live anywhere you want."

The open road Leah had always dreamed of lay before her. Her degree nearly in hand, it would be her secret password to a job in any city, possibly in any country. Outside of flying back for a few company-wide meetings, Tori could work anywhere as long as she had her laptop. The possibilities were endless, and also overwhelming. All her life she'd wanted to get out, and now she was out. They spent the last two years living in a ritzy condo overlooking the sound on the edge of Boston, enjoying the fruits of living near a metropolis. Watching plays, visiting museums, availing themselves of the beach literally across the street. They danced in nightclubs too tame for Leah and too dark for Tori. They slept in the same luxurious bed on sheets with a ridiculous thread count and woke every day in each other's arms. They did all of this far away from the town in which they'd fallen in love. Far away from any home Leah had ever known. Yet she didn't feel lost, and that made her feel…

"I feel guilty," Leah admitted softly. "Like I'm betraying my family by not going back. It's just…it's always been the three of us, you know? Especially after my grandparents cut us out of their lives. We only have my *abuelos*, but they don't live close. So, we relied on each other for everything."

Tori rose from her lap to sit on the edge of her desk instead. The contemplative look on her face transformed more into Business Tori, CEO. Business Tori was very intimidating and incredibly sexy, but Leah paid attention as best she could. "Let me ask you something. Where did your mom grow up?"

"Syracuse, then Brooklyn."

"And your dad?"

"Mexico, then Queens."

"Right. And your mom's parents, where do they live?"

"Syracuse. Tori, you know all of this already."

"Humor me," she replied. "And your grandparents?"

"South Jersey."

"And your dad has sisters who live in Mexico, your mother has basically her entire family in Syracuse, yet they both live in Garden Hills. Hundreds of miles away."

Leah narrowed her eyes. "Why are you talking like a GPS right now?"

"Because," Tori enunciated, exasperated with Leah in the way Leah secretly enjoyed. "Your mom's parents aside, you're still family. It's totally normal and natural to feel guilty about leaving your parents, but it's also totally normal and natural to leave them. It's a new chapter in your life, but in their lives too. They want you to be happy and to live your best life, you know they do. So, you have to ask yourself what *you* want that life to look like."

"I just want you," Leah replied with a shrug. Tori shot her an affectionate but disapproving stare. That was a given by now, and she wouldn't be eking out of this conversation with that old chestnut. "Where do I go? I've…I've never fit in anywhere. How do I know where to go?"

"Ah, now, see that's a different problem with a different solution." Tori abruptly rose from the desk and disappeared into another room. Before Leah could inquire as to what the hell, she returned carrying a thin pile of papers Leah had ignored for weeks. Job offers Leah received via email that Tori took upon herself to print. A stack about seven high, with seven different companies looking for someone with her specific skillset. "We can at least start here. One of these is even in Boston. But we can go anywhere," she said, picking them up to file through them. "Chicago, Detroit, Sacramento, whatever. You pick any one of these and I will follow you. And your parents will only be a phone call or a flight away."

Taking the papers from her, Leah harrumphed and fingered through the offers. She'd looked them over several times before squirreling them away to think about after graduation. Each offer more generous than the last—packages of high salaries and vacation and bonuses for this or that—and deep down, Leah felt undeserving of the amount of money she'd make. How could her father have worked thrice as hard his entire life and never make in a month what she would make in a week? It seemed unfair. But—

"Your parents want you to be more successful than they are, Leah. The cycle everyone wants to repeat is to give their kids a better life than they had. They built one for you, and you'll build one for our kids and they'll have opportunities we didn't have."

Leah blinked. "Our kids?"

Tori froze. Blushing up a storm, she took the papers from Leah's hands and walked them over to their kitchen island to spread them out. "I—I was saying, hypothetically. That's what all good parents want for their kids. Or so I hear, I don't know a whole lot about good parents."

Ah, Tori had fitted the lid on that conversation quite tightly. Leah knew better than to try to broach the subject head-on. Tori spun to look at her and Leah walked over to where she stood, placing her hands on Tori's hips. "Want to go for a walk? I need to get away from… all this for a little bit."

"Sure. Can we get veggie sushi on the way back?" Tori looped her arm through Leah's as she grabbed her keys and led them out of the condo.

"I'm always hungry after the veggie sushi," Leah mumbled as they strolled through the hallway toward the elevator. Every part of the place screamed money—the fancy, hexagonal tiles and the pretentious black-and-white art on the walls—and Leah had a hard time reconciling someone like her lived there. But she did, and she belonged, despite the sometimes wary stares of old white people.

Tori pushed open the door of the spacious lobby and out into the sidewalk. They were literally across the street from the beach and their favorite bench sat only a few blocks away. "Nobody is stopping you from getting an appetizer or soup with it."

"I can't keep my girlish figure that way, Victoria." Tori glared at her but also wrapped her arm around Leah's waist and pulled her close. "Speaking of girlish figures, have you talked to your dad recently?"

"Weak segue, Vasquez." Her gaze softened and Tori looked out into the ocean beside them. A sound, Tori would often correct her, not an ocean. Still, it smelled like the ocean and lapped like the ocean, so Leah figured she'd leave the pedantry to her girlfriend. "Yeah, a couple days ago. He said things are good at home. Vic is completely moved in with his fiancée and Ward is looking forward to going to Rensselaer. My mom…my mom's therapy is going okay. Ward said they're doing better."

"Oh, good. Ward messaged me online right before he told your dad he didn't want to go to Yale, super nervous. But I was like, dude, you came out to your mom at sixteen. This is gonna be cake in comparison. And it was. Your dad is hella soft, it turns out."

"They all love you so much," Tori replied. The smile on her face could've lit every boat in the harbor. "Vic thinks you're his 'fun' sister now, Ward likes that you're a nerd."

"I'm not a nerd."

"Yes, you are, but it's really cute." Leah pouted. So much for her heavy eyeliner and rouge lipstick giving her a cool reputation in high school. "But it helps me deal with not having a relationship with my mom. Knowing my dad and my brothers have your back, that they like you in my life."

Nodding along, Leah sat down on their bench and wrapped her arm over Tori's shoulder as they cuddled together against the ocean breeze. "It doesn't replace what you don't have, I get that. My mom loves you, for what it's worth."

"Does she really? It's hard to tell. She intimidates the shit out of me." Leah laughed, tracing her fingers through Tori's hair and scratching her scalp. Tori's eyes fluttered closed at the comforting gesture. "It's nice to have kind of a mother figure, though."

"Again, doesn't replace yours."

"Maybe one day we'll have…something, but it's gonna take a while. The distance helps. We can't get on each other's nerves or disappoint each other if we're never in the same room. Honestly, I'm not super bothered by it. Feels like I should be, but I can't mourn losing a relationship I never had, can I?" Leah felt Tori shrug her shoulders, but the dismissal didn't ring true. "Still, I'd give her another chance."

"Yeah?" Leah tried to hide the surprise in her voice. Most of their limited conversations about Cassandra revolved around never seeing her again, or cutting her out entirely. Tori got melancholy and angry when drunk and expressed a lot of deeply buried hurt toward her mother. Reconciliation never seemed to be on the table before. "Well, it's up to you and on your terms."

"I know. I just think about how many chances you gave me, and how grateful I am for that. I'm hoping your capacity for forgiveness rubs off or something."

"Maybe it's sexually transmitted," Leah replied, grinning. Tori fondly rolled her eyes, crossing her arms over her chest and leaning farther into Leah. "I forgave you because I love you and because holding a grudge for past hurt didn't measure up to how much I wanted to be with you. It wasn't even close. If forgiving her helps you heal, if having a relationship with her helps you heal, then I'll have your back."

"Thank you." Tori snuggled into her and Leah's heart did a happy flutter. Thick, gray storm clouds moved across the horizon in the distance, ravaging the water far enough away Leah couldn't hear it but could delight in the imagery of the lightning strikes. She'd miss watching storms roll in over the sea when they moved away, not only for their savage beauty, but because their presence pushed Tori into her arms. She'd never tire of being the port in the storm for her. "All this because of a storm."

"Hmm?" Mesmerized by the rain pelting the sea in front of them, Leah didn't understand the wistful comment. "What is?"

"Prom. We have this life, this love…because it rained on prom night."

Ah, right, the storm. The rain washing out the road Leah needed to take for her delivery, forcing her into the back road Tori walked down.

The fight that led to Tori storming out. The coy bonding. The dress burning. That night in her bed, holding Tori close and wondering if girls like her did sometimes get what they wanted. "Oh, right. Well, we also have it because you paid me a compliment in the late nineties and I held on to it for years."

Tori tilted her head back in laughter, resting her neck on Leah's forearm over her shoulders. She stared up at the listless sky and sighed. "You know, you never told me the song."

"What song?"

"Our song. The one you sang in eighth grade in the locker room. And I said I liked it and you became obsessed with me forever."

"How can it be our song if you don't even know what it is? Besides, it must've been something lame if you liked it too." Aghast, Tori laughed and kicked the side of Leah's foot with hers, mumbling a soft "jerk," but leaned into Leah's embrace anyway. "'Our song.' You're such a dork."

In fairness, she was being a bit of a jerk, because Leah knew the song. However, she planned to hold on to this precious bit of information for a while longer. For years she had only this song, this unexpected connection with the girl who quickened her pulse just by proximity, and so she kept it close to her heart. "All right. Let's go get some sushi."

"And a million dumplings," Leah replied, pulling Tori up from the bench and letting her fall into her arms. Leah squeezed Tori tightly, kissing her on the nose and on the lips. It continuously amazed her that they could do this in public—be affectionate, kiss, shout their love as loudly as Leah had always intended—after years of hiding. Not consistently without issue, but it got increasingly easier every year. "And tempura."

"Gosh, you really are high maintenance now, aren't you?"

"I don't know, you still haven't hired me a biplane to advertise my big ween."

"I thought we agreed never to say that word again?" Tori slipped on her shoes and Leah followed suit, walking hand in hand toward the vegetarian sushi bar a couple blocks away. "You know I don't like it."

"You seem to like it when I pull it out of the nightstand," Leah grumbled.

Tori's cheeks flushed a pretty pink, and she squeezed Leah's hand a little too hard. "I do mind, I just overlook it in that context."

"Hard to overlook. You know, on account of how big—"

"I get it, Leah." Leah chuckled, and her heart rested easy. Whatever road lay before them, they would take it together. One hand in hers, the other on the wheel, and nothing but open road ahead of them. Her family lived in Garden Hills, but her heart lived wherever Tori's heart lived. As long as they were together, she was home.

One day, many years later, that conversation on the beach became a distant memory, scattered by time. Other memories filled the space—Tori reconciling with her mother, and Tori convincing Leah to bring their firstborn into the world. The first time she laid eyes on their daughter, a stubborn thing with oak-brown eyes. Christmases split between the Vasquezes' and the Lockwoods', their little girl playing with Vic's twin sons in a sea of wrapping paper. Watery eyes glued to the television as the news trickled down from the highest court in the land, cementing their ability to formalize their family. Hands clasped at the front of the church pews, swearing their love before God with their feet on the ancient wood grain floor and the sun beating down through the stained glass sky. Long after they'd sailed the canals in Venice and scaled the peaks of Pyrenees. After they'd brought their brood to Leah's ancestral home in Mexico and to the Lockwoods' new summer compound on Martha's Vineyard.

One day, Tori would realize their song was no great secret, nor a lost piece of information kept only in the locked recesses of memory. One day they would be in the car, one of Leah's mixtapes playing from the dash, their daughter asleep in the back seat, and Leah driving with one hand on the wheel and the other holding Tori's hand. A faintly familiar song would trigger her memory. Curious, Tori would pull out the soft leather binder of CDs Leah still kept underneath the seat and look at each track list one by one, slowly confirming her suspicion. Their song was not lost, it couldn't be.

Leah had burned it onto every playlist she ever made.

Bella Books, Inc.

Women. Books. Even Better Together.

P.O. Box 10543
Tallahassee, FL 32302

Phone: 800-729-4992
www.bellabooks.com

CPSIA information can be obtained
at www.ICGtesting.com
Printed in the USA
JSHW030145151122
33210JS00001B/1

9 781642 474190